Praise for The Complaints

'Rankin delivers, without the help of Rebus, an excellent cop novel full of action, good dialogue, well-crafted characters and an authentic backdrop'
The Times

'Rankin is a master at what, for me, is one of the important aspects of a crime novel: the integration of setting, plot, characters and a theme which, for Rankin, is the moral dimension never far from his writing' *The Guardian*

'*The Complaints* conclusively demonstrates that its author has still got it, and can put together an ample, satisfyingly complex detective novel without a Rolling Stones-loving, ex-SAS sleuth at its centre'
Sunday Times

'Rankin explores both public and private morality in this well-plotted story' *Daily Mail*

'Rankin displays his customary droll humour and uses Edinburgh as a character in its own right: it's a city in gridlock, thanks to the work installing a new tram system, with new housing projects blighted by the credit crunch' *The Observer*

'Getting to know this man [Fox], an intriguing mix of apathy and action, is almost like a courtship – each new situation reveals something that makes the reader want to know yet more' *The Independent*

'On the evidence of *The Complaints* it looks as if Fox will be just as sure-footed a guide to the city as his grizzled predecessor' *Daily Express*

Born in the Kingdom of Fife in 1960, Ian Rankin graduated from the University of Edinburgh in 1982, and then spent three years writing novels when he was supposed to be working towards a PhD in Scottish Literature. His first Rebus novel, *Knots & Crosses*, was published in 1987, and the Rebus books are now translated into over thirty languages and are bestsellers worldwide.

Ian Rankin has been elected a Hawthornden Fellow, and is also a past winner of the Chandler-Fulbright Award. He is the recipient of four Crime Writers' Association Dagger Awards including the prestigious Diamond Dagger in 2005 and in 2009 was inducted into the CWA Hall of Fame. In 2004, Ian won America's celebrated Edgar Award for *Resurrection Men*. He has also been shortlisted for the Anthony Awards in the USA, and won Denmark's *Palle Rosenkrantz* Prize, the French *Grand Prix du Roman Noir* and the *Deutscher Krimipreis*. Ian Rankin is also the recipient of honorary degrees from the universities of Abertay, St Andrews, Edinburgh, Hull and the Open University.

A contributor to BBC2's *Newsnight Review*, he also presented his own TV series, *Ian Rankin's Evil Thoughts*. He has received the OBE for services to literature, opting to receive the prize in his home city of Edinburgh. He has also recently been appointed to the rank of Deputy Lieutenant of Edinburgh, where he lives with his partner and two sons. Visit his website at www.ianrankin.net

By Ian Rankin

The Inspector Rebus series

Knots & Crosses
Hide & Seek
Tooth & Nail
Strip Jack
The Black Book
Mortal Causes
Let It Bleed
Black & Blue
The Hanging Garden
Death Is Not the End (*novella*)
Dead Souls
Set in Darkness
The Falls
Resurrection Men
A Question of Blood
Fleshmarket Close
The Naming of the Dead
Exit Music

Other novels

The Flood
Watchman
Westwind
Doors Open
The Complaints

Writing as Jack Harvey

Witch Hunt
Bleeding Hearts
Blood Hunt

Short stories

A Good Hanging and Other Stories
Beggars Banquet

Non-fiction

Rebus's Scotland

Omnibus editions

Rebus: The Early Years (Knots & Crosses, Hide & Seek, Tooth & Nail)
Rebus: The St Leonard's Years (Strip Jack, The Black Book, Mortal Causes)
Rebus: The Lost Years (Let It Bleed, Black & Blue, The Hanging Garden)
Rebus: Capital Crimes (Dead Souls, Set in Darkness, The Falls)

All Ian Rankin's titles are available on audio.
Also available: *Jackie Leven Said* by Ian Rankin and Jackie Leven

Ian Rankin

The Complaints

An Orion paperback

First published in Great Britain in 2009
by Orion
This paperback edition published in 2010
by Orion Books Ltd,
Orion House, 5 Upper St Martin's Lane,
London WC2H 9EA

An Hachette UK company

1 3 5 7 9 10 8 6 4 2

A CIP catalogue record for this book
is available from the British Library.

ISBN 978-1-4091-1779-7

Typeset by Deltatype Ltd, Birkenhead, Merseyside

Printed and bound in Great Britain by Clays Ltd, St Ives plc

www.orionbooks.co.uk

The Complaints

Friday 6 February 2009

1

There was a smattering of applause as Malcolm Fox entered the room.

'Don't strain yourselves,' he said, placing his scuffed briefcase on the desk nearest the door. There were two other Complaints in the office. They were already getting back to work as Fox slipped out of his overcoat. Three inches of snow had fallen overnight in Edinburgh. A similar amount had stopped London dead a week ago, but Fox had managed to get into work and so, by the look of it, had everyone else. The world outside felt temporarily cleansed. There had been tracks in Fox's garden – he knew there was a family of foxes somewhere near his estate; the houses backed on to a municipal golf course. His nickname at Police HQ was 'Foxy', but he didn't think of himself that way. 'A bear of a man' – that was the way one of his previous bosses had described him. Slow but steady, and only occasionally to be feared.

Tony Kaye, a bulging folder tucked beneath one arm, walked past the desk and managed to squeeze Fox's shoulder without dropping anything.

'Nice one all the same,' he said.

'Thanks, Tony,' Fox said.

Lothian and Borders Police HQ was on Fettes Avenue. From some windows there was a view towards Fettes College. A few of the officers in the Complaints had been to private schools, but none to Fettes. Fox himself had been educated largely free of charge – Boroughmuir, then Heriot Watt. Supported Hearts FC though seldom managed even a home fixture these days. Had no interest in rugby, even when his city played host to the Six Nations. February was Six Nations month, meaning there'd be hordes of the Welsh in town this weekend, dressed up as dragons and toting oversized inflatable leeks. Fox reckoned he would watch the match on TV, might even rouse himself to go down the pub. Five years now he'd been off the drink, but for the past two he'd trusted himself with occasional visits. Only when he was in the right frame of mind though; only when the willpower was strong.

He hung up his coat and decided he could lose the suit jacket, too. Some of his colleagues at HQ reckoned the braces were an affectation, but he'd lost the best part of a stone and didn't like belts. The braces weren't the shouty kind – dark blue against a plain light-blue shirt. His tie today was a deep dark red. He draped his jacket over the back of his chair, smoothed it at the shoulders and sat down, sliding the locks of the briefcase open, easing out the paperwork on Glen Heaton. Heaton was the reason the Complaints had summoned up the brief round of applause. Heaton was a result. It had taken Fox and his team the best part of a year to compile their case. That case had now been accepted by the Procurator Fiscal's office, and Heaton, having been cautioned and interviewed, would go to trial.

Glen Heaton – fifteen years on the force, eleven of them in CID. And for most of those eleven, he'd been bending the rules to his own advantage. But he'd stepped too far over the line, leaking information not only to his pals in the media but to the criminals themselves. And that had brought him once more to the attention of the Complaints.

Complaints and Conduct, to give the office its full title. They were the cops who investigated other cops. They were the 'Soft Shoe Brigade', the 'Rubber Heels'. Within Complaints and Conduct was another smaller grouping – the Professional Standards Unit. While Complaints and Conduct worked the meat-and-potatoes stuff – grievances about patrol cars parked in disabled bays or cop neighbours who played their music too loud – the PSU was sometimes referred to as the Dark Side. They sniffed out racism and corruption. They looked at bungs received and blind eyes turned. They were quiet and serious and determined, and had as much power as they needed in order to do the job. Fox and his team were PSU. Their office was on a different floor from Complaints and Conduct, and a quarter of the size. Heaton had been under surveillance for months, his home phone tapped, mobile phone records scrutinised, computer checked and checked again – all without his knowledge. He'd been tailed and photographed until Fox had known more about the man than his own wife did, right down to the lap-dancer he'd been dating and the son from a previous relationship.

A lot of cops asked the Complaints the same question: how can you do it? How can you spit on your own kind? These were officers you'd worked with, or might work with in future. These were, it was often said, 'the good guys'. But that was the problem right there – what did it mean to be 'good'? Fox had puzzled over that one himself, staring into the mirror behind the bar as he nursed another soft drink.

It's us and them, Foxy ... you need to cut corners sometimes or nothing ever gets done ... have you never done it yourself? Whiter than white, are you? The pure driven?

Not the pure driven, no. Sometimes he felt swept along – swept into PSU without really wanting it. Swept into relationships ... and then out again not too long after. He'd opened his bedroom curtains this morning and stared at the snow, wondering about phoning in, saying he was stuck. But then a neighbour's car had crawled past and the lie had melted away. He had come to work because that was what he did. He came to work and he investigated cops. Heaton was under suspension now, albeit on full pay. The paperwork had been passed along to the Procurator Fiscal.

'That's that, then?' Fox's other colleague was standing in front of the desk, hands bunched as usual in trouser pockets, easing back on his heels. Joe Naysmith, six months in, still keen. He was twenty-eight, which was young for the Complaints. Tony Kaye's notion was that Naysmith saw the job as a quick route towards management. The youngster flicked his head, trying to do something about the floppy fringe he was always being teased about.

'So far, so good,' Malcolm Fox said. He'd pulled a handkerchief from his trouser pocket and was blowing his nose.

'Drinks on you tonight, then?'

Over at his own desk, Tony Kaye had been listening. He leaned back in his chair, establishing eye contact with Fox.

'Mind it's nothing stronger than a milkshake for the wean. He'll be after long trousers next.'

Naysmith turned and lifted a hand from its pocket just long enough to give Kaye the finger. Kaye puckered his lips and went back to his reading.

'You're not in the bloody playground,' a fresh voice growled from the doorway. Chief Inspector Bob McEwan was standing there. He sauntered in and grazed his knuckles against Naysmith's forehead.

'Haircut, young Joseph – what've I told you?'

'Sir,' Naysmith mumbled, heading back to his desk. McEwan was studying his wristwatch.

'Two bloody hours I was in that meeting.'

'I'm sure a lot got done, Bob.'

McEwan looked at Fox. 'Chief thinks there's the whiff of something septic up in Aberdeen.'

'Any details?'

'Not yet. Can't say I've any enthusiasm to see it in my in-tray.'

'You've friends in Grampian?'

'I've friends nowhere, Foxy, and that's just the way I like it.' The Chief Inspector paused, seeming to remember something. 'Heaton?' he enquired, watching Fox nod slowly. 'Good, good.'

The way he said it, Fox knew the Boss had qualms. Back in the mists of time, he'd worked alongside Glen Heaton. McEwan's take was that the man had done solid work, earned any advancement that came his way. A good officer, for the most part ...

'Good,' McEwan said again, even more distantly. He roused himself with a roll of the shoulders. 'So what else have you got on today?'

'Odds and ends.' Fox was blowing his nose again.

'Have you not shifted that cold yet?'

'It seems to like me.'

McEwan took another look at his watch. 'It's already gone lunchtime. Why not knock off early?'

'Sir?'

'Friday afternoon, Foxy. Might have something new starting Monday, so best get those batteries recharged.' McEwan could see what Fox was thinking. 'Not Aberdeen,' he stated.

'What then?'

'Could well peter out over the weekend.' McEwan offered a shrug. 'We'll talk Monday.' He made to move away, but hesitated. 'What did Heaton say?'

'He just gave me one of those looks of his.'

'I've seen men run for the hills when he does that.'

'Not me, Bob.'

'No, not you.' McEwan's face creased into a smile as he made for the far corner of the room and his own desk.

Tony Kaye had tipped back in his chair again. The man had ears as sharp as any bit of electronic kit. 'If you're heading off home, leave me that tenner.'

'What for?'

'Those drinks you owe us – couple of pints for me and a milkshake for the bairn.'

Joe Naysmith checked that the Boss wasn't watching, then gave Kaye the finger again.

Malcolm Fox didn't go home, not straight away. His father was in a care home over to the east of the city, not far from Portobello. Portobello had been quite the place at one time. It was where you'd go at the summer. You'd play on the beach, or walk along the promenade. There'd be ice-cream cones and one-armed bandits and fish and chips. Sandcastles down near the water, where the sand was sticky and pliable. People would be flying kites or tossing sticks into the surf for their dog to retrieve. The water was so cold you'd lose the ability to breathe for the first few seconds, but after that you didn't want to come out. Parents seated on their stripy deckchairs, maybe with a windbreak hammered into the sand. Mum would have packed a picnic: the gritty taste of meat paste on thin white bread; warm bottles of Barr's Cola. Smiles and sunglasses and Dad with his rolled-up trousers.

Malcolm hadn't taken his dad to the seafront for a couple of years. Some weeks he got the notion, without taking it any further. The old boy wasn't too steady on his pins – that was what he told himself. He didn't like to think it was because people might stare at the pair of them: an elderly man, melted ice cream running down the back of his hand from the cone he was holding, being directed towards a bench by his son. They would sit down and Malcolm Fox would wipe the ice cream from his father's slip-on shoes with his handkerchief, then use that same item to dab at the grey-flecked chin.

No, that wasn't it at all. Today it was just too cold.

Fox paid more for the care home than he did on his own mortgage. He'd asked his sister to share the burden, and she'd answered that she would when she could. The home was private. Fox had looked at a couple of council alternatives, but they'd been drab and acrid-smelling. Lauder Lodge was better. Some of the money Fox had shelled out had gone into the pot and come out as Anaglypta and pine freshener. He could always smell talcum powder, too, and the lack of any unpleasant aromas from the kitchen was testament to quality venting. He found a parking space round the side of the building and announced himself at the front door. It was a detached Victorian house and would have been worth seven figures until the recent crunch. There was a waiting area at the foot of the stairs, but one of the staff told him he could go to his father's room.

'You know the way, Mr Fox,' she trilled as he nodded and made for the longer of the two corridors. There was an annexe, built on to the original structure about ten years back. The walls had a few hairline cracks in them and some of the double glazing suffered from condensation, but the rooms were light and airy – the very words he'd been plied with when he'd first inspected the place. Light and airy and no stairs, plus en suites for the lucky few. His dad's name was on a typed sliver of card taped to the door.

Mr M. Fox. M for Mitchell, this being Malcolm's grandmother's maiden name. Mitch: everyone called Malcolm's dad Mitch. It was a good strong name. Fox took a deep breath, knocked and walked in. His dad sat by the window, hands in his lap. He looked a little more gaunt, a little less animated. They were still shaving him, and his hair seemed freshly washed. It was fine and silver, and the sideburns were kept long, the way they'd always been.

'Hiya, Dad,' Fox said, resting against the bed. 'How you doing?'

'Mustn't complain.'

Fox smiled at that, as was expected. You injured your back at the factory where you worked; you were on disability for years; then cancer came along and you got treated successfully, if painfully; your wife died soon after you got the all-clear; and then old age crept in.

And you mustn't complain – because you were the head of the family, the man of the house.

Your son's own marriage broke up after less than a year; he already had a problem with drink, but it got worse then, for a while; your daughter flew far from the nest and kept in touch infrequently, until landing back home with an unlikeable partner in tow.

But you couldn't complain.

At least your room didn't smell of piss, and your son came to see you when he could. He'd done pretty well for himself, all things considered. You never asked if he liked what he did for a living. You never thanked him for the fees he paid on your behalf.

'I forgot to bring you chocolate.'

'The girls fetch it, if I tell them to.'

'Turkish Delight? Not so easy to find these days.'

Mitch Fox nodded slowly, but didn't say anything.

'Has Jude been round?'

'I don't think so.' The eyebrows bunched together. 'When was it I saw her?'

'Since Christmas? Don't fret, I'll ask the staff.'

'I think she *has* been here ... was it last week or the week before?'

Fox realised that he'd taken out his mobile phone. He was pretending to look for messages but actually checking the time. Less than three minutes since he'd locked the car.

'I finally closed that case I was telling you about.' He snapped the phone shut again. 'Met with the Procurator Fiscal this morning – looks like it's going to trial. There's still plenty that can go wrong, though ...'

'Is it Sunday today?'

'Friday, Dad.'

'I keep hearing bells.'

'There's a church round the corner – maybe it's a wedding.' Fox didn't think so: he'd driven past and the place had looked empty. *Why do I do that?* he asked himself. *Why do I lie to him?*

Answer: the easy option.

'How's Mrs Sanderson?' he asked, reaching into his pocket again for his handkerchief.

'She's got a cough. Doesn't want me to catch it.' Mitch Fox paused. 'Are you sure you should be here with those germs of yours?' Then he seemed to think of something. 'It's Friday and it's still light ... Shouldn't you be at work?'

'Time off for good behaviour.' Fox rose to his feet and prowled the room. 'Got everything you need?' He saw a stack of elderly paperbacks on the bedside table: Wilbur Smith; Clive Cussler; Jeffrey Archer – books men were supposed to like. They would have been chosen by the staff; his father had never been much of a reader. The TV was attached to a bracket in a corner of the room, high up towards the ceiling – difficult to watch unless you were in bed. He'd come to visit one time and it had been tuned to the horse-racing, even though his father had never shown an interest – the staff again. The door to the bathroom was ajar. Fox pushed it open and looked in. No bath, but a shower cabinet fitted with a foldaway seat. He could smell Vosene shampoo, same stuff his mum had used on Jude and him when they'd been kids.

'It's nice here, isn't it?' He asked the question out loud, but not so his father could hear. He'd been asking the selfsame thing ever since they'd moved Dad out of the semi-detached house in Morningside. At first, it had been rhetorical; he wasn't so sure now.

The family home had needed to be cleared. Some of the furniture was in Fox's garage. His attic was full of boxes of photographs and other mementoes, the majority of which meant little or nothing to him. For a time, he would bring some with him when he visited, but they upset his father if he couldn't place them. Names he felt he should have known had been wiped from his memory. Items had lost their significance. Tears would well in the old boy's eyes.

'Want to do anything?' Fox asked, seating himself on the edge of the bed again.

'Not really.'

'Watch TV? Cup of tea maybe?'

'I'm all right.' Mitch Fox suddenly fixed his son with a look. 'You're all right, too, aren't you?'

'Never better.'

'Doing well at work?'

'Revered and respected by all who know me.'

'Got a girlfriend?'

'Not at the moment.'

'How long is it since you divorced ...?' The eyebrows knitted again. 'Her name's on the tip of my ...'

'Elaine – and she's ancient history, Dad.'

Mitch Fox nodded and was thoughtful for a moment. 'You've got to be careful, you know.'

'I know.'

'Machinery ... it's not to be trusted.'

'I don't work with machinery, Dad.'

'But all the same ...'

Malcolm Fox pretended to be checking his phone again. 'I can look after myself,' he assured his father. 'Don't you worry about me.'

'Tell Jude to come and see me,' Mitch Fox said. 'She needs to be more careful on those stairs of hers ...'

Malcolm Fox looked up from his phone. 'I'll tell her,' he said.

'What's this Dad tells me about stairs?'

Fox was outside, standing beside his car. It was a silver Volvo S60 with three thousand miles on the clock. His sister had picked up after half a dozen rings, just as he'd been about to end the call.

'You've been to see Mitch?' she surmised.

'He was asking for you.'

'I was there last week.'

'After you fell down the stairs?'

'I'm fine. A few bumps and bruises.'

'Would those bruises be facial, Jude?'

'You sound just like a cop, Malcolm. I was bringing some stuff downstairs and I fell.'

Fox was silent for a moment, watching the traffic. 'So how are things otherwise?'

'I was sorry we didn't get the chance to catch up over Christmas. Did I thank you for the flowers?'

'You sent a text at Hogmanay, wished me a Gappy New Zear.'

'I'm hopeless with that phone – the buttons are too small.'

'Maybe drink had been taken.'

'Maybe that, too. You still on the wagon?'

'Five years dry.'

'No need to sound so smug. How was Mitch?'

Fox decided he'd had enough fresh air; opened the car door and got in. 'I'm not sure he's eating enough.'

'We can't all have your appetite.'

'Do you think I should get a doctor to look at him?'

'Would he thank you for it?'

Fox had taken a packet of mints from the passenger seat; popped one into his mouth. 'We should get together some night.'

'Sure.'

'Just you and me, I mean.' He listened to his sister's silence, waiting for her to mention her partner. If she did that, maybe they could have the real conversation, the one they'd been dancing around:

What about Vince?

No, just the two of us.

Why?

Because I know he hits you, Jude, and that makes me want to hit him back.

You're wrong, Malcolm.

Am I? Want to show me those bruises and the staircase where it's supposed to have happened?

But all she said was: 'Okay, then, we'll do that, yes.' Soon they were saying their goodbyes and Fox was flipping shut the phone and tossing it across to the other seat. Another wasted opportunity. He started the engine and headed home.

Home being a bungalow in Oxgangs. When he and Elaine had bought the place, the sellers had called it Fairmilehead and the solicitor Colinton – both neighbourhoods seen even then as being more desirable than Oxgangs – but Fox liked Oxgangs fine. There were shops and pubs and a library. The city bypass was minutes away. Buses were regular and there were two big supermarkets within a short drive. Fox couldn't blame his father for misplacing Elaine's name. The courtship had lasted six months and the marriage a further ten, all of it six years back. They'd known one another at school, but had lost touch. Met again at an old friend's funeral. Arranged to go for a drink after the meal and fell into bed drunk and filled with lust. 'Lust for life,' she'd called it. Elaine had just come out of a long-term relationship – the word 'rebound' had only occurred to Fox after the wedding. She'd invited her old flame to the ceremony, and he'd come, well dressed and smiling.

A month after the honeymoon (Corfu; they both got sunburn) they'd realised their mistake. She was the one who walked. He'd asked if she wanted the bungalow, but she'd told him it was his, so he'd stayed, redecorating it more to his taste and completing the attic conversion. 'Bachelor beige' had been one friend's description, followed by a warning: 'Watch your life doesn't go the same way.' As Fox turned into the driveway, he wondered what was so wrong with beige. It was just a colour, like any other. Besides which, he'd repainted the front door yellow. He'd put up a couple of mirrors, one in the downstairs hall, one upstairs on the landing. Framed paintings brightened both living and dining room. The toaster in the kitchen was shiny and silver. His duvet cover was a vibrant green and the three-piece suite oxblood.

'Far from beige,' he muttered to himself.

Once inside, he remembered that his briefcase was locked in the car's boot. As soon as you joined the Complaints you were warned: leave *nothing* in open view. He headed out again to fetch it, placing it on the kitchen worktop while he filled the kettle. Plan for the rest of the afternoon: tea and toast and putting his feet up. There was lasagne in the fridge for later. He'd bought half a dozen DVDs in the Zavvi closing-down sale; he could watch one or two this evening, if there was nothing on the box. At one time, Zavvi had been Virgin. Their shops had gone bust. So had the Woolworth's on Lothian Road – Fox had gone there regularly, almost religiously, as a kid, buying toys and sweets when he was younger, then singles and LPs as a teenager. As an adult he'd driven past it a hundred times or more, but never with a reason to stop and go in. There was a daily paper in his briefcase: more doom and gloom for the economy. Maybe that helped explain why one in ten of the population was taking antidepressants. ADHD was on the increase and one in five primary school kids was overweight and heading for diabetes. The Scottish Parliament had passed its budget at the second attempt, but commentators were saying too many jobs depended on the public sector. Only places like Cuba were worse, apparently. By coincidence, one of the DVDs he'd bought was *Buena Vista Social Club*. Maybe he'd try it tonight: a little bit of Cuba in Oxgangs. A little bit of light relief.

Another of the stories in the paper was about a Lithuanian woman. She'd been killed in Brechin, her body dismembered and tossed into the sea, washing up again, piece by piece, along Arbroath beach. Some kids had discovered the head, and now a couple of migrant workers were on trial for her murder. It was the sort of case a lot of cops would relish. Fox hadn't worked more than a handful of murders during his previous life in CID, but he remembered each scene of crime and autopsy. He'd been present when family members had been given the news, or had been escorted into the mortuary to identify their loved ones. The Complaints was a world away from all that, which was why other cops would say that Fox and his colleagues had it easy.

'So how come it doesn't feel easy?' he asked out loud, just as the toaster finished toasting. He took everything – newspaper included – through to the living-room sofa. There wouldn't be much on the TV this time of day, but there was always the BBC news. His gaze shifted to the mantelpiece. There were framed photos there. One showed his mother and father, probably on holiday in the mid-sixties. The other was of Fox himself, not quite a teenager, with his arm around his younger sister as they sat together on a sofa. He got the feeling it was an aunt's house, but didn't know which one. Fox was smiling for the camera, but Jude was interested only in her brother. An image flashed into his mind – she was tumbling down the stairs at her home. What had she been carrying? Empty mugs maybe, or a basket of washing. But then she was at the foot of the stairs, unharmed, and Vince was standing in front of her, bunching a fist. It had happened before, Jude arguing that she'd struck first, or had given as good as she got. *It won't happen again ...*

Fox's appetite had gone, and the tea smelled as if he'd put too much milk in it. His mobile phone sounded an alert: incoming text message. It was from Tony Kaye. He was in the pub with Joe Naysmith.

'Get thee behind me,' Fox said to himself.

Five minutes later, he was looking for his car keys.

Monday 9 February 2009

2

Monday morning, Malcolm Fox spent almost as much time finding a parking space at HQ as it had taken him to drive there in the first place. Tony Kaye and Joe Naysmith were already in the office. As the 'junior', Naysmith had brewed a pot of coffee, and provided a carton of milk to go with it. Come Friday, he would ask the others to chip in. Sometimes they would and sometimes they wouldn't, and Naysmith would continue the pretence of keeping tabs on what he was owed.

'A quid outstanding,' he said now, standing in front of Fox's desk, hands bunched in pockets.

'Double or quits at the end of the week,' Fox answered, hanging up his coat. It was a beautiful bright day outside, the road surfaces free of ice. Gardens Fox had driven past on his estate had boasted blobs of white where snowmen had once stood. He removed his jacket, displaying the same dark-blue braces. His tie today was a more vibrant red than Friday's, his shirt white with stripes of yellow as fine as strands of hair. There wasn't much in his briefcase, but he opened it anyway. Naysmith had retreated to the coffee jug.

'Three sugars,' Kaye was reminding him, receiving the expected gesture in reply.

'No sign of Bob?' Fox asked.

Naysmith shook his mop of hair – his weekend hadn't included a trim – and pointed towards Fox's desk. 'Should be a message there, though.'

Fox looked, but couldn't see anything. He slid back his chair and peered beneath the desk. A slip of paper was lying on the floor, already boasting the imprint of his shoe sole. He lifted it up and turned it over, studying McEwan's writing.

Inglis – CEOP – 10.30.

CEOP meant Child Protection – Child Exploitation and Online Protection, to give it its full title. Most of the cops pronounced it 'chop'. Room 2.24, at the far end of the corridor and round the corner, was the Chop Shop. Fox had been inside a couple of times, stomach clenched at the very thought of what went on there.

'Know anyone called Inglis?' he asked out loud. Neither Naysmith nor Kaye could help. Fox looked at his watch: 10.30 was over an hour away. Naysmith was stirring a mug noisily. Kaye was leaning back in his chair, stretching his arms and yawning. Fox folded the piece of paper and placed it in his pocket, got up and slipped his jacket back on.

'Won't be long,' he said.

'We'll soldier on somehow,' Kaye assured him.

The corridor was a few degrees cooler than the Complaints office. Fox didn't rush, but it still took him only a few moments to reach 2.24. It was the very last door, and unusual in that it had its own high-security lock and entryphone. There were no names listed; the Chop Shop kept itself to itself – not unlike the Complaints. A sign on the door spelled out a warning: 'There may be disturbing sounds and images in this room. When working at screens, a minimum of two people must be present.' Fox took a deep breath, pressed the button and waited. A male voice came from the speaker.

'Yes?'

'Inspector Fox. I'm here to see Inglis.'

There was silence, then the voice again: 'You're keen.'

'Am I?'

'Ten thirty, wasn't it?'

'Says half nine here.'

Another silence, then: 'Hang on.'

He waited, studying the tips of his shoes. He'd bought them on George Street a month back, and they still rubbed the skin from his heels. Quality shoes, though: the assistant had said they'd last 'till Doomsday ... or the tram line's up and running ... whichever comes first'. Bright kid; sense of humour. Fox had asked why she wasn't in college.

'What's the point?' she'd answered. 'No good jobs anyway, not unless you emigrate.'

That had taken Fox back to his own teenage years. A good many of his contemporaries had dreamed of earning big money abroad. Some of them had succeeded, too, but not many.

The door in front of him was being opened from within. A woman was standing there. She wore a pale green blouse and black trousers. She was about four inches shorter than him, and maybe ten years younger. There was a gold watch on her left wrist. No rings on any of her fingers. She held out her right hand for him to shake.

'I'm Inglis,' she said by way of introduction.

'Fox,' he replied, then, with a smile, 'Malcolm Fox.'

'You're PSU.' It was a statement, but Fox nodded anyway. Behind her, the office was more cramped than he remembered. Five desks with just enough room between them for anyone to squeeze by. The walls were lined with filing cabinets and free-standing metal shelves. On the shelves sat computers and their hard drives. Some of the hard drives had been stripped back to show their workings. Others were bagged and tagged as evidence. The only free wall space had been covered with head shots. The men didn't all look the same. Some were young, some old; some had beards and moustaches; some were dull-eyed and shifty, others unapologetic as they faced the camera. There was only one other person in the room, presumably the man who had spoken over the intercom. He was seated at his desk, studying the visitor. Fox nodded towards him and the man nodded back.

'That's Gilchrist,' Inglis said. 'Come in and make yourself comfortable.'

'Is that even possible?' Fox asked.

Inglis looked around her. 'We do what we can.'

'Are there just the two of you?'

'At the moment,' Inglis admitted. 'High rate of attrition and all that.'

'Plus we mostly end up passing cases to London,' Gilchrist added. 'They've got a hundred-strong team down there.'

'A hundred seems a lot,' Fox commented.

'You've not seen their workload,' Inglis said.

'And do I call you Inglis? I mean, is there a rank, or maybe a first name . . .?'

'Annie,' she eventually told him. There was no one at the desk next to hers, so she motioned for Fox to seat himself there.

'Give us a twirl, Anthea,' Gilchrist said. From the way he said it, Fox got the notion that the joke was wearing thin for all concerned.

'Bruce Forsyth?' he guessed. '*The Generation Game*?'

Inglis nodded. 'I'm supposedly named after the gorgeous pouting assistant.'

'But you prefer Annie?'

'I definitely prefer Annie, unless you want to keep things formal, in which case it's DS Inglis.'

'Annie's fine by me.' Fox, seated, picked a loose thread from the leg of his trousers. He was trying to avoid the file on the desk in front of him. It was marked 'School Uniform'. He cleared his throat. 'My boss told me you wanted to see me.'

Inglis nodded. She had settled in front of her computer. An additional laptop was balanced precariously atop the hard drive. 'How much do you know about CEOP?' she asked.

'I know you spend your time rounding up perverts.'

'Well put,' said Gilchrist, hammering away at his keyboard.

'I'm told it was easier in the old days,' Inglis added. 'But now we've all gone digital. Nobody hands their photos in for processing any more. Nobody has to buy magazines or even go to the trouble of printing anything, except in the privacy of their own home. You can groom a kid from the other side of the world, only meet up with them when you're sure they're ready.'

'Good and ready,' Gilchrist echoed.

Fox ran a finger around his shirt collar. It was hellishly warm in here. He couldn't take off his jacket – this was a business meeting; first impressions and all that. He noted though that Annie Inglis's jacket was over the back of her chair. It was pale pink and looked fashionable. Her hair was cut short, almost in what would have been called a pageboy. It was a glossy brown, and he wondered if she dyed it. She wore a little make-up; not too much. And no nail varnish. He noticed, too, that unlike the rest of the offices on this floor, the windows were opaque.

'It gets hot in here,' she was telling him. 'All the hard drives we keep running. Take off your jacket if you like.'

He gave a thin smile: all the time he'd been trying to read her, she'd been reading him, too. He dispensed with the jacket, draping it across his knees. When Inglis and Gilchrist exchanged a glance, he knew it was to do with his braces.

'Other problem with our "client base",' she went on, 'is that they're getting smarter all the time. They know the hardware and software better than we do. We're always trying to catch up. Here's an example.'

She had nudged the mouse on her desk with her wrist. The computer screen, which had been blank, now showed a distorted image.

'We call this a "swirl",' she explained. 'Offenders send each other pictures, but only after they've encrypted them. Then we need to devise software to allow us to un-swirl them.' With a click of the mouse, the photo began to resolve itself into an image of a man with his arm around an Asian boy. 'You see?' Inglis asked.

'Yes,' Fox said.

'Plenty of other tricks, too. They've gotten so they can hide images behind other images. If you don't know that's the case, you might not bother stripping them out. We've seen hard drives hidden inside other hard drives ...'

'We've seen *everything*,' Gilchrist stressed. Inglis looked across at her colleague.

'Except we haven't,' she reminded him. 'Every week there's something new, something more revolting. All of it accessible twenty-four seven. You sit at your computer at home, surfing, maybe buying stuff or reading the gossip, and you're about four clicks away from hell.'

'Or heaven,' Gilchrist interrupted, eyes fixed on his own screen. 'It's all a matter of taste. We've got stuff that would make the hairs on your scrotum stand on end.'

Fox knew that the Chop Shop considered itself a breed apart, different from the other cops at Fettes HQ: thicker-skinned, resilient, toughened by the job. A macho outfit, too. He wondered how hard Annie Inglis had worked in order to fit in.

'You've got my attention,' was all he said. Inglis was tapping at her screen with the tip of a ballpoint pen.

'This guy here,' she said, indicating the man with the Asian boy. 'We know who he is. We know quite a lot about him.'

'Is he a cop?'

She looked at Fox. 'What makes you ask?'

'Why else would I be here?'

She nodded slowly. 'Well, you're right. But our man is an Aussie, based in Melbourne.'

'And?'

'And, like I say, we know a lot about him.' She opened a folder and brought out some sheets of paper. 'He runs a website for like-minded people. There's an entrance fee to be paid before they come aboard.'

'They have to share,' Gilchrist said. 'Twenty-five pics minimum.'

'Pics?'

'Of them with kids. Share and share alike ...'

'But there's a nominal cash fee, too, paid by credit card,' Inglis added. She handed Fox the top two sheets, a list of names and numbers. 'Recognise anyone?'

Fox went down the list twice. There were almost a hundred names. He shook his head slowly.

'J. Breck?' Inglis announced. 'The J's for Jamie.'

'Jamie Breck …' The name did mean something. Then Fox got it. 'He's Lothian and Borders,' he said.

'Yes, he is,' Inglis agreed.

'If it's the same Jamie Breck.'

'Credit card comes all the way back to Edinburgh. To Jamie Breck's bank, in fact.'

'You've already checked?' Fox handed back the list. Inglis was nodding.

'We've already checked.'

'Okay, then. So where do I come in?'

'As of right now, his credit card's all we've got. He's not posted the photos yet – maybe he's not going to.'

'The site's still active?'

'We're hoping they don't catch wind of us, not until we're good and ready.'

'Members in over a dozen countries,' Gilchrist broke in. 'Teachers, youth leaders, church ministers …'

'And none of them know you're on to them?'

'Us and a dozen other forces across the globe.'

'One time,' Inglis added, 'the office in London arrested a ring-leader and took over the running of his site. It took the users ten days to start suspecting something …'

'By which time,' Gilchrist interrupted again, 'there was plenty of evidence against them.'

Fox nodded and turned his attention back to Inglis. 'What do you want PSU to do?'

'Normally we would let London do the work, but this one's local, so …' She paused, fixing her gaze on Fox. 'We want you to paint us a picture. We want to know more about Jamie Breck.'

Fox glanced at the image on the screen. 'And it couldn't be a mistake?' When he turned his attention back to Annie Inglis, she was giving a shrug.

'Chief Inspector McEwan tells us you've just busted Glen Heaton. Breck works in the same station.'

'So?'

'So you can talk to him.'

'About Heaton?'

'You make it *look* as though it's about Heaton. Then you tell us what you think.'

Fox shook his head. 'I'm not a well-liked man around those parts. I doubt Breck would give me the time of day. But if he's dirty ...'

'Yes?'

'We can look into it.'

'Surveillance?'

'If necessary.' He had her attention now, and even Gilchrist had stopped what he'd been doing. 'We can look at what he gets up to on his computer. We can scrutinise his personal life.' Fox paused, rubbing at his forehead. 'The credit card's all you've got?'

'For now.'

'What's to stop him saying someone else must've used it?'

'That's why we need more.' Inglis had swivelled in her chair so that her knees were a millimetre from his. She leaned forward, elbows resting on her thighs, hands clasped. 'But he can't suspect anything. If he does, he warns all the others. We'll lose them.'

'And the kids,' Fox added quietly.

'What?'

'It's all about the kids, right? Child protection?'

'Right,' Gilchrist said.

'Right,' Annie Inglis echoed.

Fox was a few steps short of the Complaints office when he stopped. He'd put his jacket back on, and was running his fingers down the lapels, just for something to do. He was thinking about DS Anthea Inglis (who preferred to be known as Annie) and her colleague Gilchrist – he didn't even know the man's rank or first name. Thinking, too, about the whole Chop Shop operation. PSU might be called 'the Dark Side', but he got the feeling Inglis and her colleague would daily peer into more darkness than he would ever know. All the same, they were a cocky bunch. At PSU, you knew everybody hated you, but CEOP was different. Fellow cops didn't like the thought of what you'd seen, and wouldn't talk to you for fear of what you might open their eyes and minds to. Yes, that was it: the Chop Shop was *feared*. Properly feared, in a way the Complaints wasn't. Behind the locked door of 2.24 lurked a lifetime's supply of nightmare and bogeyman.

'Malcolm?' The voice came from behind him. He turned to see Annie Inglis standing there, arms folded, legs slightly parted. She came towards him, her eyes fixed on his. 'Here,' she said, holding something out in front of her. It was her business card. 'It's got my mobile and my e-mail, just in case you feel the need.'

'Thanks,' he said, pretending to study the printed lines. 'I was just ...'

'Just standing there?' she guessed. 'Thinking about everything?'

He took out his wallet, sliding one of his own cards from it. She accepted it with a little bow of the head, turned and walked back along the corridor. An elegant walk, he decided. A woman sure of her abilities, confident in her own skin, aware she was being scrutinised. Nice arse, too.

The PSU office was a lot noisier than it had been. Bob McEwan was at his desk, busy with a phone call. He saw Fox coming towards him and made eye contact, nodding to let him know it was okay. McEwan's desk was always tidy, but Fox knew this was because everything got tipped into its half-dozen drawers on a regular basis. Tony Kaye had gone looking for paracetamol one day and had called Fox and Naysmith over to take a look.

'It's like archaeology,' Joe Naysmith had offered. 'Layer upon layer ...'

McEwan put the phone down and started making a note to himself, his handwriting barely legible. 'How did it go?' he asked quietly.

Fox rested his knuckles against the desk and leaned in towards his boss. 'Fine,' he said. 'It was fine. You okay with me doing this?'

'Depends what you're thinking of.'

'Background check to start with, surveillance afterwards as needed.'

'Hack into his computer?'

Fox shrugged. 'First things first.'

'They asked you to talk to him?'

'Not sure that's such a good idea. He might be mates with Heaton.'

'That's what I thought,' McEwan said, 'so I had a quiet word.'

Fox's eyes narrowed. 'Who with?'

'Someone in the know.' Sensing that Fox was trying to decipher the handwritten note, McEwan turned it over. 'Breck and Heaton are rivals more than buddies. That gives you your excuse.'

'But our work on Heaton's done and dusted.'

'For now it is, but who's to know?'

'And you'll back me up? Sign off on the paperwork?'

'Whatever you need. DCC is already in the loop.'

Meaning the Deputy Chief Constable, Adam Traynor, whose authorisation was required for any of the small-scale covert stuff. McEwan's phone rang and he placed his hand on the receiver, ready to pick it up, gaze still locked on to Fox. 'I'll leave it to your discretion, Foxy.' Then, as Fox straightened up, readying to leave: 'Did you enjoy your long weekend, by the way?'

'Managed two nights in Monaco,' Fox replied.

As he passed Tony Kaye's desk, he wondered how much the Human Radar had picked up. Kaye appeared to be busy at his keyboard, typing in some notes. 'Anything interesting?' Fox asked.

'I could ask you the same,' Kaye responded, glancing in the direction of the Boss's corner.

'Might be room for you to climb aboard,' Fox decided there and then, scratching at the underside of his chin.

'Just give me a shout, Foxy.'

Fox nodded distractedly and made it to the relative safety of his desk. Naysmith was brewing another pot of coffee.

'Three sugars!' Kaye called to him.

Naysmith gave a twitch of the mouth, then noticed that he was being watched. He waved an empty mug in Fox's direction, but Fox shook his head.

3

The HR department were never happy to see someone from the Complaints. HR – Human Resources – used to be Personnel, a term Fox preferred. HR, meantime, would have preferred it if officers like him couldn't come swanning in as if they owned the place. HR felt prickly, and with good reason. They had to provide open access, access denied to practically anyone else. McEwan had called ahead to let them know Fox was on his way. He'd then typed and signed a letter verifying Fox's need to see the records. No names were mentioned, and this was what riled some of the HR staff – the assumption being that they couldn't be trusted with the information. If they knew who the Complaints had their eye on, they might pass the information along, crippling any inquiry at its very start. It had happened once in the past – over a decade back – since when the rules had been changed so that the Complaints had total privacy when they did their search. To this end, the head of HR had to vacate her private room, so that Fox could use it. She had to log on to her computer, then leave it available for his use. She had to hand him the keys to the many filing cabinets in the main open-plan office. Then she had to stand with arms folded, fuming, eyes averted as he went about his business.

Fox had been through the procedure many times, and had tried at the start to be cordial, apologetic even. But Mrs Stephens was not to be placated, so he'd given up. She still took some pleasure in delaying him and his ilk, reading the Chief Inspector's notification with the greatest care and attention, sometimes even phoning McEwan back to double-check. Then she would ask for Fox's warrant card and note his details on a form, which he had to sign. She would then check his signature against the one on his ID, exhale noisily, and hand over the keys, her computer, her desk and her office.

'Thank you,' he would say, usually his first and last words of the encounter.

HR was on the ground floor of Police HQ. Lothian and Borders was not the largest force in Scotland, and Fox often wondered how they filled their time. They were civilian staff – most of them women. They stared at him from above their computer screens. One might wink or blow him a kiss. He knew some of their faces from the canteen. But there was never any conversation, no offer of coffee or tea – Mrs Stephens saw to that.

Fox made sure no one was watching as he lifted Jamie Breck's file from the cabinet. He held it to his chest so the name couldn't be seen, locked the drawer and headed back to Mrs Stephens' office. Closed the door after him and sat down. The chair was still warm, which he minded only a little. Inside the slim file were the details of Breck's police career, along with earlier academic attainments. He was twenty-seven and had joined the force six years previously, spending the first two in training and in uniform, before transferring to CID. His assessments were favourable, bordering on glowing. There was no mention of any of the cases he'd worked on, but also no indication of trouble or disciplinary concerns. 'A model officer' was one remark, repeated a little later on. One thing Fox did learn was that Breck lived in the same part of town as him. His address was on the new estate close by the Morrisons supermarket. Fox had driven around the estate when it had first been built, wondering if he needed a bigger house.

'Small world,' he muttered to himself now.

The computer data added little. There had been the occasional sick day, but nothing stress-related. There had never been a need for counselling or referral. Breck's bosses at Torphichen Place – his base these past three years – couldn't get enough of him. Reading between the lines, Fox could see that Breck was being fast-tracked. He was already young for a detective sergeant, and DI looked achievable before the age of thirty. Fox himself had been thirty-eight. Breck had been educated privately at George Watson's College. He'd played rugby for the second fifteen. A BSc from the University of Edinburgh. Parents still alive, both of them GPs. An older brother, Colin, who had emigrated to the USA, where he worked as an engineer. Fox pulled out his handkerchief, found a dry bit, and emptied his nose into it. The noise was enough to have Mrs Stephens peering in at him through the narrow window next to the door. Her face had stiffened further with distaste. He'd be leaving his germs all over her office, defiling her private fiefdom. Though he didn't really need to, he blew his nose again, almost as noisily.

Then he closed the online file. Mrs Stephens knew what he would do next – shut down her whole system. Yet another precaution – he wanted his search to be erased as far as possible. But before he did that, he typed in another name – Anthea Inglis. Definitely against procedure, but he did it anyway. It only took a couple of minutes for him to learn that she wasn't married and had never been married.

That she'd grown up on a farm in Fife.

That she'd attended the local college before moving to Edinburgh.

That she'd had a variety of jobs before joining the force.

That her full name was Florence Anthea Inglis.

If one of her names had come from *The Generation Game*, he wondered if the other might have originated with *The Magic Roundabout*. Fox had to stifle a smile as he began closing everything down. He emerged from the office, leaving the door ajar, and replaced the file in its cabinet, making sure it couldn't be differentiated from any of the others. When he was satisfied, he closed and locked the drawer and made to hand the key to Mrs Stephens. She was resting her weight against the edge of a colleague's desk, arms still folded, so he placed the key down next to her instead.

'Till next time,' he said, turning away. One of the women glanced up at him as he passed, and he managed a wink of his own.

When he got back to the Complaints office, Naysmith told him there was a message waiting.

'And would I find it on my desk or under it?' Fox asked. But there it was, lying next to his telephone. Just a name and number. He looked at it, then up at Naysmith. 'Alison Pettifer?'

Naysmith just shrugged, so Fox lifted the receiver and punched the number in. When it was answered, he identified himself as Inspector Fox.

'Oh, right,' the woman on the other end said. She sounded hesitant.

'You called me,' Fox persisted.

'You're Jude's brother?'

Fox was silent for a moment. 'What's happened?'

'I live next door,' the woman stumbled on. 'She happened to

mention once that you were in the police. That's how I got your number ...'

'What's happened?' Fox repeated, aware that both Naysmith and Kaye were now listening.

'Jude's had a bit of an accident ...'

She tried to close the door in his face, but he pushed against it and her resistance evaporated. Instead, she marched back into her living room. It was a mid-terraced house in Saughtonhall. He didn't know which side Alison Pettifer lived – neither set of net curtains had twitched. Each and every house on the street boasted a satellite dish, and Jude's TV was tuned to some daytime chat-and-cookery show. She turned it off as he walked into the room.

'Well now,' was all he said. Her eyes were red-rimmed from crying. There was some faint bruising on her left cheek, and her left arm was in plaster, a sling cradling it. 'Those stairs again?'

'I'd had a drink.'

'I'm sure.' He was looking around the room. It smelt of alcohol and cigarettes. There was an empty vodka bottle on the floor next to the sofa. Two ashtrays, both full. A couple of crushed cigarette packets. A breakfast bar separated the living area from the small kitchen. Plates stacked up, next to discarded fast-food cartons. More empty bottles – lager; cider; cheap white wine. The carpet needed vacuuming. There was a layer of dust on the coffee table. One of the legs had been snapped off, replaced by a stack of four building bricks. Figured: Vince worked in the building trade.

'Mind if I sit down?' Fox asked.

She tried to shrug. It wasn't easy. He decided his safest bet was the arm of the sofa. He still had his hands in the pockets of his overcoat. There didn't seem to be any heating in the room. His sister was wearing a short-sleeved T-shirt and a baggy pair of denims. Her feet were bare.

'You look a right state,' he told her.

'Thanks.'

'I mean it.'

'You're not exactly a poster boy yourself.'

'Don't I know it.' He'd lifted the handkerchief from his pocket so he could blow into it.

'You still haven't got rid of that cold,' she commented.

'*You* still haven't got rid of that bastard of yours,' he replied. 'Where is he?'

'Working.'

'I didn't know anyone was building anything.'

'There've been lay-offs. He's hanging in.'

Fox nodded slowly. Jude was still standing up, shifting slightly from the hips. He recognised the movement. She'd done it as a kid, whenever she'd been caught out. Paraded in front of their father for a telling-off.

'You not got a job yet?'

She shook her head. The estate agent had laid her off just before Christmas. 'Who told you?' she asked eventually. 'Was it next door?'

'I hear things,' was all he said.

'It wasn't anything to do with Vince,' she stated.

'We're not in a bloody police station, Jude. This is just the two of us.'

'It wasn't him,' she persisted.

'Who then?'

'I was in the kitchen Saturday ...'

He made show of peering over the breakfast bar. 'Wouldn't have thought there was room to fall over.'

'Caught my arm on the corner of the washing machine as I went down ...'

'That the story you gave them at A and E?'

'Is that who told you?'

'Does it matter?' He was staring towards the fireplace. There were shelves either side, filled with videos and DVDs – looked like every single episode of *Sex and the City* and *Friends*, plus *Mamma Mia* and other films. He gave a sigh and rubbed his hands down his face, either side of his nose and mouth. 'You know what I'm going to say.'

'It wasn't Vince's fault.'

'You provoked him?'

'We provoke each other, Malc.'

He knew as much; could've told her that the neighbour often heard slanging matches. But then Jude would have known who'd called him.

'If we charged him – just one time – it might put a stop to it. We'd make it a requirement he got some counselling.'

'Oh, Vince would love that.' She managed a smile; it wiped years from her face.

'You're my sister, Jude ...'

She looked at him, blinking, but not about to cry. 'I know,' she said. Then, indicating the cast on her arm: 'Think I should still go see Dad?'

'Maybe leave it.'

'You won't tell him?'

He shook his head, then looked around the room again. 'Want me to tidy up? Wash some dishes maybe?'

'I'll be fine.'

'Has he said sorry?'

She nodded, keeping eye contact. Fox didn't know whether to believe her – and what did it matter anyway? He rose to his feet, towering over her, then leaned down to peck her on the cheek.

'Why does someone else have to do it?' he whispered into her ear.

'Do what?'

'Phone me,' he answered.

Outside, it was snowing again. He sat in his car, wondering if Vince Faulkner's working day would be curtailed. Faulkner was from Enfield, just north of London. Supported Arsenal, and hadn't a good word to say for football north of the border. This had been his opening gambit when the two men had been introduced. He hadn't been keen on the move to Scotland – 'but she keeps bending me bleedin' ear'. He was hoping she'd get bored and want to head south again. *She.* Malcolm had seldom heard him use her name. She. Her indoors. The other half. The bird. He drummed his fingers against the steering wheel, wondering what to do for the best. Faulkner could be working on any one of three or four dozen projects around the city. The recession had probably put the brakes on the new flats in Granton, and he reckoned Quartermile was dormant, too. Caltongate wasn't up and running yet, and the developer was in trouble, according to the local paper.

'Wild goose chase,' he said to himself. His phone vibrated, letting him know he had a text. It was from Tony Kaye.

We r at Minters.

It was gone four. McEwan had obviously clocked off for the day, giving the others no reason to loiter. Fox closed his phone and turned the key in the ignition. Minter's was a New Town bar with Old Town prices, tucked away where only the cognoscenti could find it. Never easy to find a parking space, but he knew what Kaye would have done – stuck a great big POLICE placard on the inside of the windscreen. Sometimes it worked, sometimes it didn't: depended on the mood of the warden. Fox tried to work out a way back into the city centre that would avoid the tram works at Haymarket, then gave up. Anyone who could solve that, they should give them the Nobel Prize. Before driving off, he looked to his right, but there was no sign of Jude at her living-room window, and still nobody visible in the homes on either side. If Vince Faulkner were to turn into the street right now, what would he do? He couldn't remember the name of the character in *The Godfather*, the one who'd chased the brother-in-law and thumped him with a bin lid.

Sonny? Sonny, wasn't it? That's what he'd like to think he would do. Bin lid connecting with face, and *don't you touch my sister!*

What he'd like to think he would do.

Minter's was quiet. But then it had been quiet for several years, the landlord first blaming the smoking ban and now muttering about the downturn. Maybe he had a point: plenty of banking types lived in the New Town, and they'd be wise to keep their heads down.

'Other than bankers,' Tony Kaye said, placing Fox's glass of iced cola on the corner table, 'who else can afford a house here?'

Naysmith was drinking lager, Kaye Guinness. The landlord, sleeves rolled up, was intent on a TV quiz show. Two further customers had gone outside with their cigarettes. There was a woman seated in another corner with a friend. Kaye had taken her over a brandy and soda, then explained to Fox and Naysmith that she was a pal of his.

'Does the missus know?' Joe Naysmith had asked.

Kaye had wagged a finger at him, then pointed it towards the woman. 'Her name's Margaret Sime, and if you're ever in here and I'm not, I'd better hear that you've sent a drink over ...'

'Did you get parked?' Naysmith was now asking Malcolm Fox.

'Halfway up the bloody hill,' Fox complained. Then, to Kaye: 'I see you didn't have any trouble.' Kaye's Nissan X-Trail was outside the pub's front door, on a double yellow line and with the POLICE notice wedged in between dashboard and windscreen. Kaye just shrugged and gave a smirk, making himself comfortable and attacking what remained of his pint. Wiping a line of foam from his top lip, he fixed his gaze on Fox.

'Vince has been a naughty boy again,' he said. Fox just stared at him, but it was Naysmith who provided the explanation.

'Soon as you'd left, Tony phoned the caller's number.'

'She told me about Jude's "accident",' Kaye confirmed.

'Leave it, will you?' Fox cautioned, but Kaye was shaking his head. Again, it was Naysmith who spoke.

'Tony looked up Vince Faulkner.'

'"Looked up"?' Fox's eyes narrowed.

'On the PNC,' Naysmith said, slurping at his drink.

'Police National Computer's only for south of the border,' Fox stated.

Tony Kaye gave another shrug. 'I know a cop in England. All I did was give him Faulkner's name and place of birth – Enfield, right? I remember you telling me.'

'You know a cop in England? I thought you hated the English.'

'Not individually,' Kaye corrected him. 'Look, do you want to know or don't you?'

'I doubt I could stop you telling me, Tony,' Fox said.

But Kaye pursed his lips and folded his arms. Naysmith looked keen to bursting, but Kaye was warning him off with his eyes. The two smokers were coming back into the bar. The landlord slammed the palms of both hands against the bar top and yelled at the TV, 'A schoolkid would've known that!'

'Don't be so sure, Charlie,' one of the smokers said. 'Not these days.'

'He's got previous,' Naysmith blurted out, trying to keep his voice down. Kaye rolled his eyes and unfolded his arms, reaching for his glass and draining it.

'Your shout, kiddo,' he said.

Naysmith gawped, but then sprinted towards the bar with the empty glass.

'Previous?' Fox echoed. Tony Kaye leaned in towards him, keeping his voice low.

'A few petty thefts from nine or ten years back. Couple of street brawls. Nothing too serious, but Jude might not know about them. How's she doing?'

'Her arm's in plaster.'

'Did you have words with Faulkner?'

Fox shook his head. 'I didn't see him.'

'Something's got to be done, Malcolm. Will she file a complaint?'

'No.'

'We could do it for her.'

'She's not leaving him, Tony.'

'Then it's up to us to have a word with him.'

Naysmith was back at the table, the landlord having taken his order. '*Exactly* what we should do,' he confirmed.

'You're forgetting something,' Fox said. 'We're the Complaints. Word gets out that we're running around putting the fear on members of the great unwashed . . .' He shook his head again, more firmly this time. 'We don't get to do that.'

'Then there's no fun left in life,' Tony Kaye decided, throwing open his arms. Naysmith had marched off again and returned with Kaye's drink. Fox studied his two colleagues.

His two friends.

'Thanks all the same,' he said. And then, lowering his voice still further: 'In the meantime, maybe there's *some* fun we could have.' He checked that no one else in the bar was showing an interest. 'McEwan's put me on to a cop called Breck ...'

'Jamie Breck?' Kaye guessed.

'You know him?'

'I know people who know him.'

'Who is he?' Naysmith asked, settling himself at the table. Only the top inch was missing from his lager.

'CID, based at Torphichen,' Kaye enlightened him. Then, to Fox: 'He's dirty?'

'Maybe.'

'That's why you were at the Chop Shop this morning?'

'Nothing gets past you, Tony.'

'And HR this afternoon?'

'Ditto.' Fox leaned back in his seat. He wasn't sure what he was doing, not exactly. No harm in Kaye and Naysmith being on board, but did he have anything for them to do? All he knew was, he needed to show his appreciation, and this was as good a way of doing it as any. Plus, now they could talk about work rather than Jude. And that was another thing: what did he do with the info about Vince Faulkner? Store it away? He couldn't see himself confronting Jude with it. She'd accuse him of snooping, of interfering.

My life, Malcolm, my business ... That was probably how she would put it. Of everything they had to do, all the cases they had to work, cops hated domestics the worst. They hated them because there was seldom a happy outcome, and precious little they could do to help or ease the situation. And that was how Jude would look to the majority of Fox's colleagues. Hers was most definitely a domestic. The smokers were standing at the bar. One of them was drinking whisky. Fox could smell it, and even felt the faintest of tangs at the back of his throat. It was making his mouth water.

'So tell us,' Tony Kaye was enquiring. Joe Naysmith had leaned forward, elbows on knees.

His sister's face was in his mind, and the aroma of the single malt in his nostrils. He told Kaye and Naysmith what he knew about Jamie Breck.

Tuesday 10 February 2009

4

Next morning, Fox called Jude but got no answer. He'd tried her the previous night, too. She probably had caller ID. She was almost certainly ignoring him. After breakfast, he drove to work. Kaye and Naysmith wanted to know their 'plan of action'. Fox's idea was that Annie Inglis should brief them, but there was no one at home in 2.24. He texted her mobile instead, asking her to get back to him.

'We'll wait,' he told his colleagues. 'No rush.' They were heading back to their own desks when Fox's phone rang. He picked it up, and heard a voice he didn't know asking him if he was Malcolm Fox.

'Who's this?' Fox asked back.

'My name's Detective Sergeant Breck.' Fox's spine stiffened, but he didn't say anything. 'Am I speaking to Malcolm Fox?'

'Yes.'

'Mr Fox, I'm calling on behalf of your sister.'

'Is she there? What's happened?'

'Your sister's fine, Mr Fox. But I'm afraid we're on our way to the mortuary. I asked her if there was anyone, and she ...'

The voice was professional without being cold.

'Tell me what's happened.'

'Your sister's partner, Mr Fox – do you know how to find the City Mortuary ...?'

He knew all right: it was on the Cowgate. An inconspicuous brick building you'd drive past without guessing what went on there. Traffic was hellish slow; there seemed to be roadworks and diversions everywhere. It wasn't just the trams – there were gas mains being replaced, and resurfacing at the Grassmarket. It seemed to Fox that he passed more traffic cones than pedestrians. Kaye had asked if he wanted company, but he'd shaken his head. Vince Faulkner was dead, and that was as much as Jamie Breck was going to tell him. Breck – managing to sound concerned and thoughtful. Breck – waiting at the mortuary with Jude …

Fox parked the Volvo in one of the loading bays and headed inside. He knew where they'd be waiting. The viewing room was one floor up. He flashed his ID at any staff he passed, not that they showed the slightest interest. They wore foreshortened green rubber galoshes and three-quarter-length smocks. They had just washed their hands or were on their way to do so. Jude heard his footsteps on the stairs and was running towards him as he came into view. She was bawling her head off, body shuddering, eyes bloodshot behind the tears. He held her to him, being careful of her arm. After a moment, he opened his eyes and looked over her shoulder to where DS Jamie Breck was standing.

You don't know his name's Jamie, Fox reminded himself. *On the phone, he called himself DS Breck.* Breck was walking towards him now. Fox managed to push Jude back a little, but as gently as possible. He held out a hand to the other detective. Breck was smiling, almost sheepishly.

'I'm sorry,' he said. 'I should have known it was a Fettes number.' He gestured towards Jude. 'Your sister tells me you're a DI.'

'Just plain Inspector,' Fox corrected him. 'In PSU we drop the Detective bit.'

Breck nodded. 'PSU means the Complaints?'

Fox nodded back at him, then turned his attention to Jude. 'I'm so sorry,' he said, squeezing her hand. 'Are you all right?' She shivered in response, and he asked Breck if the identification had taken place.

'Two minutes,' Breck said, pretending to look at his watch. Fox knew what was happening behind the door: they were making the corpse as presentable as possible. Only the face would be visible, unless identification necessitated the revealing of a tattoo or distinguishing feature.

'Where was he found?' Fox asked.

'A building site by the canal.'

'Where they're knocking down the brewery?'

'He wasn't working there,' Jude stated tremulously. 'I don't know what he was doing there.'

'When was he found?' Fox asked Breck, squeezing his sister's hand a little more tightly.

'Early this morning. Couple of joggers on the towpath. One got a stitch, so they stopped. Leaning against the fence, doing stretches or whatever. That's when they saw him.'

'And you're sure it's ...?'

'Couple of credit cards in the pocket. I gave Ms Fox a description of the deceased and his clothing ...'

Jamie Breck had blonde hair tending towards the curly, and a face speckled with freckles. His eyes were a milky blue. He stood an inch or so shorter than Fox, and was probably only two thirds his waist measurement. He wore a dark brown suit with all three buttons done up. Fox was trying to dismiss from his mind everything he knew about him: schooled at George Watson's ... parents both doctors... lives near the supermarket ... has yet to comply with the twenty-five-pic minimum ... He found himself stroking Jude's hair.

'They beat him up,' she was saying, voice cracking. 'They beat him up and left him for dead.' Fox looked to Breck for confirmation.

'Injuries consistent with,' was all the younger man said. Then the door of the room behind them slid open. The body lay on a trolley, swaddled except for the face. Even the hair and ears had been covered. The face was pulpy, but recognisable, even from a distance. Fox caught sight of it before his sister.

'Jude,' he cautioned her, 'I can do this if you don't want to.'

'I need to do it,' she answered. 'I need to ...'

'You'll want to go home with her,' Breck was telling Fox. Both men held plastic beakers of tea. They were standing in the Family Room. A pile of children's books had been placed on one of the chairs, and someone had pinned up a poster of a sunflower. Jude was seated a few feet away, head bowed, holding a beaker of her own – water was all she'd asked for. They were waiting for the forms, the forms she would need to sign. Vince Faulkner's battered corpse was already on its way to the autopsy suite, where a couple of the city's pathologists would get to work on it, their assistants weighing and measuring, bagging and tagging.

'What time was he found?' Fox asked quietly.

'Just after six.'

'It's still dark at six.'

'There were streetlights.'

'Was he attacked there or just dumped there?'

'Look, Inspector Fox, this can all wait ... you'll want to be with Jude now.'

Fox stared at his sister. 'There's a neighbour,' he found himself saying. 'Alison Pettifer. Maybe she could take Jude home and stay with her.'

Breck pulled back his shoulders. 'Due respect, I know you outrank me, but ...'

'I just want to see the locus. Any harm in that, DS Breck?'

Breck seemed to consider this for a moment, then let his shoulders relax. 'Call me Jamie,' he said.

Twenty-five-pic minimum, Fox thought to himself.

It was another hour before the paperwork was finalised and Alison Pettifer was fetched from her home. Fox shook hands with her and thanked her again for calling him the previous day.

'And now this,' was all she said. She was tall and slim and in her fifties. She took charge, coaxing Jude to her feet and telling her everything was going to be fine. 'You're coming home with me ...'

Jude's eyes were still raw-looking as Fox kissed her on both cheeks.

'I'll come as soon as I can,' he said. A uniformed officer was waiting for the women, his patrol car parked outside. He looked almost bored, and Fox wanted to shake him. He checked his mobile phone instead: two messages from Tony Kaye, which were actually the same message sent twice – Do u need me?

Fox started to punch in 'no', but lengthened it to 'not yet'. As he was sending it, Jamie Breck reappeared.

'Not needed at the autopsy?' Fox asked.

'They can't get to it for another hour.' Breck looked at his wristwatch. 'Means I can take you out there, if you like.'

'I've got my car.'

'Then you can drive us ...'

Four minutes into the journey, Breck commented that they'd have been quicker walking. It was a straight run – Cowgate to West Port to Fountainbridge – but traffic had stalled again: a contraflow controlled by two workmen in fluorescent jackets and toting signs saying STOP and GO.

'It can drive men mad,' Breck said, 'suddenly having all that power ...'

Fox just nodded.

'Mind if I ask something?'

Fox minded a lot, but gave a shrug.

'How did your sister break her arm?'

'She fell over in the kitchen.'

Breck pretended to mull this over. 'Mr Faulkner worked as a builder?'

'Yes.'

'Didn't seem to be dressed for the job – good-quality chinos; polo shirt and leather jacket. The jacket was a Christmas present from Ms Fox.'

'Was it?'

'Were they getting married?'

'You'd have to ask her.'

'The two of you aren't close?'

Fox could feel his grip tightening on the steering wheel. 'We're close,' he said.

'And Mr Faulkner?'

'What about him?'

'Did you like him?'

'Not especially.'

'Why not?'

'No particular reason.'

'Or too many to mention?' Breck nodded to himself. 'My brother's partner ... I don't get on too well with him, either.'

'Him?'

'My brother's gay.'

'I didn't know.'

Breck looked at Fox. 'No reason why you should.'

That's right, and no reason to know that that same brother's an engineer in America ...

Fox cleared his throat. 'So what's your feeling about this?' he asked.

Breck took his time answering. 'There's a hole in the fence, next to where the body was found. Little side road there, too, where a car or van could park.'

'The body was dumped?'

Breck shrugged and began working his neck muscles. 'I asked Ms Fox when she last saw Mr Faulkner.'

'And?'

'She says Saturday afternoon.' Fox could hear the grinding of gristle in the younger man's neck and shoulders. 'That cast looks pretty new ...'

'Happened Saturday,' Fox confirmed, keeping his voice level, concentrating on the road ahead: two more sets of traffic lights and one roundabout and they'd be there.

'So she heads to A and E and Mr Faulkner goes out on the town.' Breck stopped exercising and leaned forward a little, turning his head so he could make eye contact with Fox. 'Fell over in the kitchen?'

'That's what she told me.'

'And you repeated it for my benefit ... but your face tightened just a little when you spoke.'

'Are you supposed to be Columbo or something?'

'Just observant, Inspector Fox. You need to take the next left.'

'I know.'

'And there's that facial tightening again,' Jamie Breck said, just loud enough for Fox to hear.

The police cordon was still in place, but the uniform on duty eased up the tape so they could pass beneath. There was a couple of journalists from the local paper, but both were old enough to know they would ask in vain for a quote. A few people watched from the towpath, not that there was much to see. The Scene of Crime Unit had already picked over the area. Photos showed the body *in situ* – Breck grabbed some from a SOCO and handed them to Fox. Vince Faulkner had been found face down, arms thrown in front of him. His skull had been crushed by something heavy. The hair was matted with blood. There were grazes to the palms and fingers – consistent with someone trying to defend himself.

'We won't know about internal injuries until after the autopsy,' Breck commented. Fox nodded and looked around. It was a bleak spot. Mounds of earth and rubble from where some of the old brewery had been demolished. Warehouses remained, emptied of their contents and with windows pulverised. On the other side of the road, groundworks were under way for what would become a 'mixed social development', according to the billboard – shops, office space and apartments (no one seemed to call them flats these days). Cops in overalls were working in a line, trying to locate the murder weapon. There were tens of thousands of possibilities, from half-bricks to rocks and concrete rubble.

'Could have been tossed into the canal,' Fox mused.

'We've got divers coming,' Breck assured him.

'Not much blood on the ground.' Fox was studying the photos again.

'No.'

'Which is why you think he was dumped here?'

'Maybe.'

'In which case it's not just a mugging gone wrong.'

'No comment.' Breck looked to the skies and took a deep breath.

'I know,' Fox said, intercepting the speech. 'I can't get involved. I shouldn't make it personal. I mustn't get in the way.'

'Pretty much.' Breck had taken the photos from him so he could flick through them. 'Anything you want to tell me about your sister's partner?'

'No.'

'He broke her arm, didn't he?'

'You'll have to ask her that.'

Breck stared at him, then nodded slowly and kicked at a small stone, sending it rolling along the ground. 'How long do you reckon this'll stay a building site?'

'Who knows?'

'Someone told me HBOS were moving their corporate headquarters here.'

'That might not happen for a while.'

'I hope you didn't have shares.'

Fox gave a snort, then stuck out a hand for the younger man to take. 'Thanks for letting me come here. I appreciate it.'

'Rest assured, Inspector, we'll be doing all we can – and not just because you're a fellow traveller.' Breck gave a wink as he released Fox's hand.

Twenty-five-pic minimum ... You like looking at young kids, DS Breck, and it's my job to hang you out to dry ...

'Thanks again,' Malcolm Fox said. 'Can I drop you back at the mortuary?'

'I'm going to stay here a while.' Breck paused, as if deep in thought. 'PSU,' he eventually said, 'just got through mangling one of my colleagues.'

'It'd take more than the Complaints to mangle Glen Heaton.'

'Were you part of that team?'

'Why do you ask?'

'No real reason.'

'You're not particularly a friend of his, are you?'

Breck stared at him. 'What makes *you* ask?'

'I'm the Complaints, DS Breck – I see everything and hear everything.'

'I'll bear that in mind, Inspector,' Jamie Breck said.

*

Fox called the office from his car and told Tony Kaye they'd have to hold fire on Jamie Breck. Kaye, naturally, asked why.

'He's in charge of Faulkner.'

Kaye was making a whistling sound as Fox ended the call. When his phone rang, he answered without thinking.

'Look, Tony, I'll talk to you later.'

There was silence for a moment, then a female voice: 'It's Annie Inglis. Is this a bad time?'

'Not a great time, Annie, if I'm being honest.'

'Anything I can do to help?'

'No, but thanks for the offer.'

'I got your message ...'

The horn in the car behind Fox started blaring as he headed down a street meant only for taxis and buses.

'There's been a complication. My sister's partner's turned up dead.'

'I'm sorry ...'

'Don't be – he was an evil little sod. But I've just met the investigating officer. He's a DS called Jamie Breck.'

'Oh.'

'So the job you wanted me to do should probably go to someone else. In fact, a couple of my colleagues are already briefed.'

'Right.' She paused. 'So where are you now?'

'On my way to my sister's place.'

'How is she?'

'That's what I'm going to find out.'

'Let me know, will you?'

Fox glanced in his rearview mirror. A patrol car was behind him, blue roof-lights flashing. 'Got to go,' he said, ending the call.

It took him a whole five minutes to discuss his situation with the officers. He'd tried showing them his warrant card without letting them see he was Complaints and Conduct, but they seemed to know anyway. Was he aware he'd made an illegal manoeuvre? And did he recall the law about driving while holding a conversation on a mobile phone? He managed to sound apologetic; managed not to explain where he was headed and why – didn't see any reason the sods needed to know. In the end, they wrote him out a penalty ticket.

'Nobody's above the law,' the elder of the two cautioned him. Fox thanked the man and got back into his car. They did what they always did – tailed him a few hundred more yards before signalling right and heading elsewhere. It was what happened when you were the Complaints – no favours from your colleagues. In fact, just the opposite. Which got Fox thinking about Jamie Breck again …

He found a parking space along the street from Jude's house. Alison Pettifer opened the door. She'd closed the curtains in the living room and kitchen – out of respect, Fox surmised.

'Where's Jude?' he asked.

'Upstairs. I made her some tea with plenty of sugar.'

Fox nodded, looking around the living room. It seemed to him that Pettifer had started the process of tidying up. He thanked her and signalled that he was going to go see his sister. She pressed a hand to his arm. Didn't say anything, but her eyes told a story. *Go easy on her.* He patted the hand and went out into the hall. The stairs were steep and narrow – difficult to fall down them without becoming wedged halfway. Three doors led off the cramped landing – bathroom and two bedrooms. One bedroom had been turned into Vince Faulkner's lair. Boxes of junk, an old hi-fi and racks of rock CDs, plus a desk with a cheap computer. The door was ajar, so Fox peered in. The slatted blinds had been drawn closed. A couple of men's magazines lay on the floor – *Nuts* and *Zoo*. Their covers showed near-identical blondes with their arms covering their breasts. Fox tapped on the next door along, and turned the handle. Jude was lying on the bed with the duvet cocooned around her. She wasn't asleep, though. The tea sat untouched on the bedside table, beside an empty tumbler. The room smelled faintly of vodka.

'How you doing, sis?' He sat down on the bed. All he could see were her head and her bare feet. He smoothed her hair back from her forehead. She sniffled and started to sit up. Beneath the duvet she was fully dressed.

'Somebody killed him,' she said.

Best thing that could have happened. But what he said out loud was: 'It's hellish.'

'Do they think …?'

'What?'

'Maybe I had something to do with it.'

Fox shook his head. 'But they'll want to talk to you. Standard procedure, so don't worry about it.' She nodded slowly and he stroked her hair again. 'When did you last see him, Jude?'

'Saturday.'

'The same day he …' Fox gestured towards the plaster cast.

'I came back from the hospital and he wasn't here.'

'Did you hear from him?'

She took a deep breath and exhaled, then shook her head. 'Wasn't so unusual, to tell the truth. Some nights, I was lucky if I saw him for five minutes. He'd be out with his mates, and come home next day with the story that he'd bunked on a couch or a spare bed.'

'Did you try phoning him over the weekend?'

'Texted him a couple of times.'

'No answer?'

She shook her head. 'I expected him home on Sunday, but then ...' She gazed at her broken arm. 'Maybe he was feeling more ashamed than usual.'

'And by last night?' Fox coaxed.

Another deep breath. 'By last night ... maybe I was getting worried.'

'Or anaesthetised.' Fox gestured towards the empty glass. She shrugged as best she could. 'When I dropped in yesterday,' he went on, 'why didn't you say anything?'

'I didn't want you to know.'

'I tried calling you last night ... there was no answer.'

'You said it yourself – anaesthetised.'

'And again this morning?'

She stared at him. 'Have they sent you here to interrogate me?'

'I'm just asking the questions *they'll* ask.'

'You never liked him,' she commented.

'I can't deny it.'

'Maybe you're even glad he's dead.' Her voice was turning accusatory. Fox lifted her chin with one finger, so she was facing him.

'That's not true,' he lied. 'But he was never the man you deserved.'

'He was what I got, Malcolm. And that was plenty enough for me.'

5

He met Annie Inglis for coffee at the Fettes canteen. Apart from the staff, the place was deserted. Inglis insisted on fetching the drinks while he sat at a table near the window.

'I'm not an invalid,' he told her with a smile, as she pushed the mug towards him.

'Sugar?' She tipped half a dozen sachets on to the table. He shook his head and watched her draw her chair in. She'd chosen hot chocolate for herself. She fidgeted a little, dabbed a finger against the surface of the liquid and sucked on it. Then she made eye contact.

'So,' she said.

'So,' he agreed.

'Any idea what happened?'

'Building site by the canal. Someone did a job on him.'

'How's your sister doing?'

'Her name's Jude, short for Judith. I'm not sure how she's doing.'

'You went to see her?'

'She was tucked up in bed with a bottle of vodka.'

'Can't begrudge her that.'

'Jude has a history with alcohol.' He stared down at his coffee. It was meant to be a cappuccino, but the foam was non-existent. Inglis gave a twitch of the mouth and allowed the silence to linger.

'So,' she asked at last, 'you got to meet DS Breck?'

'Wondered how long it would take you,' he muttered.

She ignored this. 'How did he strike you?'

'I'd say he's good at his job. The conversation never really got round to his predilection for kiddie-fiddling.'

She bristled, but only for a moment. 'Malcolm,' she said quietly, 'I'm only asking.'

'Sorry.'

'And the reason I'm asking is because Gilchrist and me have been talking ...'

'Is he your boss, by the way?'

'Gilchrist?' She widened her eyes a little. 'He's my DC.'

'He's older than you.'

'So your immediate thought was that he had to outrank me?'

Fox was saved from answering by the sound of her phone. She lifted it from the table and checked the screen.

'I've got to take this,' she said. 'It's my son.' She held the phone to her ear. 'Hey, Duncan.' She listened for the best part of a minute, eyes fixed on the world outside the window. 'Okay, but I want you home by seven. Understood? Bye then.' She placed the phone back on the table, her fingers resting against it.

'I didn't think you were married,' Fox said.

'I'm not.' She thought for a moment. 'But what made you ...?'

He swallowed before answering. There was stuff about her he wasn't supposed to know. 'No wedding ring,' he eventually said. Then, a little too quickly: 'How old is Duncan?'

'Fifteen.'

'You must've been young.'

'My last year at school. Mum and Dad were furious, but they looked after him.'

Fox nodded slowly. There'd been no mention of a son in Inglis's personnel file. An oversight? He took a sip of his drink.

'He's headed to a friend's,' Annie Inglis explained.

'Can't be easy – single mum, teenage boy ...'

'It's fine,' she stated, her tone telling him things could be left at that.

Fox held the mug to his mouth and blew across it. 'You were telling me,' he said, 'that you'd been talking with Gilchrist ...'

'That's right. We're thinking that this could work out for us.'

'Me and Breck, you mean?'

She nodded. 'You're not involved in the inquiry, so it's not really a conflict of interest.'

'What you're saying is, while Breck investigates the murder, *I* busy myself keeping an eye on *him*?'

'The two of you have already met ... and you've got the perfect excuse for keeping in touch with him.'

'And it's not a conflict of interest?'

'We're only asking you for background, Malcolm, gen we can pass on to London. Nothing you do is going to come to court.'

'How can we be sure?'

She thought for a moment and shrugged. 'Gilchrist's checking with your boss and the Deputy Chief.'

'Shouldn't that be *your* job?'

She shrugged and made eye contact. 'I wanted to see you instead.'

'I'm touched.'

'Are you up to the task, Malcolm? That's what I need to know.'

Fox thought back to the piece of waste ground. *We'll be doing all we can ...*

'I'm up to it,' Malcolm Fox said.

Back upstairs, the Complaints office was empty. He sat at his desk for a good five minutes, gnawing on a cheap ballpoint pen, thinking of Vince Faulkner and Jude and Jamie Breck. The door, already ajar, was pushed all the way open by Bob McEwan. He was wearing a trenchcoat and carrying a briefcase.

'You all right, Foxy?' he asked, standing in front of the desk, feet planted almost a yard apart.

'I'm fine.'

'Heard about your brother-in-law ... compassionate leave if you want it.'

'He wasn't a relation,' Fox corrected his boss. 'Just a guy my sister fell in with.'

'All the same ...'

'I'll look in on her when I can.' The words, as they emerged from his mouth, made him think of his father. Mitch needed to be told.

'And about the Chop Shop,' McEwan began. 'Reckon you can still help them out?'

'You don't think there's a problem?'

'Traynor doesn't see one.' Adam Traynor – Deputy Chief Constable. 'I've just been speaking with him.'

'Then that's that,' Fox said, placing the pen back on the desk.

At work's end, he headed over to Lauder Lodge. One of the staff told him he'd find his father in Mrs Sanderson's room. Fox stood in front of her door and couldn't hear anything. He knocked and waited until the woman's voice invited him in. Mitch was seated facing Mrs Sanderson. The two chairs were positioned either side of the room's fireplace. This fireplace was for show only. A vase of dried flowers sat in the unused grate. He'd been in Mrs Sanderson's room once before, when his father had introduced him to his 'new, dear friend'. The old boy was doing the same thing again.

'This is my son, Audrey.'

Mrs Sanderson gave a tinkling laugh. 'I know, Mitch. I've met Malcolm before.'

Mitch Fox's brow furrowed as he tried to remember. Fox leaned down over Mrs Sanderson and placed a kiss against her cheek. She smelled faintly of talcum powder and her face was like parchment; her hands and arms, too. She'd probably always been thin, but now the skin on her face matched the exact contours of the skull beneath. Yet for all that, she was a handsome woman.

'You're feeling better?' Fox asked.

'Much better, dear.' She gave his hand a pat before releasing it.

'Twice in a few days,' Fox's father was saying. 'Am I supposed to feel flattered? And when's that sister of yours going to put in an appearance?'

There was nowhere for Fox to sit except the bed, so he stayed standing. It seemed to him that he towered over the two seated figures. Mrs Sanderson was arranging the tartan travel rug that lay spread across her lower body.

'Jude's had some bad news, Dad,' Fox said.

'Oh?'

'It's Vince. He's been killed.'

Mrs Sanderson stared up at him, mouth opening in an O.

'Killed?' Mitch Fox echoed.

'Do you want me to ...?' Mrs Sanderson was trying to rise to her feet.

'You sit back down,' Mitch ordered. 'This is your room, Audrey.'

'Looks like he got himself into a spot of bother,' Fox was trying to explain, 'and ended up taking a beating.'

'No more than he deserved.'

'Now really, Mitch!' Mrs Sanderson protested. Then, to Fox: 'How's Jude taking it, Malcolm?'

'She's bearing up.'

'She'll need all the help you can give her.' She turned to Mitch. 'You should go see her.'

'What good would that do?'

'It would show her that you cared. Malcolm will take you ...' She looked at Fox for confirmation. He managed something between a nod and a shrug. Her voice softened a little. 'Malcolm will take you,' she repeated, leaning forward and stretching out an arm. After a moment, Mitch Fox copied her. Their hands met and clasped.

'Maybe not just yet, though,' Fox cautioned, remembering the plaster cast. 'She's not really up to visitors ... She's sleeping a fair bit.'

'Tomorrow then,' Mrs Sanderson decided.

'Tomorrow,' Fox eventually conceded.

On the drive home, he thought about visiting Jude, but decided he would phone her instead, just before bedtime. She'd given Alison Pettifer the details of a couple of her closest friends, and the neighbour had promised Fox she would call them and get them to take turns with Jude.

'She won't be alone,' had been Pettifer's closing words to him.

He wondered, too, what Annie Inglis would be doing. She'd told her son to be home by seven. It was seven now. Fox had memorised her address from the HR file. He could drive there in ten or fifteen minutes, but to what purpose? He was curious about the kid. Tried to imagine what it had been like for the schoolgirl to confront her farming father with the news. *Mum and Dad were furious ... but they looked after him.* Yes, because that's what families did – they rallied round; they dug in.

But Duncan's not on your file, Annie ...

At the next set of traffic lights, he stared at an off-licence's window display. Little halogen spotlights threw each bottle into sharp relief. He wondered if Jude's friends were drinkers. Would they turn up with carrier bags and a collection of memories, tragic stories for the telling and retelling?

'Cup of tea for you, Foxy,' he told himself as the queue of traffic began its crawl across the junction.

The mail waiting for him on the hall carpet was the usual stuff: bills and junk and a bank statement. At least the Royal Bank of Scotland was still in business. There was nothing in the envelope with the statement, no letter of grovelling apology for getting above itself and letting down its customers. Lauder Lodge's monthly payment had gone out. The rest seemed to be petrol and groceries. He looked in the fridge, seeking inspiration for a quick dinner. Denied, he tried the cupboards and emerged with a tin of chilli and a small jar of jalapenos. There was long-grain rice in a jar on the worktop. The radio was tuned to Classic FM, but he changed the channel to something he'd come across recently. The station was just called Birdsong and birdsong was precisely what it delivered. He went back to the fridge and pulled out a bottle of Appletiser, sat with his drink at the table and rubbed a hand across his face and forehead, kneading his temples and the bridge of his nose. He wondered who would pay for *his* nursing home when the time came. He hoped there'd be someone like Mrs Sanderson waiting for him there.

When the food was ready, he took it through to the living room and switched on the TV. There was birdsong still audible from the kitchen; sometimes he left it on all night. He flicked through the Freeview channels until he found Dave. It was all repeats, but still watchable. *Fifth Gear* followed by *Top Gear* followed by another *Top Gear*.

'Can I stand the pace?'

He'd left his mobile to recharge on the worktop in the kitchen. When it started ringing, he considered not answering. A scoop of dinner, a half-groan, and he placed the tray on the carpet. The phone had gone dead by the time he reached it, but the readout showed two capitalised letters: TK. Meaning Tony Kaye. Fox unplugged the phone from its charger, punched in his colleague's number, and retreated to the sofa.

'Where are you?' Kaye asked.

'I'm not pubbing tonight,' Fox warned him. He could hear the background hubbub. Minter's or some place like it.

'Yes, you are,' Kaye informed him. 'We've got trouble. How soon can you get here?'

'What sort of trouble?'

'Your friend Breck's been on the blower.'

'Get him to call me at home.'

'It wasn't you he wanted – it was me.'

Fox had dug his fork back into the chilli, but now left it there. 'What do you mean?'

'You're going to have to square this, Foxy. Breck's going to be here at the top of the hour.'

Fox lifted the phone from his ear long enough to check its clock. Seventeen minutes. 'I can be there in twenty,' he said, rising from the sofa and switching off the TV. 'What does he want with you?'

'He's keen to know why I had a mate look up Vince Faulkner on the PNC.'

Fox cursed under his breath. 'Twenty,' he repeated as he grabbed his coat and car keys. 'Don't say anything till I get there. Minter's, right?'

'Right.'

Fox cursed again and ended the call, slamming the front door on his way out.

*

The same two customers were at the bar, conferring with the landlord on a question from yet another TV quiz show. Jamie Breck recognised Fox and nodded a greeting. He was seated at Tony Kaye's regular table, Kaye himself seated opposite, his face stern.

'What can I get you?' Breck asked. Fox shook his head and sat down. He noted that Kaye was drinking tomato juice, Breck a half-pint of orange and lemonade. 'How's your sister doing?'

Fox just nodded and rolled his shoulders. 'Let's get this sorted, eh?'

Breck looked at him. 'I hope you appreciate,' he began, 'that I'm trying to do you a favour here.'

'A favour?' Tony Kaye didn't sound convinced.

'A heads-up. We're not idiots, Sergeant Kaye. First thing we did was a background check. PNC keeps a record of recent searches, and that's what led us to your pal in Hull CID.'

'Some pal,' Kaye muttered, folding his arms.

'He was slow enough giving us your name, if that's any consolation. Took his boss to do a bit of the strongarm.'

'How did the autopsy go?' Fox interrupted.

Breck turned his attention to him. 'Blunt trauma, internal injuries ... We're pretty sure he was dead when they dumped him.'

'Dead how long?'

'Day, day and a half.' Breck paused, rotating his glass on its coaster. 'The PNC search was yesterday. Is that the same day you found out about Jude's broken arm?'

'Yes,' Fox admitted.

'You went looking for Faulkner?'

'No.'

Breck raised an eyebrow, though his stare remained focused on the glass in front of him. 'The man who'd just broken your sister's arm – you didn't want a word with him?'

'I wanted a word, but I didn't go looking.'

'And how about you, Sergeant Kaye?'

Kaye opened his mouth to answer, but Fox held up a hand to stop him. 'This has nothing to do with Sergeant Kaye,' he stated. 'I asked him for a background check on Faulkner.'

'Why?'

'Ammunition – if there was anything there, I was hoping maybe Jude would see sense.'

'Leave him, you mean?' Fox nodded. 'You told her?'

'Never got the chance – Faulkner was already dead, wasn't he?'

Breck didn't bother answering. Fox made eye contact with Tony Kaye, giving the slightest of nods to let him know this was how he wanted it. If there was going to be flak, it was Fox's to take.

'Remember when I asked you if there was anything you wanted to tell me about the victim?' Breck was fixing Malcolm Fox with a stare. 'How come you didn't mention his previous?'

'I don't really know,' Fox answered with a shrug.

'What else did you find?'

'Nothing.'

'But you knew he was a naughty boy?'

'Seems to have toed the line since coming north.'

'Well, it takes time, doesn't it? He'd want to be sure of the new terrain. How long had he been in town?'

'A year, year and a half,' Fox answered. The aroma was in his nostrils again: two fresh malts had just been poured at the bar.

'How did your sister meet him?'

'You'll have to ask her.'

'We'll definitely do that.' Breck glanced at his watch. 'I said I was giving you a heads-up, but time's nearly up.'

'How do you mean?'

Breck locked eyes with Malcolm Fox. 'I'm not your problem here, just remember that.' All three turned as the door to the pub was pushed open with enough force to rattle it on its hinges. The man who lumbered in was almost as wide as he was tall. Despite the plummeting temperature outside, he wore only a checked sports jacket over his open-necked shirt. Fox recognised him, and with good reason. He was Detective Chief Inspector William Giles – 'Bad Billy' Giles. Judging from the well-lined face, the black wavy hair had to be a dye job, not that anyone was about to point this out to the owner. The eyes were a cold, crystalline blue.

'Pint of eighty,' Giles ordered, approaching the table. Breck rose to his feet, but hesitated long enough to start making introductions.

'I know who they are,' Giles growled back at him. 'Three hours they spent grilling me – three hours of my life I'll never get back.'

'Glen Heaton didn't deserve the effort you put in,' Fox commented.

'You can knock a man down as often as you like,' Giles spat. 'The measure is when he keeps getting up, and Glen Heaton's a long way from being counted out by the likes of you.' The chair – Breck's chair – creaked as Giles lowered himself on to it. His eyes flitted between Tony Kaye and Malcolm Fox. 'But now you're mine,' he stated with grim satisfaction.

Billy Giles wasn't just the CID head honcho at Torphichen, not just Jamie Breck's boss – and Glen Heaton's, come to that. He was also Heaton's oldest friend. Fox was thinking back to that three-hour interview. Thinking, too, of all the obstacles Giles had placed in the way of the PSU investigation.

'Now you're mine,' Giles echoed with quiet satisfaction. From the bar, Breck made eye contact with Malcolm Fox. *I'm not your problem here …* Fox acknowledged as much with the same slight nod he'd earlier given to Tony Kaye. Then he turned his attention to Giles.

'Not quite yet,' he said, giving equal weight to each individual word. He rose to his feet, indicating that Kaye should do the same. 'You want us, you know where to find us.'

'Now's as good a time as any.'

But Fox was shaking his head as he buttoned his coat. 'You know where to find us,' he repeated. 'Just be sure to make an appointment – we're always busy in the Complaints.'

'You're maggots, the pair of you.'

Even standing, Fox wasn't much taller than the seated Giles. But he leaned down a little towards the man. 'We're not maggots,' he stated. 'You said so yourself – we're the ones in the ring, the ones who floored your pal Heaton. And last time I looked, he was still on the canvas.'

Then he straightened up, turned and walked out. It was a few seconds before Tony Kaye joined him. Kaye was knotting his tartan scarf as he emerged from the pub.

'What the hell do we do?' he asked.

'We don't need to do anything – it'll happen the way it happens.'

'We should at least tell McEwan.'

Fox nodded his agreement. 'Giles will want us interviewed at Torphichen. We stick to my story. I might get a reprimand, but I doubt it'll amount to much.'

Kaye considered this, then shook his head slowly. 'Giles won't let it go at that. Far as he's concerned, this is payback time.'

'All he'll get is small change, Tony.'

Kaye thought for a further moment. 'That bastard in Hull!'

'We ought to have realised – everyone leaves traces, even on a computer.'

Kaye breathed out noisily through his nose. 'So what now?'

Fox shrugged. 'Do you need a lift? I don't see your Nissan …'

'I parked it legally for a change. It's a couple of streets away.'

'You didn't want Torphichen nabbing you for that, too?'

Kaye shook his head. 'How come you're always so calm, Foxy?'

'No point being anything else – like I say, what happens happens.'

Kaye was staring at the door of Minter's. 'We should leg it before he comes out.'

'He's got that pint to drink, and maybe another one after it. By the way – what did you think of Jamie Breck?'

Kaye needed only a second to deliver his verdict. 'Good guy, seems like.'

Malcolm Fox nodded his agreement. *Seems like ...*

Wednesday 11 February 2009

6

Wednesday morning, Fox was brushing his teeth when the home phone started ringing. The upstairs handset needed recharging, and he knew the caller would have hung up before he could reach the living room, so he stayed where he was. He'd woken early, Tony Kaye's words in his head – *good guy, seems like*. Kaye had meant that Breck was the sort to help out a colleague. Didn't mean he couldn't be other things, too ... Just as Fox was wiping his mouth, his mobile let out its little chirrup. It was on the dresser in the bedroom, and he walked through, tossing the towel on to the just-made bed.

'Fox,' he said, pressing the phone to his ear.

'Mr Fox, it's Alison Pettifer.'

Fox's stomach tightened. 'Is Jude all right?'

'They've taken her.'

'Who?' But already knowing the answer.

'Some policemen. C Division, they said.'

Meaning Torphichen. Fox looked at his watch – half seven. 'It's just routine,' he started to explain.

'That's what they said – "routine questions". All the same, I thought you'd want to know.'

'That's kind of you.'

'Should I stay here, do you think?' Fox wasn't sure what she meant: was she suggesting she head to Torphichen herself? 'To keep an eye on them, I mean.'

Fox lifted the phone from his ear and read the display. She was calling from Jude's home phone. 'They're still there?' he asked.

'Some of them, yes.'

'With a search warrant?'

'They did get Jude to sign something,' the neighbour confirmed.

'Where are you now, Mrs Pettifer?'

'The foot of the stairs.' He heard her apologise as someone pushed past her. Heavy footsteps making for the upstairs landing. 'They don't seem to like me sticking around.'

'What happened to Jude's other friends, the ones who were going to look after her?'

'Joyce stayed the night, but she had to leave for work at six thirty. The police started arriving just after, so I got dressed and ...'

'Thanks for everything, Mrs Pettifer. You can go home now.'

'A couple of reporters came to the door yesterday evening, but I gave them short shrift.'

'Thanks again.'

'Well ... I might just nip home then, if you think that's for the best.'

Fox ended the call, fetched a fresh shirt from its hanger and decided yesterday's tie would suffice. He was halfway down the stairs when the landline started ringing again. He lifted the receiver from the sofa and pressed it to his ear.

'Fox,' he said.

'It's McEwan.'

'Morning, sir.'

'You sound harassed.'

'No, sir, just getting ready to leave.'

'So I'll see you here in half an hour?'

'Actually, I need to stop off somewhere first.'

'I don't think that's advisable, Malcolm.'

'Sir?'

'Torphichen have told me what's happening. I got the call half an hour ago. That stunt you pulled with the PNC is going to take a bit of work to defuse.'

'I was going to tell you, sir ...' Fox paused. 'Truth is, they've taken my sister in for questioning. She needs someone with her.'

'Not you, Malcolm. *You* need to be *here*.'

'They know she's my sister, Bob. They don't like what I've done to their pal Heaton.'

'I know people at Torphichen, Malcolm. I'll see to it everything's squared.'

'Yes, sir.'

'Half an hour, then. You, me and Tony Kaye are going to have a fine wee natter ...' The phone went dead in Fox's hand.

In fact, the journey took him longer than expected. His excuse:

tram works. Really, he'd detoured to Jude's street in Saughtonhall. Her front door was open. A Scene of Crime van stood kerbside. Someone had been dispatched to the corner shop – the crew were drinking from polystyrene cups and munching on pastries and crisps. He saw just a couple of plain-clothes cops – faces he recognised dimly from visits to Torphichen. No sign of either Billy Giles or Jamie Breck. A neighbour on the opposite side of the road stood watching from her window, arms folded. Fox let his engine idle, knowing there was nothing to be gained from going in. Eventually he signalled back out into the traffic. The drivers were all being polite; didn't mind braking on his behalf.

It gave them more time to gawp.

'My dabs will be all over the place,' Fox told McEwan. They weren't in the office: McEwan had found an empty meeting-room. An elliptical table and eight or nine chairs. There was a marker board on a tripod. Three words written there:

VISIBILITY

VIABILITY

VERSATILITY

Tony Kaye had found the only chair in the room with castors. He was rolling himself backwards from the table, then forward again.

'That's annoying me,' McEwan warned him.

'What are we going to do about Bad Billy?' Kaye asked, still moving.

'He's DCI Giles to you, Sergeant Kaye – and we're going to let him do his job.' He turned his head in Fox's direction. 'Isn't that right, Malcolm?'

Fox nodded. 'Only thing we *can* do. They'll feel better once they've given us a kicking.'

McEwan gave a sigh. 'How many times have I told you? PSU has to be above reproach.'

'Like I say, sir, searching the database for Vince Faulkner was my idea.'

McEwan glared at Fox. 'That's a load of balls and you know it. Tony here is the kind who'd decide a protocol could be bent – isn't that right, Sergeant?'

'Yes, sir,' Kaye admitted.

'Last night we told Giles something different,' Fox cautioned.

'Then you better stick to that,' McEwan snapped back. 'If he catches you in one lie, he'll go looking for others ...' He paused. '*Are* there any others?'

'No, sir,' both men said in unison.

McEwan was thoughtful for a moment. 'Billy Giles is all bile and bluster. Scratch the surface and there's a lot less of him to be scared of.' He held up a finger. 'Doesn't mean you should underestimate him.'

Malcolm Fox took out his handkerchief and blew his nose. 'Are they treating Jude's house as a crime scene?'

'*Possible* crime scene.'

'They won't find anything.'

'I thought you just said they'd find your prints.'

'I was there on Monday, and then again yesterday.'

'Best make sure they know that.'

Fox nodded slowly, while McEwan's attention shifted back to Kaye.

'Tony, I swear to God, if you don't stop swivelling on that damned chair ...'

Kaye leapt to his feet so suddenly, the chair rolled all the way back to the marker board. He strode over to the window and peered down at the car park. 'This doesn't feel right,' he muttered with a shake of the head. 'Foxy starts looking at Jamie Breck – next thing we know, C Division's sniffing at our balls. What if Bad Billy got wind of it and decided he'd lost enough rotten apples for one season?'

'And did what?' McEwan reasoned. 'Killed a man in cold blood? Is that seriously what you're suggesting?'

'I'm not saying he ...' But Kaye couldn't finish what he'd started. It turned into an elongated snarl instead.

'Do I put myself forward for questioning?' Fox calmly asked of his boss.

'They've already requested the pleasure of your company.'

'When do they want me?'

'Soon as this meeting's done,' McEwan said.

Fox stared at him. 'So?'

'So you're idiots, the pair of you. Nobody accesses the PNC without good reason.'

'We *had* good reason,' Kaye insisted.

'You had a good *personal* reason, Tony, and that's far from being the same thing.'

'He'd been involved in a domestic,' Kaye ploughed on. 'We were looking for evidence of priors.'

'Keep telling yourself that,' McEwan offered with a tired-looking smile.

'Sir?' Fox interrupted, needing to hear the word.

'Go,' Bob McEwan obliged.

'Is my sister all right?'

'You want to see her?' Giles asked. He was dressed in the same clothes as the previous night, but with the addition of a tie. His neck had outgrown the collar of his shirt, and the top button was undone, visible behind the tie's loose knot.

'Where is she?'

'She's not far.' They were in one of the interview rooms at Torphichen. The place had a *Precinct 13* feel to it – crumbling and circumferenced by dereliction and roadworks. There wasn't much for the tourists, once you got west of Princes Street and Lothian Road. The one-way system dragged buses, cabs and lorries around it, but it was a thankless spot for pedestrians. Inside the building there were the usual smells of mildew and desperation. The interview room bore battle scars – scratched walls, chipped desk, graffiti on the back of the door. They'd kept Fox waiting a good long time in the reception area, giving uniforms and plain-clothes officers alike the chance to come and glare at him. When he'd eventually followed Giles down the corridor towards the interview room, there had been plenty of hissing and cursing from office doorways.

'Is she all right, though?' Fox persisted.

Giles made eye contact with him for the first time since coming in. 'We've not started the waterboarding yet, if that's what you're asking. Tea and biccies and a female officer for company last time I looked in.' Giles leaned forward so his elbows rested against the table. 'It's a bad business,' he stated. Fox just nodded. 'When did *you* last see Mr Faulkner?'

'Before Christmas – November maybe.'

'You didn't have much time for him?'

'No.'

'Don't blame you. You knew he was using your sister as a punch-bag, though?' Fox stared at him but didn't answer. 'See, if that'd been my kith and kin, I'd've been on the bastard like a ton of shit.'

'I'd spoken to her about it. She told me her arm was an accident.'

'No way you believed her.' Giles leaned back again, bunching his hands into his jacket pockets. 'So how come you didn't face up to him?'

'I never got the chance.'

'Or you were yellow …' Giles let the accusation float in the air between them. When Fox didn't rise to it, he bared his teeth. 'Her arm was broken Saturday, wasn't it?'

'So she says.'

'When did you find out about it?'

There was a noise in the corridor outside. A young male by the sound of it, not exactly cooperating as he was led to or from his cell.

'That'll be Mollison,' Giles explained. 'Wee wanker's a one-man crime wave. Soon as I'm done here, I'll be having words with him.'

'Is he anything to do with …?'

Giles shook his head. 'Mollison'll break into your home or car, but it's unlikely he'd bludgeon you to death. Takes rage, that sort of attack. The sort of rage that comes from a grudge.'

'I hadn't seen Faulkner since before Christmas.'

'Did you know back then?'

'Know what?'

'That he was a wife-beater.'

'Jude wasn't his wife.'

'Did you, though?' Giles's small eyes, staring out from his fleshy face, were drilling into Fox. Though he fought against it, Fox wriggled in his chair.

'I knew their relationship was tempestuous.'

Giles offered a snort. 'You're not here to write a Mills and fucking Boon!'

'Jude always said she gave as good as she got.'

'Didn't make it right, Inspector. Seems to me you shied away from saying anything. You never pulled Faulkner aside for a quiet word?'

'After the arm I would've done, if there'd been the chance.'

'So we're back to my original question – when did you find out?'

'A neighbour called me on Monday afternoon.'

Giles nodded slowly. 'Mrs Pettifer,' he stated. Yes, stood to reason she'd have been questioned by the inquiry team … 'I'm assuming you then went looking for him?'

'No.' Fox was peering down at his hands, clasped across his lap.

'No?' Giles sounded unconvinced.

'What difference would it have made – he was already dead, wasn't he?'

'Come on, Fox – you know time of death's always open to debate … a few hours this way or that.'

'Did he turn up for work Monday morning?'

Giles paused a moment before answering, weighing up what he did and didn't want Fox to know. Eventually, he shook his head.

'So what was he doing? Where was he hiding himself from Saturday night onwards? Someone must have seen him.'

'Whoever killed him saw him.'

'You can't think it was Jude.'

Giles pursed his lips and removed his hands from their pockets, cupping them behind his head. As his shirt stretched, gaps appeared between the buttons, revealing a white string vest beneath. The room felt warm to Fox. He knew they probably kept it stuffy: didn't want suspects getting too comfortable. His scalp felt itchy, perspiration cloying there. But if he scratched or wiped, Giles would think the interview was getting to him.

'I've seen Faulkner on the slab,' the detective was saying. 'Plenty of muscle on him. Not sure a one-armed alcoholic girlie weighing all of eight stone could have outpointed him.' Giles was watching for a reaction. 'Someone could've helped her, though.'

'You're not going to find anything in the house.' In the distance, a door slammed. A truck or bus was idling outside, causing the frosted window pane to shiver noisily in its frame.

'Plenty of evidence of a chaotic lifestyle,' Giles went on. 'Even when someone's had a go at tidying up.'

'That was the neighbour; she did it out of kindness.'

'I'm not suggesting anyone was trying to cover their tracks.' Giles gave a cold smile. 'And by the way – how's your case against Glen Heaton shaping up?'

'Wondered how long it would take you …'

'He's loving it, you know – full pay, feet up at home while we shiver and scrape ice off the windscreen of a morning.' Giles's meaty hands came to rest on the table. He leaned over them. 'And exonerated at the end of it.'

'I go easy on Heaton and you lay off my sister?'

Giles tried for a look of mock outrage. 'Did I say that? I don't think I said that.' He paused. 'But I can't help feeling a sense of … what? Irony? Poetic justice?'

'A man's dead, in case you'd forgotten.'

'I've not forgotten, Inspector. You can be absolutely sure of that. Every detail of Faulkner's life is going to be pored over by my men. Your sister's going to have to get used to questions and more questions. The media are showing an interest, too, so she might want to stop answering her door and her phone.'

'Don't take this out on her,' Fox said quietly.

'Or you'll make a complaint?' Giles smiled. 'Now wouldn't *that* be the cherry on the top?'

'Are we finished?' Fox was starting to get to his feet.

'For now – unless there's anything you want to tell me.'

Fox could think of a few things, but all he did was shake his head.

Out in the hallway, he tried a few of the doors, but Jude wasn't in any of the other interview rooms. At the far end was the door leading to the station's cramped reception area, and beyond that the outside world. A familiar face was loitering on the steps when Fox emerged.

'Can we take a walk?' Jamie Breck asked, cutting short the phone call he'd been making on his mobile.

'My car's right here.' Fox nodded towards it.

'All the same ...' Breck gestured and started moving up the slope towards the traffic lights. 'How did it go with DCI Giles?'

'How do you think it went?'

Breck gave a slow nod. 'I reckoned you'd want to know how things are shaping up.'

'Is that how it works – Giles gives me a doing and then you start in with the "good cop" routine?'

'He'd kill me if he knew I was talking to you.' Breck looked over his shoulder as they rounded the corner into Morrison Street.

'Then why are you?'

'I don't like the politics – us on our side, you on yours.' Breck was walking briskly. It was a young man's gait, purposeful and strong, as if the future held a clear destination. Fox, struggling to keep up, could feel the sweat growing chill at his hairline.

'Where's my sister?' he asked.

'On her way home, I think.'

'Off the record, what's *your* view of Glen Heaton?'

Breck's nose wrinkled. 'I could see that he cut a few corners.'

'He drove on every pavement he saw.'

'That's his style – pretty effective, too.'

'I think your boss just tried to do a deal with me.'

'What sort of deal?'

'Heaton for my sister ...' Breck gave a little whistle. 'But since my sister hasn't done anything ...'

'You turned him down?' Breck guessed.

'You don't seem surprised he made the offer.'

Breck shrugged. 'All I'm wondering is why you're telling *me*.'

'When we nail Heaton, there'll be a vacancy at DI.'

'I suppose so.'

'You're not ambitious?'

'Of course I'm ambitious – isn't everyone? Aren't you?'

'Not especially.' The two men walked in silence for a few paces.

'So how *did* it go with Bad Billy?' Breck eventually asked.

'He sees the investigation as a way of getting at me, and that may colour his judgement ... take him down any number of wrong roads.'

Breck was nodding. 'Did he tell you about the CCTV?'

Fox looked at the younger man. 'What about it?'

'I'll assume he didn't.' Breck took a deep breath. 'There's a pub in Gorgie ... Faulkner wasn't exactly a regular, but he went in occasionally. They've got CCTV inside and out.'

'And?'

Breck stopped suddenly and turned to face Malcolm Fox, studying him. 'I'm not sure how much of this I should be telling you.'

'What's the pub called?'

'Marooned. Do you know it?' Breck watched the older man shake his head. 'It's only been open a year or so.'

'Vince Faulkner was caught on camera?' Fox prompted.

'Saturday night. A few rugby fans were in – Welsh guys. Words were exchanged and they took it outside.'

'They beat him up?'

Breck shook his head. 'From the footage I've seen, he pushed one of them and they gave his head a slap. Three against one ... Faulkner weighed it up and sloped off with a few final insults.'

'They didn't go after him?'

'Doesn't mean he didn't bump into them again later.'

'No.' Fox was thoughtful.

'Your sister says he doesn't have any family left down south – is that right?'

Fox shrugged. 'She'd know better than me.' He paused. 'This doesn't have anything to do with her, you know.'

Breck nodded slowly. 'All the same ... it's the way the game's played.'

'Will her house be a mess?'

'I asked the SOCOs to go easy.'

'They won't have found anything.' The two men had started walking again. When they turned left into Dewar Place, Fox realised they were doing a circuit. Another left into the lane and they'd be back at the police station and Fox's car.

'You live quite close to me,' Breck was saying.

Fox opened his mouth to reply, then made a swallowing motion instead. He'd been about to say, *I know*.

'Is that right?' was what he eventually answered.

'It came up,' Breck explained with a shrug. 'I'm on the estate behind Morrisons.'

'You married?'

'Girlfriend.'

'How serious?'

'Only a couple of months – she's not moved in yet. How about you?'

'I used to be married,' Fox replied.

'Family life's tough when you're a cop,' Breck decided.

'Yes, it is,' Fox agreed. He was thinking about the girlfriend. Plenty of abusers and offenders had partners. It made for good cover – 'the quiet family man'. Only a tiny part of their everyday life was given over to their secret self. On the other hand, there were probably lots of men out there who'd stumbled upon websites they wished they hadn't, then had lingered ... not altogether sure why. Drawn in by something.

How many, though, ended up handing over their credit card?

'Is that what you've got so far?' Fox asked. 'Marooned and some Welsh rugby fans?'

'That's about it.'

'No sightings Sunday or Monday?'

'It's early days, Inspector.'

Fox nodded and thought of something. 'Where did he work?'

'You don't know?'

'I know he was a labourer ...'

'He was on a short-term contract at Salamander Point.'

'I thought it had gone bust?'

'Not quite.' They had almost reached the end of Dewar Place Lane. Breck touched Fox on the shoulder. 'Best if we split up here.'

Fox nodded. 'Thanks for the chat.'

Breck smiled and stuck out his hand. The two men shook.

7

Fox called Lauder Lodge from the car. They asked if he wanted to speak to his father, but he told them just to pass on the message. He couldn't take Mitch to Jude's today. Maybe tomorrow.

Marooned was about halfway between Torphichen Place and Saughtonhall. It was down a side street, not far from the Heart of Midlothian stadium. Fox didn't get out of the car, just sat there long enough to get an idea of the place. The single-storey brick building dated back to the seventies. Must have been a gap site at one time, maybe a garage or builder's yard before that. Four-storey tenements flanked it, with another across the street. A chalkboard to the left of the main door promised quiz nights, karaoke and hot food. There was a double-measure/single-price deal on spirits. Just the one CCTV camera, bolted high up on the wall and protected by a wire cage. Fox knew he could go inside and flash his warrant card, ask to see the footage, but what good would it do? And if word got back to Billy Giles that he'd been there ... Instead, he executed a three-point turn and got back on to the road to Saughtonhall.

The door was answered by a woman he didn't know. He introduced himself as Jude's brother.

'I'm Sandra,' the woman said. 'Sandra Hendry.' She was around Jude's age, with dark, tired eyes and a blotchy face. The outfit – artfully ripped and patched denims; top trimmed to show her midriff – would have suited someone half her age and forty pounds lighter. Her hair resembled candyfloss, beginning to darken at its roots. Gold hoop earrings dangled from her lobes. Her nose and tongue were pierced and studded. 'Jude's in bed,' she said, leading him inside. 'Do you want to go up?'

'In a minute.' They were in the living room by now. The place looked relatively tidy. The woman called Sandra had retreated to the armchair and was crossing one leg over the other. The TV was on, but with the sound just audible. A tanned man seemed to be trying to train an unruly dog.

'Love this,' Sandra commented. Fox noticed that one of her ankles sported a tattoo of a scorpion.

'How's she doing?' Fox asked, commencing a circuit of the room.

'Just got back from the Gestapo ...' She broke off and stared at him, eyes widening as she remembered what Jude's brother did for a living.

'I've heard worse,' he reassured her.

'She was shattered, reckoned a nap might help.'

Fox nodded his understanding. Flipping open the lid of the kitchen bin, he saw that its inner bag had been removed. Forensics would be busy at their Howdenhall HQ, poring over its contents.

'I appreciate you looking after her.'

Sandra shrugged. 'My shift doesn't start till four.'

'Where do you work?'

'The Asda on Chesser Avenue.' She offered him a stick of gum, but he shook his head. The empty bottles and cans had gone. Ashtrays had been cleaned. The breakfast bar now boasted only a couple of dirty mugs and a pizza carton.

'Did you ever meet Vince?' Fox asked.

'Four of us used to go out.'

'You and your partner?'

'He works with Vince.' She paused, stopped chewing. 'Past tense, I suppose.'

'He's in construction, then?'

She nodded. 'Foreman – Vince's boss, I suppose.'

'So was it your partner who took Vince on?'

She shrugged. 'Husband, not partner. Sixteen years – you'd get less for murdering someone, that's what Ronnie says.'

'He's probably right. You and Ronnie knew Vince pretty well, then?'

'Suppose so.'

'Ever end up at a place called Marooned?'

'That shit-hole? Not if we could help it. In the better weather, the boys liked the Golf Tavern – meant they could play pitch 'n' putt on Bruntsfield Links.'

'You and Jude didn't play?'

'Dinner and a few games of roulette or blackjack – that's more my thing.'

'Which casino?'
'The Oliver.'
'At Ocean Terminal?' He'd finished looking around and was standing in the middle of the room, facing her as she stared at the TV.
'That's the one.'
'Not far from Salamander Point, then.'
'Within staggering distance.'
Fox nodded to himself. 'What did you make of him, Sandra?'
At mention of her name, she peered up at him. 'Vince, you mean?' She considered his question. 'He was all right – bit of a laugh when you got him in the right mood.'
'Meaning he sometimes wasn't?'
'I knew he had a temper – but Jude's not exactly lacking in that department either.'
'What do you think about him breaking her arm?'
'She says she fell.'
'But we both know she didn't.'
'My motto is: don't get involved. Just leads to more grief.' Her interest in him had waned. Onscreen, the dog-handler was making obvious progress.
'But you're her friend ... you must've ...' Fox broke off, thinking to himself: *you're* her brother, and *you* didn't. 'I'm going to go upstairs,' he said instead.
Sandra nodded distractedly. 'I'd offer to make you a cuppa, but we're all out.'
The door to Vince's den was wide open and Fox saw that his computer had been removed by the investigators. Jude's bedroom door was ajar. He knocked and pushed it all the way open. His sister was sitting on the bed, surrounded by piles of clothes. The fitted wardrobe had been half emptied, along with the chest of drawers. It was all Faulkner's stuff – his jeans and T-shirts, socks and pants. Jude was holding a short-sleeved shirt in her good hand, working at the cloth with her fingers. She was sniffing back tears.
'I can still smell him – on the sheets, the pillows ... Part of him's still here.' She paused for a moment and gave her brother a look. 'Know what they told me, Malcolm? They said we can't have the funeral. They need to hold on to his body. Might take weeks, they said. Nobody knows how long.'
There was a corner of the bed going spare, so Fox rested his weight there, but stayed silent.
'Sandra says we need to start cancelling stuff and telling the

proper authorities. But what's left of him after that?' She sniffed again, and rubbed her forearm across her eyes. 'They kept asking me all these questions. They think I did it ...'

'They don't.' Fox assured her, reaching out to give her shoulder a squeeze.

'That man ... Giles, his name was ... he kept on at me about Vince being an abuser – that's the word he used, "abuser". He said Vince had past convictions. He said they were for violence. Told me no one would blame me for getting my own back. But that's not what happened, Malcolm.'

'Giles knows that, Jude – they all do.'

'Then why did he keep saying it?'

'He's a prick, sis.'

She managed a fleeting smile at this. Fox wasn't letting go of her shoulder just yet, but she turned to look at his hand. 'That hurts,' she explained, and he realised the shoulder belonged to her broken arm.

'Christ, sorry.'

Another half-smile. 'There was a nicer detective ... Breck, I think. Yes, because we read that book one holiday when we were kids.'

'*Kidnapped*,' Fox reminded her. 'The hero's called Alan Breck. You wanted me to read it to you.'

'At bedtime.' She nodded, remembering. 'Every night for two weeks. And now look at us ...' She turned to him, tears running down her cheeks. 'I loved him, Malcolm.'

'I know.'

She started wiping her tears on the shirt she was holding. 'I'm not going to cope without him.'

'Yes, you are ... trust me. Can I get you anything?'

'How about a time machine?'

'Might take a while to build. Sandra says you're out of tea and coffee – I could go to the shop and fetch some.'

She shook her head. 'She's going to bring some back from Asda – says there's a discount for staff.'

'She was telling me the four of you used to go to the casino. I never knew you liked a flutter.'

Jude took a deep breath and exhaled. 'It wasn't me so much as the other three. I liked the meal and a few drinks ... They were always good nights.' She paused. 'They had people here, you know, rifling through all our stuff. I had to sign for some things they took. It's why ...' She gestured towards the clothes surrounding her. 'Drawers were already open, so I thought I might as well …'

Fox nodded. 'I'll leave you to it, if you're sure there's nothing I …'

'Does Mitch know?'

'Yes. I've put him off visiting.'

'I'll go see him. That would be easier, wouldn't it?'

'I can take you. How about later – three o'clock, four?'

'Shouldn't you be at work?'

Fox just shrugged.

'Okay then,' Jude said. Her brother started to get to his feet. He was at the door when she thought of something. 'Monday night, someone came to the house.'

Fox paused with his hand on the handle.

'Said he was looking for Vince,' Jude went on. 'I told him I didn't know where he was. Closed the door on him and that was that.'

'You didn't know him?'

Jude shook her head. 'Tall guy, dark hair. I went to the window and watched him leave, but all I saw was his back.'

'Did he get into a car?'

'Maybe …'

'You told Giles this?'

She shook her head again. 'Mad as it seems, I wasn't in the mood. Maybe you could tell him instead?'

'Sure. One thing, though, Jude …'

'What?'

'Was Vince in any sort of trouble? Maybe he'd been on a shorter fuse than usual?'

She considered this, holding the shirt up to her nose. 'He was just Vince,' she told Fox. 'Always will be. But Malcolm …?'

'Yes?'

'Did you know about the convictions?' She watched him as he gave a slow nod of the head. 'You never told me.'

'By the time I found out, he was already dead.'

'You could still have told me. Better to hear it from you than that vile man.'

'Yes,' Fox agreed. 'Sorry, sis. But how about you? Did you really not know?'

It was Jude's turn to shake her head. 'Doesn't matter now,' she said, her attention drifting back to her dead lover's shirt. 'Nothing matters now …'

*

At Fettes, there was a message that DS Inglis wanted to see him.

'She delivered it herself,' Tony Kaye teased as Fox read the note. 'Tidy body on her …'

'Where's the boss?' Fox asked.

'Knocked off early; says he's got a speech to write.' When Fox looked at him, Kaye just shrugged. 'Some conference in Glasgow.'

'Methods of Policing an Expected Surge in Civil Unrest,' Joe Naysmith recited. 'All down to the credit crunch, apparently.'

Kaye tutted. 'They'll be lynching bankers next.'

'What's that got to do with the Complaints?' Fox asked.

'If our lads go in a bit too hard at the protesters,' Kaye explained, 'might end up coming to us.' He had risen from his desk and was moving towards Fox's. 'Good to see you escaped unscathed – kept you there long enough.'

'Bad Billy Giles was doing his Torquemada impression.'

'Only to be expected. How's your sister bearing up?'

'Fine, so far. I went to see her after Torphichen.'

'Did you learn anything?'

'Faulker had a run-in with some rugby fans Saturday night.'

'Oh?'

'Seemed to peter out.'

'All the same … Is that the last sighting?' Kaye watched his colleague nod. 'And Jude's been interviewed?'

'By both Giles and Jamie Breck.'

'Did she have anything to tell them?'

'I don't think so.' Fox was pinching the bridge of his nose. He wished the head cold would either explode into life or else burn itself out. At the moment, all it was doing was shadowing him like a stalker.

'Are you going to go see the talent?'

'What?' Fox looked up at Kaye.

'The Chop Shop glamour puss.' Kaye gestured towards the note. 'I can always nip along on your behalf, pass on a message.'

'It's fine,' Fox said, getting back to his feet. Kaye shrugged and turned away.

'Hey, Starbuck,' he called to Joe Naysmith, 'get the coffee on …'

Fox walked the short distance to the CEOP office and pressed the buzzer. Annie Inglis herself opened the door. Just an inch at first, checking it was him. She beamed a smile and ushered him inside. DC Gilchrist nodded a greeting. The blinds were drawn against the low mid-afternoon sun.

'I haven't got long,' Fox warned Inglis.

‘Just wondered how things were.’ She held her hand out towards the same chair he’d taken on his first visit. He sat down opposite her, their knees brushing for a moment. She was dressed in a skirt and black tights, and an open-necked white blouse with a string of pearls around her neck. The pearls looked old; maybe some sort of heirloom.

‘Things are fine,’ he said. Gilchrist, his back to them, was lifting the casing from a hard drive, peering inside for anything of interest.

‘Our opposite numbers in Melbourne are readying to jump the gun,’ Inglis said.

‘How do you mean?’

‘The cop down there, the one I showed you …’ She indicated her desk monitor. ‘They’re worried he has friends on the force, meaning he’ll find out we’re on to him.’

‘They’re getting ready to question him?’

Inglis nodded. ‘We might lose any number of his UK clients.’

‘The ones who’ve coughed up the cash,’ Gilchrist added without looking up, ‘but not the rest of the joining fee. They’ll have to be let off with a caution.’

‘Breck still hasn’t sent any pictures?’

Inglis shook her head. ‘Hasn’t posted anything on the group’s message board either.’ She paused. ‘This has happened before – information gets leaked, leaving plenty of time for evidence to disappear or be tampered with.’

‘But you’ve *got* the evidence.’ It was Fox’s turn to gesture towards the monitor.

‘We’ve just scratched the surface, Malcolm.’

‘Tip of the iceberg,’ Gilchrist agreed as he started to dismantle the drive unit. ‘What we could really do with …’ he seemed to be talking to himself, ‘…is access to the suspect’s home computer.’

Fox looked at Inglis. She was staring back at him. ‘Thing is,’ she said, ‘we’d have to apply for a search-and-seize. Breck’s bound to have a friend somewhere in the system who might be tempted to alert him.’

‘You on the other hand,’ Gilchrist added, still seemingly intent on his task, ‘can do a bit of breaking and entering – and all of it above board. The Complaints have got powers beyond us mere mortals.’

‘I thought it was general background you wanted?’

‘A bit of evidence would be nice,’ Inglis mused.

‘We’d get a gold star from London,’ her colleague continued.

‘Is that what this is about?’ Fox asked. ‘Impressing the big kids?’

‘You want them to think we’re all amateurs north of the border?’ Inglis waited for a response, which didn’t come. ‘He’ll have a store of images at home – either on his hard drive or a memory stick,’ she continued quietly but determinedly. ‘Even if he’s transferred them, they’ll have left traces.’

‘Traces?’ Fox echoed.

She nodded slowly. ‘It’s like forensics, Malcolm – everyone leaves a bit of a trail.’

‘Or a trail of bits,’ Gilchrist added, in what Fox assumed was a private joke. Inglis certainly offered her colleague a smile. Fox leaned back in his chair, thinking of the trail Tony Kaye had left on the PNC.

‘Nice line of patter the two of you have got. All for my benefit, or is it a tried and tested routine?’

‘Whatever it takes,’ Inglis said.

‘Thing is, though,’ he told her, ‘we don’t just go breaking into people’s homes without okaying it first.’

‘But permission can be granted retrospectively,’ Inglis stated.

‘It has to be justified to the Surveillance Commissioner,’ Fox cautioned.

‘Eventually,’ Inglis agreed. ‘As far as I understand it, in emergencies you’re allowed to act first and consult later.’

‘But this isn’t my case,’ Fox said quietly. ‘I’m not the one investigating Jamie Breck. In point of fact, he could argue that *he’s* investigating me. And how’s that going to look?’

There was silence in the room for a moment. ‘Not great,’ Inglis eventually conceded. The glimmer of hope had vanished from her eyes. She looked to Gilchrist, and received a shrug in reply.

‘We had to try,’ she told Fox.

‘We hate to lose one,’ Gilchrist added, tossing a small screwdriver on to the desk.

‘Maybe there’s some other way,’ Fox offered. ‘For B and E, we need the Surveillance Commissioner’s okay … but if Breck’s using his home computer, we could set up the van outside, zero in on his keystrokes and find out what he’s doing.’

‘You don’t need judicial approval for the van?’ Inglis asked, her spirits lifting.

‘Fox shook his head. ‘DCC can give the go-ahead, and even then it can be retrospective.’

‘Well, the DCC’s on our side,’ Inglis commented. She had nudged the mouse on the desk next to her. The computer screen sprang back into life, showing the same photograph as before – the Melbourne cop with the Asian kid. 'You know what their defence is?' she asked. 'They call it a victimless crime. They share photos. In most cases that's all they say they do. They're not the ones doing the actual abusing.'

'Doesn't mean it's not abuse,' Gilchrist stated.

'Look,' Fox said with a sigh, 'I appreciate the job you're trying to do—'

'With one arm tied behind our backs,' Inglis interrupted.

'Let me see if I can help,' Fox went on. 'The surveillance van's a real option, if he is what you say he is …'

'If?'

Gilchrist's voice had risen. He was staring hard at Fox. But Inglis calmed him with a wave of her hand. 'Thanks, Malcolm,' she said to Fox. 'Anything at all would be appreciated.'

'Okay then,' Fox said, rising to his feet. 'Leave it with me.'

Her hand touched his forearm. They locked eyes and he nodded. She mouthed three words as he readied to leave.

Anything at all.

Back in the Complaints, he crooked a forefinger at Tony Kaye. Kaye approached Fox's desk, arms folded.

'How would you feel,' Fox asked him, 'about a night-time stint in the van?'

Kaye gave a snort and a grin. 'What's she giving you in return?'

Fox shook his head. 'But how would you feel?' he persisted.

'I'd feel grumpy and tired. Is this in the hope that we catch Breck drooling over internet porn?'

'Yes.'

'He's not our customer, Foxy.'

'He could be, if he's doing what the Chop Shop say he is.'

'A joint operation?'

'I think DS Inglis or her colleague would need to be in the van …'

'Is her colleague as tasty as she is?'

'Not quite.' Fox looked over towards the coffee machine. 'You'd need Naysmith, too, of course.'

Kaye seemed to deflate. 'Sadly, that's true.' Naysmith was the one who knew how to get the best out of the technology.

'But while he's breaking sweat,' Fox added, 'you'll have plenty of time to work your charm on DS Inglis.'

'Also true,' Kaye agreed, perking up again. 'But where would you be?'

'I can't get involved, Tony.'

Kaye nodded his acceptance of this. 'Tonight?' he asked.

'Sooner the better. The van's not on other duties?'

Kaye shook his head. 'Cold night for it. Might need to snuggle up for warmth.'

'I'm sure DS Inglis would like that. Go tell Naysmith and I'll let the Chop Shop know.'

Fox watched Kaye retreat, then picked up the telephone and punched in the number for CEOP. Inglis answered, and he cupped his hand to his mouth so Kaye wouldn't overhear.

'We can do a surveillance tonight. It'll be two of my men – Kaye and Naysmith.'

'Nights are ...'

Fox knew what she was about to say. 'Difficult? Yes, with your son and everything. But as it happens, Sergeant Kaye would be a lot more comfortable with a male officer.'

'Gilchrist would be up for it,' Annie Inglis stated. Then, prickling: 'Why's Kaye uncomfortable working with a woman officer?'

'It's women in general, Annie,' Fox explained in an undertone.

'Oh,' she said. Kaye and Naysmith were approaching his desk, so Fox ended the call.

'That's sorted, then,' he told them.

Tony Kaye just rubbed his hands together and smiled.

8

On his way home that evening, Fox stopped off at a Chinese restaurant. He'd half a mind to take a table, but the place was empty – it would just have been him and the staff. So instead he ordered some food to eat at home. Fifteen minutes later, he was in the car, the carrier bag on the passenger seat: chicken with fresh ginger and spring onion; soft noodles; Chinese greens. The owner had offered him a helping of prawn crackers on the house, but Fox had declined. Once home, he emptied the whole lot on to a plate, then decided it was too much and scooped half the noodles back into their container. He ate at the dining table, a dishtowel tucked into his shirt collar. There had been no messages on his phone, and no mail waiting for him. A couple of dogs were having an argument a street or two away. A motorbike passed the house, being driven too quickly. Fox turned the radio on to the Birdsong channel, poured himself a glass of Appletiser, and thought back to the visit to Lauder Lodge.

He'd picked Jude up at four as agreed, the two of them not saying much on the drive. The staff at the care home had tried not to look too interested in Jude. It wasn't just the cast on her arm – they'd been reading their papers and watching the local TV news. They knew who she was and what had happened.

'I forgot to wear my mourning veil,' Jude muttered to her brother as they headed down the corridor to their father's room. Mitch was waiting for them. He insisted on getting to his feet so he could offer Jude a consoling embrace. As they all sat down, two staff members arrived to ask if they wanted a cup of tea. Mitch decided this would be acceptable. But after the tea had been fetched, another staffer stuck her head round the door to see if they might like a biscuit.

Malcolm Fox decided enough was enough, and closed the door. But almost immediately there was a knock. This time they wanted Mr Fox to know that it was whist night, starting straight after supper.

'Yes, I know,' he said. 'Now bugger off and leave us in peace.'

He turned his attention back to his daughter. 'How are you, Jude?'

'I'm okay.'

'You don't look it. It's hellish about that man of yours.'

'His name's Vince, Dad.'

'Hellish,' Mitch Fox repeated, staring at her arm.

'Sorry, Dad,' Fox apologised. 'I should have told you ...'

'What happened?'

'I fell in the kitchen,' Jude blurted out.

'I'm sure you did,' her father muttered.

The visit hadn't been a complete disaster. Mitch had managed not to say anything like 'I told you so' or 'He was never right for you'; Jude had managed to say nothing to offend her father.

'You're quiet,' Malcolm's father had chided him at one point. Fox had just shrugged, making show of concentrating on the cup of tea he was holding.

Afterwards, he'd driven Jude home, asking her if she wanted any company. She'd shaken her head, told him Alison was going to look in. Then she'd pecked him on the cheek before exiting the car.

Sitting at his dining table, reflecting back on that moment, Fox wasn't sure why he'd been so startled by Jude's gesture. Maybe it was because, like many another family, they so seldom showed affection. There might be a kiss or a hug at Christmas. Or at funerals, of course. But he hadn't seen Jude this past Christmas, and the last family funeral had been an aunt the previous summer.

'Thanks,' Jude had said, closing the car door. He'd watched her all the way into her house. She didn't pause to wave. And after her front door was closed and the living-room light came on, she hadn't come to the window to offer a signal of goodbye.

Back at Lauder Lodge, Mitch had asked if he should give Audrey Sanderson a buzz – 'I'm sure she'd like to see you.' But Jude had asked him not to, and Fox got the feeling Mrs Sanderson herself was keeping well out of the way, not wishing to interfere.

Scraping the leftovers into the bin, Fox wondered what his father thought of him. Mitch could have been living here with him – there was plenty of space. The stairs might have been an issue – the very argument Fox had used to himself when deciding his father's future. Besides, at Lauder Lodge the old boy had made friends. True, that might have happened in Oxgangs as well – there was a daily get-together of older people at the local church. But no ... Lauder Lodge had been the best option and outcome. Lauder Lodge had been the right thing to do.

He started to make himself some tea, but stopped – the taste of the cup he'd drunk at Lauder Lodge was still at the back of his throat, dissuading him from repeating the experience. There was more Appletiser in the fridge, but he didn't fancy it. He didn't know what he wanted. Through in the living room, he tried all the TV channels, without finding anything he was willing to waste time on. He supposed he could have an early night, catch up on some reading, but it wasn't even nine o'clock. Two hours until the Breck surveillance was due to start. Joe Naysmith had asked the obvious question – 'Is everything in order?'

Meaning paperwork. Meaning the green light from on high. Naysmith: cautious and scrupulous. Fox had assured him it was 'in the post', shorthand for 'to be dealt with at a later date'. Kaye had told the younger man not to worry, ruffling his hand through Naysmith's hair. Their excuse: McEwan's absence. Plus the Chop Shop's stipulation that it was an emergency.

'We'll be fine,' Fox had stated.

Everything would be fine.

A DVD ... maybe he could watch a film. But nothing jumped out at him as an obvious candidate. He thought of the DVDs in Jude's house, none of them Vince Faulkner's choices – romantic comedies; dreams of another, less imperfect life. He tried to remember what Jude's ambitions had been, back when they'd both been kids, but nothing came to mind. What about him – had he always wanted to be a detective? Yes, pretty much. The Hearts first team had never come calling, and vacancies for film stars seemed not to be advertised. Besides, he'd liked telling friends, *I'm going to be a cop*, relishing the words and the effect they had on some people.

Cop, copper.

Filth, pig.

He'd been called worse, too, down the years – and sometimes by his own kind, colleagues who'd crossed the line, gone bad, been found out. He imagined Jamie Breck, clean and shiny on the surface, heading home and locking the door after him. Shutting the curtains. All alone, no prying eyes, warming up his computer, allowing his secret self to breathe. And unaware of the van parked outside, picking up every key he tapped, every site he visited.

Everything he viewed, the people in the van viewed too. Fox had seen it in action. He'd felt a shiver up his spine as love affairs were revealed, criminal connections confirmed, frauds and frailties exposed.

That how you get your kicks? Peeping fucking Tom ...

Yes, he'd been called worse. *Twisted bastard ... shafting your own kind ... Lower than slime ...*

Lowest of the low. But still better than you – the only response possible.

Still better than you.

He was about the try the words out aloud when his doorbell sounded. He checked his watch. It was half past nine. He stood in the hall for a moment, listening for clues. When the bell rang again, he opened the door an inch.

'Hiya,' Jamie Breck said.

Fox opened the door all the way. He glanced to right and left. 'This is a surprise,' was all he managed to say.

Breck gave a little laugh. 'I'd be lying if I said I was just passing, but in a way it's true. I sometimes take a walk at night, just clearing my head. When I saw the sign for your street, it dawned on me where I was. Maybe I'd planned to end up here all along.' He offered a shrug. 'The subconscious is a wonderful thing.'

'Is it?' Fox was weighing up his options. 'Well, you better come in.'

'Only if I'm not disturbing you ...?'

Fox led Breck into the living room. 'Do you want something to drink?'

'Are you having anything?'

'I don't drink.'

'I don't think I knew that.'

'Well, now you can add it to my profile, can't you?'

Breck smiled at this. 'No alcohol in the house, not even for visitors?' He watched Fox shake his head. 'Meaning you don't trust yourself with the stuff – am I right?'

'What can I do for you, DS Breck?'

'This isn't an official visit, Malcolm – call me Jamie.'

'What can I do for you, Jamie?' Breck was seated on the sofa, Fox in the armchair to his right. Breck had twisted himself round so he was facing the older man. He had changed his clothes since leaving work – a denim jacket, black cords, purple polo neck.

'Nice place,' he said, studying the room. 'Bigger than mine, but then mine's newer – they tend to build smaller these days ...'

'Yes,' Fox agreed, waiting to hear what Breck really wanted to say.

'We've done what we can with the footage from outside the pub,' Breck duly obliged. 'I don't think we're going to get anything useful by way of an ID. Might let the police in Wales take a look anyway, just on the off-chance … Thing is, only a few minutes after the spat, the rugby lads were back inside Marooned, laughing it off and ordering more drink.'

'Says who?'

'A couple of regulars – the Welsh stood them a round. Even apologised for having a go at Faulkner.' He paused. 'Plus there was CCTV inside the bar as well as outside – the story stacks up. So unless they bumped into him again later on in the evening …'

'You're ruling them out?'

'We're not ruling out anything, Malcolm.'

'Why are you telling me?'

'Thought you'd want to know – just between us, you understand.'

'And what do I give you in return?'

'Well … seeing how this is a dry house, I'm not too sure.'

Fox managed a smile, and eased himself a little further back in his chair. 'There's one thing,' he said at last. 'Jude didn't give it to Billy Giles because she didn't like his attitude …'

'Yes?' Breck prompted, leaning forward.

'Monday night, someone turned up at her door asking for Faulkner.'

'If the pathologist is right, Faulkner was already growing cold by then.'

Fox nodded. 'It's probably nothing,' he agreed. 'And all I got from her by way of description was that the caller was a man.'

It was Breck's turn to smile. 'Well, thanks for that, Malcolm. A man? That certainly narrows things down …' The two sat in silence for a moment until Breck started shaking his head slowly. 'I don't know why they bother with CCTV,' he declared.

'Deterrent value,' Fox suggested.

'Or comfort blanket,' Breck countered. 'People are fitting it in their houses now, did you know that? To make them feel safer. There was a housebreaking in Merchiston a few months back. Glen Heaton took me along for a look. The footage was so grainy the guys responsible looked barely human. They got half a million in antiques and jewellery – know what Heaton told the owners? Sell the cameras and buy a dog.'

Fox nodded his agreement.

'Preferably a big one,' Breck continued, 'and keep it half starved.'

'Did you work with him often?'

'Hardly at all – I'm assuming that's why you never bothered to interview me.'

'We had everything we needed.'

'But you still gave Billy Giles a grilling?'

'Just for a spot of fun.'

'I didn't think "fun" was in the dictionary, so far as the Complaints are concerned.' Breck considered for a moment. 'I dare say by now you know more about Glen Heaton than I do – how long did you have him under surveillance?'

'Months.' Fox shifted in his chair, less comfortable now.

'Should we even be discussing him?' Breck asked, seeming to take the hint.

'Probably not. But now you know he was breaking every rule in the book, how do you feel about him?'

'Way Billy Giles tells it, Heaton only broke a rule if he stood to gain a result. He'd trade gen with criminals, but the stuff he got in return put plenty of bad guys away.'

'And that makes it all right?' When Breck shrugged, Fox gave a sigh. 'Change of subject – any other news on Vince Faulkner?'

'We still don't have any sightings from Sunday or Monday.'

'And no pools of blood to report from the vicinity of that building site?'

Breck shook his head. 'Billy Giles thinks he was maybe killed Saturday night and kept somewhere ... By Monday, the killer's nerve was starting to go, and that's when the body got dumped.'

Fox nodded slowly, staring down at the carpet.

'One last thing,' Breck added. 'Two youths were seen having a bit of a shouting match with a guy at a bus stop on Dalry Road – not too far from Marooned and about thirty or forty minutes after Faulkner left the place.'

'Meaning what sort of time?'

'Around half past nine.'

'Does the description fit?'

'There isn't much of a description. A woman saw it from her tenement window. She was two floors up and fifty yards across the other side of the street. But she's a law-abiding busybody, so she came forward to tell us.'

'What does she say happened?'

'Couple of younger guys arguing with an older guy. He seemed to be waiting for a bus as they were walking past. Words were exchanged. A taxi came along and the man stuck his hand out. Got in, and one of the kids gave the back of the cab a bit of a kick as it headed off.'

'Which direction?'

'Haymarket.'

Fox was thoughtful. 'Which buses go that route?'

Breck shook his head. 'Needle in a haystack, Malcolm – they go all over: west towards Corstorphine and the Gyle, north to Barnton, east to the likes of Ocean Terminal ...'

'Vince used to go to a casino near Ocean Terminal,' Fox mused. 'Him and his gaffer, plus the gaffer's wife and my sister ...'

'Is that the Oliver?' Breck asked, sounding interested. Fox nodded.

'Why?' he asked.

'No real reason. You ever been there?'

'No.'

'Me neither.' Breck had something on his mind. He was rubbing the underside of his jaw with the back of his hand.

'Are you trying to track down the taxi driver?' Fox asked into the silence.

'Yes.'

'Shouldn't be too hard – if nothing else, he'll remember the kicking his cab got.'

'Mmm.' Breck seemed to make up his mind, slapping his hands against his knees. 'I really do fancy a drink, Malcolm – are you allowed to join me?'

'I don't drink.'

'I meant, can you come out to the pub?'

'Sure,' Fox said after a moment's hesitation. He checked his watch. They'd have picked up the van by now ... checked its equipment. They'd be discussing tactics before heading out. 'But it's getting pretty late.'

Breck looked at his own watch and raised an eyebrow. 'It's not even ten.'

'All I meant was, just a quick one.'

'A quick one,' Breck agreed. 'Is it all right if we take your car?'

'Where did you have in mind?'

'The Oliver. I'm guessing it'll have a bar.'

Fox's eyes narrowed. He wasn't thinking about options now, but consequences. 'Why there?'

'Maybe we can ask if Vince Faulkner visited on Saturday night.'

'That's not exactly going by the rules, Jamie. Your boss'll have a fit if he finds out.'

'Rules are there to be broken, Malcolm.'

Fox wagged a finger. 'Careful who you say that to.'

Breck just smiled and got to his feet. 'Are you game?' he asked.

'Long way to go for one drink ...' Breck was neither budging nor about to say anything. With a sigh, Fox placed his hands on the arms of his chair and began to rise.

The area around Ocean Terminal was an odd amalgam of dockside wasteland, warehouse conversions and new buildings. Ocean Terminal itself was a shopping centre and cinema complex, with the royal yacht *Britannia* berthed permanently as a tourist attraction in a marina to the far side of the building. Nearby a vast, shiny construction housed the city's army of civil servants – or at least a few battalions of them. A handful of lauded restaurants had opened up, perhaps with one eye on the cruise ships that occasionally docked in Leith. The Oliver was rotunda-shaped, and liked to think that it had been the harbourmaster's residence at some time. Fox wasn't even sure they'd be allowed inside – Breck was wearing trainers – but Breck had waved his objection aside and reached for his warrant card.

'Accepted nationwide,' he'd said, waving it in Fox's face. So they'd parked between a Mercedes and a sporty Toyota in the car park. Liveried doormen stood guard at the well-lit entrance. Breck pointed out the CCTV camera to Fox, though Fox had already spotted it. He was wondering if he should text Kaye to let him know there was no point in tonight's stakeout. On the other hand, if they did only stay for the one drink ...

'Good evening,' one of the doormen said. It sounded more warning than greeting.

'How are you doing?' Breck asked. 'Busy, is it?'

'Just starting to be.' The man looked him up and down, eyes lingering on the denim jacket. 'Sightseeing trip, is it?'

Breck patted his pocket. 'I've got some cash burning a hole.'

The other man was staring at Fox. 'This one's a cop,' he informed his colleague. 'I'd bet my life on it.'

'Are cops not allowed a night off?' Fox asked him, taking a step forward so he was in the man's face.

'Long as you're not looking for freebies,' the first doorman said.

'We can pay our way,' Breck assured him.

'You better,' the man warned him. And then they were in. Breck left his jacket at the cloakroom, which helped him blend in a little. At first glance the place offered glitz, but it was fairly casual: businessmen playing some tables, their wives and girlfriends the others. A few onlookers stood around, sizing things up. One of them looked to Fox like the waiter who'd taken his order earlier at the Chinese restaurant – confirmed when the man grinned and waved and gave him a little bow.

'Friend of yours?' Breck asked.

There were slot machines as well as the tables for cards, dice and roulette, plus a well-lit bar. Each croupier had someone from the house staff watching over them, just to be on the safe side. Fox had heard stories of croupiers who were too regular in their actions; meant the players could work out which quadrant of the wheel the roulette ball was most likely to stop, cutting the odds. Down the years, a few cops had got into trouble over gambling debts, entering the orbit of the Complaints as a result – not everyone was good at reading cards and roulette wheels.

A curving staircase, each step artfully illuminated, led to the mezzanine level. Fox followed Breck up. There was another bar here, and the casino's restaurant off to one side. The restaurant itself was just half a dozen booths and three or four extra tables, doing no business at all tonight. All the stools at the bar were taken, and other drinkers were watching the action beneath from the relative safety of the balcony.

'What can I get you?' Breck asked.

'Tomato juice,' Fox said. Breck nodded and squeezed between two of the bar stools. The barman was pouring a cocktail into an old-fashioned champagne glass. Fox joined the other drinkers and peered down towards the floor below. The added attraction seemed to be that you could occasionally catch a glimpse down the front of a woman's dress, but the tables had been angled and lit so that it was impossible to make out the contents of any hand of cards. The man nearest Fox nodded a half-greeting. He looked to be in his early sixties, his face deeply lined, eyes rheumy.

'Table three's the lucky one tonight,' he offered in an undertone. Fox puckered his mouth, as if considering this.

'Thanks,' he said. He had three twenty-pound notes in his pocket, and knew he would have to offer to break one of them to buy Breck back a drink. Hopefully Breck wouldn't accept, and they'd go home instead. Fox certainly had no intention of handing any of the cash to the tables, even lucky number three.

'Virgin Mary,' Breck said, handing him his drink. Fox thanked him and took a sip. It was spiced to the hilt: Worcestershire Sauce, Tabasco, black pepper. Fox felt his lips go numb.

'Reckoned that's how you'd like it. Cheers.'

Breck was holding a chunky glass filled with ice and a dark concoction. 'Rum and Coke?' Fox guessed, receiving a nod of confirmation.

'Used to be my dad's drink,' Breck said.

'Used to be?'

'He's like you – off the booze. Being a doctor, he's seen more than his fair share of damaged livers.'

The man next to them had been listening in. 'What doesn't kill you,' he said, offering it up as a toast, the iced remains rattling in his whisky glass as he tipped it to his mouth.

'Gentleman here,' Fox informed Breck, 'thinks table three's the good one.'

'That right?' Breck peered over the balcony. Table three was hosting blackjack, and Breck turned back towards Fox. 'What do you think?'

'I'm enjoying my drink,' Fox replied, taking another fiery sip. 'But don't let me stop you …'

It was after Fox bought them their second – 'and final' – round that Breck decided he might 'have a flutter'. Over the course of the next fifteen minutes, he lost the best part of thirty quid, while Fox watched from the wings.

'Ouch,' was all Breck said as he ended the experiment.

'Ouch indeed,' Fox agreed. They retreated to a spot near the machines. 'Why did we come here, Jamie?' Fox asked.

Breck studied his surroundings. 'Not exactly sure,' he appeared to admit. Then, spotting that Fox's glass was empty: 'One for the road?'

But Fox shook his head. 'Home,' was all he said.

On the drive back, Breck started talking about chance and how he didn't really believe in it. 'I think we decide how things are going to be, and we make those things happen.'

'You reckon?'

'You don't agree?'

Fox shrugged. 'Far as I'm concerned, stuff just happens and goes on happening and there's not a lot we can do about it.'

Breck studied him. 'Have you heard of a band called Elbow?

They've got a song about how when we're drunk or just happy we can start to believe that we've created the whole world around us.'

'But that's an illusion.'

'Not necessarily, Malcolm. I think we shape each and every moment. We *choose* the way our lives are going to go. That's why I get such a buzz from games.'

'Games?'

'Online games. RPGs. There's one called Quidnunc that I play a lot. I've got an avatar who roams the galaxy having adventures.'

'How old are you?'

Breck just laughed.

'I don't believe we have any control over the world,' Fox went on. 'My dad's in a care home – *he* has almost no control over his daily life. People just come and do things around him, making decisions for him – same as politicians and even our bosses do for us. They're the ones who run our lives. Adverts tell us what to buy, government tells us how to live, technology tells us when we've done something wrong.' In demonstration, Fox undid his seat belt. A warning light came on, accompanied by the ping-ping-ping of an alarm. He slotted the buckle home again and glanced in Breck's direction. 'Ever managed to use a computer without it asking if you need help?'

Breck was smiling broadly. 'Free will versus determinism,' he stated.

'I'll take your word for it.'

'I'm betting you don't have a Facebook page or anything like that?'

'Christ, no.'

'Friends Reunited?'

Fox shook his head. 'It's getting hard enough to hold on to any sort of private life.'

'My girlfriend likes to Twitter – know what that is?'

'I've heard of it and it sounds like hell.'

'You're one of life's spectators, Malcolm.'

'And that's the way I like it …' Fox paused. 'You didn't ask the staff about Vince Faulkner.'

'Another time,' Breck said with a shrug.

Fox knew he had a decision to make. Ideally, he would drop Breck on the main road and let him walk the final few hundred yards home. That way, the three residents of the surveillance van wouldn't spot him. But if he failed to take Breck all the way home, would Breck himself become suspicious of his motives? And once his suspicions had been aroused, might he spot the van? In the end, it was Breck who made the decision. They'd just turned on to Oxgangs Road when he asked if Fox could pull over and let him out.

'You don't want me to drop you nearer home?'

Breck shook his head. Fox was already signalling to stop at the kerb. 'I want to finish that walk I was taking,' Breck explained. When Fox pulled on the handbrake, he saw that Breck had his hand outstretched for him to shake.

'Thanks,' Breck said.

'No, Jamie, thank you.'

Breck smiled and opened the door, but once outside, he stuck his head back into the car again.

'This stays strictly between us, right? Wouldn't do either of us any good otherwise.'

Fox nodded slowly, and watched as Breck drew himself upright. But then the head dipped back into the car again.

'One thing you need to know,' the younger man said. 'We're not all like Glen Heaton – or Bad Billy Giles, come to that. Plenty of us at Torphichen were cheering when you nailed him. So thanks for that, Malcolm.'

The passenger door was pushed closed. A hand slapped twice against the car roof. Fox signalled back out into the road and released the handbrake. He drove home with his thoughts swirling and eddying, refusing to coalesce.

Thursday 12 February 2009

9

Fox had been in the office three hours when Tony Kaye arrived, looking bleary.

'Well,' Kaye said, 'that's a chunk of my life I'm not getting back.'

'What happened?' Fox paused in his typing. He was making a record of a meeting he'd just had with two lawyers from the Procurator Fiscal's office. They'd warned him that the case against Glen Heaton would take 'no little time to prepare'. The pair had been young – one male, one female. They could almost have been brother and sister, the way they dressed, moved and spoke. It was as if they'd spent their whole life together, to the point where Fox had asked if they were an item.

'An item?' The female lawyer hadn't seemed to understand the term.

'We're not,' her colleague had stated, blood colouring his neck.

'What happened?' Tony Kaye was saying now, mimicking Fox's question as he sloughed off his overcoat. '*Nothing* happened, Malcolm. The sod didn't get home until midnight. He'd left a light on upstairs, so we didn't know. Then, when he finally arrives, he logs on to the computer straight off. That's when we think we've got him. Know what he does?' Kaye had hung up his coat and placed his leather satchel on the floor next to his desk.

'What?'

'He starts looking at some online RPG. Know what that is?'

'A role-playing game.'

Kaye gave him a look, surprised by his colleague's breadth of knowledge. 'Joe Naysmith had to tell me,' Kaye admitted. 'Playing his game takes him over an hour, after which he catches up on e-mails – really exciting stuff like one to his brother in the US and another to his niece and nephew.'

'I thought the brother was gay.'

Kaye looked at him again. 'What makes you say that?'

He told me, Fox thought to himself. But he didn't want Kaye to know how intimate some of his chats with Breck had become, so he shifted in his chair and explained that the info had been in Breck's personnel file.

'Now that's what I call full disclosure ... The guy from the Chop Shop says maybe he's grooming them, but that's just paranoia talking.' Kaye paused. 'And that's something else you and me will be having words about, old friend.' Kaye nodded in Fox's direction, to reinforce the point. 'No sign of DS Inglis. She's got a son to tuck in, so she swaps with the world's most boring man. And surprise surprise – *he* gets on like a house on fire with Naysmith. Take a guess why.'

'They like computer games?'

'They *love* computer games. And gadgets, new technology, blah blah blah ... Ten minutes in and they're showing one another their mobiles. Another ten after that, it's modems and streaming and God knows what. I had four hours of it.' Kaye gave a sigh and stared in the direction of the lifeless coffee machine. 'Don't tell me Naysmith's still in bed.'

Fox blew his nose. 'Haven't seen him,' he admitted.

'And McEwan's still at his conference,' Kaye added. 'Maybe I'll just tuck a duvet around myself at my desk.'

'Be my guest.'

'Breck went to bed around two. We waited to see if he'd maybe taken his laptop with him, but there was nothing, so we left it at that.'

'Does the Chop Shop want another try?'

Kaye shrugged. 'Wouldn't surprise me, if only so Gilchrist and Naysmith can compare Freeview boxes.' Kaye sighed again. He wasn't yet seated; in fact had taken a couple of steps in the direction of Fox's desk and was looking at him.

'What?' Fox prompted.

'One other thing, compadre ... He Googled your name.'

Fox's eyebrows dipped. 'He did what?'

Kaye shrugged by way of reply. 'And that took him to some media websites. He wasn't long, so we reckon he was printing stuff off rather than reading it online.'

'He won't have found much.'

'Except that he Googled "Complaints and Conduct", too. Pretty much everything we've done in the media eye this past couple of years.' Kaye paused. 'Including Heaton, of course.'

'Why would he be doing that?'

Kaye shrugged again. 'Maybe he just likes you.'

Fox was considering telling his colleague about Breck's unannounced visit to his home, and their little jaunt to the Oliver. But Kaye was speaking again.

'On the other hand ... the guy who beat up your sister has just found himself deceased. Billy Giles is on the hunt for suspects.'

'Using Breck as his bloodhound?' Fox was thoughtful for a moment. 'I got the feeling there wasn't much love between those two.'

'Could be a front. Breck *wanting* you to think that ...'

Fox nodded slowly.

'Have you seen him recently?' Kaye asked.

'Who? Breck?' Fox reached into his pocket for his handkerchief and started blowing his nose again, playing for time. The door swung open and Joe Naysmith walked in. He was carrying his notebook in one hand and a newspaper in the other.

'Says here,' he began, laying the paper on Fox's desk, 'that detectives are making progress.'

The story was prominent on page three of *The Scotsman*. Not so surprising: Edinburgh wasn't exactly a murder capital – maybe one a month on average, usually cleared up quickly. When they did occur, the local media were keen to react, usually at length. There was a large photo of the scene of crime with a grainy inset of a smiling Vince Faulkner, and a smaller shot of Billy Giles, looking no less fierce than in the flesh.

'Eyes like lasers,' Naysmith commented.

'Where did the paper come from?' Kaye was asking. 'Thought you were a *Guardian* reader.'

'Helen said she was finished with it.'

'Helen?'

'In HR ... the desk nearest the door ...'

Kaye rolled his eyes. 'We just about merit the time of day, and he's on first-name terms with them.' He wagged a finger at Naysmith. 'Next you'll be telling me Mrs Stephens shines your shoes while you've got your feet under her desk.'

'She's all right,' Naysmith mumbled, making for the coffee machine. 'They all are ...'

'Three sugars!' Kaye called out.

'He knows that by now,' Fox stated.

'Never makes it sweet enough.' Kaye turned his attention to Fox. 'What does it say?'

'Not much. Marooned gets a mention. They're asking for people to come forward if they saw the victim elsewhere that weekend.'

'Memories are short,' Kaye commented. 'What's Marooned?'

'A pub in Gorgie – Vince got into an argument with some Taffs.' Fox scanned the story again. 'They don't say anything about the bus stop ...' He was talking to himself, but loud enough for Kaye to overhear.

'What bus stop?'

'After the rugby fans, Vince headed for Dalry Road. Looks like he was going to catch a bus but he ended up in a shouting match with some kids.'

Kaye's eyes narrowed.

'He took a taxi instead,' Fox finished.

'And how have you come by this information, Inspector Fox?'

Fox licked his lips. 'I have my sources, Sergeant Kaye.'

'Breck?' Fox couldn't deny it, so kept quiet instead. Kaye rolled his eyes once more. 'What have we just been talking about? He's dangling worms in front of you so you can't see Giles hiding behind him with the hook!'

'Nicely put,' Naysmith called out.

'Shut up, Joe,' Kaye spat back. He was pressing the palms of his hands against Fox's desk, leaning down over it. 'Tell me you get that. Tell me you can see right through him.'

'Sure,' Fox stated, not really sure of very much any more. He bit down on the pen he was holding, felt the plastic casing crack.

There was a health club just in front of the Asda on Chesser Avenue. Fox knew this because he'd had a trial membership when it first opened. He'd never been inside the supermarket, though, and was surprised by its size. He selected a hand basket and added a couple of items, then headed for the checkout. The woman in front of him in the queue pointed out that there was another checkout nearby where he wouldn't have to wait to be served. She was emptying the extensive load from her trolley while her young son sucked a lollipop. He was seated inside the trolley, swinging his legs in repeated attempts to connect with Fox's basket.

'I'm not in a hurry,' Fox told the woman. She looked at him strangely, then got on with the task of filling the conveyor belt.

Transaction complete, she paid not with a credit card but with handfuls of notes from her purse. The checkout assistant counted these into the till and handed the woman a receipt like a length of ticker tape. She then smiled towards Fox and asked him how he was.

'Not too bad, Sandra,' he replied.

Sandra Hendry had already finished running his items through the scanner. At mention of her name, she looked him in the face for the first time. 'It's you,' she stated. Then: 'Cooking Indian tonight?'

Fox considered the items he'd bought: basmati rice, Madras sauce. 'Yes,' he said.

'How's Jude?' There was no one behind Fox, so Sandra reached under her till and, for want of any other job, started wiping down the conveyor belt with the cloth stored there.

'She's okay,' Fox said.

'I'm looking in on her later.'

'She'll appreciate that.' Fox paused. 'You know you said you sometimes went to the Oliver? I was just wondering if you and your husband were there on Saturday.'

'Saturday?' She considered this. 'Saturday I was at my sister's. Bunch of us had a night on the town.'

'But not at the Oliver?'

Sandra Hendry shook her head. 'Too far from the centre for Maggie. George Street's what she likes.'

'Was your husband with you?'

'Ronnie? On a girlie night?' She gave a snort. 'Joking, aren't you?'

'So he was at home then?'

Having finished wiping, she fixed him with a stare. 'What's this all about?'

Fox had his answer prepared. 'We think Vince may have gone to the Oliver. Just wondering if he was on his own.'

She considered this and nodded slowly, accepting the explanation as being reasonable.

'Did he know anyone else who frequented the casino?' Fox asked.

'No idea.' The tone she used, he knew he was losing her – too many questions. In her eyes, he'd stopped being Jude's brother and turned back into a cop.

'Times you went there with him, he didn't bump into people he knew?'

She shrugged, straightening up as a new customer approached and started emptying his trolley. The man was unkempt and unshaven, eyes bloodshot. He was buying enough booze to kickstart Hogmanay. Sandra Hendry wrinkled her nose as she made eye contact with Fox. Her meaning was clear: one of her regulars, but by no means a favourite.

'Is Ronnie at work just now?' Fox asked her quickly.

'Unless they've laid him off ... Nobody's safe these days.'

Fox nodded his agreement, picked up his shopping, and thanked her for everything.

When Fox had driven into the Asda car park, a black Vauxhall Astra had been thirty yards behind him. Now, driving away, he caught the same car in his rearview mirror. It wasn't close enough for him to make out the licence plate. He kept to a crawl of ten miles an hour as he headed towards the main road, but the Astra never came any closer. His phone rang and he answered it.

'Where are you?' Tony Kaye asked.

'Keeping busy,' Fox replied.

'Want to hear some news?'

'Good or bad?'

'Vince Faulkner did indeed take a cab. Driver remembers interrupting the rammy and his cab taking a dunt in the process.'

'How did you find out?'

'You're not the only one with sources – and there aren't that many cab outfits in Edinburgh. Giles's boys got hold of the info about an hour before I did.'

'Does the cabbie remember where he dropped Vince?'

'The casino near Ocean Terminal. Driver got out to inspect the damage.'

'He saw Vince go into the Oliver?'

'You sound like you already know all this ...'

'I had an inkling, but the confirmation is greatly appreciated.' Fox said his goodbyes and ended the call, rewarding himself with a little smile. He didn't know why he'd come up with the Oliver as Vince's probable destination, but he'd been proved right. He'd never been the type to rely on gut instinct – at every step, he worked from the evidence presented. He liked to think this was one reason the Complaints had maintained their near-perfect record. But maybe instinct had its place.

As he neared the city centre, he lost sight of the Astra. Could be it had turned off. The area around Haymarket was as bad as ever. A sandwich board outside a newsagent's informed him that the day's *Evening News* was leading with a dispute between the local council and the German company behind the construction of the tram system. The Germans wanted more money, because of sterling's weakened exchange rate.

'The best of British luck to you,' Fox muttered, awaiting his turn through the contraflow. He was wondering if he should have taken another route – cut straight across the south of the city maybe. But then there were delays there too. It really did feel as if the whole city – with the blessing of those empowered to manage and nurture it – was grinding to a halt. For want of anything better to do, he lifted his phone from the passenger seat and punched in the number for Jamie Breck's mobile. Listening to it ring, he happened to glance in the rearview mirror again. A familiar-looking black Astra was three cars behind him.

'Hello?'

'Jamie, it's Malcolm Fox.'

'Morning, Malcolm. Thanks again for playing chauffeur last night.'

'No problem. I was just wondering if there was any news.'

'Taxi driver remembers Vince Faulkner. Dropped him outside the Oliver.'

'So you'll be talking to the staff?'

'Somebody on the team will. I'm a bit busy elsewhere just at the minute.'

'I'm interrupting you?'

'No, but I can't talk for long. Was there anything else?'

Fox realised there probably wasn't – all he'd wanted to know was whether Breck would share with him about the taxi, and Breck had passed that test. Besides, traffic had eased and Fox wasn't far from his destination. The Astra seemed to have taken a turning, but now Fox was wondering about the green Ford Ka – it was a couple of cars back, and how long had it been there?

'Nothing else,' Fox said in answer to Breck's question. He ended the call and took a right turn at the next set of lights, pulling over to the kerb and stopping. He watched in his rearview as the Ka went straight ahead at the junction instead of following him. 'Just because you're paranoid, Malcolm,' he muttered to himself, not bothering to complete the sentence.

There were plenty of signposts showing potential buyers the way to Salamander Point. A few blocks were already finished – curtains and blinds in some of the windows; plants sitting in pots on the corner balconies. But it was a huge site, and foundations were under way on a further four high-rise constructions. Large billboards attached to the fence around the site showed an approximation of the finished 'city within the city by the sea'. There were capitalised buzz-words such as EASE and QUALITY and SPACE drifting into the blue-painted sky, below which the artist had depicted smiling people walking past a café, outside which other shiny people sat at tables with their espressos and cappuccinos. This was their LIFESTYLE, but the present reality was somewhat different. The occupants of Salamander Point were living in the middle of a building site that resembled, to Fox's eye, a World War One battlefield, all mud and trench-digging, noise and diesel fumes. A corner of the site had been turned into an encampment for the workforce – ten or twelve Portakabins were stacked at double height, fronted by scaffolding and ladders. Men in high-visibility jackets and yellow hard hats scanned blueprints as they pointed with their fingers. Diggers were digging, cranes lowering pipes and slabs of concrete into place. The single extent of finished pavement led to the door of a temporary sales office. Behind the windows, Fox could see a young woman seated at her desk. She had no customers to deal with, and her phone didn't seem to require answering. The glazed look on her face indicated to him that this had probably become her daily routine.

Nobody was buying.

In a moment, he would walk up the path and she would see him, and there would be a momentary lifting of her spirits, dashed when he introduced himself and asked to see the gaffer. But first he locked his car, leaving it by the kerb. A truck rumbled past, kicking up a mini dust storm. Fox held his hands over his eyes and mouth until everything had settled, then headed up the path. When his phone started ringing, he answered it.

'Fox,' he stated.

'Anything you want to tell me, Malcolm?' It was Breck's voice.

'How do you mean, Jamie?'

'Take a look to your left, over by the Portakabins.'

With the phone still held to his ear, Fox turned his head, knowing what he would see. Breck was standing on the scaffolding. There was a hard hat on his head and another on the man standing next to him. Breck waved and spoke into his phone. A split second later, his words reached Fox.

'Come on over, then ...'

As he moved away, Fox caught sight of the saleswoman. She had risen from her desk, ready to greet him. He offered a shrug and a sheepish smile, and began picking his way across the treacherous terrain towards the site office. At the top of the ladder, Breck introduced him to Howard Bailey.

'This is Mr Bailey's show,' Breck explained, stretching out an arm towards the expanse of the site. Then, turning to Bailey: 'Could you give me a minute with my colleague?'

'I should really fetch him a hard hat.'

'He won't be staying.'

Bailey nodded and headed for the door at the far end of the platform. Breck slid his hands into his pockets and stared at Fox.

'Has that given you enough time to come up with a plausible story?' he asked.

'You know why I'm here – same reason you are.'

'Not quite, Malcolm. *I'm* here because I'm part of the inquiry team. You, on the other hand, are here to stick your oar in.'

'I was just hoping for a quiet word with Vince's friend Ronnie.'

'That'll be Ronnie Hendry – Vince's foreman. Mr Bailey was telling me the two of them were friends off-site as well as on.'

'You're going to speak to him?'

Breck nodded slowly. 'And ask him the same questions you probably would.' After a moment's pause, Breck gave a sigh and looked down at his muddied shoes. 'What if it had been Billy Giles waiting here instead of me? He'd have had you on report – not the sort of thing I'd imagine your boss would be thrilled with.'

'My sister's lost her partner. I'm just after a word with that partner's best friend. Could be I want to discuss the funeral arrangements … ask Ronnie to be a pall-bearer.'

'You really think Giles would fall for that?'

Fox shrugged. 'I'm not really that worried about Billy Giles.'

'You should be – and you know it.'

Fox turned and rested his hands against one of the scaffolding poles. The warehouses across the street were going to be redeveloped too, by the look of things. Their windows had been boarded up, and a small tree was doing its best to grow from the edge of the mossy roof. A car was driving past – a black Astra.

'You're not having me tailed by any chance?' Fox asked Breck.

'No.'

'Could Billy Giles be doing it without you knowing?'

'I doubt we've got men to spare. And why would he want you tailed?'

'A black Vauxhall Astra? Green Ford Ka?'

Breck shook his head. 'Odd thing, though ...'

'What?'

'After I'd walked home last night, there was a van parked outside. Just after I got into bed, I heard it leave.'

'So?' Fox was still pretending to be taking in the view. His grip on the pole had tightened.

Breck had taken off his hard hat to rub a hand through his hair. 'We're all getting a bit twitchy,' he decided. Below them, a man had come into sight. He was dressed for work, his spattered denims tucked into thick grey woollen socks and those socks emerging from steel-toed boots. He wore his hard hat cocked high on his head, and under his high-visibility jacket was a denim one, not unlike Breck's from the previous night. Fox knew it had to be Ronnie Hendry. He turned to face Breck.

'Let me sit in,' he said.

Breck stared back at him. Hendry had reached the foot of the ladder and was starting to climb.

'Please,' Fox said.

'You don't say anything,' Breck warned him. 'Not one word. Has he met you before?'

Fox shook his head.

'You've said it yourself,' Breck went on, 'he'll see you at the funeral if not before. He'll know then that he's seen you somewhere ...' He rubbed a finger down his nose, obviously in a quandary. Then, as Hendry's head appeared through the gap in the flooring, he uttered the one word Fox wanted to hear.

'Okay.'

Fox stood back as Breck introduced himself to Ronnie Hendry and shook the man's hand. Hendry had been wearing leather workmen's gloves, but stuffed them into his pocket.

'Mr Bailey's letting us use this office here,' Breck told Hendry, opening the door nearest them. 'My colleague's going to sit in.' Breck was leading them inside, giving Hendry no time to study Malcolm Fox. It was a utilitarian space, just a desk with a plan lying on it, weighted down at all four corners with chunks of masonry. There were three folding chairs, a free-standing electric heater, and not much else. Hendry held his hands to the heater and rubbed some warmth back into them.

'Not much of a job in this weather,' Breck sympathised. Hendry gave a nod of agreement and removed his hard hat. His first name had been felt-penned across the back of it, and from what Fox could see of the gloves, they'd been name-tagged too. It was a building site, after all. Things would tend to go for a walk. Hendry's hair was short-cropped and beginning to silver at the temples. He would be in his late thirties, Fox guessed. He was short and wiry – a physique not unlike Vince Faulkner's. The face was lined and pitted, Hendry's eyebrows black and bushy. He had now seated himself opposite Breck at the table, Fox opting to stay standing at the far end of the room, arms folded, making himself as inconspicuous as possible.

'I wanted to ask you about Vince Faulkner,' Breck told Hendry.

'Hellish thing.' The voice was gruffly local.

'The two of you were friends.'

'That's right.'

'You didn't see him last Saturday?'

Hendry shook his head. 'Got a text from him in the afternoon.'

'Oh?'

'Just a comment about the football half-times.'

'You didn't speak to him?'

'No.'

'Did you hear from him after that?'

Hendry shook his head again. 'Next thing I knew, I was hearing he was dead.'

'Must've come as a shock.'

'Too true, pal.' Hendry shifted in his chair.

'The two of you worked together?'

'Sometimes. Depends which gang you end up in. Vince was a solid worker, so I'd always pitch for him.'

'Did he specialise in anything?'

'He could lay bricks, mix the cement. He'd trained as a brickie, but he would turn his hand to pretty well anything you asked.'

'He was English,' Breck stated casually. 'Was that ever a problem?'

'How do you mean?'

'Did the guys ever give him stick?'

'If they had, he'd've given them pelters.'

'He was a bit hot-headed, then?'

'I'm just saying he stood up for himself.'

'Did you know he sometimes hit his partner?'

'Jude?' Hendry thought for a moment before answering. 'Sandra tells me she's got a broken arm.'

'And that doesn't exactly surprise you?'

'The pair of them liked a good rammy. Oftentimes it was Jude who started it. She'd just keep having a go at him until he started to snap.'

'I've known women like that.' Breck was nodding his apparent agreement. 'They seem to get a buzz out of it ...'

Fox shifted his weight a little and bit down on his bottom lip. *He's only doing his job*, he told himself, *getting the man to open up ...*

'So you can imagine him getting into a fight on Saturday night?' Breck was asking.

'I suppose so.'

'When he didn't turn up for work Monday morning, what did you think?'

Another shrug. 'I was up to my eyes. Didn't really have time *to* think. Tried phoning him ...' He paused. 'Or did I? I know I texted him for definite.'

Breck nodded. 'We checked his phone. The text was there, but no one had read it. We took a look at all the messages he had stored. There were a fair few to and from you.'

'Oh aye?'

'And mention of the Oliver ...'

'It's a casino. Just around the corner from here, actually. We sometimes took the wives there.'

'He liked gambling?'

'He didn't like losing,' Hendry said with a thin smile.

'We think maybe he went there Saturday night. Would that have been like him – going there without you?'

'If he'd had an argy-bargy with Jude ... gone out drinking ... Yeah, maybe.'

'What about you, Mr Hendry – what did you get up to on Saturday?'

Hendry puffed out his cheeks and expelled a ball of air. 'Long lie-in the morning, as per ... shopping at the Gyle with Sandra, also as per ... football results and an evening kick-off on Sky. I fetched an Indian ...' He paused again, remembering something. 'Hang on, that's right – Sandra was out with her sister and some mates. I ate enough curry for two and fell asleep in front of the telly.'

'And Sunday?'

'Not much different.'

'So there's no weekend overtime going on?'

'Phase One there was, but nobody's buying now we're in Phase Two. I'd say we're a fortnight away from lay-offs. Another fortnight after that, the whole site could be mothballed.'

'Not so nice for the people who're already living here.'

'We reckon if they tried selling up, they'd get half to two thirds what they paid originally.'

'So there are bargains to be had?'

'If you're interested, make Helena in sales an offer. She'll probably throw in a lap-dance.'

'I'll bear that in mind.' Breck managed a smile.

'Tell you what's really worrying the bosses, though,' Hendry went on. 'They can't see an end in sight. This whole development – council sold the land for almost six million. Lucky if it would fetch a third of that.'

'Ouch,' Breck sympathised.

'Well, that's one way of putting it. The guys reckon the only reason we'll finish the next high-rise is so the developer can top himself by jumping from it.'

'What's the developer's name?' Breck asked.

'Charlie Brogan – you going to put him on suicide watch?'

'Reckon we should?'

This got a bark of laughter from Ronnie Hendry. 'Not before his bills are paid,' he said.

Breck offered another smile and decided on a change of direction. 'Did you know that Vince Faulkner has a criminal record?'

'Plenty of guys in the building trade could say the same.'

'So you knew?'

'He never made it a secret – it was there on his job application.'

'His partner doesn't seem to have known.'

'Jude?' Hendry gave a shrug and folded his arms. 'That's between the two of them.'

'Did he ask you not to mention it in front of her?'

'What does it matter if he did? Ancient history's what it was.'

It was Breck's turn to shrug. 'Okay, so let's say he's had a fight with his partner. Her arm gets broken and she heads to A and E. Vince opts not to go with her and heads out on the lash instead. Ends up at the Oliver and loses some money ... What do you think he would do next, Mr Hendry?'

'No idea.' Hendry's arms were still folded. He was definitely on the defensive. Fox decided an interruption was in order.

'His partner says he sometimes stayed out all night, slept at friends' houses ...'

'Yeah, that happened once or twice.'

'So it could have happened that night?' Breck asked.

'Not at mine,' Hendry stated with a shake of the head.

'Where then?'

'You tell me – you lot are supposed to be the ones with the brains.'

Jamie Breck's car was parked on the site, just next to the Portakabins. It was a red Mazda RX8, low-slung and sporty. Breck leaned his elbows against its roof as he watched Ronnie Hendry go back to work.

'Anything I forgot to ask?'

Fox shook his head. 'I don't think so.'

'What did you make of him?'

'I can see why Faulkner liked him. He's the sort who'd back you up in a fight, but at the same time he's probably canny enough to calm things down so the fight never quite happens.'

'He didn't seem exactly numb with shock, did he?'

'Isn't that the Scottish way?'

'Bottling it up for later?' Breck guessed. Then he nodded slowly in agreement.

'Sorry for butting in like that.'

'It was a fair point, though. I didn't know he was prone to sleeping around.'

'Jude never mentioned other women,' Fox stipulated. 'By the way, have you done anything about Jude's mystery visitor?'

'It's now a matter of record,' Breck confirmed.

'So where next?' Fox asked. 'The Oliver?'

Breck looked at him. 'And you'll be wanting to tag along, I presume?'

'Might as well,' Fox said. 'Last one there's a scabby dog ...'

But in fact, by the time he'd unlocked his Volvo and executed a three-point turn, the Mazda was a hundred yards ahead. As he pulled into the casino car park, Breck was standing by the door of the building, trying to look as if he'd been there for hours.

'Hiya, Scabby,' Breck said in greeting. 'Any suspicious-looking Astras to report?'

'No,' Fox admitted. Then he pulled open the door. 'After you,' he said.

Although the casino was open for business, no actual business was taking place. There was nobody on duty at the cloakroom, and only one croupier stationed at a blackjack table, practising her skills in front of three empty stools. A couple of tiny, foreign-looking women in tabards were polishing the brass fittings and rails. The downstairs barman looked to be doing a stock check, ticking off items on a clipboard. Upstairs, Fox could hear a vacuum cleaner at work.

'Boss around?' Breck asked the young croupier. She had blonde hair tied back in a ponytail, and was dressed in regulation black waistcoat with a white blouse and sky-blue bowtie.

'You'll need to talk to Simon.' She gestured towards the barman.

'Thanks,' Breck said. He started walking in that direction, pulling his warrant card from his pocket. 'Need a word with you, Simon.'

'Oh, aye?' The barman hadn't bothered looking up from the task in hand, but Fox knew he'd noticed the warrant card ... and recognised it for what it was.

'You in charge here?' Breck was asking.

'Boss is due back in quarter of an hour.'

'Would you mind looking me in the eye when you speak?' Breck was managing to sound polite, yet there was steel just below the surface. Simon took a few moments before complying. 'Thank you,' Breck said. 'Okay if I put my ID away now? You're satisfied you're talking to a detective and not some neighbourhood divvy?'

The barman gave a half-smirk, but Breck had his attention. Fox noticed that his colleague had roughened his natural voice and was bringing in more glottal stops.

'If it's anything to do with licences or that,' Simon was saying, 'it's the boss you need to speak to.'

'But the boss isn't here, so it's your job to answer a few questions.' Breck had put his warrant card away, but was now producing a photograph from the same pocket. It was a snap of Vince Faulkner. Fox reckoned it had been lifted from Jude's house.

'This guy's a regular,' Breck was saying, 'so I'm assuming you know him.'

The barman looked at the photo and shrugged.

'Actually,' Breck went on, 'I should've stipulated that he *was* a regular. Poor sod got himself killed at the weekend, after visiting this place.'

'Which night?'

'Saturday.' The barman didn't say anything for a moment. Breck decided to speak for him. 'You're trying to work out the odds, aren't you? Do you lie or tell the truth – which is going to work out best? And that means just one thing, Simon – you were here Saturday night.'

'It was busy,' the barman admitted with another shrug.

'But he was in here.' Breck waved the photo to and fro. 'And it was out of character, because whenever you'd seen him in the past, he'd always been with people.'

'So?'

Fox had been scanning the corners of the ceiling. 'We'll need to see the recordings,' he commented. 'From your security cameras ...'

Breck stiffened a little. He'd had a flow going, and Fox had broken it.

'My colleague's right,' he stated eventually.

'Talk to the boss.'

'We will,' Breck confirmed. 'But you *do* remember Vince Faulkner?'

'I never knew his name.'

'You saw in the papers that he was dead?'

'Suppose so.' The admission was grudging at best. Simon was running a finger down the clipboard, as though hoping they would take the hint and leave him to his task. Fat chance, Fox thought to himself.

'You saw him in here Saturday night?'

'Can't remember.'

'He got here around ten.'

'Place was heaving by then.'

'But Mr Faulkner was on his own, and I'm betting that meant he'd be sitting on one of these stools.' Breck slapped the seat of the bar stool next to him.

'There's another bar upstairs.'

'But all the same ...' Breck decided to let the silence linger.

'He was half cut when he got here,' Simon finally admitted. 'Doormen should never have let him in.'

'Did he cause trouble?'

The barman shook his head. 'But he had the look of a loser.'

'And that's not good for the ambience?' Breck nodded his understanding.

'Just sat slumped at the corner of the bar.'

'How many drinks did he have?'

'No idea.'

'What was he drinking?'

'Shorts ... that's all I remember. We had three staff working the bar that night.'

'Did he meet anyone? Talk to them?'

'Dunno.' The fingers were now drilling against the clipboard, tapping out the sound of horses' hooves at full gallop.

'Did you see him leave?'

Simon shook his head.

'What about Sunday or Monday?'

Another shake of the head. 'I was off both nights.'

Breck glanced at his watch. 'Your boss is running late.'

'Bosses get to do that.'

Breck smiled and turned his head towards Fox for the first time. 'Simon likes to think he's smart.' But every trace of humour had left Breck's face by the time he turned back to the barman. 'So do the smart thing, Simon – get thinking of anything else you can tell us about Saturday night or about Vince Faulkner in general.' Where the snapshot had been, there was now a business card. 'Take it,' Breck commanded. The barman did as he was told. 'How old are you, Simon?'

'Twenty-three.'

'Been in the trade long?'

'Started bar work when I was at uni.'

'What did you study?'

'I didn't study much of anything – that was the problem.'

Breck nodded his understanding. 'Ever see any trouble around here?'

'No.'

'Not even once the punters get outside? A good evening gone sour?'

'By the time I've closed the bar, cleaned up and done a tally, people are long gone.'

'Do the management stand you to a cab home?' Breck watched as the barman nodded. 'Well, that's something at least.' Then, turning to leave: 'Jot a few thoughts down and give me a call. Plus, pass the number on to your boss. If I haven't heard back by end of play today, I'll be round tonight with some squad cars and uniforms. Got that?'

Simon was studying the writing on the card. 'Yes, Mr Breck,' he said.

It was strange to step out of the gloom – the casino boasted no natural light at all – and find that it was still daytime in Edinburgh, the sky overcast but boasting enough glare to have Jamie Breck slipping on a pair of Ray-Bans. He'd taken up the same position as after the meeting with Ronnie Hendry – elbows resting against the roof of his Mazda. Fox squeezed the bridge of his nose and squinted into the light. It had been quite a performance: Breck was a natural. Just the right mix of authority and empathy. Too bullish and the barman would have blustered or clammed up …

I like you, Fox thought. Even though you've been checking up on me behind my back. Even though you may not be what you seem ...

'You really got into character there,' Fox complimented him. 'I liked what you did with your voice.'

'That's the thing about RPGs and avatars – you get to pretend to be someone you're not.'

'Handy training for CID.' *And for other things*, Fox thought to himself. 'So what now?'

'Nothing much. I'll head back to base, write up what I've got – might leave out a *few* salient details.' Breck glanced in Fox's direction.

'Sorry I butted in again,' Fox apologised. 'Broke my promise ...'

'I'd have got round to the cameras in my own time, Malcolm.'

'I know you would.'

Both men turned at the sound of a car approaching. It was a 'baby' Bentley, the GT. Glossy black bodywork and tinted windows. The engine stopped and the driver's-side door opened. Fox caught a glimpse of burgundy leather upholstery. The woman who stepped out was wearing high heels, black tights and a black knee-length skirt. The skirt clung to her. White silk blouse, open at the neck to show a pendant of some kind. Cream-coloured jacket with a little padding at the shoulders. Her hair was auburn, thick and flowing. She had to push some back from her face as a gust of wind caught her. Red lipstick and, when she removed her oversized sunglasses, dark eyeshadow and a hint of mascara. She gave them an inquisitive look as she headed towards the door of the casino.

'Simon will tell you all about it,' Breck called to her. She ignored this and headed inside. Fox turned to Breck.

'Shouldn't we talk to her?'

'She's going to call me, remember?'

'But she's management, right?'

'Later.'

'Don't you want to know who she is?'

Breck smiled. 'I *know* who she is, Malcolm.' He pointed at a spot just above the casino's main door. There was a plaque sited there, announcing that the premises were licensed for the sale of alcohol. The name of the licensee was J. Broughton.

'Who's J. Broughton?' Fox asked.

Breck opened the door of the Mazda and started to get in. 'Stick to watching the detectives, Malcolm. Let us other cops do the *real* work ...'

10

'Does it mean anything to you?'

Fox was back in the Complaints office, standing in front of Tony Kaye's desk. Kaye mouthed the name a few times. As usual, he had pitched his chair back, and now swung slowly backwards and forwards.

'Wasn't there a villain called that?' he said at last. 'Well, by "villain", obviously I mean an upstanding local businessman whose tangled web of dodgy dealings Lothian and Borders Police could never unravel.' Kaye paused. 'But he'd be in his seventies now … haven't heard his name in years.'

'Will he be in the system somewhere?' Fox nodded in the direction of Kaye's computer hard drive.

'I can check, just as soon as you give me the reason.'

'Vince was at the Oliver on Saturday night. Licence is in the name of J. Broughton.'

'Jack Broughton – that was your man.' Kaye stared at his colleague. 'But Vince isn't really your territory, Foxy. Shouldn't you be busying yourself liaising with the Fiscal's office about Glen Heaton? Or readying a report on Jamie Breck to send to the Chop Shop?'

'Just do it, will you?' Fox turned and walked over to the coffee machine. Breck's words were still niggling at him – *us other cops … the* real *work* … He knew that a lot of CID felt that way. The Complaints was for the cold fish, the oddities, the cops who could never make it as bona fide detectives. It was for voyeurs with chips on their shoulders. Joe Naysmith was opening a fresh consignment of coffee and Fox watched him at work. Naysmith didn't fit the description; nor did Tony Kaye, come to that …

'I love that smell,' Naysmith commented, holding the bag to his nose.

‘Tell me something, Joe – why the Complaints?’

Naysmith raised an eyebrow. ‘You’ve had six months to ask me that.’

‘I’m asking now.’

Naysmith considered for a moment. ‘It suits me,’ he eventually offered. ‘Isn’t that why we’re all here?’

‘Christ knows,’ Fox muttered, pinching the bridge of his nose. Then he asked if Naysmith was planning another evening in the van.

‘DC Gilchrist thinks we should.’

‘Well, I don’t,’ Fox stated. ‘Far as I can see, you’d be wasting your time. So why don’t you trot along the hall and tell him so?’

‘I’m making the coffee . . .’

Fox snatched the bag from him. ‘Not any more. Now hop it.’ He gave a jerk of the head as added incentive and watched Naysmith leave the room. He poured the coffee into the filter, slid it home, and filled the water reservoir before placing the emptied glass jug on its hotplate.

‘I like it better when Joe makes it,’ Kaye chided him. He’d risen from his chair and walked over to the room’s shared printer. It was in the process of churning out a final sheet of paper. ‘You’ll see a note at the bottom,’ he explained. ‘Says there’s a bit more in the DFW.’

DFW: the Dead Files Warehouse. Every now and again, the police stations in and around the city had a clear-out. Files were dusted off, their existence recorded for posterity, and they were then sentenced to life imprisonment on a shelf in a vast warehouse on Dumbryden Industrial Estate. Fox had had reason to visit the facility at times in the past. By rights everything in the archives should have been transferred to digital format – the process had been green-lighted by a previous Chief Constable – but funding had become an issue. When Kaye handed Fox the three A4 sheets, the first thing Fox did was study the foot of the final page. There were several references to the DFW. The references were dated – 1968, 1973, 1978. The computer printout listed further brushes with the law in 1984 and 1988. One was for aiding and abetting a fugitive. It never made it to trial. The other was for receiving stolen goods – again, charges dropped. Jack Broughton’s year of birth was given as 1937, making him seventy-one, going on seventy-two.

‘Over twenty years since he was in any trouble,’ Fox commented. ‘And now he’s the same age as my dad.’

Kaye was reading the report over Fox's shoulder. 'I remember one of the older cops telling me about him when I was a probationary. Guy definitely had a reputation in those days.'

'At the casino, there was a woman in her thirties – I think she's front-of-house.'

'You've been there?'

Fox glowered at him. 'Don't ask.' He started reading the next page. Jack Broughton had two sons and a daughter, but both sons had predeceased their father, one dying in a car crash, the other in a bar brawl gone wrong. 'I wonder if it's the daughter ...'

'The licensing board will know,' Kaye informed him. 'Want me to get on to them?'

'You know someone there?'

'Might do.' Kaye started to retreat to his desk. 'Bring me over a mug when it's brewed, will you?'

'Three sugars?' Fox asked, with just a hint of sarcasm.

'Heaped,' Tony Kaye confirmed.

But Joe Naysmith was back before the machine had finished its business. He seemed concerned that something terrible might have happened to the percolator in his absence.

'How did it go with Gilchrist?' Fox asked him.

'DS Inglis wants a word with you.' Naysmith was avoiding eye contact.

'Why? What have I done?'

'She just said she wants a word.'

'Better run along and see her, Foxy,' Kaye said, his hand pressed over the telephone receiver. 'Maybe a quick skoosh of Lynx beforehand ...'

But when Fox looked, Annie Inglis was standing in the doorway, arms folded. She gave a twitch of the head, signalling for him to meet her in the hall. Fox handed Naysmith the empty mug he'd been holding. Then he made his exit, closing the door after him.

'Why?' she asked without preamble.

'Why what?'

'Why pull the surveillance on Breck?'

'It didn't get us anywhere last night.'

Her eyes narrowed. 'You've had meetings with him, haven't you?'

'You having me followed, DS Inglis?'

'Just answer the question.'

'Answer mine first.'

'No, I'm not having you followed.'

'He's investigating a murder pretty close to home, unless you'd forgotten – I'm keeping tabs on it, so yes, I've talked to him.'

'From what I hear, he puts up a good front: conscientious, likeable, generous ...'

'So?'

'They *all* do, Malcolm. It's how they win the trust of children and sometimes even the kids' parents. It's why we don't catch them nearly often enough – they're *good* at this. They're good at acting as if they're just like you and me ...'

'He's not like me,' Fox stated.

'Is that what's getting to you?'

'Nothing's getting to me.' There was irritation in his voice. Inglis looked down towards the floor and gave a sigh. 'He spent an hour last night on an online role-playing game called Quidnunc. He has an avatar. You know what that is?'

'Yes.'

'It's someone he creates so he can hide his true self – it lets him become someone else.'

'Him and a few million other players.'

She looked up at Fox. 'He told you about it?'

'Yes.'

Inglis was thoughtful for a moment. She pushed the hair back from her forehead, taking her time. 'Is there any possibility he knows we're on to him?'

Fox thought back to what Breck had told him – the van outside his home, driving away soon after he'd gone to bed. 'I don't think so,' he said.

'Because if he does, he'll start getting rid of the evidence.'

'I don't think he does,' Fox repeated.

She considered this for a few moments more. 'It fits with offender profiling,' she said at last, her voice softening. 'These men, they'll join online communities, pretend to be fourteen or fifteen, ask others in the group to send them photos ...'

'I get it,' Fox told her.

'They're good at role-playing. They hone their skills by playing online games. Sometimes they even get to meet other players along the way ...'

'You want Gilchrist and Naysmith to go out again tonight?'

'They're keen.'

Fox nodded slowly. 'Can they park further away? Same spot two nights running and there's more likelihood of them standing out.'

Inglis nodded back at him, and reached out to touch his arm. 'Thank you,' she said, turning to go. But then she paused.

'Your sister's boyfriend – is there any news?'

Fox shook his head and watched her retreat. Then he took out his phone and called Jude, guilty that he hadn't done so earlier. But there was no answer, so he left a message and went back into the office.

'You're out in the wagon again tonight,' he told Naysmith.

'Tell me I'm not needed,' Kaye pleaded. He had just put down his receiver, and was holding a slip of paper.

'That for me?' Fox asked.

'The very name you wanted.' Kaye waved the slip.

'All right,' Fox told him, 'you're exempt from holding Joe's hand tonight.'

'You've got Gilchrist for that, haven't you, Joe?' Kaye teased, folding the piece of paper into a glider and sending it flying towards Fox's desk. It landed on the floor, and Fox stooped to retrieve it. A name was printed there. The J in J. Broughton didn't stand for Jack.

It was Joanna, the daughter.

Fox thought back to the woman who'd pulled up outside the Oliver. Pulled up in her Bentley and sauntered inside. She hadn't stopped to ask them what they were doing in her car park, because she'd had a bit of training at her father's knee – she could smell a cop a mile off.

Joanna Broughton. Fox called Jamie Breck on his mobile.

'The J is for Joanna, right?' he asked without introduction. There was a smile in Breck's voice as he answered.

'Fast work.'

'And I'm assuming you know who she is?'

'Jack Broughton's daughter?' Breck pretended to guess.

'So is she fronting the place for him or what?'

'You're assuming the woman we saw earlier today is Ms Broughton.'

'I'm not assuming anything,' Fox corrected him. 'But I think *you* know it was. What is it about the Oliver and her? Something you're holding back on me, Jamie?'

'I'm working on a murder inquiry, Malcolm. There may be times when I can't open my heart to you.'

'Is this one of them?'

'Maybe I'll tell you later. For now, I need to get back to work.' Breck ended the call and Fox placed his mobile phone on his desk and settled himself in his chair. His braces were cutting into his shoulders, and he adjusted both straps. Inglis's words were bouncing around his head: *conscientious ... likeable ... generous ... Is that what's getting to you?* When his mobile rang, he picked it up and studied the number on the screen – Jude.

'Hey, sis, thanks for getting back to me ...' There was silence on the line, but for a muffled sound, very like someone sobbing. 'Jude?' he prompted.

'Malcolm ...' Her voice cracked halfway through his name.

'What's going on?'

'They're digging in the garden.'

'What?'

'The police – *your* lot – they're ...' She gulped down another sob.

'I'm on my way,' Fox told her. Ending the call, he shrugged his arms back into his jacket. Kaye asked him what was happening.

'Got to go,' was all Fox said. Out in the car park, the interior of his car still retained a trace of warmth.

Some of Jude's neighbours were at their windows again. Three patrol cars, two white vans. Jude's front door was open. There was no sign of any disruption in the front garden. The back could be accessed only from a door in the kitchen. It wasn't much of a garden either, maybe sixty feet by twenty, most of it paving slabs and weeds. There was a uniformed officer on duty at the front door, but Fox was waved inside when he showed his warrant card. The interior of the house was ice cold – both front and rear doors open, defeating anything the radiators could do.

'Who let you in?' DCI Billy Giles roared. He was standing in the kitchen, holding a mug of tea in one hand and a half-eaten Mars Bar in the other.

'Where's my sister?'

'Next-door neighbour's,' Giles stated, chewing on the snack. Fox had advanced far enough into the room to be able to see out of the rear window. There was a team hard at work with shovels and pickaxes. They were digging in some spots, lifting the paving slabs in others. Muck had been trailed into the house, so recently cleaned by Alison Pettifer. Someone from Forensics was running a hand-held scanner down the walls in the living room, seeking any microscopic bloodstains.

'You still here?' Giles growled, tossing the empty chocolate wrapper on to the floor.

'What are you playing at, Giles?'

'I'm not playing at anything – I'm *being* a cop.' He glowered at Fox. 'Something your lot don't seem to like. I'm beginning to think it's jealousy.'

'I can't decide what this smacks of more – intimidation or desperation.'

'We got a call from a concerned neighbour,' Giles said. His voice was coarse, his breathing ragged as he bore down on Fox. 'Heard digging in the garden Sunday night. Horticulture at midnight – is that something your family makes a habit of?'

'Did this neighbour give a name?' Giles didn't say anything to that, and Fox barked out a laugh. 'Are you really going to lend an ear to every nutter who phones you? Did you bother trying to track them down?' Fox paused. 'I'm assuming you noted their number?'

'Pub in Corstorphine,' Giles stated. Then, snapping his head round as one of his team walked in from the garden: 'Anything?'

'A few bones ... been there for years – Phil says a pet cat or maybe a puppy.'

'What is it you think you're going to find?' Fox asked into the silence. 'You know damned well this isn't about cats or puppies ... it's about the wild goose you've been sent to chase.'

Giles pointed a stubby finger at him. 'This man's contaminating my crime scene and I want him out of here!'

A hand grabbed Fox's arm from behind. He made to shrug it off, but turned and saw that it was Jamie Breck.

'Come on, you,' Breck said sternly, leading Fox towards the front door.

Outside on the path, both men kept their voices low. 'This is horseshit,' Fox hissed.

'Maybe so, but we're duty-bound to follow any and all leads. You know that, Malcolm.'

'Giles is trying to get at me and mine, Jamie – that's what this boils down to. You've got to tighten his leash.'

Breck's eyebrows went up. 'Me?'

'Who else is going to stand up to him?'

'You looked to be doing a pretty good job ...' There was a tapping sound. Fingers against the window of the house next door. 'You're wanted,' was all Breck said. Fox turned to look, saw Alison Pettifer gesturing for him to join her. Fox held up his hand, signalling that he was on his way, but then turned back to face Jamie Breck.

'Tighten his leash,' he repeated, making for the door of the neighbouring house.

*

He'd stayed for the best part of an hour, downing two mugs of tea while both women sat on the sofa, Pettifer occasionally taking Jude's hand and patting or stroking it. He'd asked the neighbour if he could unlock her back door, take a look over the fence as another flagstone was lifted. Giles had glowered at him, but there was nothing he could do.

'Can't you stop them?' Jude had asked her brother more than once. 'Surely you can make it stop.'

'I'm not sure I can,' he'd answered defensively, knowing how weak it made him sound. He could have added that it was precisely *his* fault it was happening. Giles couldn't get to him, so he was getting at his loved ones instead. Fox knew he could make a complaint to McEwan, but he knew, too, that the complaint would make him look foolish. It was simplicity itself for Giles to defend the charge: *there's been a murder … we have to pursue every avenue … I can't believe a fellow officer wouldn't appreciate that …*

No, he couldn't take it to McEwan. He'd considered telling Jude to get a lawyer, but he knew how *that* would look – and all cops, the Complaints included, had a deep-seated mistrust of lawyers. The truth was, he couldn't take it anywhere, and Giles knew as much. So instead Fox had said goodbye, pecking Jude on the cheek and shaking Pettifer's hand. Then he'd sat in his car for five minutes, trying to decide whether to go back to Fettes or not. Mind made up, he'd driven to the supermarket in Oxgangs, lugging the bags into his house and spending half an hour putting away the food, checking the sell-by dates of everything so he could arrange what needed eating when – stuff for later to the back of the fridge and stuff for sooner to the front. Fresh pasta with pesto sauce for his evening meal. At the supermarket, he'd found himself in the drinks section, wondering about buying a couple of bottles of alcohol-free beer, then had walked past the wines and spirits, noting that some whiskies were actually cheaper than when he'd last bought any of them. The pricier bottles had little neck-band alarms to deter shoplifters. Back at one of the chill cabinets, he'd picked up a litre carton of mango and pear juice. Better for you by far, boy, he'd told himself.

After the meal, he tried watching TV, but there was nothing to grab his attention. He kept swimming back through the day's events. When his phone bleeped with a message, he sprang towards it. Tony Kaye was inviting him to Minter's. It took Fox all of five seconds to make up his mind.

*

'It's almost as if we have nothing better to do with ourselves,' Fox said as he made for the usual table. There was a different barman on duty – much younger, but still glued to a quiz show on TV. Two clients standing at the bar – Fox recognised neither of them. Margaret Sime, Kaye's friend, was at her own table. She nodded a greeting. On the way back into town, Fox had taken the slightest of detours past Jamie Breck's house. No sign of life, and no van parked in the vicinity.

'Cheers,' Kaye said, taking delivery of the fresh pint and placing it beside the one he was halfway to finishing. Fox placed his own tomato juice on a coaster and slipped out of his sports jacket. He had left his tie at home, but was still wearing the same shirt, braces and trousers.

'So what was happening at Jude's?' Kaye asked.

'Bad Billy had his men digging up the garden. Anonymous caller said they heard some activity on Sunday night.'

'That's Billy's excuse anyway,' Kaye sympathised with a shake of the head. 'Hope you didn't leave any prints at the locus, Foxy. If he sees an opening, he's going to come at you with teeth bared and claws out.'

'I know.'

'Bastard put a lot of trust in Glen Heaton … defended him to the hilt.'

Fox stared at his colleague. 'You don't think Giles knew what Heaton was like?'

Kaye shrugged. 'We can't know for sure one way or the other. All I'm saying is, I can appreciate the man is hurting.'

'If he goes on tormenting my sister, he'll really get to know that feeling.'

Kaye chuckled into his glass. Fox knew what he was thinking: *You've no ammo, Foxy, no stomach for that kind of fight*. Maybe. Maybe not. He sipped at his own drink.

'Would it kill you to put a dash of vodka in there?' Kaye chided him. 'It makes me feel like the town drunk when I'm sitting with you.'

'You asked me to come.'

'I know I did; I'm just saying …'

'The first one wouldn't kill me,' Fox said after a moment's thought. 'But it would be a start. Somebody like me, Tony, a start's all they need.'

Kaye wrinkled his nose. 'You're not an alky, Malcolm. I've *seen* alkies, used to hose their cells down when I was a probationary.'

'Drink doesn't like me, Tony. Besides ...' He picked up the tomato juice again. 'This gives me the moral high ground.'

Both men drank in silence. A group of three new faces had arrived. Fox, his back to the door, watched Kaye make a quick appraisal. That was what you did when you were a cop – you watched the door for trouble. Trouble was the guy you'd once arrested; the guy whose uncle or cousin you once gave evidence against; the guy you'd persuaded to turn informer one time so he'd save his own skin. City the size of Edinburgh, it was difficult sometimes to escape your own history – things you'd done; people you'd used. But Kaye was back to concentrating on his drink: no reason to fret. Fox gave the men a quick glance anyway. Suits and ties – businessmen at day's end, maybe with a curry-house appointment later.

When the door opened again, Fox watched Kaye, saw an eyebrow rise, and turned round to look. It was Joe Naysmith. He was dressed for a long, cold night in the van. Lumberjack shirt beneath Shetland sweater, sweater beneath jerkin, jerkin beneath duffel coat. He was shedding these layers as he approached the table.

'Boiling in here,' he complained. He unbuttoned the shirt, to show a plain black T-shirt.

'Had a tiff with the boyfriend?' Kaye asked slyly.

Naysmith ignored him and asked them what they were drinking.

'Usual for me,' Kaye was quick to say, while Fox shook his head. His eyes met the younger man's.

'So what *did* happen?' he asked.

'We were doing a final check on the van. Gilchrist gets a call and tells me we don't need to go out.' Naysmith shrugged and started to head for the bar.

'Who was the call from?' Fox persisted. Naysmith just shrugged again and went to fetch the drinks.

'You think something's happened?' Kaye asked Fox.

'I'm not a soothsayer, Tony.'

'Nice excuse to call DS Inglis at home, invite her out for a late-night pow-wow with beverages supplied ...'

'She's got a kid.'

'Then invite yourself round there; take a bottle.' Kaye broke off and rolled his eyes. 'Except you don't drink.'

'That's right.'

'So it's soft drinks for you, and a few hefty Bacardis for the lady.'

Naysmith was coming back, a pint in either hand. 'I'd packed sandwiches and everything,' he went on complaining. 'Loaded some videos on to my phone to show him ...'

'And he didn't say who the call was from or what was said?' Fox watched Naysmith shake his head. 'You couldn't hear any of it – not even what *he* was saying?'

'I was in the back of the van; he was out front.'

'This was in the garage at Fettes?'

Naysmith nodded and gulped down the first inch and a half of beer, exhaling with satisfaction and wiping thumb and forefinger across his lips.

'Inglis seemed keen enough earlier,' Fox stated.

'Maybe she came round to your point of view,' Naysmith suggested.

'Maybe,' Fox conceded. 'So where's Gilchrist now?'

'He said he didn't fancy a drink.'

The three men sat in silence, and when the conversation resumed they were soon discussing other cases – past and present – moving on from there to McEwan's current 'jolly'.

'It'll be an hour of discussion over tea and biscuits, then four hours on the golf course,' Tony Kaye proposed.

'Does McEwan even play golf?' Fox asked, rising to get the next round in. He was debating whether to stay. Maybe he'd get a pint apiece for Kaye and Naysmith, then tell them he had to be leaving. But as he waited to be served, he glanced up at the TV. The quiz show had finished, and the local news was on. A dapper-looking man was giving some sort of statement in what looked like his office. Reporters held microphones to his face. Then a still photograph appeared onscreen: a man and woman standing on the deck of a yacht, dressed to the nines and grinning for the camera, arms around one another. Fox thought he recognised the woman.

'Turn that up,' he ordered the barman. But by the time the remote control had been located, the news had moved to another story. Fox gestured to be given the remote, and used it to switch from TV to text, running down the list of options until he found 'Regional News'. He clicked on Scotland and waited for the items to appear on the screen. Third story down he saw what he was looking for.

Property Tycoon Missing At Sea

Fox hit the button again and scrolled down the story. Charles Brogan, 43, millionaire property developer ... took his boat out from its Edinburgh mooring ... boat found deserted and drifting at the mouth of the Firth of Forth ...

‘What is it?’ Kaye asked. He was standing by Fox’s shoulder, studying the TV screen.

‘The guy behind Salamander Point. I heard his company was in trouble, and now he’s missing from his boat.’

‘Hara-kiri?’ Kaye guessed.

Fox laid the remote on the bar and paid for the round. Without having been asked, the barman had poured him another tomato juice. They took the drinks to the table.

‘Something on the news?’ Naysmith prompted.

‘Nothing for you to worry your pretty little head about,’ Kaye replied, tousling Naysmith’s hair. ‘Hadn’t you better get a trim before Jack Nicklaus gets back?’

‘I had it cut last month.’

Fox was rising from his chair again. ‘I need to make a phone call,’ he explained. ‘Back in a tick.’

He went outside and the cold hit him. Thought about retreating indoors for his jacket, but resisted the urge. Another urge was taking precedence. He punched Jamie Breck’s number into his mobile.

‘Wondered how long it would take you,’ Breck answered.

‘I just saw it on the news.’

‘Me too.’

‘You didn’t know?’

‘Looks like the wife’s first call was to her PR guy.’

‘That’s who was giving the statement?’

‘His name’s Gordon Lovatt. As in Lovatt, Meikle, Meldrum.’

‘Never heard of them.’

‘Big PR firm. They do lobbying, too.’

‘You’ve done your research.’

‘They’ve strayed into my orbit on occasion . . .’ Breck’s voice drifted off. Fox could hear a siren. He lowered the phone from his ear to confirm that it was coming from the earpiece. ‘You’re out somewhere,’ he stated.

‘I’m headed to Torphichen.’

‘Why?’

‘No real reason.’

‘Is it because of Joanna Broughton? Did she ever get back to you about the CCTV?’ Fox moved aside as two of the drinkers emerged from the bar to smoke a cigarette. They coughed a few times and continued the conversation they’d been having.

‘Which pub?’ Breck asked. ‘Minter’s?’

‘I was asking about Joanna Broughton. How come I just saw her on TV?’

'She's married to Charlie Brogan. Didn't change her name, but they've been together three or four years.'

'Has his body washed ashore yet?'

'It's dark out, if you hadn't noticed. Coastguard have called off the search until daybreak.'

'But you're still going into the station.' It was a statement rather than a question.

'Yes,' Jamie Breck answered.

'Will you let me know if you find out anything?'

'If it's pertinent to the case. I don't doubt I'll be talking to you sometime tomorrow . . . whether I like it or not. Meantime, Inspector, take the rest of the evening off.'

'Thanks, I'll do that.'

'Or at least try,' Breck said, ending the call.

Fox headed back indoors, rubbing some heat back into himself.

'Good news is,' he told Naysmith, 'you'd have been wasting your time anyway.'

'Breck's not at home?' Kaye guessed.

'The office,' Fox confirmed.

'Is that why Gilchrist cried off?' Naysmith asked. 'Could he have known?'

'Doubtful,' Fox answered after a moment's thought.

Friday 13 February 2009

11

Next morning, he was in the office early, but no one was at home in Room 2.24. Fox went downstairs to the canteen and found Annie Inglis there, slumped over a black coffee with a half-eaten scrambled-egg roll pushed to one side.

'You look rough,' he offered as he pulled out a chair and sat down opposite her.

'Duncan,' was all she said.

'What's he done?'

She rubbed her hands down her face. 'Nothing really. He's just at that age ...'

'Rebelling against Mum?'

She offered a tired smile. 'He stays out late – later than I like. He always comes home eventually ...'

'But you wait up for him?'

She nodded. 'And if it's a school night, next morning's like trying to raise the dead.'

'Is he running with the wrong crowd?'

She managed another smile, this time at his wording. 'When you're a mother, *everyone's* the wrong crowd.'

'Right.'

'I think they drink a little ... take drugs a little.'

'Not skunk?'

She shook her head. 'Duncan just seems a bit ...' She sought the right description. 'Tipsy,' she eventually decided, 'on occasion. Plus, the school say he's falling behind, not handing in homework.'

'He's got O Grades next year?'

'Standard Grades, they call them these days.' She tried shaking some life back into herself and picked up the coffee. 'Third one of these I've had.'

'Want a fourth?'

But, having drained the cup, she shook her head.

'Does he see his dad?' Fox asked, but she wasn't about to answer.

'Was there something you wanted, Inspector?' she asked instead.

'Yes, but it can wait.'

'Tell me. Might help get this brain of mine started.'

'You know the surveillance got pulled last night?'

She looked at him. 'No,' she said.

'It's just that ... you were so keen for it to go ahead. I was wondering what had changed.'

'I've not seen Gilchrist this morning.'

'They were getting the van ready. Gilchrist took a call, and told my guy it wasn't happening.'

'I'll ask him when I see him. Maybe something else came up.'

'Maybe,' Fox conceded.

'I'll ask him,' Annie Inglis repeated.

'Okay.' Fox got back to his feet. 'Sure about that coffee? We actually make better stuff upstairs – four-star leaded.'

'We can smell it every time we walk past.'

'Feel free to drop in.'

She thanked him. 'Malcolm ... what I was saying about Duncan ...'

'My lips are sealed,' Fox assured her, turning to leave.

In the Complaints office, McEwan was back.

'Did you bring us a souvenir?' Fox asked him.

McEwan snorted, then asked if things had been quiet in his absence.

'As the grave,' Fox stated, moving towards the coffee machine. But there was hardly any coffee left in the tin. He considered heading downstairs again to the canteen, but decided against it. There were tea bags, and he could boil some water. No milk, though. He checked his watch. Naysmith could have no excuses this morning – no surveillance to explain away a late start. He'd be here inside the quarter-hour.

'RBS headquarters has its own Starbucks,' McEwan commented, as though reading his mind.

'We're not the RBS,' Fox replied.

'Thank Christ for small mercies.'

'How was the conference?'

'Boring.'

'Are riots likely this summer?'

'Couple of the pundits seem to think so. Rising unemployment ... unrest ... people fearful of the future ... tension needing to be broken somehow ... And plenty of extremists ready to make it happen.'

'An Edinburgh riot would be something to see.' Fox was back at his desk.

'Plenty of them in times past, Malcolm – the mob was a thing to be feared.'

Fox was shaking his head. 'Not these days. Even when they're protesting outside the RBS boss's house, they use placards for the graffiti so as not to damage anything – *that's* your Edinburgh mob, Bob.'

'I hope to God you're right.' McEwan sneezed three times, then picked up his phone. 'On top of everything, I've caught that cold of yours.'

'Happy to share, sir,' Malcolm Fox told him. 'Mine's actually a little better.' He watched as Joe Naysmith walked into the room. Naysmith held up the plastic bag he was carrying – coffee and milk. Fox offered him the thumbs-up and received a gesture in return – Naysmith's palm held out as if for money. It was Friday – accounts day as far as the coffee was concerned. Fox ignored Naysmith and got down to the first of the day's chores. Copies of testimony in the Heaton case were beginning to arrive from the lawyers in the Fiscal's office, queries and comments attached to most of the pages. Fox would pass some off to Naysmith and some to Kaye, keeping the juiciest ones for himself. Half an hour later, Kaye sauntered in, rolling his eyes as he saw McEwan was back.

'What time do you call this?' McEwan complained.

'Sorry, sir,' Kaye replied, reaching for the coffee Naysmith had poured him. Then he drew a newspaper from his coat pocket and tossed it on to Fox's desk. 'Page three,' he said. 'No topless shots, though ...'

It was the morning's *Scotsman*. The story took up the whole page. There were photos of Brogan, his boat, Joanna Broughton and her father Jack. None of the pictures looked particularly recent, except for one of Gordon Lovatt at the press conference. The story itself was long on background and short on substance. Brogan's company owned swathes of commercial land and property in the city. Debt had become an issue. Brogan was a 'keen weekend sailor' who kept his million-pound yacht moored at South Queensferry. His wife was owner of the successful Oliver casino and his father-in-law a wealthy and retired 'local businessman, known for his cavalier approach'. Fox had a little smile to himself at that. When he looked up, Kaye was watching him.

'Doesn't add much,' Fox commented.

'Maybe because there's not much to add. Did you check the TV this morning?'

Fox nodded. 'Body's still out there somewhere.'

'Empty bottle of posh wine left on the deck, plus a smattering of sleeping tablets as prescribed to the wife.' Kaye paused, angling his head towards the newspaper. 'She's a looker, though – wonder what first attracted her to the pot-bellied, balding tycoon.'

'Says here they live in the penthouse of one of his developments.'

'Top three storeys of a new-build by Inverleith Park,' Kaye confirmed. 'It was in the papers at the time – priciest flat in Scotland.'

'But that was before the slump.'

'I doubt she needs to sell – Daddy's on hand to bail her out.'

'Begs the question why he hasn't done the same for his son-in-law.'

'You two,' Naysmith broke in, 'are like a couple of checkout girls with the latest copy of *Heat*.'

The phone on Fox's desk rang and he picked it up.

'Hallway in two,' Annie Inglis said, before the line went dead. Fox put the phone back down and patted the stacks of paperwork in front of him.

'Which is mine?' Kaye asked. Fox tapped the relevant pile.

'And mine?' Naysmith added. Another tap.

'Meaning yours is the smallest, Malcolm,' Kaye said with his usual frown.

'As per,' Naysmith agreed.

'Tough,' Malcolm Fox told them, getting to his feet.

Outside in the corridor, Annie Inglis was already waiting. She was leaning with her back to the wall, one foot crossed over the other, hands behind her.

'It's been pulled,' she said.

'That much I knew.'

'We won't be pursuing a case against DS Breck.' Her face was as stony as her voice.

'Why?'

'Orders.'

'Says who?'

'Malcolm ...' Her eyes fixed on his. 'All you need to know is, we no longer require the assistance of Complaints and Conduct.'

'Is that how you were told to phrase it?'

'Malcolm ...'

He took a step towards her, but she was already on her way back to her office. As his eyes followed her, he saw her head go down. She knew he was watching, knew he'd take it as a sign.

A woman who'd just done something she wasn't happy about, and wanted him to know.

At lunchtime, he told the office he was going out. He took a detour into the canteen, hoping Inglis might be there, but she wasn't. As he drove out of the compound he offered up a prayer that his parking space would still be vacant on his return, while knowing from experience that there was maybe a cat-in-hell's chance. As had become his custom, he kept a regular watch on any traffic behind him, but there were no black Astras or green Kas. Within ten minutes he was parking outside the Oliver. Simon was again behind the bar, chatting up one of the female croupiers while another eked out a shift at the blackjack table for the two hunched punters who were providing the casino's only custom.

'I already told you you'd need to talk to the boss,' Simon said, recognising Fox.

'Actually, it was my colleague you told that to, and we did consult with Ms Broughton.' Fox paused. 'Thought you might have been closed today as a mark of respect.'

'Nuclear war, that's about all we close for.'

'Lucky for me.' Fox pressed his palms against the bar counter. Simon stared at him.

'She said you could watch the tapes?' he guessed.

'Of Saturday night,' Fox confirmed. Then: 'Go call her; she'll tell you.' But they both knew Simon wasn't about to pick up the phone to Joanna Broughton. For one thing, she had other things on her mind. For another, Simon didn't have the clout – not that he would want the slim blonde croupier across the bar from him to suspect as much, which was why he told Fox it was fine, and that he could use the office. Fox nodded his thanks, inwardly congratulating himself on having read the young man correctly, and explained that he would be out of their way in no time at all.

The office was cramped. Simon sat at the desk while he set up the playback. The recording could be viewed directly on the screen belonging to the desktop computer.

'Hard-drive recorders,' Simon explained.

Fox nodded as he studied the room: a couple of chairs, three filing cabinets, and a bank of CCTV screens, alternating between a dozen different cameras.

'Do you depend on this to catch the cheats?' Fox asked.

'We have staff watching the floor. Sometimes we'll put someone on a table, pretending to be just another punter. Everyone's trained to be on the lookout.'

'Have any scams actually worked?'

'One or two,' Simon admitted, using the mouse to navigate the screen. Eventually he was happy, and swapped places with Fox. He started asking if there was any news about 'Mr Brogan'.

'Did you know him?' Fox asked back.

'He came by pretty regularly. Didn't gamble much, but liked to see Joanna.'

Simon looked as if he might hang about, so Fox told him he could get back to work. The young man hesitated, but then seemed to remember the blonde croupier. He nodded and left. Fox leaned in towards the screen and hit 'play'. There was a time code at top right, showing him that it was nine o'clock Saturday evening. He fast-forwarded to ten. At times, the camera would zoom in to pick out one particular player, or even that player's hand movements as they studied their cards. The place was busy, but, the tape being silent, there was a surreal quality to the footage, and the colour had a washed-out look. The cameras seemed to be focusing on the tables. Little attention was being paid to the doormen or the lobby or either of the bars. Fox couldn't see Vince Faulkner anywhere. Simon had told Breck he'd been drunk, seated on a stool by the corner of the downstairs bar, but Fox was damned if he could find him. When a tapping came at the door, he let out a hiss of air.

'Look,' he called out, 'I'm not halfway finished here!'

The door opened slowly. 'Oh, but you are,' a voice crooned. DCI Billy Giles was standing there, filling the whole doorway.

'Gotcha,' he said.

Torphichen police station.

Not the same room as before – one of the *proper* interview rooms.

And set up for a *proper* interview, too – video camera pointing down at the table from the ceiling. Once it was operational, a red light would blink to indicate that recording was in progress. A tape deck plugged into the wall socket – two tapes, one for each party. One microphone on its stand in the centre of the table. The walls whitewashed, decorated with nothing but a reminder that smoking was punishable by a fine – as if any of the room's usual inmates would worry about that. A foetid smell; the place had only recently been vacated.

They'd left Malcolm Fox there to stew in his own juices. No offer of tea or even water. Giles had asked him for his mobile; Fox had told him to get stuffed.

'How do I know you won't go calling chat lines on my tab?' was his reasoning.

There was a uniform in the room with him, standing to one side of the door. Doubtless this man would have been chosen for his gift of recall – every station had one. So Fox pretended to be texting instead of making calls. Thing was ... who was he supposed to tell? Who could help him clamber out of the midden he'd nosedived into? So he just pushed buttons at random, hoping he was getting on the uniform's nerves. It was a further ten minutes before the door opened. Giles was followed into the room by two other detectives. One of them was a woman in her thirties; Fox seemed to remember seeing her around the place when he'd been working on Heaton, but couldn't recall if he was supposed to know her name.

The male detective was Jamie Breck.

It was the woman's job to make sure the tapes were spooling, the recorder picking up their voices. She also checked that the camera's little red light was flashing, then gave Giles the nod. He had seated himself opposite Fox. He placed a folder and a large envelope on the table between them. Fox resisted looking interested in either.

'DS Breck,' Giles said with a nod of the head. The nod was directed towards the empty chair next to Fox. Breck seated himself slowly, avoiding eye contact, and Fox realised that the pair of them were in the selfsame mess. They sat side by side, with Giles across the desk from them like a headmaster with a pair of truants, and the woman officer replacing the uniform by the door.

'Where do I start?' Giles muttered, almost to himself. He was running his fingers over the folder and the envelope. Then he looked up, as though he'd just had an idea. 'How about the pictures? Camera never lies and all that ...' He tipped the contents of the envelope on to the table. There were dozens of photos. They'd come from a desktop printer, and weren't of the best quality.

But good enough, all the same.

'You'll see the time and date on each one,' Giles was saying, turning them around so Fox and Breck could view them more clearly. 'That one's you, DS Breck. You're visiting Inspector Fox at his home. The two of you then took a little trip to a casino.' Giles paused for effect. 'Happens to be the same one Vince Faulkner visited the night he disappeared.' He held up the appropriate photo. It was grainy, shot with a telephoto lens from some distance. Fox and Breck were depicted having their little word with the two doormen, prior to entering the Oliver. 'What else have we got here?' Giles made show of sifting through the photos again. 'The pair of you at Salamander Point. DS Breck was there to gather information on our murder victim.' Another pause. 'Not sure why *you* were there, Inspector Fox. Hardly part of your remit as a member of Complaints and Conduct.' Giles gave a little sniff. The man was loving every second, playing up to the camera and the microphone both. Fox thought back to the car – the *two* cars. He had his answer now. Even if you're paranoid, he said to himself, it doesn't mean they're not after you.

'Trying to influence the investigation, Inspector Fox?' Giles was asking. 'Barging in on the locus at your sister's house?'

'Her house isn't a crime scene,' Fox snapped back.

'Until I say otherwise, that's exactly what it is.' The huge man's voice was so calm, he could have been inhaling Prozac rather than oxygen.

'That's because you're an arrogant prick.' Fox decided a pause of his own was in order. 'For the record,' he concluded.

Giles took a few moments to shepherd his emotions back into the pen. 'What were you doing when you were apprehended, Inspector?'

'I was being a cop.'

'You were in the office of the Oliver casino, viewing that venue's CCTV footage for the night Vince Faulkner went missing.'

Fox could sense Jamie Breck's disquiet at this news.

'On whose authority did you go there?

'Nobody's.'

'Did DS Breck tell you it would be all right? The pair of you had already been to that establishment not once, but twice.' Giles sifted out another photo – Breck and Fox in daylight, standing beside Breck's car just seconds before Joanna Broughton turned up.

'This has nothing to do with DS Breck,' Fox argued. 'I went to Salamander Point on my own. It was coincidence he was there at the same time.'

Giles had turned his attention to Breck. 'But you let the Inspector sit in on your interview with Mr Ronald Hendry?'

'Yes,' Breck admitted.

'I outrank him,' Fox began to explain. 'I *ordered* him …'

'Whether you did or you didn't, here's the thing …' Giles opened the folder and produced a typed sheet. 'DS Breck left that particular detail out of his account of the interview.' Giles let the piece of paper fall on to the table. 'And the night he came to your home – had you *ordered* him to put in an appearance?' Giles allowed the silence to run its course. 'Seems to me the two of you have become a bit too pally.' He glared at Breck, while his finger stabbed in Fox's direction. 'He's a suspect! *You* knew that! Since when do we get cosy with suspects?'

'Glen Heaton did it often enough,' Fox commented in an undertone.

Giles's eyes were full of fire, his voice just about under control.

'Listen to the hypocrisy of the man,' he growled. Then he leaned back in his chair, rolling his shoulders and neck. 'None of this looks good. Time was, maybe the force would have dealt with it in its own way …' He pretended a rueful sigh. 'But with all the checks and balances these days, the need to be whiter than white …' He was staring straight at Fox. 'Well … you of all people, Inspector, you know how it is.' And he offered a shrug. Almost on cue, there was a knock at the door. The woman officer opened it, and two men entered. One was Chief Inspector Bob McEwan. The other was in uniform, carrying his peaked hat tucked beneath one arm.

'A bloody disgrace!' were the man's opening words. Giles had risen to his feet, as had Breck and Fox. It was what you did when the Deputy Chief Constable announced his presence. And he *did* have presence. He'd stuck it out at Lothian and Borders while rejecting the advances of other forces; stuck it out while several Chief Constables had been promoted over him or drafted in from outside. His name was Adam Traynor and he was ruddy-cheeked, steely-eyed, tall and barrel-chested. 'A copper's copper' was the consensus; admired by the lower ranks as well as the higher-ups. Fox had met the man several times. Minor cases of misconduct could be dealt with by the DCC. Only the more serious cases had to go to the Procurator Fiscal.

'Disgrace,' Traynor was repeating to himself, while McEwan had eyes only for his errant employee. Fox remembered their conversation of that morning. *Have things been quiet in my absence?* McEwan had asked. *As the grave,* Fox had answered. Now Traynor's attention turned to McEwan and Giles. 'Your men,' he was telling them, 'will have to be suspended pending the outcome of the inquiry.'

'Yes, sir,' McEwan muttered.

'Sir,' Giles agreed.

'Don't fret,' Traynor went on, half turning his head in the direction of Fox and Breck. 'You'll be on full pay.'

Giles's eyes were on Fox too, and Fox knew what his nemesis was thinking: *Just like Glen Heaton ...*

'Excuse me,' the woman officer interrupted. 'We're still taping ...'

'Then switch it off!' Traynor roared. She did so, having first informed the microphone that the interview was ending at two fifty-seven p.m.

'Internal inquiry, sir?' Bob McEwan was asking.

'Bit late for that, Bob – Grampian have had your man under surveillance these past four days.' Traynor was sifting through the photographs on the table. '*They'll* be the ones sorting it all out, same as we'd do for them if the tables were turned.'

McEwan was frowning. 'My officer has been under surveillance?'

The Deputy Chief Constable silenced him with a glare. 'Your man's been misbehaving, Chief Inspector.'

'And no one saw fit to inform me,' McEwan stated.

'A topic for later discussion.' Traynor was glaring at McEwan, but McEwan's attention was concentrated on Malcolm Fox, and there was an unspoken question there: *what the hell is going on here?*

'Right,' Traynor said, straightening up and running a thumb along the brim of his cap. 'Is that all clear enough for you?'

'I've got paperwork I could do with finishing,' Breck said.

'Not a chance,' Traynor barked back at him. 'Don't want you trying to cook the books.'

The blood rose up Jamie Breck's neck. 'With all due respect, sir ...'

But the Deputy Chief Constable was already in the process of leaving.

'We'll need your warrant cards and any pass keys,' Billy Giles was stating, hand held out in preparation. 'You walk out of here and you don't go near either of your offices, even to pick up a jacket or bag. You go home and you stay home. Grampian Police will doubtless be in touch – you'll know the protocol off by heart, Inspector Fox …'

McEwan had followed Traynor out of the room as if keen to collar the man, and without so much as a backward glance. But Fox trusted his boss. He'd be arguing Fox's case, fighting his corner.

'Warrant cards,' Giles repeated, fingers twitching. 'After which you'll be escorted from the premises.'

'The Federation has lawyers,' the woman officer piped up. Giles gave her a hard stare.

'Thanks, Annabel,' Jamie Breck said, throwing his warrant card down well short of Billy Giles's hand.

12

There was a pool hall on the corner, and that was their first stop, if only because they needed a place to sit and take it all in. Breck seemed to be known to the proprietor. A table by the window was wiped down for their use, and coffees arrived 'on the house'.

'No, we'll pay for them,' Breck insisted, producing a handful of coins from his pocket. 'One man's gift is another man's bung.' His eyes met Fox's and the two men managed wary smiles.

'Not exactly the most pressing of our worries,' Fox offered. 'Annabel was right, though – there are lawyers we could be consulting.'

Breck shrugged. 'At least you were right when you said you were being tailed. Might explain that van outside my house …'

'Yes,' Fox commented, feeling suddenly awkward.

'So what happens now? I'd say you're the resident expert here.'

Fox didn't answer immediately. He listened to the sounds around him – pool balls clacking against each other; mild cursing from the players; the low rumble of traffic outside. *Now we're in the same boat*, he thought.

'What was the last you heard about Brogan's yacht?' he asked.

Breck stared at him. 'We're not interested in any of that, Malcolm. We're suspended from our jobs.'

'Sure.' Fox shrugged. 'But you've got friends, right? Annabel – she's one of them? That means you can keep tabs on what's happening.'

'And if it gets back to Billy Giles?'

'What's the worst he can do? We're Grampian's problem from now on.' Fox picked up the cup and blew across its surface. He knew it was going to be the cheapest brand of powdered instant; knew the cup wasn't as clean as it could be. But he would remember the smell and the taste and the pattern on the saucer for the rest of his life.

'We're civilians now, Jamie,' he went on. 'That gives us more room to manoeuvre, not less.'

'I'm not sure what you're saying.'

Fox proffered a huge shrug. 'I thought you were the risk-taker, Jamie, the one who reckons we all make our own luck, affect the way our lives are going to turn out?'

'And you're the one who thinks the opposite.'

Fox just shrugged again. A couple of players had come in. They carried their two-piece cues in little travel cases. One of the men had a rolled-up copy of the day's *Evening News* in his pocket. When he slipped out of his jacket and made to hang it up, Fox sauntered over.

'Mind if I take a look?' he asked. The man shook his head, so Fox retreated to his table with the paper. Charlie Brogan had made it to the front page – not that there was much to report.

'Remember what you said, Jamie? Joanna Broughton's first phone call seems to have been to this PR agency. The media knew about the boat before we did. What does that say to you?'

'That the lady has skewed priorities.' Breck paused. 'What do *you* make of it?'

'I'm not sure ... not yet.'

'You're not just going to go home and put your feet up, are you?'

'Probably not.'

'Who's to say they'll stop tailing you?'

'That's another thing – I want to know precisely how long it's been going on.'

'Why?'

'Because timing is everything, Jamie.' Fox stared at Breck. 'You really didn't know I was under surveillance?'

Breck shook his head determinedly.

'Traynor said four days – that takes it back to Monday.'

'Vince's body wasn't found till Tuesday.'

Fox nodded. 'I still want to know what's on the CCTV footage from the Oliver.'

'I doubt it'll be useful.'

Fox leaned back in his seat. 'Maybe it's time for you to tell me why you seem to know so much about the place.'

Breck considered for a moment, weighing up how much to say. 'It was a few months back,' he began. 'Just someone we were trying to build a case against ...'

'Who?'

'A councillor – suspected of being a naughty boy. There were rumours of a meeting at the Oliver, so we asked Joanna Broughton for any recordings.'

'And?'

'And there weren't any – not by the time we went looking.'

'They'd been wiped?'

'Story we got was, there'd been a glitch of some kind.'

'But I've seen the tapes from Saturday night – I know *they're* there.'

'Doesn't mean there won't be another glitch. The Oliver is Broughton's pride and joy – her way of saying she can make it on her own.'

'Without Father Jack, you mean?'

Breck nodded. 'She doesn't want the place getting a rep – dodgy meetings; last known sightings of murder victims ...'

'That's why she uses the PR company?'

'Lovatt, Meikle, Meldrum,' Breck recited.

Fox thought for a moment. 'The night we went to the Oliver, you told me you'd never been to the Oliver in your life.'

'I lied.'

'Why?'

'Empathy?' Breck suggested. He'd taken the paper from Fox, skimming the front page and then flipping to the leader column. 'Seen this?' he asked. Then he started to quote from the piece: '"The value of the various development sites along the Edinburgh Waterfront has dropped by £220 million over the past year ... Land in the city has fallen from a high of £2 million an acre to less than a quarter of that ..." Fountain Brewery project in trouble ... Ditto Caltongate and the projected new town at Shawfair. Eighty per cent of the land holdings in Edinburgh now have no development value at all ...' He placed the newspaper on the table in front of them. 'No development value at all,' he repeated. 'Seems to me Charlie Brogan had every reason to walk the plank.'

'Hard to disagree.' Fox was scanning the piece for himself. 'Fountain Brewery,' he mused. 'That's where Vince was found.'

Breck nodded.

'Would Brogan have been one of the developers?'

'It's possible,' Breck conceded.

'Hundreds of millions of pounds that have just vanished into thin air,' Fox commented.

'The land's still there,' Breck argued. 'Only thing that's gone is the confidence. Banks stop lending, everyone gets the jitters.' He thought for a moment. 'So what *are* you going to do, Malcolm?'

'Maybe go see Jude, check how she's doing. What about you?'

'Been a while since I could dedicate a whole day to Quidnunc.' Breck broke off, staring down at the table. 'I'm not sorry I did what I did.'

'Don't worry about it – this is all my fault, not yours. Tell it just the way it happened – I railroaded you, pulled rank, maybe even lied ...' He was on the verge of saying it: *by the way, I'm not the only one who's been under surveillance*. But he swallowed the words back and gave a sigh instead. 'You could have told me about the casino and the councillor.'

Breck just shrugged. 'Giles was right, though – I never should have allowed you within a million miles of the case. He's probably more furious with me than he is you – you're the enemy he knew about, but me ... turns out I'm Judas.'

'I'm sure Judas had his good points.'

They shared a half-hearted laugh as they got to their feet, coffees unfinished. Stood facing one another and shook hands. Fox replaced the newspaper in the pool-player's jacket and offered a wave of thanks. When he turned towards the door, Jamie Breck had already left.

Tony Kaye exited Police HQ with a scuffed briefcase swinging from one hand. He was whistling through his teeth, scanning the car park. When a horn sounded, he headed in that direction. The Volvo's passenger-side door was already open, so he got in and closed it after him, handing the briefcase to its owner.

'What happened?' he asked.

'They wouldn't let me past the front desk,' Malcolm Fox explained. 'Word must already have gone out that I'm radioactive.'

'McEwan has a face like fury.'

'What's he been saying?'

'Not a cheep. He had some meeting in the DCC's office, and there's another scheduled for later.' Kaye paused. 'I'm hearing a lot of strange accents about the place ...'

'Grampian Police,' Fox explained. 'From the Complaints, I suppose. They've got me under investigation.'

Kaye puckered his lips to give a proper whistle. 'Grampian Complaints? What's going on, Foxy?'

'I've walked right into it, Tony. Nobody to blame but myself.'

'Did Breck grass you up?'

Fox thought for a moment, then shook his head. 'They were looking at me before I'd even met him.'

'Looking's one thing, but did they have any ammo until he came along? And why were they looking at you in the first place? Anything I should know about?'

Fox didn't have even the beginnings of an answer. He unlocked his briefcase and peered in. 'Where are the queries from the Fiscal's office?'

It was Kaye's turn to shake his head. 'McEwan has already divvied them up.'

'He's bringing someone else in?'

'Only temporary, till you're back on your feet.'

'Who said I wasn't on my feet?' Fox snapped. Then: 'Who is it?'

'Gilchrist.'

Fox stared at him. 'Chop Shop Gilchrist?'

Kaye nodded slowly. 'So now I'll have him in one ear, Naysmith in the other, the pair of them vying to out-geek each other. And you know what that means ...'

'What?'

'Means you've got to get his thing quashed pronto, before I go postal.'

Fox managed a tired smile. 'Thanks for the vote of confidence.'

'It's *me* I'm thinking of, Foxy.' They sat in silence for a moment, staring through the windscreen. Then Kaye gave an elongated sigh. 'You going to be all right?' he asked.

'Don't know.'

'Anything I can do to help?'

'Keep your ear to the ground. Call me once a day so I know what's happening.' He paused. 'Whose idea was it to bring in Gilchrist?'

'No doubt Naysmith put in a good word ...'

'But from what I've seen, the Chop Shop's short-handed as it is. With Gilchrist elsewhere, that only leaves Inglis.'

Kaye offered a shrug. 'Not your problem, Foxy.' He was opening the car door. 'Minter's later? Friday night, remember ...'

'I doubt I'll be in the mood.'

Kaye was halfway out of the car when he paused and stuck his head back in. 'By the way, Joe wanted me to remind you – you're three weeks behind with the coffee kitty.'

'Tell him the debt's transferred to the new boy.'

'I like your style, Inspector Fox,' Kaye said with a grin. 'Always have ...'

*

Instead of going straight home, Fox stopped outside Jude's house. There was no sign of any activity – no vans or officers. He rang her bell and she answered with a shout from the other side of the door.

'Who is it?'

'Your brother.'

She opened the door and let him in. 'Had reporters round?' he guessed.

'They wanted to know why your lot had been excavating my garden.' She accepted his peck on the cheek and led him into the living room. She'd been smoking: a stub was still smouldering in the ashtray. But there was no evidence that she'd had a drink, other than coffee. A fresh jar of instant sat on the breakfast bar, alongside the kettle and a mug and spoon.

'Want one?' she asked, but he shook his head.

'That cast looks different,' he commented.

She lifted her arm a fraction. 'Brand new this lunchtime. Bit less cumbersome, and at least I got to have a good scratch when they took off the old one.'

He smiled at this. 'Didn't you break your other arm once?'

'Wrist,' she corrected him. 'I wondered if you'd remember.'

'Mum took me along when you went to the hospital to have the cast removed.'

Jude was nodding. She had returned to her favoured armchair and was preparing to light a fresh cigarette.

'You've just put one out,' Fox reminded her.

'Meaning it must be time for another. Didn't you used to smoke?'

'Not since leaving school.' He settled himself on the sofa across from her. The TV was playing with the sound turned down – looked like a nature documentary.

'Seems a lifetime ago,' Jude was saying.

'It *was* a lifetime ago.'

She nodded, growing solemn, and Fox knew she was thinking of Vince. 'They still can't tell me when they'll release the body,' she said in an undertone.

'I was wondering something,' Fox began, leaning forward a little. 'I'm not sure you've ever told me how the two of you met.'

She stared at him. 'I didn't think you were interested.'

'I am now.'

Jude drew on her cigarette, screwing shut her eyes against the smoke. She had slid around in the armchair so that her legs hung over one of its arms. Fox was reminded that his sister had a good figure. The jeans she was wearing were tight, showing the lines of her slender thighs and hips. Just the beginnings of a roll of fat around her waist. No bra discernible beneath the T-shirt, which was baggy at the sleeves, allowing glimpses of the flesh either side of her breasts. She'd been bright at school, a bit of a swot. The rebel in her had only come to light later, with her first tattoo – a red rose on her left shoulder, complete with a thorny stem. Fox recalled that Sandra Hendry, too, boasted a tattoo – a scorpion on her ankle. And Vince Faulkner's arms had been scarred by the amateur needle-and-ink methods of his youth.

'Vince,' Jude was saying, drawing the name out beyond its natural length. 'Vince was drinking with some of his friends in the West End. It was a Sunday night and I was out with this girl, Melissa, from the office. It was her birthday and, tell the truth, she was called the Frumpster behind her back. She'd asked half a dozen of us to go out that night, and I'd said yes before realising that everybody else had made some excuse.' Jude sighed. 'So there were just the two of us, and that had its compensations.'

'How so?'

'Being out with the Frumpster meant I got all the attention.'

'Beauty and the Beast?'

'She wasn't *that* bad, Malcolm.' But the putdown was half-hearted at best. 'Anyway, we ended up in a pub on St Martin's Lane or somewhere ... You don't know London, do you?' She watched Fox shake his head. 'You'd hate it – too big, too full of itself ...' She seemed to be drifting away, but managed to stop herself. 'Vince was in a crowd of half a dozen. There'd been a football game that lunchtime and it looked like they'd been celebrating ever since. They insisted on buying us drinks ...' She paused again, lost in thought. 'Vince was the same as them but different. He didn't seem to have put as much away as his pals. He was quieter, almost shy. He wrote his mobile number on the back of my hand, said he'd leave the rest to me.'

'It was up to you to take the initiative?'

'I suppose ...'

'And it turns out you did.'

But Jude was shaking her head. 'I had a shower the next morning, and the number was gone. Far as I was concerned, he was just a fella in a Sunday-night boozer. But Melissa had hooked up with one of the guys. Week later, he turned up to fetch her from the office ...'

'Vince was with him?'

She smiled. 'Wanted to know why I hadn't called.'

'The four of you went out together?'

'The four of us went out together,' she confirmed. 'Melissa broke up with Gareth after about a fortnight.' Her eyes were glassy with tears, but she blinked them back. 'I never expected us to last.'

Fox watched his sister rub her eyes against either shoulder of her T-shirt. There was writing on the front of the shirt, along with an illustration. It was from a rock tour, and Fox remembered that Vince Faulkner had often taken Jude to concerts. They'd travelled as far afield as Paris and Amsterdam for certain bands.

'You never really knew him,' Jude was saying. 'You never made the effort.'

All Fox could do was nod his agreement.

'He wasn't all candyfloss and ice cream, Jude.'

'Because he'd been in trouble with the law?' Her eyes were fixing on his. 'That's the thing, though – people like *you* can't see past that. It was ancient history, yet that man Giles kept harping on about it, and the papers keep saying it.'

'And he kept it from you, Jude. He didn't want you to know.'

'Because it wasn't *him* any more!' Her voice was rising. 'And don't start saying he was beating me up – I don't want to hear it! The papers have got hold of that, too, and who is it's been feeding them all this crap if not *your* lot?'

'They're not my lot,' Fox said under his breath. 'Not any more.'

He spent much of the evening lifting books from the bookshelves in his living room and placing them on the coffee table. His intention was to put them in alphabetical order, maybe with a split into two categories – ones he'd read; ones he hadn't. But then he wondered if maybe some of them couldn't go to a charity shop. And of the ones left for reshelving, should he initiate a further subdivision into fiction and non-fiction? He'd eaten chicken curry for his supper, using up the ingredients bought from Asda when he'd gone there to talk to Sandra Hendry. The chicken had come from a Co-op on the way back from Jude's. He was now suffering from discomfort, having eaten too much.

'Maybe they could all go,' he told himself, staring at the piles of books. That would mean he could dispense with the shelving, creating more space. But space for what, exactly? A bigger TV, one of those home cinema systems? He would just end up watching more rubbish than ever. When his mobile trilled, he was happy to answer it. It was a text message from Annie Inglis, inviting him to lunch on Sunday. She provided her address and ended her message with the simplest of questions:

OK?

Fox ran his fingers through his hair and found that he was sweating from his work with the books. Never the world's most expert texter, it took him three trial runs before he decided he was happy with his reply. Only then did he press the 'send' button. His message had been a succinct OK, no question mark required.

Saturday 14 February 2009

13

Saturday, Fox slept late, but then he hadn't fallen asleep until two. By eleven, he was seated at the kitchen table with three newspapers – *Scotsman*, *Herald* and the very earliest printing of the *Evening News*. He was looking for background on Charlie Brogan, and Scottish journalism was happy to oblige. Working-class roots, raised and schooled in Falkirk. His father had been a joiner, Charlie picking up some skills even before school had kicked him out. His CV was copious and wide-ranging, taking in everything from carpet-fitting to door-to-door selling. The two had combined eventually, Brogan setting up a company that sold floor coverings to factories and businesses. By twenty-three, he had enough money going spare that he could afford a punt – buying flats and either letting them out or refurbishing them for resale. The economy was buoyant and Brogan prospered further, moving into full-scale land development and rubbing shoulders with the rich and influential. He enjoyed the hospitality of bankers and other businessmen, dated some of Scotland's most eligible young women and eventually met and married Joanna Broughton.

The papers carried several snapshots of Joanna. She'd always been a looker, but there was a hardness to her features and her stare. Even smiling, she let the photographer know she was the boss. The interior of the Inverleith penthouse featured in one picture, its walls festooned with art. A sidebar had been contributed by a professional psychologist who warned that more tragedies involving one-time high-flyers might be the inevitable outcome of the credit crunch.

The sole public failure in Brogan's long career had come when his attempt to join the board of Celtic FC was rebuffed. One of his friends reminisced for the *Herald* about the incident: 'Charlie never got used to people saying no to him. It festered to the extent that he discussed switching his allegiance to Ibrox – that's the kind of guy he was.'

The hot-headed kind, Fox thought to himself. Not the kind to rationalise a snub if he could stew about it instead. A man who would see the economy's doldrums as a personal affront. But that phrase about Ibrox ... about not giving in but getting even ... it didn't hint that Brogan was the sort to just give up. He would want to fight back. The psychologist had focused on the economy without bothering to debate the most important question: could Charlie Brogan have been classed as a suicide risk? There was no mention that any note had been left; no evidence that he had tidied up his affairs before taking the plunge. But then maybe that was fair enough – he'd taken his boat out, drifting further and further from his troubles, tranquillising himself with pills and alcohol. He could have gone on deck, stumbled and fallen overboard. Or that impetuous streak might have suggested to him suddenly that he should finish things properly. Not a planned suicide, but absolutely of the moment.

There had been no comment from the family, apart from the original statement issued through Gordon Lovatt. Fox stared at Joanna Broughton's photograph.

'You made sure you had a media angle,' he told her, 'before you let anyone else in on it.'

Was that cold? Was it calculating? Or just a smart woman being smart? Fox stared and stared and couldn't decide. He took a break, stretching his spine and loosening his shoulders. Through in the living room, he saw that the coffee table was covered in books. There were more on the floor in front of the shelves, the shelves themselves denuded. Dust hung in the air. So far, he'd found only half a dozen titles that he felt no further use for, heavily outnumbered by those he wanted to read again. When his phone rang, he had to hunt for the handset. It was hidden between two of the piles.

'Malcolm Fox,' he said by way of greeting.

It was Lauder Lodge. Mitch wanted to know if he'd be visiting today or tomorrow. He wanted to see him. Fox was about to suggest Sunday until he remembered lunch with Annie Inglis. He glanced at his watch, then asked the caller to tell his father he was on his way.

He took the city bypass to the Sheriffhall roundabout, and headed for The Wisp, cutting through Niddrie and reaching the care home in under twenty minutes. Mitch was seated in reception, dressed in coat, scarf and hat.

'I want to go out,' he told his son.

'Sure,' Fox agreed. 'I can bring the car round.'

'My legs haven't seized up entirely.' So they walked around the corner to where Fox had found a parking space. He had to help his father with his seat belt, and they took the short drive to Portobello, parking on a side road by the promenade.

'We should have invited Mrs Sanderson.'

'Audrey's spending the day in her bed,' Mitch explained. 'She's got a cold coming.' Then, as Malcolm unclipped his seat belt for him: 'I asked them to phone Jude for me, but she wasn't answering.'

'She's been getting a lot of calls from journalists. Or it could be she's next door with a neighbour.'

'How is she?'

'Bearing up.'

'Are you any nearer catching whoever did it?'

'It's not my case, Dad.'

'I'd hope you'd be keeping a bloody eye on it, though.'

Fox nodded slowly. 'I don't think there's been much progress ...'

The sun was shining, and the seafront was busy. There were dog-walkers and children down on the beach itself. Kids with in-line skates were being guided along the concrete walkway by their parents. A sharp wind was whipping across the Firth of Forth. Fox wondered if Charlie Brogan's boat would have been visible from here. According to the papers, it had been towed to North Queensferry, which meant that Fife Constabulary were vying with Lothian and Borders for jurisdiction. The respective Chief Constables would sort it out, with Edinburgh the likely winner, much as the Fife cops might fancy a few days or weeks stationed in the capital.

'What are you thinking?' Fox's father asked him. They were standing by the sea wall, staring out at the view.

'Weekends aren't for thinking,' Malcolm stated.

'Meaning you had your mind on work.'

Fox couldn't deny it. 'Things have been a bit rough,' he admitted.

'You need a holiday.'

'I had a decent break at Christmas.'

'And did what exactly? I mean a proper holiday with sunshine and a hotel swimming pool and meals served on the terrace.' Mitch

Fox paused. 'You could well afford it, if you didn't have my bills hanging over you.'

Fox looked at his father. 'Lauder Lodge was a godsend, Dad. I don't begrudge a penny of it.'

'I'm betting your sister doesn't chip in.'

'She doesn't need to – I can afford it.'

'But it leaves things tight, doesn't it? I know damned well how much my room costs, and I can guess how much you make ...'

Fox gave a short laugh, but said nothing.

'What if you meet a nice girl and want to take her away somewhere?' his father continued.

'What's brought this on?' Fox asked with a smile.

'I'm not going to be here much longer, Malcolm – we both know that. I just want to be sure in my mind that my son and daughter are all right.'

'We're fine.' Fox touched the sleeve of his father's coat. 'And you shouldn't be talking like that.'

'I think I've earned the privilege.'

'Maybe so, but all the same ...' Fox blew his nose and looked up and down the promenade. 'Let's get something to eat,' he said.

They ate fish and chips from the paper, seated by the sea wall. 'Sure you're not too cold?' Fox asked his father. The old man shook his head. 'The smell of vinegar,' Fox confided, 'always takes me back to holidays and high days.'

'A treat on Saturday night,' Mitch Fox agreed. 'Except your mother was never so keen on the fish – had to be chicken or steak pie for her.'

'What was the name of the chippie near us?' Fox was frowning in concentration, but his father thought for a moment and shook his head.

'Can't help.'

'Maybe I should ask Lauder Lodge if there's a room there for me ...'

'You'll get it eventually.'

'The room, or the name of the chippie?'

Mitch Fox smiled at this. He'd had enough to eat, so offered the remainder to Malcolm, who shook his head. They rose to their feet and started walking. Mitch was stiff at first, but tried not to show it. People they passed either nodded a greeting or said hello. There were plenty of gulls around, but Fox dumped the remains of the food in a bin instead.

'Are Hearts home or away?' Mitch asked.

'Couldn't even tell you who they're playing.'

'You loved going to a game when you were a kid.'

'I think it was the swearing I liked. And I've not been to a match all season.' Fox's father had paused again, leaning against the sea wall.

'Are things really okay, son?' he asked.

'No, not really.'

'Do you want to tell your old man about it?'

But all Malcolm Fox could do was shake his head.

They found a pub and went inside, Mitch selecting their table while Malcolm fetched the drinks – a sparkling water and a half of IPA. His father asked him how long it was since he'd had a 'real' drink, and confessed that Audrey Sanderson kept a supply of brandy in her bedside cabinet. Fox sat in silence for a minute, then took a deep breath.

'Do you really want to know why I stopped drinking?'

'Because you realised it was going to end up killing you?' his father guessed. But Fox shook his head.

'After Elaine left, I took to it hard. Kept pestering her, to the point where I could probably have been done as a stalker. I went round to see her one night. I'd had a skinful, and I ended up punching her.' He went quiet, but his father wasn't about to interrupt. 'She could have had me prosecuted. My career would have been in tatters. When I phoned her to apologise … well, it took some persuading before she'd even talk to me, and then all she said was "stop drinking". And I knew she was right.'

'Why are you telling me this?' Mitch asked quietly. 'Why now?'

'Because of what happened to Vince,' his son explained. 'I've always hated him, hated the way he treated Jude, but now that he's dead …'

Mitch waited for Fox to make eye contact. 'You're not like him,' he stated. 'Don't go thinking you are.'

They settled back to watch the football on TV, staying for the results. It was five o'clock and nearly dark when they emerged. Fox drove his father back to Lauder Lodge in silence, receiving a firm look from one of the staff members. Mr Fox, it transpired, was late for supper.

'Lucky we've kept it for you,' the woman advised.

'That's debatable,' Mitch muttered, stretching a hand out towards his son. The two men shook.

On his way home, Fox thought about stopping and buying some flowers for Annie Inglis. She had texted him her address, unaware that he already knew it. He wondered, too, if he should buy something for her son. But what? And might flowers not start to wilt overnight? Straight home then, to dinner from the fridge and more sorting of books. He thought back to the pub. *You're not like him … don't go thinking you are.* When he unlocked his door, there was a note inside his letter box. It was from Jamie Breck.

CALL ME WHEN YOU GET IN.

Fox took out his phone but then paused, tapping it against his teeth. He locked the door after him and got back into his car. Five minutes later, he was parking on the street outside Breck's home. The houses had their own driveways and garages, meaning there was plenty of space kerbside. It struck him, though, that the surveillance van really must have stood out because of this. As he pressed the remote-locking button, he noticed that a young woman was just coming out of Breck's, shrugging her arms into her coat and wrapping a scarf around her neck. She was heading towards Breck's Mazda, but saw him and managed to place him. She gave a wave and a smile.

'Just nipping out for pizza – do you want any?'

Fox, halfway down the path by now, shook his head. 'It's Annabel, isn't it?'

She nodded and got into the driving seat. 'There's a bottle of wine open,' she informed him, giving another wave before driving off. Fox rang the doorbell and waited.

'Forgotten something?' Jamie Breck was asking as he opened the door. Then his eyes widened. 'Oh, it's you.' He was dressed in T-shirt and denims, his feet bare. There was music playing – it sounded vaguely Brazilian to Fox.

'Didn't mean to interrupt,' Fox began.

'Annabel's just gone for pizza …' Breck broke off. 'How did you know where I live?'

Yes, Malcolm, good question … 'I thought I knew the street,' he explained. 'Then I just got lucky – saw Annabel coming out and recognised her from Torphichen.'

'So now my guilty little secret is out.'

'She's your girlfriend?' Fox deduced.

'Yes.'

'Does Giles know?'

'I reckon he suspects, not that it's a state secret or anything. It's just that we'll both take a ribbing when it gets out.'

'What rank is she?'

'Detective constable – her surname's Cartwright, if you want to keep things nice and formal.' Breck broke off again. 'Come in, won't you?'

Fox followed him inside. The place had a very modern feel – well decorated and laid out. The music was coming from an MP3 system and there was a flat-screen TV attached to one wall. The lights had been dimmed but Breck powered them up again. On the floor by the sofa sat a wine bottle, two glasses and Breck's shoes and socks.

'Look, I don't want to interrupt anything,' Fox said.

'Not a problem, Malcolm. I think I'm still in shock from yesterday – how about you?'

Fox nodded and slipped his hands into his coat pockets. 'You had something to tell me?' he prompted.

Breck had collapsed on to the sofa. He stretched out a hand towards his wine glass and lifted it to his mouth. 'It's your friend Kaye,' he said before drinking.

'What about him?'

'Annabel told me this afternoon. I was going to phone you, but I thought maybe it was best done in person. We were heading out for a drive, so we dropped by and when you weren't home I put that note through your door.'

'You were saying about Tony Kaye ...?'

Breck sloshed the wine around in his glass. 'Remember you told me about your sister's mystery visitor on the Monday night?' He stared at Fox above the rim of the glass.

'Kaye?' Fox guessed.

'Seems that a "concerned citizen" called to let police know of a car parked illegally in Jude's street – one front and one back tyre up on the pavement.' Breck managed the faintest of smiles. 'You've got to love Edinburgh's army of nosy parkers.' He lifted a remote control from the sofa and used it to turn down the music. 'Anyway, they called it in and eventually someone noticed it. Turns out our concerned citizen had made a note of the make and model of car, plus a partial registration. Nissan X-Trail.'

'That's what Tony Kaye drives.'

'And his registration matches.'

'Partially,' Fox stressed.

'Partially,' Breck conceded. 'But it's enough to satisfy Billy Giles.'

Fox thought for a moment. 'It doesn't mean anything,' he said.

'Maybe not.' Breck took another mouthful of wine. 'Anyway, I thought you'd want to know, since Kaye doesn't seem to have mentioned it to you himself.'

Fox didn't know how to answer, so nodded slowly instead. 'Does he know he's been rumbled?'

'His presence at Torphichen has been requested first thing tomorrow.'

'Giles has the team working a Sunday?'

'He reckons the budget will stretch to it. Will you stay and have some pizza?'

'I can't. Listen ... thanks for letting me know. I wouldn't want Annabel to get into trouble ...'

'Annabel's cleverer than you and me combined – and wilier, too.' Breck had risen to his feet.

'Sorry again to burst in on you ...'

Breck waved the apology aside. He opened the front door for his guest and stood there as Fox made his way back along the path towards the pavement.

'Malcolm!' Breck called out, causing Fox to stop and turn towards him. 'How did you know my street? The night you dropped me off, I don't remember mentioning it.'

But instead of waiting for a reply, Breck just closed the door. A few seconds later, the music had been turned up again. Malcolm Fox was still rooted to the spot.

'Shit,' he said, reaching into his pocket for his phone.

Tony Kaye was in a restaurant with his wife. He seemed to have excused himself from the table and was dodging waiters and other diners as he talked. Fox was back at his car by this time, seated behind the steering wheel but with the key not yet in the ignition.

'Just exactly what did you think you were doing?' he asked. 'And when were you going to tell me?'

'I've got a more interesting question for you, Foxy – who the hell told *you*?'

'Doesn't matter. Is it true?'

'Is what true?'

'You went round to Jude's Monday night.'

'What if I did?'

'Why in God's name did you do that?' Fox was massaging the bridge of his nose with his fingers.

'Christ, Foxy, you'd just told me he'd broken your sister's arm.'

'*My* problem, not yours.'

'But we both know, don't we? We know you weren't planning on doing anything about it!'

'And what were *you* going to do, Tony? Take a swing at him?'

'Why not? Might've stopped him doing it again.'

'And both of them would think I'd put you up to it.'

'What does it matter?' Kaye's voice was rising. 'He wasn't at home.'

Fox gave an elongated sigh. 'Why didn't you say something?'

'Your sister was paralytic – I reckoned she'd have forgotten about it by morning.'

'Instead of which, you're now going to have Billy Giles crushing your nuts in a vice.'

'Make a change from the wife.'

'Don't go thinking this is funny – it isn't. Giles is going to want to know everything you did on Monday evening. If there are gaps, suddenly you're a suspect. McEwan's already lost one man, Tony ...'

'Yeah, yeah.'

'Giles would love to blow our whole show to smithereens.'

'Received and understood.'

Fox paused for a moment. 'Which restaurant?'

'Cento Tre on George Street.'

'Special occasion?'

'We're celebrating not killing each other so far this weekend. Mind you, that makes it like every other weekend. Did you catch the Hearts game?'

'Be careful tomorrow.'

'You mean at Torphichen? It's a Sunday away from home... far as I'm concerned, that's a holiday and a lotto win rolled into one.' The background noises had changed – Kaye had obviously stepped outside. There were shrieks of drunken female laughter and the sound of a car horn. 'You'd think people would have the decency to stop having fun,' Kaye commented. 'Does nobody realise this is Credit Crunch Ground Zero?'

'Be careful tomorrow,' Malcolm Fox repeated, watching the woman detective called Annabel returning with the pizzas in Jamie Breck's Mazda. 'And let me know how it goes.'

Sunday 15 February 2009

14

Annie Inglis lived on the top floor of a Victorian tenement in Merchiston. Her name was on the intercom, and when Fox pressed the buzzer a male voice answered.

'Who is it?'

'Is that Duncan? My name's Malcolm Fox.'

'Okay.'

Fox pushed open the door and found himself in a tiled stairwell with two bicycles parked just inside the entrance. He climbed the stairs slowly, peering up towards the glass cupola, through which the lunchtime sun was streaming. His morning had comprised coffee, shopping, and more newspapers. He carried a bag within which lay a bottle of wine and a bunch of early daffodils for his hostess, along with an iTunes token for her son. Duncan was waiting for him at the top, loitering just outside the door to the flat. Fox tried to make light of the climb.

'Must keep you fit,' he offered. Duncan just grunted. He had lank brown hair falling into his eyes, and was tall and gangly. His chosen outfit of denims and T-shirt would have fitted someone twice his girth. He headed indoors and crooked a finger to let Fox know he should follow. The flat's main hallway was long and narrow with half a dozen doors off. The original flooring had been sanded and varnished. There was a cycle helmet next to the phone on the only table, above which was fixed a row of hooks with keys dangling from them.

'Mum's …' Duncan pointed vaguely, before disappearing into his bedroom. There was a 'Legalise Cannabis' sticker on the door, and Fox could hear the low hum of a computer's cooling fan. At the far end of the hall was an open door leading to the drawing room. It looked spacious, with a bay window allowing views across the chimneypots north to the city centre and beyond. But just before Fox reached it, he heard sounds from the room to his immediate right. The door was open an inch, allowing him a glimpse into the kitchen. Annie Inglis was stirring a pot. Her face was red and she seemed flustered. He decided to leave her be, and walked into the drawing room. A table had been set next to the window, laid for three. Fox placed his carrier bag on it and took a look around. Sofa and chairs, TV and hi-fi, shelves filled with books, DVDs and CDs. There were framed photos, too – Annie and Duncan, an elderly couple (presumably her parents), but no indication that Duncan's father played any role in the family's life.

'You're here.' She was standing in the doorway, carrying three wine glasses.

'Duncan let me in.'

'I didn't hear you.' She placed the glasses on the table, then noticed the bag.

'For you,' he said. 'And something for Duncan, too.'

She peered inside and smiled. 'That's kind of you.'

'If you're busy in the kitchen, don't worry – I can entertain myself. Or I can come and help …'

She shook her head. 'Nearly done,' she said, grabbing the bag. 'Just give me two minutes.'

'Sure.'

'I can fetch you a drink.'

'I'm not really a drinker.'

'Cranberry juice? It's just about the only source of vitamins Duncan gets.'

'Cranberry juice is fine.'

'Two minutes,' she repeated, making her exit. Fox recommenced his tour of the room. Her preferred Sunday paper was the *Observer*. She liked the novels of Ian McEwan and films with subtitles. Her taste in music stretched from Alan Stivell to Eric Bibb. All of which left Fox not much the wiser. He returned to the view, envying her this sweep of the city and of the firth to its north.

'Mum says to say thanks.' It was Duncan in the doorway this time. He was waving the credit-card-sized token.

'I wasn't even sure if you used downloads,' Fox said.

Duncan nodded to let him know he did. Then he waved the token a final time and was gone again. Fifteen years old – Fox tried to think back to himself at that age. There'd been rows with Jude, and plenty of them. He could always wind her up until she was at screaming point. Throwing things at him, even. Fifteen … he'd started drinking by that stage. Bottles of cider in the park with his pals. Screw-top wine and quarter-bottles of whisky.

'Here you go …' It was Annie Inglis again, bringing him his tall glass of cranberry juice. She looked around. 'I told Duncan to …'

'He did. Seems a nice kid.'

She handed him the glass. 'Why don't you sit down? I'll just fetch my drink.'

It was white wine in a tumbler. She decanted it into one of the proper wine glasses on the table, then brought it over and sat next to him on the sofa.

'Cheers,' she said, chinking glasses.

'Cheers. And thanks for the invite.'

'We don't normally do Sunday lunch.' Her eyes widened a little. 'You're not vegetarian, are you?'

'Perish the thought.'

'I've got pork and apple sauce. Plus a burger for Duncan.'

'He won't eat pork?'

'He'd pick at it.' She took a mouthful of wine and exhaled. 'That's better.' She smiled at him. 'Not that I need it, you understand.'

'Your secret's safe with me.'

'Did you hear about Gilchrist?'

Fox nodded. 'I was going to ask if you knew.'

'I don't know what it is the Complaints have got that CEOP hasn't.'

'It's only temporary, though.'

'He was quick enough to accept.'

'You think they should have offered it to you?'

'I'd have turned it down,' she said quickly. 'And not just because it's *your* job we're talking about.' She trained her eyes on him. 'How are you feeling?'

'I'm fine. You know that sign on the CEOP door, the one that says two people have to be present when you look at anything …?'

'Working solo is going to present problems,' she agreed.

'I don't know how you can do the job you do,' he stated with a slow shake of the head.

'The secret is, you never focus on what's happening in the photo – you look for the clues in the background, anything that can identify where the abuse took place …'

'But it must get to you – you've got a kid of your own.'

'We limit our time on the computer to a couple of hours a day, plus three times a year we get counselling – mandatory counselling. When I come home, the office doesn't come with me.'

'It still sounds tough.'

'It's a job,' she said, taking another gulp of wine. Then: 'What about you, Malcolm? What's going to happen?'

He shrugged and lifted his own drink to his mouth. 'What are you going to do about Breck?'

'What *can* I do?'

'Can you at least talk about it?'

She shook her head.

'Why not?' When she just stared at him, he lifted his hands in a show of surrender.

'I'll check on the meat,' she said, getting back to her feet. She was wearing tight black cords and a cream-coloured woollen sweater. Fox couldn't help enjoying his view of her as she left the room.

Lunch itself was fine. Duncan said almost nothing, hiding behind his curtain of hair. The pork was tender, and accompanied by mountains of veg, Duncan partaking of two boiled potatoes and one roast to accompany his burger. There was trifle for dessert, which the teenager asked if he could take to his room. After a theatrical sigh, his mother relented. With dessert finished, Fox helped her clear the table. The kitchen was a mess, but she insisted she'd clean up later – 'Duncan will help, trust me.' So they settled back on the sofa with coffee and little cubes of home-made tablet. She'd put his flowers in a vase of water.

'You've been married, right?' she asked.

'Right.'

'No kids, though?'

'We weren't together long enough.'

'What happened?'

'We hooked up for all the wrong reasons.'

'Oh?'

'I'm not about to bore you with the details.' He crossed one leg over the other. 'How does Duncan feel about your job?'

'He knows not to ask questions.'

'Fair enough, but he knows what you do, and he has to tell his mates something ...'

'We've never talked about it much.' She tucked her legs beneath her, having kicked off her shoes. Fox could hear some sort of brass instrument being practised nearby.

'Is that Duncan?'

She shook her head. 'One of the kids downstairs. Tuba, his mum tells me. And there's a drummer through that wall.' She nodded in the direction of the shelving unit.

'How about Duncan?'

'An electric guitar for his birthday last year, but he won't take lessons.'

'I was like that when my parents bought me a set of golf clubs – reckoned I'd teach myself.'

'Teenage boys can be stubborn. Are your parents still alive?'

'My dad is.'

'And how's your sister doing? There'll be the funeral to plan, I suppose.'

'Might take a while for them to release the body.'

'And there's still no news?' It was his turn to shake his head. 'So you started making your own enquiries …'

'As a result of which, I get a nice paid holiday.'

'Are you thinking of going somewhere?'

'I might just stay close to home.' He paused. 'Is there any point in me asking Gilchrist a few questions?'

She looked at him. 'I wouldn't think so, Malcolm. You *do* understand what the word "suspension" means?'

'Of course.'

A smile spread across her face. 'I wouldn't have taken you for a rebel.'

'That's because I wear braces with my suit.'

Now she laughed. 'Maybe.'

Duncan stuck his head around the door. 'I'm just going out.'

'Where?' his mother asked.

'Princes Street.'

'Meeting up with anyone?' He shrugged. 'Okay, then. Say goodbye to Malcolm.'

'Bye,' Duncan said. 'Thanks again for the …'

'Maybe see you again,' Fox replied. He sat in silence with Inglis until the front door had closed.

'I thought he was going to help you in the kitchen,' Fox said.

'He'll do it when he comes back.'

'Must be hard.' Fox paused. 'Not having his dad around, I mean. Do your parents still help out?'

'We see them some weekends.'

'Are they still in Fife?'

She gave him a look. 'I never told you I grew up in Fife.'

'You must have.'

But she was shaking her head slowly, never taking her eyes off him. 'You saw it in my file, didn't you?'

'I like you, Annie ...'

'So you had a trawl through my personnel file. Find out anything interesting, Inspector?'

'Only that you never bothered to mention Duncan.'

Her voice was steely. 'I didn't want anyone seeing me as a single parent first, and a cop second.'

'I can understand that.'

'I can't *believe* you checked up on me!'

'It's what I do.' He paused. 'What I used to do,' he corrected himself.

'It was still out of order, Malcolm.'

He was trying to shape an explanation, but Annie Inglis had risen to her feet.

'Time for you to leave, I think.'

'Annie, I just wanted to know a little more about you ...'

'Thanks again for the wine and the flowers and ...' She looked about her, avoiding eye contact, then turned towards the door. 'I need to get started in the kitchen.'

He watched her go. He was standing by this time, still holding his coffee cup. He placed it on the table and put his jacket back on. She had closed the kitchen door. He could hear her moving stuff around. His fingers brushed the door handle, without enough force to open it. He stayed there a further minute, willing her to come out. But she had switched the radio on. Classic FM: same station he sometimes listened to.

Out of order, Malcolm ...

He could open the door and apologise. But instead, he padded down the hall and let himself out. On the pavement outside, he craned his neck. There was no one watching from the bay window, or from the next window along. The car next to Fox's was being washed by its owner.

'Nice day, for a change,' the man said. Fox drove away without responding. He was halfway home when his phone rang. He answered it, hoping to hear Annie's voice. But it was Tony Kaye.

'What do you want?' Fox asked.

'You were the one who told me to ring,' Kaye complained. 'And it went okay, thanks for asking.'

Fox remembered then: Torphichen. 'Sorry, Tony. I was lost for a minute there.'

'Bad Billy wants me in the frame for Faulkner's demise – he

wants it *a lot*, but he knows it's not going to happen, and that's driving him nuts.'

'Good,' Fox said.

'Other scenario he's got is *you* thumping Faulkner and me acting the messenger. He said maybe it wasn't my idea, or even yours – maybe Jude got you to do it.' Kaye paused. 'She didn't, did she?'

'Look, Tony, I've just had lunch round at Annie Inglis's flat.'

'Nice one.'

'It ended badly. She worked out that I'd taken a look at her personnel file.'

'Christ, when did that happen?'

'I was down at HR for background on Jamie Breck ...'

'And thought you'd take a peek at Annie while you were at it? Seems fair enough to me.'

'She didn't see it that way.'

'Sounds like an overreaction.'

Fox thought so too, but he still had a favour to ask. 'I need you to have a word with her.'

'What?'

'Let her know I'm not some sort of stalker.'

'Well, I've only got your word for that ...'

'It'll give you something to do tomorrow while Naysmith and the new boy are getting cosy.'

Kaye let out a hiss of air. 'I'd forgotten we were getting lumbered with Gilchrist.'

'While the Techie Twins are chatting, you can be at the Chop Shop.'

'Interceding on your behalf? I'd've thought Annie Inglis was the least of your worries.'

'Can't afford any more enemies right now, Tony.'

'Good point. Consider it done. But if she starts falling for my charms in place of yours ...'

'I'll be sure to let your wife of twelve years know.'

'You miserable sod.' Kaye gave a laugh. 'I bet you would, too.'

'Are you all done with Torphichen?'

'I dare say Giles will drag me in again. Plus, Grampian will want a word, apparently.'

'The Complaints?'

'Giles was quick to tell them about me turning up at your sister's. No chance of them investigating your misdemeanours without dragging me into it too.'

'Things just get better and better, don't they?'

'Look on the bright side – the restaurant last night forgot to charge me for our second bottle of wine.'

Fox managed the beginnings of a smile, then reminded Kaye to talk to Annie Inglis.

'Relax,' Kaye told him. 'So what are you doing the rest of the day? Want to meet up at Minter's?'

'I've got stuff to do.'

'Such as?'

'Alphabetising my bookshelves.' Fox ended the call and drove home in silence.

The rest of the day, he couldn't really concentrate on anything. The piles of books sat untouched. There were sections of the various papers still unbrowsed. The TV proved little comfort and he had no view from his window other than the house identical to his across the street. Then, at eight o'clock, someone rang his doorbell. He ticked off possible visitors – Jamie, Tony Kaye, Annie Inglis ...

It was Jude. The taxi that had just dropped her was leaving. Her arm was still in a sling, so she'd only managed to drape her three-quarter-length coat around her shoulders.

'Good to see you,' he said, pecking her cheek and ushering her inside.

'Are you moving out?' she asked when she saw the state of the living room.

Fox shook his head. 'Been a while since you were last here,' he commented.

'We never seemed to get invited.' She had shrugged off her coat. Fox walked into the kitchen and started filling the kettle.

'DCI Giles phoned me,' she explained from the doorway. 'He says the man who came to my door on Monday night was a friend of yours.'

'He works with me.'

'Giles thinks you sent him.'

'I didn't.'

'Sent him to do your dirty work,' she continued. 'His name's Kaye ... I think you've mentioned him to me before. How did he know where I live, Malcolm?'

Fox turned towards her. 'Jude ... this man Giles is trying every trick he knows in an effort to fuck things up for me.'

'You told Kaye where I live?'

'At some point I must have. But I didn't know he was going to come to your house.'

'He was looking for Vince. Only reason he'd be doing that is if you told him what happened ... told him about my arm.'

'So?'

She was blinking back tears. 'DCI Giles thinks maybe you had Vince killed.'

'I didn't.'

'Then why send your friend round?'

'I didn't send him. He was looking for Vince, remember? But Vince was already dead, Jude – and that means Tony Kaye didn't know.' Pain was thrumming in Fox's temples. He opened a drawer and took out a packet of paracetamol tablets, popping two of them from the blister pack and washing them down with water from the tap. Jude waited until she had his full attention again before she spoke.

'Giles says Vince could have been killed Monday night. He says the tests always have a margin of error.'

'He's lying. Pathology has Vince dying on the Saturday or the Sunday.'

A single tear was running down Jude's left cheek. 'I just want this to be over,' she said, her voice cracking. Fox stepped forward and placed his hands gently on her shoulders.

'I know,' he said, as she buried her face in his chest.

They spent the next hour and a half talking quietly in the living room. She drank the tea he prepared for her, but didn't feel like eating. She promised him she had eaten something at lunchtime. She promised him she would have breakfast. He brought out a packet of Weetabix from the kitchen and said she'd be taking it home with her. When he offered milk, she gave a little laugh and told him to stop making such a fuss. But he got the feeling she liked it really.

He called a taxi for her and pressed a ten-pound note into her hand. Then he pecked her on the cheek again and closed the door of the cab for her, waving as she was driven away. She'd asked him if he'd seen their father and he had lied – because he hadn't wanted her to feel left out. Next time he was visiting Mitch, he would take her along. She belonged there just as much as he did. She was family.

Malcolm Fox made himself a last mug of tea and headed for bed. It wasn't yet ten, but he couldn't think of anything else to do.

Monday 16 February 2009

15

Malcolm Fox's alarm woke him at seven as usual. He was in the shower before he realised there was no necessity to be up this early. Nor did he have to wear a clean shirt and a fresh tie, or his suit and braces, but that didn't stop him putting all of them on. As he was eating breakfast, there was a phone call. It was a woman called Stoddart from Grampian Police PSU. She was 'inviting' him to a meeting at Fettes HQ.

'Shall we say three p.m.?'

'Three's fine,' Fox informed her.

The day was cold and overcast. Snowdrops were starting to appear in his front garden, and he reckoned there'd be some brave crocuses already sticking their heads above the parapet in the Meadows and the city's other parks. He tried to work out a route that would take him through the Meadows on his way to Leith. It would be circuitous, but with the added bonus of a drive through Holyrood Park. Besides, he wasn't exactly in a hurry.

A few years back, Fox and his team had investigated an officer based at Leith Police Station. He'd been taking backhanders and turning a blind eye. One of his own men had come to them, but only with a promise of anonymity. Meetings had taken place at a greasy spoon near the docks, and this was Fox's destination today. The café was called The Marina, its paintwork peeling, interior walls shiny with grease. There were half a dozen Formica-topped tables and a ledge by the window where you could stand and eat if you preferred. The owner was a large, red-faced woman who did much of the cooking while an Eastern European girl worked the till and the tables. Fox had been seated for fifteen minutes, nursing a mug of industrial-strength tea, when Max Dearborn walked in. Dearborn saw him and his whole body seemed to sag. He'd put on half a stone or more since they'd last met, and had developed jowls. There was still acne around his mouth, and his dark hair was slick-looking, combed straight down. More than ever, he resembled Oliver Hardy's Scottish nephew.

'Hiya, Max,' Fox said.

Dearborn's breathing was hoarse as he wedged himself into the seat opposite Fox.

'Is this just some horrific coincidence?' the young man pretended to guess.

Fox was shaking his head. The waitress had arrived, and he ordered a bacon roll.

'Usual for you, Max?' she asked Dearborn, who nodded a reply, keeping his eyes on Fox. When she moved away, Fox spoke in an undertone.

'I hear you're a DS these days – congratulations.'

Dearborn responded with a twitch of the mouth. Fox remembered him the way he'd been – a detective constable with ideals and principles still intact, yet fearful of alienating his colleagues. 'Serpico', Tony Kaye had called him.

'What do you want?' Dearborn was asking. He'd taken a good look around the café, seeking out enemies and sharp ears.

'Are you working the Charlie Brogan drowning?' Fox could feel sweat forming on his back. His heart was beating far too fast. The tea had enough tannin in it to fell an ox, so he pushed the mug to one side.

'It's not a drowning yet,' Dearborn corrected him. 'And what's it to you anyway?'

'I'm just interested. Reckon maybe you owe me a favour.'

'A favour?'

'For keeping your name under wraps.'

'Is that some sort of threat?'

Fox shook his head. Dearborn's coffee had arrived and he shovelled two spoonfuls of sugar into it, stirring noisily.

'Like I say, I'm just interested. I'm hoping someone can keep me up to date.'

'And that's me, is it?' Dearborn stared at him. 'Why the interest?'

Fox shrugged. 'Brogan might tie in to another case.'

'To do with the Complaints?' Dearborn was suddenly less hostile, and more interested.

'Maybe. It's all hush-hush, but if anything *did* come to light, I'd be willing to share the credit.' Fox paused. 'You know my boss had a say in your promotion?'

'Thought he might have.'

'It can happen again, Max ...' Fox let his voice drift away. Dearborn took a slurp of coffee and then another, and started to do some thinking. Fox just sat there, hands in his lap, not wanting to rest any part of his suit against the surface of the table. The waitress was returning with their food – Fox's filled roll; Dearborn's fry-up. The young man's plate was heaped, and he turned towards the cook and gave her a nod and a smile. She smiled back. Fox had peeled open his roll. The bacon looked pale and stringy. He closed it again and left it on the plate. Dearborn was squeezing brown sauce across the array of bacon, fried egg, sausage, beans and mushrooms.

'Looks good,' Fox commented. Dearborn just nodded and took his first mouthful, eyes on Fox as he chewed.

'Body's still not surfaced,' Dearborn said.

'Is that unusual?'

'Not according to those in the know. Currents are irregular in the channel. He could have been swept out into the North Sea. A container ship's propeller could have snagged him and turned him to mush. Coastguard were out again at first light. We've got patrols working both seashores, north and south.'

'I heard Fife Constabulary was claiming jurisdiction.'

Dearborn shook his head. There were already traces of egg yolk either side of his mouth. 'That'll never wash. We've asked for their cooperation, but this is D Division territory, fair and square.'

'So where's the boat?'

'Dalgety Bay.'

'Last time I looked, that was in Fife.'

'It's going to be towed to Leith later today.'

'I'm assuming you've already given it a once-over?'

'Forensics have,' Dearborn confirmed.

'Evidence of alcohol and pills,' Fox stated.

'You're well informed. No suicide note, but I'm told that's not so unusual. He'd contacted his solicitor a few days back to check some of the details of his will.'

Fox's eyes narrowed. 'When exactly?'

'Tuesday afternoon.'

'Did he want to change anything?'

Dearborn shook his head.

'I'm assuming everything will go to the widow?'

'That depends on us finding a body. If we don't, then she's got a wait on her hands – it's a legal thing.' Dearborn concentrated on his food, then decided to share something with Fox. 'His shoes have been found. Deck shoes, they're called. Bobbing in the water off Inchcolm Island.' He paused. 'Supposing this does tie in to whatever you're working on ... how do I get my share of the spoils without anyone on my side knowing I've been talking to you?'

'There are ways,' Malcolm Fox said. 'Trust me.'

When the meal was finished, their waitress asked if something was wrong with the bacon roll.

'Just not hungry,' Fox reassured her. Then, to Dearborn: 'Let me get this.'

'Your money's no good in here.'

'How come?'

Dearborn offered a shrug. 'There was a break-in a few months back. I made sure we put in an extra bit of effort ...'

'You sure you should be telling this to someone from the Complaints?'

Max Dearborn winked and, with a certain amount of effort, got back to his feet. He insisted on leaving first. Fox watched him go and speculated as to a future of high blood pressure and diabetes, maybe even the odd coronary. About a year back, his own doctor had foretold much the same for him. Since when he'd dropped a stone, while feeling little better for it. He stood outside the café, listening to the screaming of gulls on the nearby roofs. Then he started walking. D Division HQ was on Queen Charlotte Street. As with Torphichen, it boasted a solid if drab Victorian exterior, but unlike Torphichen its interior still held traces of a certain faded grandeur – marble floors, carved wooden balustrades, ornate pillars. Dearborn would be inside by now. His last words to Fox had consisted of a promise to keep him posted. Fox had given him a card with his mobile number – 'Your best bet for catching me,' he'd said. Last thing he wanted was Dearborn calling his Fettes office and being told that Inspector Malcolm Fox was out of the game. Word would spread fast enough – Billy Giles would see to that – but meantime Dearborn might prove useful. He'd already given Fox something to think about.

Tuesday morning – Vince Faulkner's body is found.

Tuesday afternoon – Charlie Brogan contacts his solicitor.

Thursday – his boat is found drifting, its owner missing.

Missing presumed dead.

Without really meaning to, Fox found that he'd strolled the

quarter-mile to Leith Police Station. He walked as far as the corner of Constitution Street, then turned. He was just passing the building's public entrance when a woman came out, sliding her oversized sunglasses back on to her face. She was dressed not in black but coordinated brown. She reached into her leopard-print handbag for cigarettes and lighter, but the breeze kept foiling her attempts.

'Let me,' Fox said, opening his suit jacket so it provided a windbreak. She got the cigarette lit and gave him a nod of thanks. Fox nodded a response and then moved off. Once back at his car, he made a U-turn and headed in the direction of the police station. She was still standing there, looking up and down the street. Fox pulled to a halt next to her and slid down the passenger-side window.

'It's Ms Broughton, isn't it?'

She took a moment to recognise him as her nicotine saviour, then leaned down a little towards the open window.

'I take it you've just been talking to my colleagues?' he asked her.

'Yes,' she said, her voice less husky than he'd imagined it would be.

'Looking for a taxi?' She was peering up and down the street again. 'I'm headed in your direction, if you're interested.'

'How do you know?'

Fox offered a shrug. 'Casino or Inverleith – they're both on my route.'

She studied him for a moment. 'Can I smoke in the car?' she asked.

'Sure,' he said with a smile. 'Hop in.'

They drove in silence for the first couple of sets of traffic lights. As they stopped at the third, she noticed that he had wound his window halfway down.

'You didn't mean it about the smoking,' she said, flicking the remains of her cigarette out of her own window.

'Where do you want dropped?' he asked.

'I'm going home.'

'By Inverleith Park?'

She nodded. 'SeeBee House.'

Fox worked it out. 'Your husband's initials?'

She nodded again. 'I suddenly realise something,' she began, twisting in her seat so she was facing him. 'I've only got your word for it that you're a police officer. I should ask to see some ID.'

'I'm an inspector. What did my colleagues want with you?'

'More questions,' she answered with a sigh. 'Why it can't be done over the phone ...'

'It's because the face says a lot about us – we give things away when we talk. I'm assuming it wasn't DS Dearborn you saw?'

'No.'

'That's because I had a meeting with him at the same time.'

She nodded, as though accepting that he had proved his credentials. Her phone trilled and she plucked it from her handbag. It was a text message, which she responded to with quick, sure movements of her thumbs.

'Long nails help,' Fox commented. 'My fingers are too pudgy for texting.'

She said nothing until she'd sent the message. Then, just as she was opening her mouth, her phone trilled again. Fox realised that it was mimicking the sound of an old-fashioned bell on a hotel reception desk. Broughton busied herself punching buttons again.

'Messages from friends?'

'And creditors,' she muttered. 'Charlie seems to have had more of the latter.'

'You know his shoes have surfaced?' He saw her give him a hard look. 'Sorry,' he apologised, 'not the best turn of phrase ...'

'They told me at the station.' She was back to her texting again. But then another phone sounded from inside her handbag. She rummaged until she found it. Fox recognised the ringtone – it was the theme from an old western.

'Sorry about this,' Broughton said to him as she answered. Then, into the phone: 'I can't talk now, Simon. Just tell me everything's all right.' She listened for a moment. 'I should be there by six or seven. If you can't cope till then, start writing out your resignation.' She ended the call and dropped the phone back into her bag.

'Staff problems?' Fox asked.

'My own fault for not having a proper deputy.'

'You don't like to delegate?'

She looked at him again. 'Have we met somewhere before?'

'No.'

'You look familiar.' She had slid her sunglasses down her nose and was peering at him. When she'd applied the make-up around her eyes this morning, her hand hadn't been too steady. Close up, her hair was clearly a dye job, the tan probably fake. There was some crêping of the skin around her neck.

'I get that a lot,' Fox decided to reply. Then: 'I was sorry to hear about your husband – and I'm not just saying that. Guy I know used to work for him ... only had good things to say.'

'What's your friend's name?'

'Vince Faulkner. I say he worked for your husband, but really he worked on the site at Salamander Point.'

Joanna Broughton didn't say anything for a moment. 'A lot of people liked Charlie,' she eventually affirmed. 'He was easy to like.'

'It's when you get into trouble, though, that you find out who your *real* friends are.'

'So they say ...' She had twisted towards him again. 'I never caught your name.'

It took Fox a second to decide not to lie. 'Inspector Malcolm Fox.'

'Well then, Inspector Malcolm Fox, are you trying to get me to say something?'

'How do you mean?' Fox tried for a hurt tone.

'I didn't *know* Charlie was going to do it. I certainly didn't aid and abet. And despite appearances, I'm torn to shreds inside – *all* of which I've repeated time and again to you and your kind ...' She looked out of the window. 'Maybe you should drop me off here.'

'It's only another five minutes.'

'I can walk that far.'

'In those heels?' Fox exhaled noisily. 'I'm sorry, and I suppose you're right. Once you're a cop, it's hard to switch off the mechanism. No more questions, okay? But at least let me drive you the rest of the way.'

She pondered this. 'All right,' she said at last. 'Actually, that's ideal. Your colleagues want to see Charlie's business diary – you can take it back and save me the trouble.'

'Sure,' Fox agreed. 'Happy to.'

SeeBee House was a five-storey apartment building comprising mainly steel and glass. It sat within a compound of brick walls and metal security gates. Broughton had her own little remote-control box, which she pressed, initiating the mechanism on the gates. There was an underground car park, but she told Fox to stop at the main door. He turned off the ignition and followed her towards the building. The foyer was almost as big as the ground floor of his house. There were two lifts against one wall, but Broughton was marching over to the opposite wall, where a single, narrower lift stood.

'Penthouse has its own,' she explained as they got in. Sure

enough, when the lift doors opened again, they stepped directly into a small carpeted lobby with just the one door off. Broughton unlocked it and Fox followed her inside. 'They call it a triplex,' she informed him, shrugging off her coat and pushing her sunglasses up on to the crown of her head, 'but that's a cheat – one floor has nothing but a couple of terraces.'

'It's still incredible,' Fox said. There was glass on three sides, floor to double-height ceiling, and views across the Botanic Gardens towards the Castle. Turning to his left, he could make out Leith and the coastline. To his right he could see as far as Corstorphine Hill.

'Great for entertaining,' Joanna Broughton agreed.

'Place looks brand new.'

'One of the benefits of having no children.'

'True enough – and a sort of blessing, too, I suppose.'

'How do you mean?'

'Not having to explain things to them ...' Fox watched her begin to nod her understanding. 'The worker who died didn't have any children either.'

'What worker?'

'My friend, the one I was telling you about – did your husband not mention him?'

She ignored the question and instead told him to wait while she fetched the diary. Fox watched her as she started climbing the glass staircase to the next floor, then turned his attention to the room he was standing in. It was much as he remembered it from the newspaper photo. An L-shaped open-plan with pale stone flooring and modern furniture. The kitchen area was just around the corner. When he looked up, he could see a landing, probably with bedrooms and office off. The living area's back wall – the only wall made of something more substantial than glass – seemed to have been stripped of its art. There were still a few hooks, plus holes where hooks had been removed. Fox remembered the newspaper article. It had described Brogan as 'a collector'. He took a step back and watched as Joanna Broughton descended the stairs, taking her time, holding on to the handrail. She was keeping her high heels on, even at home. They added over an inch to her height, and he wondered if that was the reason.

'Here you go,' she said, handing over the large, leather-bound diary.

'Any idea why they want it?' Fox asked.

'You're the detective,' she said, 'you tell me.'

He could only shrug. 'Just being thorough,' he guessed. 'See if there was any unusual activity prior to your husband's ...' He swallowed back the end of the sentence.

'You're wondering at his state of mind? I don't mind saying it again – he was absolutely fine when he left here. I hadn't the slightest inkling.'

'Look, I said I wasn't going to ask anything ...'

'But?'

'But I'm wondering if it hurt you, him not leaving a note.'

She considered this for a moment. 'I'd like to know why, of course I would. Money worries, yes, but all the same ... we could have worked it out. If he'd asked, I'm sure we could have put our heads together.'

'Maybe he was too proud to ask for help?'

She nodded slowly, arms hanging loosely by her sides.

'Did he sell all his paintings?' Fox asked into the silence. She nodded again, then started as the intercom sounded. She walked over to it.

'Yes?' she demanded.

'Joanna, it's Gordon. I've got Jack with me.'

Her face relaxed a little. 'Come on up,' she said. Then, turning to Fox: 'Thanks again for the lift – I'd probably still be waiting there.'

'My pleasure.'

She held out her hand and he shook it. The diary was too big for any of his pockets, so he carried it with him into the lobby. When the lift doors opened, Gordon Lovatt emerged, momentarily surprised to find someone facing him. Lovatt was dressed to the nines in what looked like a bespoke three-piece pinstripe suit. A gold watch chain dangled from the pockets of the waistcoat. His silk tie boasted an extravagant knot and his hair looked freshly barbered. He nodded a greeting but then decided more was needed.

'Gordon Lovatt,' he said, holding out his hand.

The two men shook. 'I know who you are,' Fox told him, not bothering to reciprocate with an introduction. The man next to Lovatt was much older, but dressed in what looked like an even more expensive suit. He too held out his hand.

'Jack Broughton,' he announced.

Fox just nodded and squeezed past both men, turning to face them once he was inside the lift. He pressed the button for the ground floor, and waited for the doors to close. Jack Broughton seemed already to have dismissed him, and was entering the penthouse, greeting his only surviving child with a kiss. Lovatt, on the other hand, had stayed in the lobby to stare at Fox, the same enquiring look on his face.

'Going down,' the lift's automated female voice said. The doors slid shut and Fox let go of the breath he'd been holding.

There was no sign of the PR man's car outside, so he'd either left it in the car park or come by taxi. If the car park, then he had to have some way of accessing the compound. But then the same was true if he'd been dropped off from a cab – he still had to get past the gates. So then maybe Joanna had gifted her father one of the small black remote-control boxes ...

Fox got into his own car and placed Charlie Brogan's diary on the passenger seat. Then he stared at it, wondering what the Grampian Complaints would make of his recent activities. He'd been very careful all morning – watching for cars tailing him, for people loitering or following him. It had been easy for them to keep tabs on him the previous week – he'd not been alerted to the probability. But now he knew he'd been under surveillance, that made things a great deal harder for any team trying to track him. Then again, if he was going to keep pulling stunts like this one ... It took him a further three or four minutes to decide, but at last he picked up the diary and flipped it open.

He started with the Monday of the previous week, but found nothing immediately of interest. It wasn't that Brogan used a code, but like most people he used initials and abbreviations. The J in '8 p.m. – J – Kitchin' Fox assumed was Joanna Broughton. The Kitchin was a fancy restaurant in Leith, run by a chef with the surname Kitchin. There were notes of meetings, but it hadn't exactly been an action-packed week. Flipping back to January, Fox found that Brogan had been far busier. By February, he'd been reduced to noting TV shows he was planning to watch.

After quarter of an hour, Fox closed the book and turned the ignition. On his way back to Leith Police Station he made two stops. One was at a stationer's, where he bought a padded envelope big enough to take the diary. The other was at a phone shop, where he bought a pay-as-you-go mobile, using his credit card. If he was still under surveillance, this new phone wouldn't keep him off the radar for long ... but maybe long enough.

And it was certain to annoy any Complaints team when they eventually worked out what he'd done.

He parked his car outside the police station just long enough to drop the envelope off at reception. He'd written Max Dearborn's name on the front. It would puzzle Max, perhaps, but Fox didn't mind that in the least. Back in the car, his old mobile started ringing. Fox checked the caller ID but made no attempt to answer. When the ringing stopped, he used his new phone and called Tony Kaye back.

'Who's this?' Kaye asked, not recognising the number.

'It's Malcolm. This is how to get me from now on.'

'You've changed phones?'

'In case they're tracking me.'

'You're paranoid.' Kaye paused. 'Good thinking, though – reckon I should do the same?'

'Have they spoken to you again?' *They*: Grampian Complaints.

'No – how about you?'

'Later today. So why were you calling?'

'I just wanted a moan. Hang on a sec …' Fox listened as Kaye moved from the Complaints office to the hallway. 'Those two are driving me nuts,' he said. 'It's like they've known one another since the playground.'

'Other than that, how's Gilchrist settling in?'

'I don't like that he's sitting at your desk.'

'Then offer to swap.'

'He's not having my desk.'

'Then we're stuck with it. Has McEwan been in?'

'He's not speaking to me.'

'We've piled his plate high with shit,' Fox conceded.

'And not even tied a bib around his neck,' Kaye added. 'Is your afternoon grilling to be courtesy of a woman called Stoddart?'

'Any tips for handling her?'

'Asbestos gloves, Malcolm.'

'Great, thanks.' Fox thought for a moment. 'Can you get Naysmith for me?'

'What?'

'I want a word with him – but out of Gilchrist's earshot.'

'I'll fetch him.' It was Kaye's turn to pause. 'Are you playing it cool, or has it actually slipped your mind?'

Fox realised immediately what he meant. 'Have you had a chance to talk to her?'

'She hasn't been in this morning. Gilchrist had to fetch something from his desk at the Chop Shop, so I went along with him and took a look. I asked him if she had any meetings, but he didn't know.'

'Well, thanks for trying.'

'I'm not giving up yet. Joe!' Fox realised that Kaye was calling from the doorway. 'Here he comes,' Kaye said. The phone was handed to Naysmith. 'It's Foxy,' Fox heard Kaye explain.

'Malcolm,' Naysmith said.

'Morning, Joe. I hear you and Gilchrist are getting on famously.'

'I suppose.'

'So there's no reason why you shouldn't invite him out for a drink after work.'

'No ...' Naysmith drew the word out way past its natural length.

'You'd probably suggest Minter's, and you'd be there by five thirty.'

'Right.' Again the word took on elasticated form in Naysmith's mouth.

'No need to tell him it was my idea.'

'What's going on, Malcolm?'

'Nothing's going on, Joe. Just take him for that drink.' Fox ended the call. He had plenty of time to kill before his meeting at Fettes. At a newsagent's, he bought the *Evening News,* a salad roll and a bottle of water, then headed in the general direction of Inverleith, parking by the north entrance to the Botanics. He located Classic FM on the radio and ate his roll while flicking through the paper. Charlie Brogan was no longer news, and neither was Vince Faulkner. People were foaming at the mouth about the former RBS boss's pension and perks. The tram dispute had entered its 'eleventh hour', with the council telling the contractors there was no more cash to put on the table. And now the Dunfermline Building Society was in trouble. Fox seemed to remember the Prime Minister was from Dunfermline ... No, Kirkcaldy, but Dunfermline was in his constituency. Fox's parents had held an account with the Dunfermline – he wondered if Mitch still had money there. Fox's own money was in the Co-op. It was the one bank he hadn't heard anything about. He wasn't sure if that was reassuring or not.

The piece of music finished and the announcer declared that it had been by Bach. Fox had recognised it – he recognised a lot of the tunes on Classic FM without being able to name them or their composer. He looked at his watch again, checking that it hadn't stopped.

'Hell with it,' he said, closing the newspaper and turning the ignition key.

He'd just have to turn up early to his crucifixion.

16

The officer on duty at the reception desk – a man Fox had known for a couple of years – had the good grace to apologise that he would have to take a seat. Fox nodded his understanding.

'You're just following orders, Frank,' he said. So Fox sat down on one of the chairs and pretended an interest in his newspaper, while other officers came and went. Most of them gave him a glance or an outright stare – word had gotten around – and one or two paused to offer a word of sympathy.

When Stoddart made her entrance, she was flanked by two heavyset men. Stoddart herself was tall and elegant with long fair hair. If someone had told Fox she sat on the board of a bank or corporation, he wouldn't have been surprised. She had a visitor's pass around her neck, and ordered Frank to get one for Fox. Fox took his time getting to his feet. He closed his paper, folded it, slipped it into his pocket. Stoddart didn't offer to shake hands; didn't even bother to introduce herself or her henchmen. She handed the pass to Fox and turned on her heels.

'This way,' she said.

It wasn't a long walk. Fox didn't know whose office they had commandeered. The bulletin board and desk gave few clues. There was space for a circular coffee table and several chairs, which looked to have been borrowed from the canteen. On the desk sat a laptop and some cardboard folders. There was another laptop on the coffee table. A video camera had been fixed to a tripod and aimed at the desk.

'Sit,' Stoddart commanded, walking around to the far side of the desk. One of her goons had seated himself at the coffee table.

The other was peering into the camera, making sure it didn't need adjusting. He came forward and handed Fox a tiny microphone.

'Can you clip that to your lapel?' he asked. Fox did so. A wire ran from the mic to the camera. The officer had slipped a pair of headphones on, and was checking the apparatus again.

'Testing, testing,' Fox said into the mic. The man gave him the thumbs-up.

'Before we get started,' Stoddart began. 'You'll appreciate how awkward this is. We don't like finding out a complaint has been made against one of our own—'

'Who made the complaint?' Fox interrupted. She ignored him, her eyes on the laptop's screen as she spoke.

'But these things have to be done properly. So don't expect any favours, Inspector Fox.' She nodded towards the cameraman, who pressed a button and announced that they were rolling. Stoddart sat in silence for a moment, as if collecting her thoughts, then she announced the date and time.

'Preliminary interview,' she went on. 'I am Inspector Caroline Stoddart and I am accompanied by Sergeant Mark Wilson and Constable Andrew Mason.'

'Which is which?' Fox interrupted again. Stoddart gave him a stare.

'Constable Mason is operating the camera,' she informed him. 'Now, if you'll identify yourself . . .'

'I'm Inspector Malcolm Fox.'

'And you work for the Complaints and Conduct department of Lothian and Borders Police?'

'That's right.'

'Specifically the Professional Standards Unit?'

'Yes.'

'How long have you been based there?'

'Four and a half years.'

'And before that?'

'I was at St Leonard's for three years, and Livingston before that.'

'This was in your drinking days?'

'I've been sober for five years. Didn't realise my tippling was a matter of record.'

'You've never looked at your personnel file?' She sounded unconvinced.

'No,' he told her, crossing one leg over the other. In doing so, he dislodged the newspaper, which fell from his pocket on to the floor.

He stooped to pick it up, stretching the microphone cord so that it came unplugged from the camera.

'Hang on,' Mason said, removing his headphones. Fox apologised and straightened himself, his eyes on Caroline Stoddart.

'Having fun?' she asked.

'Are we speaking on the record or off?'

Her mouth twitched, and she went back to checking whatever was on her computer screen. 'Your sister likes a drink too, doesn't she?'

'This isn't about my sister.'

'Ready,' Mason announced.

Stoddart took a moment to collect her thoughts again. 'Let's talk about Vincent Faulkner,' she said.

'Yes, let's. He was found dead on Tuesday morning of last week – when did you get the word to put me under surveillance?'

'He was living with your sister?' Stoddart asked, ignoring his question.

'That's right.'

'And you'd recently discovered that there had been an argument between the two of them, during which her arm was broken?'

'A week ago, yes.'

'What were you working on at that time?'

'Not much. My team had just finished expending considerable effort putting together a case against DI Glen Heaton of C Division.'

Stoddart was scrolling down a page. 'Anything else in your in-tray?'

'I'd been asked to take a look at someone …'

'This would be Detective Sergeant Jamie Breck?'

'That's right.'

'Also stationed at C Division?'

'Yes.'

'What were the circumstances of the request?

'My boss, Chief Inspector McEwan, had been contacted by CEOP. DS Breck had come on to their radar and they wanted him checked out.'

Stoddart reached over to the top folder and opened it. There were surveillance photos inside, the same ones Giles had had at Torphichen.

'Bit of a conflict of interest,' Stoddart mused. 'You're looking at Breck, while he's looking into your sister's partner's murder …'

'I was aware of that.'

'You didn't attempt to distance yourself from the case?'

'Which case?'

'Either, I suppose.'

Fox gave a shrug. 'How are things in Aberdeen?' he asked.

The change of direction didn't appear to have any effect on Stoddart.

'We're not here to talk about me,' she drawled, pushing her hair back behind her ears. 'You seem to have become friendly with DS Breck in a very short space of time.'

'The relationship was always professional.'

'That's why he came to your house on Wednesday night? You went to a casino together.'

'It was work-related. Besides, CEOP had asked for my assessment of DS Breck.'

'Yes, there was a Complaints van parked outside his home. Did you advise them they were wasting their time?'

'He headed back there eventually.'

'But you told them about the trip to the casino?'

'No,' Fox admitted.

'So two of your colleagues were sitting in a surveillance van on a cold February night ...'

'It's what we do.'

She looked at him, then back to the screen again. Fox enjoyed a momentary fantasy of punching his fist through it. When he peered over his shoulder, Wilson was busy studying his own laptop.

'Is it patience you're playing there, or Minesweeper?' Fox asked him. Wilson didn't respond.

'DS Breck,' Stoddart was saying, 'was at the casino because Vincent Faulkner might have visited it the night he died?'

'He did visit it,' Fox corrected her.

'And that visit was on the Saturday, after he'd broken your sister's arm?'

Fox nodded. 'And I didn't find out about her arm until Monday.'

'Mr Faulkner's body was found on Tuesday morning?'

'That's right.'

'Your sister was visited on Monday evening by one of your colleagues?'

'Sergeant Kaye.'

'Did you know that was happening?'

'No.'

'You'd told him about her arm?'

'Yes.'

A phone started to ring. Stoddart realised it was hers. She signalled for Mason to pause the recording, then reached into her jacket pocket.

'One moment,' she advised the room, getting to her feet and making for the door. After she'd gone, Fox stretched his spine, feeling the vertebrae click.

'This is interesting,' he commented. 'Being on the receiving end for a change. So how *are* things in Aberdeen? Got anything on the go?'

The two Grampian officers shared a look. It was Wilson who spoke. 'Grampian's pretty clean these days,' he offered.

'Must be a nice change then, visiting Gomorrah. Have they given you a decent hotel?'

'Not bad.'

'Well then, you'll want to string this out as long as possible.'

Mason managed a smile, but only for a second. Stoddart was coming back into the room. She returned her phone to her pocket and settled back down behind the desk.

'Ready,' Mason advised. Stoddart stared at Fox as she began forming her next question.

'What,' she asked, 'were you just doing at the home of a woman called Joanna Broughton?'

Fox took a moment to collect himself. 'I gave her a lift. She was standing outside Leith Police Station and I happened to be passing and recognised her. She's just lost her husband and seemed a bit upset, so I offered to drop her somewhere.'

The room was silent until Stoddart asked: 'You expect me to believe that?'

Fox just shrugged, while inwardly uttering a stream of curses.

'She employs a public relations company,' Stoddart went on, 'and they got straight on the telephone screaming harassment.'

'I can assure you I did anything but harass her – ask her, if you like. Besides which, it's got nothing to do with any of this.'

He knew what Stoddart would say to that – same thing he'd have said if he'd been her side of the desk – and she duly obliged.

'I'll be the judge of that, Inspector.' Then: 'You say you were just passing Leith Police Station? Isn't it rather a long way from anywhere?'

'Not particularly.'

'So if I go asking, none of the officers there will tell me they spoke with you this morning?'

She watched Fox shake his head, and went back to looking at her computer again.

It was another three quarters of an hour before she decided they'd take a break for the rest of the day.

'You're not thinking of heading off somewhere?' she asked, closing the lid of her laptop. 'A holiday or anything?'

'I won't be leaving the country,' he assured her, as Mason unclipped the microphone. 'Same time tomorrow?'

'We'll let you know.'

Fox nodded, then thanked them, and made for the door. He paused with his hand on its handle. 'One last thing,' he said. 'DS Breck has no inkling that he's being investigated. If news leaks to him, all three of you will be suspects ...' He opened the door and closed it after him. Since he was in the building, he climbed to the next floor, removing his visitor's pass and stuffing it in his pocket. He walked past the door of the Complaints office and headed for 2.24. But there was still no one home, so he returned to his old haunt, peering around the door to make sure Bob McEwan wasn't on the premises. Then he rapped against the frame with his knuckles, announcing his arrival. Gilchrist was seated next to Naysmith at the latter's desk while Naysmith showed him something on his computer. Kaye was tipped back in his chair, hands behind his head. Fox managed not to stare at his own desk, though he couldn't help catching a glimpse of Gilchrist's stuff scattered across it.

Kaye got to his feet. 'You been to the headmaster's office?' he asked.

'Yep.'

'Got a sore bottom?'

'Nope.'

Kaye smiled, shrugging himself back into his jacket. 'Let's go to the canteen,' he said.

Out in the hallway, he gripped Fox by the sleeve. 'Gilchrist could bore for Scotland.' He rolled his eyes and shook his head in exasperation. Then: 'So how did it really go?'

'They didn't come up with much I wasn't expecting. Seemed to know about my relationship with the demon drink.'

'Must be in your files somewhere.'

'Meaning one of my previous bosses must have noticed ...'

'But never said anything?' Kaye made a clucking sound. 'Just hoping the problem would go away.'

'Well, it did.'

'They trying to say you're an alkie?'

'I'm not sure. Maybe they were told to ask.'

'What did you think of Stoddart?'

'She's the Ice Queen.'

'Wouldn't mind trying to thaw her out.'

They had reached the canteen. Half a dozen people were dotted around the tables, mostly staring into space as they chewed their snacks. 'You sure you want to be seen with me?' Fox asked.

'Maybe some of that rebel glamour will rub off on me.' Kaye placed two mugs on a tray. 'Still haven't seen hide or hair of DS Inglis,' he admitted. 'What did you do to her?'

Fox ignored this. His old phone was buzzing, so he held up a finger to let Kaye know he was taking it. Turning away and walking towards the windows, he pressed the 'receive' button.

'Malcolm Fox,' he said.

'It's Dearborn.'

'Max – can I assume you've got something for me?'

'My boss is apoplectic. He gets a call from Gordon Lovatt, complaining about a D Division cop called Fox. The only Fox anyone has heard of is you, and when Lovatt is given the description, he says it's spot-on.'

'After we'd had our little chat,' Fox explained, 'I saw Joanna Broughton looking up and down the street for a non-existent taxi. She seemed a bit distraught so I offered her a lift. She must have assumed I was stationed in Leith.'

'So it was you she gave her husband's diary to?'

'Happy to help, Max.'

Fox listened as Dearborn expelled some air. Kaye had taken the tray to one of the tables, having added two chocolate bars to his purchases. He was already unwrapping one of them.

'Is there anything else?' Fox asked into the phone. 'Any news of Charlie Brogan?'

'Give me a break,' Dearborn muttered, hanging up. Fox called him straight back.

'One last thing,' he said, by way of warning. 'Grampian Complaints may come sniffing around. Best if you don't tell them we shared breakfast.'

'You're bad news, Fox.'

'Tell me about it.' Fox managed to end the call before Dearborn could, then went over to the table and seated himself opposite Kaye. He tried to work out if he'd been bought tea or coffee. The look and aroma weren't giving much away.

Kaye had stopped chewing. He was looking over Fox's shoulder.

When Fox turned his head, he saw why. Mason and Wilson had just entered the canteen.

'Bugger,' Kaye said through a mouthful of chocolate. Fox, however, waved the two men over. They seemed to discuss it for a moment, then shook their heads and took a table as far away from Fox's as possible. Each man had opted for a bottle of still water and a piece of fresh fruit.

'They're bound to tell Stoddart,' Kaye commented.

'Nobody's banned us from seeing one another, Tony. It's not like we have ASBOs or anything. You can say you were already here ... the whole thing just a chance meeting.'

'She won't believe it.'

'But she'll have to *accept* it – same as we would if we were doing her job.'

'I'm a bollock-hair away from joining you on the subs' bench.'

'You haven't done anything wrong, Tony.'

'But I'm like you, Foxy – guilty until proven otherwise. And all because everybody hates us.'

'Do you want this?' Fox was offering Kaye the spare chocolate bar. Kaye took it and put it in his pocket. 'And answer me something – what the hell is it we're drinking?'

Kaye stared down at his mug. 'I thought it was tea.'

'But you're not sure?'

'Maybe I asked for coffee ...'

Having handed his pass back to Frank at the front desk, Fox went out to the car park. He passed his own Volvo and kept walking. There were spaces at the furthest corner of the compound, next to the playing fields. They were marked for the use of visitors, and that was where he found the black Astra and the green Ka, parked side by side. The stickers on their back windows identified them as having been bought at garages in Aberdeen. There was a fresh-looking graze to the metallic paintwork on the Ka, and Fox hoped that local traffic was to blame.

He returned to his own car, exited the car park and crawled up the long steep slope back into town until he reached Queen Street. An auction house had its headquarters there, and Fox seemed to remember they specialised in paintings. He didn't have any trouble finding a parking bay. Drivers were either counting the pennies or else had been dissuaded from coming into town by the tram works. Fox put a pound coin in the parking meter, attached the sticker to his windscreen and headed inside. There was a long counter in the main reception area, and at the end of it a couple of windows resembling the tellers' positions in a bank. A customer was standing at one of the windows, writing out a cheque for a recent purchase.

'Can I help?' the woman behind the counter asked.

'I hope so,' Fox said. 'I'm a police officer.' In lieu of a warrant card, he offered her one of his printed business cards. They were about three years out of date, but looked nice and official. 'I've got a problem I'm hoping one of your experts can help me with.'

The woman, having studied his card, asked him to wait while she fetched someone. The man who eventually appeared was younger than Fox had been expecting. He wore a pinstriped shirt and pale yellow tie and shook hands vigorously, introducing himself as Alfie Rennison. His voice was educated Scots. He, too, was pleased to receive one of Fox's business cards.

'What is it I can do for you?' Rennison asked.

'It's about some paintings.'

'Modern or classical?'

'Modern, I think.'

Rennison lowered his voice. 'Fakes?' he hissed.

'Nothing like that,' Fox assured him. The young man looked relieved.

'It happens, you know,' he said, keeping his voice low. 'People try to offload all kinds of stuff on us. Follow me, will you?'

He led Fox towards the back of the premises until they reached a stairwell. A red rope provided the sole deterrent to anyone wishing to descend to the next level, and Rennison unhooked it long enough for both men to pass through. Fox followed him down into the bowels of the building, which proved far less grand than the public areas. They squeezed past canvases stacked against walls, and manoeuvred between busts and statues and grandfather clocks.

'Sale coming up,' Rennison explained. 'Viewing's next week.'

They reached his office, which consisted of two rooms knocked into one. Fox had believed them below ground, but there were frosted windows, albeit barred on the outside.

'This was somebody's house at one time,' Rennison was saying. 'I'm guessing the kitchen, laundry and servants' quarters would have been down here. Four upper storeys of Georgian elegance, but with the engine room hidden below.' He smiled and gestured for Fox to take a seat. Rennison's desk was disappointingly bland. Fox reckoned it was an IKEA kit-build. On it sat a laptop computer, hooked up to a laser printer. There was only one painting in the whole room. It measured about six inches by four and sat on the wall behind Rennison's chair.

'Exquisite, isn't it? A French *plage* by Peploe. I can hardly bear to part with it.'

Fox knew next to nothing about art, but he liked the thick swirls of paint. They reminded him of melting ice cream. 'Is it going into the sale?'

Rennison nodded. 'Should fetch fifty to sixty.'

'Thousand?' Fox gazed at the work with new respect, mixed with a stunned sense that this was a world he was going to have trouble comprehending.

Rennison had clasped his hands together, elbows on the desk. 'So tell me about these paintings.'

'Have you heard of a man called Charles Brogan?'

'Alas, yes – the latest victim of our challenging times.'

'But you knew of him before he drowned?'

Rennison was nodding. 'There are several auction houses in the city, Inspector. We work hard to maintain a client's fidelity.'

'You're saying he bought from you?'

'And from some of the city's actual galleries,' Rennison felt duty-bound to add.

'You've seen his collection?'

'Much of it.'

'Had he started selling it off?'

Rennison studied him, resting his chin against the tips of his fingers. 'Might I ask why you're interested?'

'We're looking into the reasons why he would kill himself. You mentioned finances, and it's just that Mr Brogan's decision to sell his paintings might chime with that theory.'

Rennison nodded to himself, happy with this explanation.

'Some pieces he sent to London; some he sold here. Three or four are actually consigned to our next auction. Naturally, we'll hold them back until we know what his estate wants us to do.'

'How many are we talking about in total?'

Rennison did a quick calculation. 'Fourteen or fifteen.'

'Worth . . .?' Fox prompted.

Rennison puffed out his cheeks. 'Half a million, maybe. Before the recession, it would have been closer to seven fifty.'

'I hope he didn't buy at the height of the market.'

'Unfortunately, mostly he did. He was selling at a loss.'

'Meaning he was desperate?'

'I would say so.'

Fox thought for a moment. 'Have you ever met Mr Brogan's wife?'

'She accompanied him to a sale once. I don't think it was an experience she was keen to repeat.'

'Not an art-lover, then?'

'Not in so many words.'

Fox smiled and started getting to his feet. 'Thanks for taking the trouble to talk to me, Mr Rennison.'

'My pleasure, Inspector.'

As they shook hands, Fox took a final look at the Peploe.

'You're thinking of melted ice cream?' Rennison guessed. Then, seeing the look on Fox's face: 'You're by no means the first.'

'Fifty grand buys a lot of Cornettos,' Fox told the man.

'Maybe so, but what would their resale value be, Inspector?'

Rennison led the way back to the ground floor.

17

Fox was parked fifty yards from Minter's when Naysmith and Gilchrist arrived. They'd come by taxi, obviously intending to have more than just the one drink; no driving home for either of them. Fox gave it another twenty minutes, by which time Kaye, too, had arrived, parking on a double yellow and slapping his POLICE sign on the windscreen. He was checking messages on his phone as he headed inside. Fox was listening to Radio 2, tapping his fingers on the steering wheel in time to the music. But when a quiz was announced, two listeners vying for the 'star prize', he switched channels. There was some local news, so he listened to that without taking much of it in. More economic grief; more trams grief; a spell of good weather imminent. The travel report warned of long tailbacks on the Forth Road Bridge and eastbound on the ring road.

'And the city centre is its usual rush-hour mayhem,' the report concluded. Fox felt snug in the parked car, cosseted from chaos. But the time came to turn off the radio and get out. He'd finally plucked up the courage to send Annie Inglis a text message:

Hope u can forgive me. Wd like us 2 b pals.

He wasn't sure now about the 'pals' bit. He was attracted to her, but had never had much luck with women, Elaine excepted – and even that had proved to be a mistake. Maybe it wasn't Annie who intrigued him, but rather the combination of the woman and the career she had chosen. For the past half-hour he'd been hoping she might send a return message, or call him, and as he pushed open the door to the pub, his old phone started buzzing. He plucked it from his pocket and pressed it to his ear.

'Hello?'

'It's me,' the voice said.

'Annie … thanks for getting back to me.' He had retreated to the pavement, narrowly avoiding a pedestrian. 'Look, I just wanted you to know how sorry I am about what happened yesterday. I know I was stupid …'

'Well, *I'm* sorry I blew up at you. Maybe I wasn't thinking straight. Duncan had got me wound up as usual.' Fox waited for more, but she had come to a stop.

'Doesn't mean I wasn't in the wrong,' he said into the silence. 'And I really enjoyed the meal and seeing you and everything. Maybe I can repay the favour?'

'Cook for me, you mean?'

'The word "cook" may be a bit strong …' When she laughed, a weight fell from him. 'But I'm an expert on the local carry-outs.'

'Okay,' she said. 'We'll see.'

'Any night this week is good for me.'

'I'll let you know, Malcolm.' She paused. 'That's Duncan coming home.'

'I came looking for you, to apologise in person,' Fox told her.

'At Fettes? I thought you were suspended?'

'Grampian Complaints had me in for a chat.'

'You've a lot you should be focusing on, Malcolm. Maybe we should give this week a miss.'

'You'd be doing me a favour, Annie – honestly.'

'Okay then, let me think about it. I've got to go now.'

'Say hello to Duncan for me. Tell him I want to know what music he buys with that token.'

'Trust me, you won't want to hear any of it.'

The phone went dead, and Fox managed a smile as he stared at its tiny glowing screen. Then the screen went dark, and he took a deep breath, adjusting his demeanour before walking into the pub.

Tony Kaye saw him first. Kaye wasn't at the usual table, but the one next to it, giving Naysmith and Gilchrist some space to themselves. He had been reading the evening paper, but with little apparent interest in it. His eyebrows lifted when he saw Fox, but then he bounded to his feet and reached the bar before him.

'Let me get this one,' he stated, delving into his trouser pocket for money.

'Glad to see me?' Fox asked.

'You better believe it. I feel like the spare prick at an orgy.' He twitched his head in the direction of the corner table. 'Half the stuff they drone on about I can't understand, and the other half bores the knackers off me.' He paused and stared at Fox. 'Just passing by, were you?'

'Actually, I wanted a word with Gilchrist.'

Kaye thought about this. 'That's why you spoke to Naysmith? He's baited the trap for you?'

Fox just shrugged and asked the landlord for a tomato juice. The man nodded and brought a bottle from the glass-fronted fridge, shaking it vigorously before pouring.

'Did you see *Deal or No Deal*?' he asked, not waiting for an answer. 'Dealt at seventeen and a half; had the hundred grand.' He shook his head at the idiocy of some people.

'I love it when they lose,' Kaye commented, handing over the money and asking for a half-pint for himself.

'Remember you're driving,' Fox chided him.

'Pint and a half, that's all I'm having.'

'All the office needs now is for you to fail a breathalyser – McEwan would have a seizure. Besides which, are you sure you can trust Gilchrist not to clype?'

Kaye gave a snort, but changed his order to orange and lemonade. Naysmith and Gilchrist were watching them as they approached the table with their drinks. Kaye moved the newspaper and seated himself. Fox took the chair closest to Gilchrist.

'All right, lads?' he asked, noting that Gilchrist was near to finishing his first gin and tonic of the evening. 'Settling in, are you?'

'Look, I know it's awkward ...'

Fox cut Gilchrist off with a wave of his hand. 'I'm fine with it; none of it's your fault, is it?' It sounded like a rhetorical question, but Fox's eyes told a different story. Gilchrist held the man's gaze, then shook his head slowly.

'No,' he eventually said.

'No,' Fox echoed. 'So that's all right, then. Makes things hard on DS Inglis, though ...' He took a sip of tomato juice.

'Yes,' Gilchrist agreed.

'Bit sudden, too, the way you were plucked from the Chop Shop ...'

'They knew I was keen to try something different.' Gilchrist paused. 'It's only temporary, after all.'

'Course it is,' Kaye stressed, while Naysmith nodded along.

Fox smiled at the show of support, but his eyes were still on Gilchrist. 'What's happening about Jamie Breck?' he asked. Gilchrist gave a shrug. 'Has the Aussie inquiry started crumbling?'

'Far as I know, they think they've got enough.'

'So they'll be bringing the main suspect to trial.' Fox nodded his understanding. 'But what about his clients?'

Gilchrist gave another shrug. 'I can do a bit of digging, if you like.'

Fox reached over and patted Gilchrist on his thigh. 'Don't worry about it. You're in the Complaints now – you've got different fish to fry. Same again?' Fox signalled to the glasses on the table.

'Thanks, Malcolm,' Naysmith said, but Gilchrist was shaking his head.

'I was only staying for the one,' he explained. This seemed to come as news to Naysmith, but Gilchrist was draining his glass. 'Meeting someone in town ...' He was already rising to his feet. 'See you all tomorrow, eh?'

'Not me,' Fox reminded him.

'No ... But good luck.'

'You think I need it?'

Gilchrist didn't answer this. He was pulling on his thermal jacket. Fox reached out and grabbed him by the arm.

'Who was it pulled the surveillance on Breck? *You* got the call – who was it on the other end of the line?'

Gilchrist wrestled the arm free, his jaw clenched. With a wave in Naysmith's direction, he was gone.

'Did you get what you wanted?' Kaye asked Fox.

'I'm not sure.'

Naysmith was holding his empty pint glass. 'Kronenberg, please,' he told Fox.

'Buy your own, you little quisling,' Malcolm Fox replied.

'Is it all right if I come in?' Fox asked.

It was nine in the evening and he was standing on Jamie Breck's doorstep. Breck had just opened the door to him and was wearing an open-necked polo shirt and green chinos, with socks but no shoes on his feet.

'If it's inconvenient ...' Fox continued, his voice trailing off.

'It's fine,' Breck eventually conceded. 'Annabel's at her place tonight.' He turned and padded back down the short hallway into the living room. By the time Fox got there, Breck had switched on some of the lamps. The TV was off, and so was the stereo.

'I was on the internet,' Breck seemed to feel it necessary to explain. 'Bit bored, to be honest with you.'

'Playing Quidnunc?'

'How did you guess? Four or five hours today ...' Breck paused. 'Maybe longer, actually ...'

Fox nodded and settled himself on the sofa. He'd been home and tried to eat a ready meal, giving up halfway through. 'I had a talk with the Grampian Complaints,' he said.

'How did it go?'

'It went.'

'They want to see me in the morning ... a woman called Stoddart.'

'You'll be fine.'

Breck fell into one of the armchairs. 'Sure about that?'

'Has Annabel come up with anything?'

'You mean about Vince Faulkner?' Breck gave a twitch of the mouth. 'Seems to be getting nowhere. Instead of ploughing on, Giles is going over old ground, seeing if the team's missed something.'

'It's a lazy strategy,' Fox commented.

'They got access to the footage from the casino ...'

'And?'

Breck shrugged. 'No sign of Faulkner on any of it. But guess what – there were gaps in the recording.'

'Someone had tampered with it?'

'A "glitch", according to the management.'

'Just as you predicted. Was Joanna Broughton there to explain matters?'

Breck shook his head. 'She was nowhere to be seen. It was the guy behind the bar – he's obviously had a promotion. Plus someone from Lovatt, Meikle, Meldrum.'

'What's it got to do with them?'

'Their client had asked them to be present. I told you, Malcolm, she doesn't want anything tarnishing the Oliver's rep.' Breck broke off. 'Sorry, I should have asked if you wanted a drink.'

'I'm fine,' Fox assured him. The two men sat in silence for a moment.

'Might as well spit it out,' Breck said with the thinnest of smiles.

'What?'

'Something's eating you.'

Fox looked at him. 'How do I know I can trust you?'

Breck gave a shrug. 'I get the feeling you need to trust *someone*.'

Fox rubbed a finger across his forehead. He'd spent the past hour and a half thinking much the same thing. 'Maybe I'll have that drink,' he said, playing for time. 'Water will do.'

Breck was already on his feet and heading out of the room. Fox looked around, barely taking his surroundings in. It had been a long day. Dearborn and Broughton, Stoddart and Gilchrist … Breck was coming back with the tumbler. Fox accepted it with a nod. His stomach felt full of acid. His eyes stung when he blinked and there was a persistent throbbing at his temples.

'Do you need an aspirin or something?' Breck was asking. Fox shook his head. 'You look shattered. I'm guessing not all of it courtesy of Inspector Stoddart.'

'There's something I'm going to tell you,' Fox blurted out. 'But I'm not sure how you're going to take it.'

Breck hadn't quite sat down. Instead, he rested his weight against the arm of his chair. 'In your own time,' he coaxed.

Fox took another sip. The water had a slightly sweet aftertaste, reminding him of the way tap water had tasted in his childhood, on a hot day after running around outside.

'You've been under investigation,' he stated, avoiding eye contact. 'Up to and including surveillance.'

Breck thought for a few seconds, then nodded slowly. 'That van?' he said. 'Yes, I sort of knew about that. And about you, too, of course.' The two men fixed eyes. 'You seemed to know a bit too much about me, Malcolm. Remember when I told you my brother was gay? You said you didn't know, but that meant you knew I had a brother in the first place. Then when you came round here, you couldn't really explain how you knew my street.' He paused. 'I was hoping you might eventually get round to saying something.'

'And here I am …'

'I thought maybe you were trying to tie me to Glen Heaton.'

'We weren't.'

'What then?' Breck sounded genuinely curious.

'Your name appeared on a list, Jamie. Subscribers to a website …'

'What sort of website?'

Fox angled his head so he was staring at the ceiling. 'I shouldn't be doing this,' he muttered.

'Bit late for that,' Breck told him. Then: 'What sort of website …?'

'Not the sort you'd want Annabel knowing about.'

'Porn?' Breck's voice had risen a little. 'S and M? Snuff …?'

'Underage.'

Breck was silent for a moment, until a laugh of incredulity exploded from his mouth.

'You paid by credit card,' Fox went on. 'So CEOP had us run a check.'

'When did all this start?'

'Beginning of last week. I started backing off once we'd met face to face …'

Breck had slid from the arm of the chair into the seat itself. 'My credit card?' he asked. Then he sprang up and left the room, returning a minute later with a folder. He held it over the coffee table and tipped out its contents, crouching down to sift through everything. There were bank statements, receipts, mortgage letters and credit card statements. Fox couldn't help noting that Breck's savings account was well into five figures. Breck himself was plucking out the credit card statements.

'Australian dollars, most likely,' Fox explained.

'There's nothing here …' Breck was running a finger down the columns. He used his card a lot – supermarkets, petrol stations, restaurants, clothing companies. Plus his internet and TV packages.

'Wait a second,' he said. The tip of his finger was running along one entry. 'US dollars, not Australian. Ten dollars translates as eight pounds.'

Fox looked at the description. 'SEIL Ents,' he read.

'I never paid any attention …' Breck was almost talking to himself. 'Sometimes I buy downloads from the States … Is this it, do you think?'

'Have you bought anything else in dollars recently? This goes back five weeks.'

'I swear to God, Malcolm …' Breck was wide-eyed. He broke off from staring at the sheet of paper and got back to his feet. 'Come on, there's something I want to show you.' He left the room, Fox following him. They entered what would have been the home's second bedroom. This was Breck's office. The computer was switched on, the screen-saver active. Breck nudged the mouse. His chosen wallpaper was a head-and-shoulders photo of Annabel.

'Sit down,' he was commanding Fox, indicating the swivel chair. 'Take a look for yourself. I doubt I've browsed online porn more than half a dozen times in my life – and never anything … I mean, just the normal stuff.'

'Look, Jamie …'

Breck spun around to face him. 'I don't know anything about this!' he shouted.

'I believe you,' Fox said quietly.

Breck stared at him. 'Right, because you had that van parked outside ...' He ran a hand through his hair. 'You were tapped into my system somehow ... No, not *you*, not you personally ... you were with me at the Oliver that night. Some of your guys, right? And someone from CEOP, too.'

'His name's Gilchrist. He's got his feet under my desk at the Complaints.'

Breck's eyes narrowed as he digested this. 'We've got to talk to him, find out how this could have happened.'

Fox nodded slowly. 'I had a word with him earlier on, but he wasn't exactly cooperating.'

'I need to talk to someone about this,' Breck was saying. Then, eyes boring into Fox: 'All the time we've been ... and I let you ... and you thought I was a *paedophile*?'

Fox couldn't think of anything to say to this. Breck had taken a couple of steps towards the window and was peering around the edge of the blind.

'It was just the one night,' Fox explained. 'We were planning another, but it got pulled – CEOP's decision.'

Breck turned to look at him. 'Why?'

'I don't know.'

'They realised it was a mistake?'

Fox offered a shrug. Breck ran his hand through his hair again. 'This is a fucking nightmare,' he said. 'You've met Annabel – I've got a *girlfriend*.'

'Sometimes they do.'

'Paedophiles, you mean?' Fox could see that Breck's mind was racing. 'You had a *van* watching me! It's like the Gestapo or something.'

'One thing the equipment in the van picked up ...'

Breck looked at him. 'What?'

'You did some online digging into *me*.'

Breck thought for a moment, then nodded slowly. 'That's true,' he said. Then he fell silent, staring at the computer screen. 'What's the site called?' he eventually asked. 'We've got to contact them, find out how it happened.'

'That's the last thing you want to do,' Fox cautioned.

'They got my credit card number – how is that possible?'

'It's possible,' Fox argued. 'You've said it yourself – you buy stuff online. Do you pay a subscription to Quidnunc? Because if you do, your card details are out there ...'

'This is a nightmare,' Breck repeated, staring blindly at the walls around him. 'I need a drink ...' He fled the room, leaving Fox standing there. Fox waited a moment, then scrutinised the icons on the computer screen. He saw nothing out of the ordinary. Quidnunc had been minimised, and he put it back on to full screen. Breck's avatar seemed to be a muscular blond warrior toting a complicated-looking handgun. He was standing in a valley surrounded by mountains, beyond which explosions were going off, fighter jets or spaceships occasionally flying over. His hair fluttered in the breeze, but otherwise he would stand there until Breck came back to the game. Fox hit the 'minimise' icon again and left the room.

Jamie Breck was in his kitchen. It was spotless, but Fox had the feeling the place got used. There was a fruit bowl filled with oranges and plums, and a breadboard with half a wholemeal loaf sitting on it. Breck had brought ice cubes from the freezer and was pouring whisky over them.

'There are occasions,' he said, voice trembling slightly, 'when only local remedies will do.' He waved the bottle in Fox's direction, but Fox shook his head. It was Highland Park: he'd tried it plenty of times in the past. Soft peat and sea spray ... Breck downed half the drink without pausing. He squeezed shut his eyes and opened his mouth in a loud exhalation. Fox's nostrils flared. Yes, that was the tang he remembered ...

'This isn't happening,' Breck said. 'I'm being fast-tracked, everybody knows it. Another year and I'll be a DI.'

'That's what your file seemed to say.'

Breck nodded. 'And that's how you knew all about me – you'd seen it in my personnel file.' His eyes fixed on Fox. 'So why own up now, Malcolm?'

Fox poured himself another glass of tap water. 'You said it yourself, Jamie – I need somebody I can trust.'

'And you think that's me?' Breck waited until Fox had nodded. 'Well, thanks for that at least – or does it just mean I'm your very last hope?'

'Thing is, Jamie, there's a lot going on that I'm not even close to understanding. I think maybe you can help.'

'What you're saying is, me being a suspected paedophile is the least of your worries? And my girlfriend could come in useful along the way?'

Fox managed a smile. 'Something like that, yes.'

Breck gave a snort as he smiled into his drink. 'Well, at least we know where we stand. Is there any point in me contacting my credit card company? They must be able to trace the transaction back.'

Fox offered a shrug. 'Worth a try,' he said.

'Meantime I can run a check on SEIL Ents.'

'A word of caution – the guy behind the site is a cop in Australia. They're on to him but they definitely don't want him to know that. If he finds out and shuts everything down …'

'There'll be some who might think I'd warned him off?' Breck nodded slowly. 'How near are they to nailing him?'

'I don't really know.'

'Can you find out?'

Fox nodded.

'And I'll make sure Annabel keeps in touch with Billy Giles and all his doings – does that sound fair?'

Fox gave another nod and watched Breck hold up a finger.

'But I don't want Annabel to know about this.'

'She won't hear it from me,' Fox promised.

'Does Stoddart know?' Breck asked.

'Yes.'

'But I don't want to let her know that *I* know?'

'That's up to you, Jamie.'

'They'd realise it was you who told me. And that would look even worse for us.'

'True.'

Breck had turned round, so that the small of his back rested against the edge of the black marble work surface. The glass was still in his hand, half an inch of liquid left in it.

'Look at the pair of us,' he said with another tired smile. And then, raising his glass in a toast: 'But thanks for taking me into your trust, Malcolm – better late than never.' He tipped the glass to his mouth, finishing the whisky and tossing the ice into the sink. 'So,' he said, smacking his lips, 'do you have a particular plan of action in mind?'

'I'm the one who thinks stuff just happens to us, remember? It's *you* that thinks we control our destinies.'

'Seems to me you're in the process of changing.'

'Speaking of changing …' Fox lifted a card from his pocket and handed it over. 'I've bought myself a new mobile phone.'

'You think I should do the same?' Breck studied the card. Fox's old mobile number had been scored out and the new one written in biro. He looked up at Fox. 'The Complaints can tap my phone?'

'Not easily. But they *can* grab the records of any calls in or out.'

'You said "they" rather than "we" ...' Fox didn't say anything to this, and Breck was thoughtful for a further few seconds. 'Why am I being set up, Malcolm?' he asked quietly. 'Who'd do something like that? An Australian porn site?' He shook his head slowly. 'It doesn't make any sense.'

'It will,' Fox stated, straightening his shoulders. 'We just need to work at it.'

Tuesday 17 February 2009

18

Tuesday morning, Fox was waiting for Annie Inglis outside her tenement. Duncan appeared first, slouching his way to school under the weight of his backpack. Ten minutes later, it was Inglis's turn. Fox, seated across the road in his car, sounded his horn and waved her across. Traffic was busy – people on their way to work or dropping their kids off at the school gates. A warden had paused his scooter beside Fox's car, but had scuttled off again when he saw that the indicators were flashing and there was someone behind the steering wheel. Annie Inglis stood her ground for a moment, and when she did cross the road she didn't get into the car. Instead, she leaned down so her face was at the passenger-side window. Fox slid the window down.

'What are you doing here?' she asked. He handed her a business card, on the back of which was written the number of his new mobile phone.

'That's in case you need to reach me,' he explained. 'But keep it to yourself.' Then: 'I need a favour, Annie.'

'Look, Malcolm …'

'It would be easier to talk if you got in. I can even give you a lift.'

'I don't need a lift.' When he made no answer to this, she sighed and opened the door. He'd removed the sweet-wrappers from the passenger seat. There was a street map on the floor, which she handed to him. He tossed it into the back.

'Is it to do with Jamie Breck?' she asked.

'Gilchrist's being obstructive.'

'You're suspended, Malcolm! It's not his job to help you out.'

'All the same …'

She gave another heavy sigh. 'What is it you want?'

'A contact at the Australian end – someone from the team there. Name, phone number, e-mail ... anything at all, really.'

'Do I get to ask why?'

'Not yet.'

She looked at him. Her work face differed from the one she wore at home – there was a little more make-up. It hardened her features.

'They're going to know it was me,' she stated. She didn't mean the cops in Australia; she meant Fettes.

'I'll say it wasn't.'

'That's all right, then – after all, there's no reason for them not to take you at your word, is there?'

'No reason at all,' he said with a smile.

Annie Inglis opened her door and started to get out. She was still holding his business card. 'What's the matter with your old phone?' she asked. Then: 'No ... on second thoughts, I really don't want to know.' She closed the door after her and crossed the road again, unlocking her own car.

It took Fox five minutes to drive to the café on Morningside Road, but another five to find a parking space. He put enough coins in the meter for an hour, and walked the short distance to his destination. Jamie Breck was already there, plugging his laptop into one of the power sockets next to the corner table he'd secured.

'Just got here,' he told Fox as the two men shook hands.

'How are you feeling?'

'I didn't get much sleep, thanks to your confession.'

Fox's mouth twitched at the word. He shrugged off his coat and asked what Breck wanted to drink.

'Americano with a spot of milk.'

Fox did the ordering, adding a cappuccino for himself. 'Anything to eat?' he asked Breck.

'Maybe a croissant.'

'Make that two,' Fox told the assistant. By the time he got back to the table, Breck had angled the laptop so that the low sun wouldn't hit the screen. Fox drew a chair round to Breck's side of the table. This had been Fox's idea, and looking around at the other customers he felt vindicated. Even if someone was outside in a surveillance van – and he'd taken a good look, spotting no obvious candidates – there were half a dozen people in the café logged on to the internet, courtesy of the free wi-fi. Most looked like students, the others business people. Naysmith had told him once how hard it was to untangle one user from another in such a cluster.

'So what is it we're looking for?' Breck asked. He looked and sounded businesslike, the shock of the previous night assimilated and squeezed into a compartment in his mind.

'Something you said a while back,' Fox began, leaning forward in his chair. 'You've come across the PR company before.'

Breck nodded. 'Lovatt, Meikle, Meldrum have a lobbying arm.' He got online and searched the firm's name, coming up with the home page of their website. A further couple of clicks later, he was showing Fox a photographic portrait. The man was bald and bullet-headed and smiling. 'Paul Meldrum – LMM's political Mr Fixit. I was telling you about the local councillor – Paul here bent my ear about it. He said he was representing the council.'

'Who was the councillor?'

'Ernie Wishaw.'

'I've never heard of him.'

'He runs a lorry business out by the Gyle.'

'What's he supposed to have done?'

'One of his drivers was delivering a few packages too many ...'

'Dope?'

Breck nodded. 'Drug Enforcement got him, and he's due to serve five years. But they wondered how far up the ladder things went. Wishaw had a meeting at the Oliver with the driver's brother-in-law. DEA reckoned maybe it was hush money to be given to the wife. If she was kept sweet, the driver wouldn't go blabbing.'

'How come you got involved?'

'DEA wanted local knowledge. Their boss was tight with Billy Giles, so they got us.'

Fox frowned. 'Was Glen Heaton part of the team?'

Breck nodded. 'Up until then, I hadn't really doubted him.'

'Something changed your mind?'

Breck offered a shrug. 'I think they were on to us from the start – don't ask me why; it was just a feeling I got.'

'So you weren't surprised when there was nothing from the Oliver's CCTV?'

'No,' Breck agreed.

Fox took a sip of coffee. 'How long ago did you say this was?'

'Best part of six months.'

'It never came up.' Breck looked as if he didn't quite understand. Fox enlightened him: 'We'd been looking into Glen Heaton for nearly a year, and this is the first I've heard of it.'

Breck shrugged again. 'He didn't do anything wrong.'

'You could have voiced your suspicions.'

'Seemed to me you were doing fine on your own. And like I say, I'd nothing to back them up.' Breck reached for his own drink, then changed his mind and bit into a croissant instead, brushing crumbs from his trousers. Fox stared at the photo of Paul Meldrum.

'The drug-smuggling had nothing to do with the council,' Fox stated. 'How come LMM got involved?'

'Good question.'

'Did you ask it at the time?'

'Ernie Wishaw had bought out a rival firm a few years earlier. It all got a bit ugly, and he used LMM to win round the media.'

Both men looked up as a new customer entered the café. But she was pushing a baby buggy, so they dismissed her. When they made eye contact, they shared a smile. Better safe than sorry …

'So they might have been working for him personally, rather than the council?' Fox asked.

Jamie Breck could only shrug once more. 'Anyway, the whole thing ended up going nowhere. DEA dropped it and thanked us for our help.'

Fox concentrated on his breakfast, until he thought of something else to say.

'You're not the only one who was under surveillance, Jamie. The Deputy Chief Constable let slip that I'd been watched all last week, but Vince's body wasn't found until Tuesday morning – it takes a bit of time to decide that a cop might be breaking the rules and you should put a watch on him.'

'How long did it take till you decided I merited the van?'

'Not long,' Fox conceded. 'But that's beside the point. I was being watched *before* I started misbehaving.'

'Then there's something you're obviously hiding from everybody.'

'I'm honest as the day is long, DS Breck.'

'This is winter, Inspector Fox – the days are pretty short.'

Fox ignored this. 'In the interview room at Torphichen, when Traynor was spelling it all out and Billy Giles was trying hard not to do a little dance around the table, there was a look my boss gave me …'

'McEwan?'

Fox nodded. 'I don't think he knew. I mean, he *knew*, but he hadn't been in the loop for long. He was asking himself what was going on.'

'Maybe he can find out for you.'

'Maybe.'

'You don't trust him?'

'Hard to know. But here's the thing – the tail on me coincides with the new assignment I'd been given.'

'By "assignment" you mean me?'

'Yes.' The caffeine was getting to Fox; he could feel it pounding through him. When his mobile started ringing, he didn't recognise the tone. It was the first time someone had called him on his new phone.

'Hello?' he answered.

'I've got something for you,' Annie Inglis said. She was speaking so softly, he could hardly hear her. He held the phone more firmly to his ear, and pressed a finger into his other ear.

'Is there anybody else there?' he asked.

'No.'

'Then why are you whispering?'

'Do you want this or not?' she asked, sounding irritated. Then, without waiting for his answer, she reeled off a phone number.

'Hang on,' he said, scrabbling for a pen and brushing flakes of croissant from the paper napkin on his plate. While she repeated the number, Fox jotted it down.

'Her name's Dawlish. Cecilia Dawlish.' Inglis ended the call before Fox could utter any form of thanks.

'What's the code for Australia?' he asked Breck. It took Breck thirty seconds and a few keystrokes to come up with the answer.

'Zero-zero-six-one,' he said. 'They're eight to ten hours ahead of us.'

Fox looked at his watch. 'Meaning it's evening there – and hellish expensive.' He held up his new phone. 'This is pay-as-you-go,' he explained.

'My treat,' Breck responded, handing over his own Motorola.

'They might be able to trace the number back to you,' Fox warned him, but Breck just shrugged.

'I'm not the one making the call, though, am I?' he countered.

It turned out that the number Inglis had given Fox was for a mobile. Dawlish was in her car when she answered.

'It's Detective Constable Gilchrist here,' Fox explained, concentrating his attention on the world outside the café window.

'Yeah?'

'CEOP Edinburgh. You had us looking into a local officer called Breck?'

'Yeah.'

'Is this a bad time to talk?'

'I'm headed home, DC Gilchrist. What is it you need?'

'I've been put in charge of the paperwork.'

'Just bear in mind what we told you at the start – the more who know about this, the tougher it is to keep it quiet.'

'Understood.' Fox paused. 'So you've not arrested him yet?'

'We'll let you know when that happens.'

'Right,' Fox said, turning his attention to the listening Breck. 'So what is it you want us to do with Breck?'

'Just get us anything you can. Now tell me about these bloody forms you're filling in.'

'Just wondered if it was okay to put you down as our main contact.'

'Sure.'

'And this phone number?'

'Seems to be the one you've got.'

'I suppose so, yes.' Fox thought of something. 'We managed to gain entry to Breck's home.'

'Yeah?'

'His computer was clean, but we took a look at his latest credit card bill – SEIL Ents.'

'That's the one.'

'What do the letters stand for?'

'The bastard's initials – Simeon Edward Ian Latham. Sim to his mates.'

'The payment was in US dollars ...'

'He's got an account in the Caribbean. Latham's been running this thing for years without us knowing – he's learned all the old tricks and invented a few of his own.' Dawlish paused. 'This is a secure line, right, Gilchrist?'

'Absolutely,' Fox assured her. 'And thanks for your help.'

'Paperwork's killing this job,' Dawlish commented, ending the call.

Fox stared at Jamie Breck. 'Far as the Aussies are concerned, you're still in the frame.'

'Thanks for not setting the record straight.'

'Thing is, Jamie, we did one night's surveillance on you, and the second night was pulled. Thinking seemed to be that the Aussies didn't need you any more, or had crossed your name off their list. When I spoke to Gilchrist last night, he as good as said the same thing – Sim Latham was headed for trial.'

'And he's not?'

'Inquiry's ongoing, according to Dawlish.'

'So why did Gilchrist tell you different?'

'Maybe we should ask him.'

'I can go solo on this,' Breck said, 'if you'd rather keep out of it.'

But Fox shook his head before attacking the final chunk of croissant.

'Are we done here?' Breck asked, tapping the edge of his laptop's screen. Fox glanced at his watch: fifteen minutes left on the meter.

'There's one final thing,' he said. 'And that computer of yours could come in handy.' He wiped the pastry crumbs from his mouth. 'Something I asked you when we were at the pool hall.'

'Yes?'

'I asked if Charlie Brogan could have been one of the developers.'

'We can take a look,' Breck said, busying himself at the keyboard. Within a couple of minutes, he had found enough information to confirm that CBBJ was indeed part of the consortium.

'CB stands for Charles Brogan,' Fox commented, 'but what about BJ?'

'Broughton, Joanna?' Breck guessed.

'That makes sense, I suppose.' Fox was peering at the screen. 'I got a look at his diary, you know ...'

'What?' Breck was staring at him.

'Brogan's diary. Joanna Broughton asked me to drop it into Leith Police Station.' Fox paused. 'It's a long story.'

Breck folded his arms. 'I've got time, partner.'

'I recognised her when she was standing outside the station. Offered her a lift home.'

'To the penthouse?'

Fox nodded. 'Triplex, actually.'

'You were inside? She knew you were a cop?'

Fox kept nodding. 'Leith wanted to see Brogan's appointments diary. She asked me if I'd take it.'

Breck was chuckling. 'It's always the quiet ones you have to watch out for. I can't believe you got away with it.'

'I didn't. On the way out, I bumped into Gordon Lovatt. She told him who I was, and he got on to Leith, who got on to DI Stoddart and her merry men.'

Breck gave a low whistle, then was thoughtful for a moment. 'Was the diary worth the effort?' he eventually asked.

'Not really. Work was drying up for Charlie Brogan. He spent more time planning what TV shows to watch than scheduling meetings.' Fox paused to collect his thoughts. 'Think it through, though. Vince Faulkner works on one of Brogan's projects. He's last seen in a casino owned by Brogan's other half. He winds up dead and his body's dumped at yet another site owned by Brogan's company. Then, just to put some icing on top, Brogan goes for a swim in the Forth and doesn't bother coming up for air.'

Breck was rubbing the stubble on the underside of his chin. 'You should take this to Billy Giles.'

'Oh, sure,' Fox replied. 'Because I'm dead sure DCI Giles would take me seriously.' Breck had opened his mouth, but Fox stilled him with a gesture of the hand. 'And *you* can hardly go to him with it, because you're his little Judas. So where exactly does that leave us?' When Breck didn't answer, Fox glanced at his watch again. 'I need to put more money in the meter,' he said.

'Let's finish up here and I'll come with you.' Breck had already started shutting down the laptop. Fox noticed that he'd left most of his coffee untouched.

'Where are we going?' he asked.

'Back to Salamander Point.'

They used the same Portakabin as before. Breck had asked the site manager what would happen now that the developer was dead.

'We keep working until we're ordered to stop – or the wages dry up,' the man had replied.

But Malcolm Fox had noticed some changes. The sales office was locked shut, no sign of life inside. And once they'd climbed the ladder to the upper level of temporary offices, he could see that over to one side of the site an impromptu game of football was in progress, piles of bricks substituting for goalposts. When Ronnie Hendry arrived, he was sweating and breathing hard.

'We're waiting for a delivery of ready-mix,' he explained, removing his hard hat and wiping a sleeve across his face.

Breck gestured for him to sit at the table. The three men were then positioned as before, Fox maintaining his silence.

'Just a couple of follow-up questions,' Breck was telling Hendry. 'How have things been since Charlie Brogan jumped ship?'

Hendry stared at him, wondering how to react to the pun, but Breck remained stony-faced.

'The men are worried about pay day.'

'Your gaffer just said much the same thing.'

'He's got more at stake, money he makes for standing around all day with his dick in his hand and not a clue in his head.'

'You sound aggrieved.'

Hendry wriggled in his chair. 'Not really.' But he folded his arms across his chest – a defensive gesture, in Fox's eyes. 'You any closer to finding out who killed Vince?'

'We think the "why" might help answer that. But meantime, I wanted to ask about Mr Brogan.'

'What's he got to do with it?'

'Well, now that he's gone the same way as Vince Faulkner ...' Breck's voice drifted off.

'But there's no connection,' Hendry stated, eyes shifting from one detective to the other. 'Is there?'

'We can't know that for sure. I'm assuming Mr Brogan visited Salamander Point?'

'He was pretty hands-on,' Hendry agreed.

'How often did you see him?'

'Maybe once a week, twice a week sometimes. Gaffer would be able to say for sure.'

'But it's *you* I'm asking. Did he just sit in here with a mug of tea and the plans spread out in front of him?'

Hendry shook his head. 'He liked to give the whole site a good look-see.'

'So you'd have met him, then?'

'Spoke to him a few times. He always had a couple of questions. Seemed like a good guy – not all developers are.'

'How do you mean?'

Hendry shifted in the chair again. 'Some jobs I've worked on, they turn up wearing pinstripe suits and shiny brogues – one or two from CBBJ were that way inclined. But Mr Brogan ... with him it was work boots and jeans. And he always shook your hand without brushing the dirt off after.' Hendry was nodding slowly at the memory. 'Like I say, a good guy.'

'Did Vince Faulkner think the same?'

'Never said any different, not to me.'

'He met Brogan, too?'

Hendry nodded again. 'Mr Brogan knew most of the guys by name. And he remembered who you were. There was always some detail or other he'd toss into the conversation.'

'Gleaned from the personnel files?' Fox interrupted. Hendry turned his head towards him.

'Maybe,' he said.

'How often did the two of them meet?' Breck asked, drawing Hendry's attention back to him.

It took the man a few seconds to answer. 'Don't know,' he eventually stated.

'You see what we're getting at?' Breck persisted.

'Not really.'

'If the two of them knew one another … well, you add Vince Faulkner's death to anything else happening in Mr Brogan's life …'

'And he goes and tops himself?' Hendry seemed to consider this. He offered a shrug, his arms still folded.

'Last time we spoke,' Breck continued, 'you said you sometimes went out for the evening – a meal and some drinks at the Oliver casino.'

'Right.'

'You knew it was owned by Mr Brogan's wife?'

'Sure.'

'Ever see him there?'

'Probably.'

'You can't be sure?'

Hendry had unfolded his arms and was pressing his palms against his thighs, preparing to stand up.

'I've got to get back to work,' he said.

'What's the rush?'

'There's nothing I can tell you about Charlie Brogan or why he decided to end it all.' He was on his feet now, and readying to put his yellow hard hat back on. Breck got up from the table too.

'Maybe we're not finished,' he said.

'You're clutching at straws,' Hendry stated. 'You've hit a wall with Vince, so you're focusing on Brogan instead. But there's no connection between the two.'

'You're sure of that?'

'Definitely.'

'What makes you such an expert, Mr Hendry?'

Hendry glared at him. He seemed to try half a dozen answers for size, dismissing each of them in turn. With a cold smile, he opened the door and exited the Portakabin. Fox closed the door and rested his weight against it, eyes on Breck.

'Well?' Breck asked him.

'About three quarters of the way through …'

Breck was nodding. 'He'd been cagey enough before that.'

'But he started holding back. I wonder why.'

'Might be different if we were talking to him at Torphichen. Maybe having cautioned him first ... But we can't do that, can we?'

Fox shrugged his agreement. They moved out of the room and on to the wooden walkway. Hendry was clambering over foundations and lengths of pipe and ducting, heading back to the football game. The sun had come out, and a few of the men were now topless.

'Makes you proud,' Fox commented. 'Temperature's halfway to double figures, but at the slightest glimmer of sunshine ...'

'The Scotsman in his prime,' Breck agreed, as he started back down the ladder.

They were leaving the site when a car pulled up, two men climbing out. Breck cursed under his breath.

'Dickson and Hall,' he muttered.

'I know the faces,' Fox confirmed. They were Torphichen CID; Bad Billy Giles's men. Both were smiling, without a trace of humour between them.

'Well, well,' Dickson said. He was the older and heavier of the two. His partner was, as Fox's father would have put it, 'twa ply o' reek', but with a shaven head and Ray-Bans.

'What brings you here?' Breck asked, hinting to Fox at their strategy here – namely, brazen it out.

Dickson managed a chuckle as he slid his hands into his trouser pockets. 'That's more than a bit rich, Jamie. But since you ask ...'

Hall took his cue. 'Billy Giles has got us retracing your steps. He's worried you might have left gaps in the paperwork or maybe tweaked your reports.' He angled his head slightly to take in Malcolm Fox. 'With a bit of help from Inspector Fox here ...'

'You're wasting your time,' Breck stated.

'And yet here you are, Jamie – the pair of you,' Dickson said, leaning forward a little from the waist and reminding Fox of one of those toddlers' toys that you could rock to and fro without them ever falling over.

'And you'll be reporting all of this back, of course,' Breck was saying.

'You think we shouldn't?' Hall asked, feigning amazement. 'Last I heard, you two were suspended from duty.'

'So?'

'So it begs the question what could you possibly be doing *here*?'

'I'm in the market for a flat,' Fox interrupted. 'And if you ever watch those property shows on TV, you'll know it's advisable to bring a friend to the viewing – they can spot things you might miss.'

'Billy Giles told us you were a smart-arse.'

Dickson leaned a little further forward without shifting his stance. 'Remember me, Fox? You had a few questions for me about Glen Heaton ...'

'And you thought you were doing him a favour, not answering any of them.'

A grin spread across Dickson's face. 'That's right,' he said.

'Thing is, though,' Fox confided, 'as soon as we sussed he had friends like you, we knew he had to be dirty.' He turned towards Breck. 'We're done here.' But as he made to move past Dickson, the man stuck a hand out into his chest. Fox grabbed the hand and yanked it sharply downwards, the rest of the body following. He watched as Dickson dropped to the ground. The mud was crusted on the surface, but wet just beneath. Hall was helping his colleague to his feet, Dickson swearing and spluttering and wiping his face clean.

'We're done,' Fox repeated. Without bothering to look at Breck, knowing he'd be following, he made his way to the waiting car.

19

They drove in silence for the first half-mile or so. Fox was behind the steering wheel, Breck in the passenger seat. Eventually, Breck found the right form of words for what he wanted to say.

'What was that all about?'

'What?'

'Back there – you and Dickson.'

'Just wanted to check his centre of gravity, Jamie. Didn't think he'd go down so easily.' Fox made eye contact, then gave a wink.

Breck smiled, but he was shaking his head. 'It's not the way to play Dickson and Hall. That's two enemies for life, right there.'

'It was worth it,' Fox stated.

'Suddenly you're Action Man …'

'Some of us don't have avatars to fall back on.'

Breck turned his attention to the world outside the car. 'Where are we going?'

'My sister's.'

'Does she live in an underground bunker?'

'She lives in Saughtonhall.'

'Might not be protection enough. Billy Giles is going to want to talk to us.'

'Talk *at* us, you mean.'

'Okay, but he's going to haul us in if we don't go to him first.'

'You're the guy who likes to take risks and show initiative …'

'And that's what you were doing back there?'

'Was I being passive?'

'Not really.' Breck managed a short-lived laugh. 'So why are we going to see your sister?'

'You'll see.'

But when they got there, Jude wasn't at home. Fox rang the bell next door and Alison Pettifer answered. She had an apron tied around her and was wiping her hands on a towel.

'Sorry,' Fox said. 'Is Jude with you?'

'She went to the shops.' Pettifer looked up and down the road. 'Here she comes now ...'

Jude had seen them but couldn't wave, with one arm still in plaster and the other holding a full shopping bag. Fox thanked Pettifer and went to meet his sister, taking the bag from her.

'What have you got in here?' he asked. 'Coal?'

'Just some food.' She smiled at him. 'Reckoned it was time I learned to fetch for myself.'

Fox thought of something. 'How are you doing for money?'

She gave him a look. 'You're already paying for Dad's care home ...'

'There's some to spare if you need it.'

'I'm fine for now.' But she leaned her head in towards his shoulder, her way of saying thanks. Then: 'I seem to know him ...' They were walking up the path towards her front door, where Jamie Breck was waiting.

'DS Breck,' Fox explained. 'He was on the inquiry team.'

'Was?'

'Long story.'

Breck greeted Jude with a slight bow of the head as she unlocked the door. 'Lucky I got some coffee,' she told both men. 'In you come, then.'

Fox told her he'd help put the shopping away, but she shooed him off. 'I can manage.' And she did – filling the kettle and switching it on; placing her purchases in the fridge or a cupboard. Then she spooned coffee into three mugs and poured on the boiling water, adding milk.

When all three were seated in the tidied living room, Fox asked her how she was doing.

'I'm managing, Malcolm – as you can see.'

Fox nodded slowly. He knew that people had ways of dealing with grief and loss. But keeping busy could lead to problems later, if all it meant was that you were in denial. Still, the lack of mess and empty bottles perhaps boded well.

'You don't mind talking a little about Vince?' he asked her.

'Depends,' she answered, starting to light a cigarette. 'Has there been any progress?'

'Precious little,' Breck admitted. She turned her attention to him.

'I remember you,' she said, blowing smoke through her nostrils. 'You were here the day they dug up the back garden.'

Breck gave another bow of his head, acknowledging the fact. Fox cleared his throat until she focused on him again.

'Did you hear about Charles Brogan?' he asked.

'It was in the paper. Fell from his yacht.'

'You know he was married to Joanna Broughton?'

'So the paper said.'

'Did you know she owns the Oliver?'

Jude nodded and removed a sliver of tobacco from her tongue. 'They showed her picture – I recognised her.'

'From your nights at the casino?'

'She was sometimes there. Always looked very glam.'

'How about her husband? Did you ever see him?'

Jude was nodding. 'Once or twice. He sent us over a bottle of champagne.'

'Charles Brogan bought you champagne?' Breck asked, seeking verification.

'Didn't I just say that?' Jude took a slurp of coffee. 'Cast's coming off next week,' she informed her brother.

'Why?' he asked.

'Typical NHS balls-up. Turns out it's a fracture – less serious than a break.'

'I meant, why did Charles Brogan send you over a bottle of champagne?'

She looked at him. 'Well, both Vince and Ronnie worked for him, didn't they?'

'Not exactly.'

She pondered this. 'Okay,' she agreed, 'not exactly. But he'd met them on the site; he knew who they were.'

'Was it good champagne?'

Breck had asked the question, and Jude turned her head towards him. 'It was Moët … or something like that. Thirty quid or thereabouts in Asda, so Sandra said.'

'More like a ton in a casino.'

'Well, it's his wife's place, isn't it? I doubt he was paying full whack.'

Fox decided to step in. 'It was a nice gesture, all the same. Did he come over and say hello?'

Jude shook her head. 'Not that time.'

'Another time, though?'

Now she was nodding. *And Vince's friend Ronnie didn't want us to know,* Fox thought. 'He handed Sandra and me twenty quid's worth of chips – each, mind you.' She paused. 'I think he was showing off.'

'Is that what Vince thought?'

'Vince thought he had *style*. When the champagne arrived, Vince had to go shake him by the hand. Brogan just patted him on the shoulder, like it was no big deal.' She shrugged. 'Maybe it wasn't.'

There was a phone ringing. It was Breck's. He apologised as he lifted it from his pocket and checked the screen. His glance towards Fox confirmed what Fox had already been thinking: Billy Giles.

'Don't answer,' Fox was saying, but Breck had already placed the phone to his ear.

'Afternoon, sir,' he said. Then, after listening for a moment: 'Yes, he's with me.' And a few seconds later: 'Right ... yes ... understood ... Yes, I was there when it happened, but it was really more of a misund—' Breck broke off and listened some more. Fox couldn't hear what Giles was saying, but his tone was splenetic. Breck actually eased the phone away from his ear as the diatribe continued.

'Sounds narked,' Jude whispered for her brother's benefit. Fox nodded back. By the time the call ended, blood had risen up Breck's neck and into his cheeks.

'Well?' Fox asked.

'Our presence is requested,' Breck explained, 'at Torphichen, any time within the next half-hour. Any later, and there'll be patrol cars out trawling for us.'

Jude stared at her brother. 'What have you done? Is it to do with Vince?'

'It's nothing,' Fox assured her, while locking eyes with Jamie Breck.

'You were always a terrible liar, Malcolm,' his sister remarked.

Torphichen: not an interview room this time, but Bad Billy Giles's inner sanctum. The office lacked any whiff of personality. There were no framed family snaps on the desk; no citations or certificates on the walls. Some people liked to brighten up their drab surroundings, but Giles was not among them. You could tell nothing about the inhabitant of this space, other than that he was behind with his filing. There were boxes awaiting storage elsewhere, and a three-foot-high pile of paperwork balanced precariously atop the only cabinet.

'Cosy,' Fox said, manoeuvring his way in. The place was crowded. Giles was behind his desk, swivelling slightly in his chair and with a pen gripped in his hand like a dagger. Bob McEwan was seated next to the filing cabinet, hands clasped in his lap and with Caroline Stoddart alongside him. She stood with arms folded. Then there were Hall and Dickson. Dickson had given himself a wash and changed into a spare set of clothes, which looked like the result of a whip-round of the other officers in the station. The ill-fitting brown cords did not match the pink polo shirt, which in turn clashed with the green blouson. He was also wearing tennis shoes, and his furious eyes never left Fox for a second.

Breck had managed to squeeze into the room behind Fox, but gave up on trying to close the door. Giles tossed his pen down on to the desk and looked towards McEwan.

'With your permission, Bob …' Permission was granted with the curtest of nods, and Giles turned his attention back to Fox and Breck.

'One of my officers wants to make a complaint,' he told them. 'Seems he was manhandled to the ground.'

'That was a misunderstanding, sir,' Breck explained. 'And we're sorry about it. We'll pay the dry-cleaning costs or any other reasonable expense.'

'Shut up, Breck,' Giles snapped. 'You're not the one who needs to do the grovelling.'

Fox pulled his shoulders back. 'Dickson went for me first,' he stated. 'I'm not sorry for what I did.' He paused for a beat. 'I just didn't expect him to go down like a sack of spuds.'

'You prick,' Dickson snarled, taking half a step forward.

'Dickson!' Giles cautioned. 'My office, my rules!' Then, to Fox: 'What I want to know is what you and the Boy Wonder were doing there in the first place.'

'I told Dickson and Hall at the time,' Fox replied calmly. 'I'd already paid one visit to Salamander Point and I liked what I saw. There's a sales office, and not having much else to do, I decided to see if I could snag a bargain in these straitened times.'

'Taking DS Breck with you?'

'Except,' Hall interrupted, 'that's not what happened. You'd asked to speak to Mr Ronald Hendry. He wasn't happy at being pulled away from his game of football, and even less happy when I asked for him again not ten minutes later.' He offered Fox a cold smile. Giles allowed the silence to linger, then snatched up his pen and stabbed it in Stoddart's direction.

'I think maybe it would be wise,' she said on cue, 'if I brought forward my interview with DS Breck.'

'To when?' Breck asked.

'Directly after this meeting.'

He offered a shrug. 'Fine by me.'

'Wouldn't matter if it wasn't,' Giles snapped back. 'And afterwards, I'm ordering the pair of you to cease communication.'

'And how are you going to enforce that?' Fox asked. 'Have us tagged, maybe? Or kept under surveillance?' As he said this, he glanced in McEwan's direction.

'I'll use whatever methods I think necessary,' Giles growled. Then, for Breck's benefit: 'You're not doing your prospects much good, son – it's high time you saw sense!'

'Yes, sir,' Jamie Breck replied. 'Thank you, sir.' Fox gave him a look, but Breck wasn't about to make eye contact. He was standing with his hands behind his back, feet slightly apart, head bowed in a show of contrition. 'And just to reiterate, sir,' Breck went on, 'I'd be more than happy to pay whatever compensation's warranted for DS Dickson's distress.' He then leaned past Fox, hand stretched out towards Dickson. Dickson stared at the hand as if it might be booby-trapped.

'Good man,' Giles said by way of encouragement, leading Dickson to accept the handshake, but with a baleful stare directed at Fox.

'Well then ...' Giles was half rising to his feet. 'Unless Chief Inspector McEwan has anything to add?'

But McEwan didn't, and neither did Stoddart. She was telling Breck she had a car waiting outside. Their little chat would take place at Fettes. Giles had already ordered Hall and Dickson back to work. 'We've a case to clear up,' he reminded them.

Fox waited to see if there'd be any further admonishment, but Giles was removing some paperwork from his desk drawer. *You're not important enough*, he seemed to be telling Fox. Jamie Breck offered him the briefest of nods as he left.

Fox moved swiftly through the station, not knowing if Dickson and Hall might be ready to spring out at him. When he reached the pavement, Bob McEwan was standing there, knotting his coffee-coloured scarf around his neck.

'You're a bloody idiot,' McEwan told him.

'It's hard to deny it,' Fox offered, sliding his hands into his coat pockets. 'But something's behind all this – don't tell me you don't feel it too.'

McEwan looked at him, then gave a single, slow nod of the head.

'That time in the interview room,' Fox pressed on, gesturing towards the police station, 'there was a moment where we caught sight of it. The Deputy Chief said I'd been under surveillance most of the week. But that means it was in place *before* any of this other stuff. So I'm asking you, sir ...' Fox planted himself firmly in front of his boss. 'How much do you know?'

McEwan stared back at him. 'Not much,' he eventually conceded, adjusting the knot in his scarf.

'Not too tight, Bob,' Fox advised him. 'If you end up strangling yourself, they're bound to find a way to pin it on me.'

'You've not done yourself any favours, Malcolm. Look at it from *their* point of view. You've interfered in an inquiry, and when ordered to stop you seemed to push your foot to the pedal that bit harder.'

'Grampian Complaints already had me in their sights,' Fox stressed. 'Is there any way you can look into that?' He paused. 'I know I'm asking a lot under the circumstances ...'

'I've already set the ball rolling.'

Fox looked at him. 'I forgot,' he said, 'you have friends in Grampian CID.'

'I seem to remember telling you that I've friends nowhere.'

Fox thought for a moment. 'Say that there *is* something rotten in Aberdeen. Could they be trying for a pre-emptive strike?'

'It's doubtful. The job I mentioned up there has gone to Strathclyde instead of us. And besides – why pick on you? If I were them, I'd have zeroed in on Tony Kaye. *He's* the one with the history.' McEwan paused. 'Are you going to heed the warning and keep away from Breck?'

'I'd rather not answer that, sir.' Fox watched his boss's face cloud over. 'I think he's being set up, Bob. There's not a shred of evidence that he's got inclinations that way.'

'Then how did his name end up on the list?'

'Someone got hold of his credit card,' Fox said with a shrug. 'Maybe you could ask DS Inglis if that's possible. Could someone have signed up in Breck's name without his knowledge?' Fox broke off and held up a cautionary hand. 'Best if Gilchrist doesn't know, though.'

McEwan's eyes narrowed. 'Why?'

'The fewer the better,' Fox offered.

McEwan shuffled his feet. 'Give me a single good reason why I should go out on a limb for you.'

Fox considered this, then gave another shrug. 'To be honest, sir, I can't actually think of one.'

McEwan nodded slowly. 'That's the word I was looking for.'

'What word, sir?'

'Honest,' Bob McEwan said as he marched towards his car.

Home felt like a cage. Fox did everything but dismantle the landline to look for bugs. Thing was, that was straight out of *The Ipcress File*. These days, you eavesdropped in other ways. A couple of months back, the Complaints had attended a series of seminars at Tulliallan Police College. They'd been shown various bits of new technology. A suspect might be making a phone call, but it was software doing the listening, and it would only start to record if certain pre-programmed keywords came up. Same went for computers – the gadgets in the van could isolate an individual laptop or hard drive and withdraw information from it. Fox kept walking over to the windows and peering out. If he heard a car engine, he'd be at the window again. He held his new phone in his hand, wondering who he could call. He'd made toast, but the slices sat untouched on their plate. When had he last eaten something? Breakfast? He still couldn't summon up any appetite. He'd made a start at replacing the books on the living-room shelves, but had given up after the first few minutes. Even the Birdsong channel had begun to annoy him, and he'd switched the radio off. As night fell, his lights remained off, too. There was a car parked across the street, but it was just a parent picking up her son from a friend's house. The same thing had happened before, so he decided he could dismiss it. Then again ... He tried to recall if any of the houses nearby had come on the market recently. Had any 'To Let' signs come and gone? Could a surveillance team be sitting in its own darkened living room, surrounded by the same equipment he'd been shown at Tulliallan?

'Don't be so bloody stupid,' he admonished himself.

Making a mug of tea in the unlit kitchen, he poured in too much milk, and ended up tipping the drink down the sink. Drink ... now there was a thing. The supermarket was open late. He could almost recite from memory the bottles in its malt whisky display: Bowmore, Talisker, Highland Park ... Macallan, Glenmorangie, Glenlivet ... Laphroaig, Lagavulin, Glenfiddich ...

At half past eight, his phone gave a momentary chirrup. He stared at it. Not a call, but a text. He tried to focus on the screen.

Hunters Tryst 10 mins.

Hunters Tryst was a pub nearby. Fox checked the texter's identity: Anonymous Caller. Only a handful of people had his new number. The pub was a ten-minute walk, but there was parking. Then again, it might be good to arrive early: reconnaissance and all that. And why was he going anyway?

Well, what else was he going to do?

But when he eventually headed out to the Volvo, he looked up and down the street, then, once in the car, made a circuit of his estate, slowing at every corner and junction, until he was confident no one was following.

A week night in February: the Tryst was quiet. He walked in and took a good look around. Three drinkers in the whole place: a middle-aged couple who looked as if they'd fallen out a decade before, each still waiting for the other to offer the first apology; and an elderly man whose face was known to Fox. The guy had owned a dog, used to walk it three times a day. When he'd stopped being visible, Fox had assumed he'd croaked, but now it looked as if the dog had been the victim rather than its master. There was a young woman behind the bar. She managed a smile for Fox and asked him what he was having.

'Tomato juice,' he said. His eyes lingered on the row of optics as she shook the bottle and prised off its top.

'Ice?'

'No thanks.'

'It's a bit warm,' she warned him.

'It'll be fine.' He was reaching into his pocket for some coins when the door opened again. The couple who entered had their arms around one another's waist. The middle-aged couple gave a disapproving look.

'Look who's here,' the male half of this new couple said. Breck held out his hand for Fox to shake.

'This is a coincidence,' Annabel Cartwright added. She wasn't much of an actress, but then maybe she thought the charade unnecessary.

'What are you having?' Fox asked.

'Red wine for me, white for Annabel,' Breck said. The barmaid had perked up at the arrival of customers with a bit of life to them. She poured what seemed to Fox's eye generous measures.

'Let's grab a table,' Breck said, as though chairs were at a premium. They headed for the furthest corner, and got themselves settled, removing coats and jackets. 'Cheers,' Breck said, chinking glasses.

'How was it?' Fox asked him without preamble.

Breck knew what he was referring to and pretended to give it some thought. 'DI Stoddart's a piece of work,' he told Fox, keeping his voice low, 'but I didn't think much of those two blokes she's saddled with – and I don't think she reckons them much cop either ... if you'll pardon the pun.'

Fox nodded and took a sip of his drink. The barmaid had been right: it was like soup that had been left to cool for a few minutes. 'What's with the text?' he asked. 'You changed your number?'

'New phone,' Breck explained, waving the handset in his face. 'Rental, believe it or not. Visitors from the States and suchlike use them all the time. I'd no idea till I started looking ...'

'What he means is, he asked me and *I* told him.' Annabel Cartwright gave Breck's arm a playful punch.

'So what's with the pow-wow?' Fox asked.

'Again, that was Annabel's idea,' Breck said.

She looked at him. 'I wouldn't go that far ...'

Breck turned to face her. 'Maybe not, but you're the one with the news.'

'What news?' Fox asked.

Cartwright looked from Fox to Breck and back again. 'I could get in so much trouble for this.'

'That's true,' Fox said. Then, to Breck: 'So why don't *you* tell me, Jamie? That way, we can say hand on heart that the only person Annabel told was her boyfriend.'

Breck thought for a moment and then nodded. He asked Cartwright if she wanted to leave them to it, but she shook her head and said she'd just sit there and finish her drink. Breck leaned a little further over the table, elbows resting either side of his glass.

'To start with,' he said, 'there's new information on Vince. Another cab-driver's come forward. This one had been waiting for fares outside the Oliver. He reckons he picked Vince up around one in the morning.'

'He's sure it was Vince?'

Breck nodded. 'The team showed him photos. Plus, he ID'd Vince's clothes.'

'So where did he take him?'

'The Cowgate. Where else are you going to go if you want to keep drinking at that time of night?'

'It's a bit ...'

'Studenty?' Breck guessed. 'Trendy?'

But Fox had thought of something else. 'Isn't the Cowgate closed to traffic at night?'

'Driver knew all the little short cuts and side streets. Dropped him outside a club called Rondo – do you know it?'

'Do I look the type?'

Breck smiled. 'Annabel dragged me there once.' She jabbed him in the ribs by way of complaint and Breck squirmed a little. 'Live music in the back room, sticky carpets and plastic glasses in the front.'

'That's where he was headed?'

'Driver wasn't sure. But it was where he got out.'

'Meaning he was still alive in the small hours of Sunday morning?'

Breck nodded. 'So now the inquiry team's going to be doing a sweep of the Cowgate – must be about a dozen pubs and clubs; more if they widen the search to the Grassmarket. They're printing up flyers to hand out to the clubbing fraternity.'

'Doormen might remember him,' Fox mused. 'He probably wasn't typical of their clientele. Did the cabbie say what sort of state he was in?'

'Slurring his words and a bit agitated. Plus he didn't tip.'

'Why was he agitated?'

'Maybe he was wondering what was waiting for him back home,' Breck offered. 'Maybe he was just the type who gets that way after a skinful.'

'I'd like to listen to the interview with the cabbie ...'

'I could probably get you a transcript,' Cartwright offered.

Fox nodded his thanks. 'The first cab would have dropped him at the Oliver around ten – means he was in there three hours.'

'A fair amount of time,' Breck agreed.

'Well, it's progress, I suppose. Cheers, Annabel.'

Cartwright gave a shrug. 'Tell him the rest,' she commanded Breck.

'Well, this is just something Annabel picked up when she was talking to a colleague based at D Division ...'

'Meaning Leith and Charlie Brogan?' Fox guessed.

'The inquiry team's beginning to wonder why no body's been washed ashore. They're digging a bit deeper into the whys and wherefores.'

'And?'

'Brogan had recently sold a large chunk of his art collection.'

Fox nodded again. 'Worth about half a million.'

Annabel Cartwright took up the story. 'Nobody seems to know where that money is. And Joanna Broughton's not exactly being cooperative. She's got her lawyers setting up their wagons in a circle. She's also got Gordon Lovatt reminding everyone involved that it won't look good if we start harassing a "photogenic widow" – his very words.'

'Leith think the suicide was staged?'

'As Jamie says, they're definitely beginning to wonder.'

'Has any other cash gone AWOL?'

'Hard to know until the lawyers stop denying access. We'd need a judge to issue a warrant, and that means convincing him it's right and proper.'

'There's no way of knowing if any of Brogan's accounts or credit cards are still being used?' Fox didn't expect an answer. He lifted his glass, but paused with it halfway to his mouth. 'When I was in her flat, I saw the spaces on the wall where those paintings had been.'

'You've been to her house?' Cartwright asked.

'There wasn't any paperwork lying around, but then she had to fetch Brogan's diary from elsewhere. Must be a room he uses as an office.'

'He could always have siphoned some cash off from CBBJ,' Breck added. 'We've got specialist accountants for that kind of digging.'

'But there still needs to be a judge's signature,' Cartwright cautioned.

Fox shrugged. 'If Joanna Broughton's being obstructive,' he argued, 'I'd have thought that might be reason enough.'

'I'm sure they'll fight their corner,' Breck said, running his finger down the wine glass.

'Any more revelations?' Fox's eyes were on Annabel.

'No,' she said.

'I really do appreciate this.' Fox got to his feet. 'So much so that I'm going to buy you another drink.'

'This one's on us,' Breck said, but Fox was having none of it. When he placed the order, the barmaid smiled and nodded towards the table.

'Nice when you bump into friends, isn't it?'

'Yes,' Malcolm Fox replied. 'Yes, it really is.'

20

At midnight, he was standing at the foot of Blair Street, staring towards the illuminated doorway of Rondo. There was just the one doorman. They usually operated in pairs, so the partner was either inside or on a break of some kind. The street was almost deserted, but wouldn't have been at the same sort of time on a Saturday. Plus the Welsh rugby fans had been in town the night Vince died, gearing up for Sunday's encounter – some of them would have known that the Cowgate was the late-licence district.

Fox stood at the corner, hands in pockets. This was where Vince had been dropped. Access to the main thoroughfare was curtailed between ten at night and five in the morning. Fox knew that this was because the Cowgate boasted narrow pavements. Drunks kept stumbling from them into the path of oncoming traffic. Cars had been banned because people were stupid. But then no one surely would pass this way sober at dead of night. It was a dark, dank conduit. There were homeless hostels and rubbish-strewn alleys. The place reeked of rat piss and puke. But there were plenty of little oases like Rondo. Lit by neon and radiating warmth (thanks to the heaters above their doors), they coaxed the unwary inside. As Fox crossed to the other side of the road, the doorman sized him up, loosening his shoulders under his three-quarter-length black woollen coat.

'Evening, Mr Fox,' the man said. Fox stared at him. There was a smile playing at the edges of the mouth. Stubble on the scarred chin. Shaven head and piercing blue eyes.

'Pete Scott,' the man eventually said, having decided that Fox needed help.

'You've shaved your hair off,' Fox replied.

Scott ran a hand over his head. 'I was beginning to lose it anyway. Long time no see.' He held out a hand for Fox to shake.

'How long have you been out, Pete?' Fox remembered Scott now. Six years ago, in his pre-Complaints life, he'd helped put him away. Housebreaking, a string of convictions stretching back to adolescence.

'Almost two years.'

'You served four?'

'Took me a while to see the error of my ways.'

'You battered someone?'

'Another con.'

'But you're doing okay now?'

Scott shuffled his feet and made show of looking up and down the street. There was a Bluetooth connected to his left ear. 'Keeping out of trouble,' he eventually offered.

'You've a good memory for names and faces.'

Scott just nodded at this. 'You having a night out?' he asked.

'Working,' Fox corrected him. 'There was a murder the weekend before last.'

'They've been round already.' Scott reached into his coat and pulled out a sheet of paper. Fox unfolded it and saw that it was a head-and-shoulders photo of Vince Faulkner, with a few salient details and a phone number. 'They've left them on the tables inside, with another stack on the bar. Won't do any good.'

Fox handed back the sheet. 'Why do you say that?'

'Guy didn't come in here. I was on the door that Saturday. I'd have known about it.'

'Did you see him get out of the cab?'

'Might've done – taxis drop people off all the time.'

'You saw somebody like him?'

Scott just shrugged. The scrawny nineteen-year-old Fox had interviewed had bulked up, but the eyes had definitely softened.

'There was a guy wandered off in that direction.' Scott was nodding towards the east. 'Wasn't too steady on his pins, so I was glad he hadn't tried coming in.'

'You'd have stopped him?'

Scott nodded. 'But there was just something about him ... don't ask me what. It made me think he'd have relished it.'

'Relished being turned away?'

'Yeah.'

'Why?'

'Because it would have given him every excuse.'

'For a fight, you mean?'

'The guy was wound tight, Mr Fox. I think that's what I'm trying to get at.'

'Did you tell this to the other cops, Pete?' Fox watched Scott shake his head. 'Why not?'

'They never thought to ask.' Scott was distracted by the arrival of two teenage girls. They wore teetering high heels, miniskirts and plenty of perfume. One was tall and skinny, the other short and plump. Fox could sense that they were cold but trying not to show it.

'Hiya, Pete,' the shorter one said. 'Any talent in tonight?'

'Plenty.'

'That's what you always say.' She patted his cheek as he held open the door.

'The job has its compensations, Mr Fox,' Pete Scott told the detective.

As he walked eastwards along the Cowgate, Fox wondered just how invisible he'd become. Neither girl had paid him the slightest attention. On the other hand, it was good that Scott didn't hold a grudge. Good, too, that he was holding down a job – any kind of a job. Before Fox had left, the young man had confessed that he was now the father of an eighteen-month-old daughter called Chloe. He was still seeing Chloe's mum but living together hadn't worked out. Fox had nodded and the two had shaken hands again. The meeting had made Fox feel better, though he couldn't say exactly why.

He knew that if he kept walking, he'd come to the St Mary's Street junction. Past that and he'd soon be at Dynamic Earth and the Scottish Parliament. He was coming to the end of the short strip of bars and clubs. There were shops, but with their windows empty or boarded up. The city mortuary was along here, but he'd no desire to pay a visit. He assumed Vince's body would still be in the fridge there. Across the road, a church had decided that the best way to raise funds was to build a hotel in its grounds. The hotel seemed to be doing reasonable business; Fox wasn't sure if the church could say the same thing. He decided to turn and retrace his route. There were too many paths Vince could have taken: narrow lanes and flights of steps. He could have headed towards Chambers Street or the Royal Mile. For all Fox knew, he could have checked into the hotel and slept things off. He was trying to see the area's attraction for Vince. Yes, it was full of bars, but then so was Lothian Road. Vince would have paid good money to have a cab bring him here from Leith. On the way, he would have passed dozens of places still open at that hour. He had to have had a destination in mind. Maybe Fox could talk to the cabbie; maybe Annabel would find out the man's details for him.

'Maybe,' he muttered to himself.

The temperature was dipping still further. He had pulled up the collar of his coat, trying to protect his ears. There was a chip shop at the Grassmarket, but that suddenly seemed like a long haul. Besides, would it still be open? The curfew was in place, meaning all traffic had ceased. His own car was parked near the top of Blair Street. Five more minutes and he would be snug – there was nothing for him here.

But then he saw another neon light. This one was down a narrow alley – a dead end, in fact. He hadn't spotted it before, but now that he looked there was a sign on the brick wall, pointing towards the lit doorway. Just one word above the sign's arrow – SAUNA. He wondered if any of the team had got round to leafleting this particular business. He took a couple of steps deeper into the alley so he could better see the door. It was solid wood, painted gloss black, with a tarnished brass handle and an assortment of graffiti tags. There was a video intercom off to one side. Edinburgh's sex industry liked to keep itself to itself, which was fine by the police.

Fox was readying to turn and head back to the car when a massive force detonated between his shoulders, sending him flying. His face hit the ground. He'd had just enough time to half turn his head, so that his nose escaped the worst of the impact. The weight bore down on him – someone was kneeling on his back, punching the air out of his lungs. Dazed, Fox tried to wrestle free, but a foot had connected with his chin. A black shoe, nothing fancy or memorable about it. It snapped his head back and he felt himself spiralling into the dark ...

When his eyes blinked open, the shoe was back. It was jabbing at his side. He lashed out a hand to grab it.

'Wake up,' a voice was saying. 'You can't sleep here.'

Fox clambered to his knees and then his feet. His spine ached. So did his neck and his jaw. The man standing in front of him was old, and Fox thought for a second that he knew him.

'Too much to drink,' the man was saying. He'd taken a step away from Fox. Fox was checking himself for damage. There was no blood, and no teeth seemed to have been dislodged.

'What happened?' he asked.

'You'd be better going home to your bed.'

'I'm not drunk – I don't drink.'

'Are you ill, then?'

Fox was trying to blink away the pain. The world sounded off-kilter, and he realised it was the blood surging in his ears. His vision was blurred.

'Did you see him?' he asked.

'Who?'

'Pushed me to the ground and swung a kick at me ...' He rubbed his jaw again.

'Did they take anything?'

Fox checked his pockets. When he shook his head, he felt like he might throw up.

'It's a bad part of town.'

Fox tried to focus on the man. He had to be in his seventies – cropped silver hair, liver-spotted skin ... 'You're Jack Broughton.'

The man's eyes narrowed. 'Do I know you?'

'No.'

Broughton stuffed his hands into his pockets and moved in until his face was a few inches from Fox's. 'Best keep it that way,' he said. Then he turned to leave. 'You might want to get yourself checked out,' was his parting nugget of advice.

Fox rested for a moment, then shuffled back towards the main road. He angled his watch towards a street lamp. Twelve forty. Could only have been out cold for a matter of minutes. He held on to some of the buildings for support as he made his way back along to Rondo. His back felt like fire whenever he inhaled. Pete Scott saw him coming and stiffened his stance, mistaking him for trouble. Fox held up a hand in greeting and Scott moved towards him.

'Did you trip or something?' he asked.

'Have you seen anybody, Pete? Had to be a big guy ...'

'There've been a few,' Scott conceded.

'In the time since I saw you?'

Scott nodded. 'Some of them are inside.'

Fox gestured towards the door. 'I'm going to take a look,' he said.

'Be my guest ...'

The bar was rammed, with a sound system that could loosen fillings. The queue was three deep for drinks. Young men in short-sleeved shirts; women sipping cocktails through dayglo straws. Fox's head took a fresh pummelling from the bass speakers as he squeezed his way through. In the back room, the stage was lit but no band was playing. More drinkers, more noise and strobing. Fox didn't recognise anyone. He found the gents' toilets and headed inside, gaining some respite from the din. There were paper towels strewn across the floor and none at all in the dispenser. He ran water over his hands and dabbed at his face, staring at his reflection in the smeared mirror. His chin was grazed and his cheek had swollen. The bruising would come soon enough. His palms stung where they'd connected with the ground, and one of his lapels had been ripped at the seam. He took off his coat and checked it for evidence of the force that had hurled itself at him, but there was nothing.

His attacker hadn't taken anything – credit cards, cash, both mobile phones, all accounted for. And once he was unconscious, it didn't appear as if they'd continued the beating. He took a good look at his teeth and then manipulated his jaw with his hand.

'You're okay,' he told his reflection. Then he noticed that one button was missing from his waistband. It would need replacing, or his braces wouldn't sit right. He took a few deep breaths, ran the water over his hands again and dried himself off with his handkerchief. One of the drinkers from the bar came weaving in, paying him almost no attention as he headed for a urinal. Fox put his coat back on and left. Outside, he nodded towards the doorman. Pete Scott was busy talking to the same two women as before. They'd stepped out for a cigarette and were complaining about the lack of 'hunks'. If Fox had been invisible to them before, he seemed more so now. Scott asked him if he was really okay, and Fox just nodded again, heading across the road to where his car waited. Someone had left the remains of a kebab on the Volvo's bonnet. He gave it a swipe on to the roadway, unlocked the doors and got in.

The journey home was slow, the lights against him at every junction. Taxis were touting for business, but most people seemed content to walk. Fox tuned his radio to Classic FM and decided that Jack Broughton had not recognised him. Why should he have? They had met for approximately ten seconds at the triplex penthouse. Broughton hadn't known until some minutes later that the man waiting for the lift was a cop. Could Broughton himself have been the attacker? Doubtful – and why would he have hung around? Besides, his shoes had been brown brogues; not at all the same as the one Fox had watched connect with his chin.

Pete Scott on the other hand ... Pete's shoes had been black Doc Martens, and Pete was strong enough ... But Fox didn't think so. Would Pete have deserted his post for a spot of small-minded revenge? Well, maybe he would, but Fox had him down as a 'possible' rather than a 'probable'.

Once home he stripped off his clothes and stood under a hot shower, training the water on to his back for a good nine or ten minutes. It hurt when he tried towelling himself dry, and he was able to get a look at himself in the bathroom mirror – no visible damage. Maybe it would be different in the morning. Slowly, he pulled on a pair of pyjamas and went downstairs to the kitchen, finding an unopened bag of garden peas in the freezer compartment, wrapping a tea towel around it and holding it to his jaw while he boiled the kettle for tea. There was a box of aspirin in one of the drawers, and he swallowed three tablets with a glass of water from the tap.

It was nearly two o'clock by the time he settled himself at the table. After a few minutes of staring at the wall, he got up and went through to the dining room. His computer sat on a desk in the corner. He got it working and started a search of three names: Joanna Broughton, Charlie Brogan and Jack Broughton. There wasn't much on the last of these – his heyday had been before the advent of the internet and the twenty-four-hour news cycle. Fox hadn't thought to ask him what he was doing in the Cowgate at that time of night. But then Jack Broughton was no ordinary seventy-one-year-old. Probably he still fancied his chances against the majority of the drunks and chancers.

Fox couldn't get properly comfortable. If he leaned forward, he ached; if he leaned back, the pain was greater. He was grateful for the lack of alcohol in the house – it stopped him reaching for that quickest of fixes. Instead, he held the bag of peas to his face and concentrated on Charlie Brogan, finding several interviews culled from magazines and the business pages of newspapers. One journalist had asked Brogan why he'd become a property developer.

You're creating monuments, Brogan had replied. *You're making a mark that's going to outlast you.*

And that's important to you?

Everybody wants to change the world, don't they? And yet most of us, all we leave behind is an obituary and maybe a few kids.

You want people to remember you?

I'd rather they noticed me while I'm here! I'm in the business of making an impression.

Fox wondered to himself: an impression on who? Joanna Broughton? Or her successful dad, maybe? Didn't men always want to prove themselves to their in-laws? Fox recalled that he'd been nervous when he'd met Elaine's parents, even though he'd known them when he was a school-kid. He'd been to birthday parties at their house. But flash forward two decades and he was greeting them as their daughter's boyfriend.

'Elaine tells us you're in the police,' the mother had said. 'I'd no idea you were that way inclined ...' The tone of voice said it all: our lovely, talented daughter could have done so much better. So much better ...

Fox could well imagine Brogan's first encounter with Pa Broughton. Both sons were dead, meaning there was a lot for Joanna to prove. She'd left it late to get married. Fox reckoned her doting and protective father would have chased off many a previous suitor. But Charlie Brogan knew what he wanted – he wanted Joanna. She was glamorous and her family had money. More than that, her father had about him the whiff of power. When you got hitched to the daughter, you kept her father's name in your pocket like a number for the emergency services. Anybody tried to turn you over, the name would be dropped into the conversation.

Not that Fox could imagine Jack Broughton liking that.

So when CBBJ started hitting the skids, there was no insurance policy. Maybe Brogan had approached the old boy on the quiet – *definitely* wouldn't want Joanna knowing about it – but if he had, he'd given Jack the perfect opportunity to tell his son-in-law just how useless he'd always reckoned him. *You say you lost all your money in the downturn? Well, Charlie, I didn't know you were that way inclined.*

And by the way, my lovely talented daughter could have done so much better.

'Poor sod,' Fox said to himself.

Half an hour later, he was done with the three of them. He found a link to Quidnunc but couldn't enter the game without the relevant software. Instead, he stared at the website's home page with its colourful graphics. Some sort of monster was being dispatched by half a dozen muscle-men.

'The Warrior Is In You' ran the strapline. Fox thought of Jamie Breck. He hadn't been much of a warrior in Billy Giles's office. Breck: losing himself in this fiction while a real life with Annabel was kept on pause. Fox wondered what sort of role he himself had played throughout his life. Had he used alcohol the same way Breck used the online game – sinking into a virtual world as an escape from the real thing? He wondered, too, whether he really *did* trust

Jamie Breck. He thought he did, but then again, Breck had said it himself: *does it just mean I'm your very last hope?* Failing to come up with an answer, he set the computer to 'sleep' mode and headed for bed. He lay on his side, the only way he could rest without pain. The curtains were illuminated by the sodium glare of a street lamp. The peas were defrosting in their bag. Birdsong was playing on the radio ...

Wednesday 18 February 2009

21

At seven next morning, his mobile phone – his old one, rather than the pay-and-go – chirruped to let him know he had a message. It was from DI Caroline Stoddart. She wanted him at Fettes at nine for another interview. Fox texted back: unwell, sorry – can we postpone?

Did 'unwell' cover it, though? He'd had colds and flu and earache and migraines, but never anything like this. Had he just gone three rounds with a grizzly bear? It took him over a minute to cross from his bed to the bathroom. Face nicely swollen and chin scabbed over but stinging when touched. And from what he could see of his back, bruising either side of his spine in the perfectly legible shape of two human paws. After twenty minutes in the shower, he found another text waiting for him in the bedroom. It was from Stoddart.

Tomorrow then, it said.

Fox decided he would stay at home the rest of the day. He had milk and bread, enough food to see him through. By nine he was lying along the sofa nursing his second mug of coffee and with the BBC's news channel on the television. When his doorbell sounded, he considered not answering. Maybe it was Stoddart, checking his story. But curiosity got the better of him and he crossed to the window. Jamie Breck had taken a couple of steps back from the door and was staring straight at him. He lifted a grocery bag and gave a smile. Fox went to let him in.

'I got croissants from the supermarket,' Breck was saying. But then he got his first close-up of Fox's damaged face. 'Christ! What happened to you?'

Fox led the way back into the house. He was still in his pyjamas with his dressing gown wrapped around him. 'Somebody jumped me,' he explained.

'Last night? Between Hunters Tryst and here?' Breck sounded incredulous.

'The Cowgate,' Fox corrected him. He'd switched the kettle on and found a clean mug for his visitor. 'Coffee or tea?' he asked.

'Because Vince took a taxi there?' Breck was nodding to himself. 'After Hunters Tryst you headed down for a recce? So who was it gave you the doing?'

'They came at me from behind; I didn't see anything. But when I woke up, Jack Broughton was standing over me.'

'Say that again.'

'You heard the first time. Tea or coffee?'

'Tea's fine. What was Jack Broughton doing there?'

'He didn't say.'

'Was he the one who ...?'

'I don't think so.' The two men stood in silence for a minute or so as the kettle came to the boil. When the tea was made, they headed through to the living room. Fox brought a plate for each of them, and they shared the croissants. Breck sat on the very edge of his chair, leaning well forward.

'I just thought we'd have a quiet breakfast.'

'We still can.'

'You doing a spot of spring-cleaning?' Breck gestured towards the piles of books.

'Anything takes your fancy, it's yours.' Fox lifted his plate from the table, trying not to hiss in pain as he stretched. 'Something I wanted to ask you ...' He bit into the croissant.

'Fire away.'

'Why don't you want Annabel to know?'

Breck chewed thoughtfully, then swallowed. 'You mean about SEIL Ents and my credit card? I'm still weighing up the pros and cons.'

'If she finds out the hard way, she's not going to be too happy,' Fox said. 'And we really need her on our team ...'

'So you're not just thinking of my best interests?'

'Perish the thought.'

Breck picked crumbs from the knees of his trousers. 'She keeps asking, though, why I've not gone to the Federation to ask them for a lawyer.'

'It's a fair question – why haven't you?'

Breck decided not to answer. Instead, he had a question of his own. 'What in God's name did you hope to find in the Cowgate?'

'Torphichen had been along, handing out flyers.'

'So at least you know they're doing their job. Where were you when you got thumped?'

'There's an alley with a sauna down it ...' Fox noticed the change in Jamie Breck's face. 'You know it?' he guessed.

'There's a sign, just says "Sauna"? Narrow little lane?'

'Spit it out.'

But Breck needed some tea first. He placed his plate on top of some of the books on the coffee table, half the croissant still untouched. 'I went there once with Glen Heaton,' he admitted.

'What?'

'Not inside,' Breck quickly corrected himself. 'We'd been out to Jock's Lodge ... talking to a witness. On the way back, Heaton said to take the route through the Cowgate. Then he sent a text, and told me to pull up when we reached that lane. He got out of the car and a woman came out of the building. She was wearing a raincoat, but I got the feeling there wasn't a whole lot underneath. The two of them did some talking. At the end, she pecked him on the cheek. I think he might even have given her some money.' Breck's face was creased in concentration. 'She was tiny – had to stand on tiptoe to reach his face. Younger than him; maybe late twenties. Anyway, she headed back indoors and he got into the car.' He gave a shrug.

'Did he tell you her name?'

'No. I asked him what it was all about and he just winked and hinted that she was a contact of some kind.'

'An informer?'

Breck gave another shrug. 'There were things I knew it was best not to ask. Glen had a way of letting you know ...'

'How long ago was this?'

'Last autumn.'

Fox thought for a moment. 'She was tiny, you say?'

'Under five foot.'

'Curly blonde hair?' Breck stared at him, and Fox decided to explain. 'We had Heaton under surveillance for months – checked his e-mails, taped his phone calls, followed him. There was a woman he was seeing behind his wife's back. Worked as a lap-dancer on Lothian Road. Little slip of a thing called ...' But Fox couldn't summon up her name.

'Looks like she's holding down two jobs,' Breck commented. Then, fixing Fox with a stare: 'You don't think ...?'

It was Fox's turn to shrug. 'Whoever it was, they just wanted to dole out a bit of punishment – not a huge amount; just enough.'

'Glen Heaton would have motive,' Breck agreed. Fox was already punching Tony Kaye's number into his phone.

'Wondered when I'd be hearing from you,' were Kaye's answering words. 'Give me a sec, will you?'

Fox listened as Kaye got up from behind his desk and moved into the corridor. 'Can I assume Gilchrist's hard at work?'

'McEwan's got him busy on a few bits and pieces,' Kaye acknowledged. 'I'm assuming this is purely a social call?'

'I need you to look something up for me, Tony – might mean a trip to the Fiscal's office, if they're the ones with the paperwork.'

'Or I could just call them …'

'Fewer people in the know, the better I'll like it,' Fox countered.

'Fair enough – so what do you need?'

'Info on Glen Heaton's squeeze.'

'The lap-dancer?'

'Do you recall her name?'

'We never bothered interviewing her. She was going to be leverage, remember? If we needed Heaton to 'fess up.'

'Just get me what you can, Tony.'

'Mind telling me why?'

'Later.' Fox ended the call and made to tap the phone against his chin, before remembering that it would sting.

'What was Jack Broughton doing there?' Breck was asking himself.

'Customer maybe – his wife's dead and the old bastard's probably still got some juice.' Fox paused. 'Or could he be the proprietor?'

'A pimp, you mean?'

Fox shook his head. 'Might own the building, though … maybe he's the landlord or leaseholder.' He looked at Breck. 'Could Annabel do some digging?'

'Under what pretext?'

'The inquiry team's not finished with the Cowgate – she could be looking for background …'

Breck puffed his cheeks and expelled some air. 'I suppose so,' he said. 'You want me to call her?' He had his own phone in his hand.

'Why not?' Malcolm Fox said.

Breck started to make the call. 'I'm just wondering …'

'What?'

'Now that I think about it, why did Heaton do that? Why take me with him when he went to see his bit on the side?'

'He was showing off,' Fox decided. 'Pure and simple.'

Breck considered this, then nodded. His call had been picked up. 'Hey, Annabel,' he said, his face breaking into a smile. 'You'll never guess what I'm after ...'

By mid-afternoon, Fox knew several things.

Courtesy of Tony Kaye, he now knew that the lap-dancer's name was Sonya Michie and that she lived in a block of flats in Sighthill. She was a single mum with two kids at the local primary school. There was no mention in her file of any employment in a sauna, and she had no arrests to her name.

The information from Annabel Cartwright was more intriguing still. The building in which the sauna was housed was owned by a Dundee-based company called Wauchope Leisure Holdings Limited. Wauchope Leisure owned all sorts of interesting properties in the city, mostly saunas and strip clubs. The list happened to include the lap-dancing bar where Sonya Michie worked. Cartwright had sourced the register of directors, including a certain J. Broughton. Just to be on the safe side, Jamie Breck had asked her to verify the first name. A further hour later had come confirmation: John Edward Alan Broughton.

'Better known as Jack,' Fox had commented.

'So at least he had a reason to be there,' Breck had added. 'Business rather than pleasure, I mean.'

'At that time of night?'

But Cartwright hadn't been finished. Wauchope got its name from Bruce Wauchope, who was currently serving fifteen years at Her Majesty's Pleasure for his role in a drug-smuggling scheme in the north-east.

'Fishing boats working out of the likes of Aberdeen,' she explained. She'd arrived at Fox's house with a sheaf of photocopied pages – mostly newspaper articles about Wauchope, but also the transcript of the interview with the cabbie who'd dropped Vince off at the Cowgate. It hadn't added much.

Took him the best part of a minute to decide he was getting out, the cab-driver stated. *I thought he was going to change his mind ...*

Cartwright had been offered a drink and decided on water. Breck had given her a kiss. Her cheeks were flushed, and she appeared energised by completion of her tasks. She had noted Fox's injuries but hadn't asked anything, knowing she'd be told if necessary. Nor had she mentioned the piles of books, which had been lifted from the coffee table and now sat on the floor, threatening to fall over at any moment.

'Nobody noticed what you were up to?' Fox thought to check, receiving a shake of the head in answer.

'The trawlers would meet with other boats out in the North Sea,' she explained between sips of water. 'The drugs would come ashore, finding a ready market with fishermen and oil workers ...'

Fox was studying a grainy photograph of a scowling Bruce Wauchope. The man would be in his early fifties.

'He looks like a right thug,' Jamie Breck offered.

'Wait till you see his son.' Cartwright sifted through the paperwork. The photo she found was small, and accompanied a news report from Bruce Wauchope's trial. 'His name's Bruce, too – Bruce Junior, I suppose – but he goes by the nickname "Bull".'

Fox and Breck studied the article while Cartwright added a few details.

'He's got a fierce reputation in Dundee. Kicked out of half a dozen schools by the time he was fifteen. Ran a local gang. No doubt made his dad proud of him. With Wauchope Senior out of action, Bull's the one in charge.'

'In charge of what exactly?'

'For that, I'd probably need to chat up Tayside CID – either of you got a contact there?'

'I might know someone,' Breck admitted.

'Does Wauchope own anything else in Edinburgh?' Fox asked, still intent on his reading.

'Again, that would need a bit more work.' Cartwright paused. 'Why is it so important?' The question had been asked of Breck, but he fixed his attention on Fox, who could only shrug. The room remained quiet as Fox continued to pore over the photocopies. Breck had walked over to the window.

'I don't see your car,' he commented.

'I left it round the corner,' Cartwright explained. 'Didn't want anyone seeing it here.'

'Probably wise.' Fox glanced up from his reading.

She was checking her watch. 'I've got to get back. Doesn't normally take me this long to buy a sandwich.'

'Thanks for all this,' Fox said.

'I just hope it helps.' She slung her bag over her shoulder. Jamie had already left the room and opened the front door for her. Fox couldn't make out what was said, but he heard a final wet-sounding kiss before the door closed. Breck came back into the room and watched her from the window.

'She's too good for you,' Fox told him.

'Don't I know it.' Breck turned and came back to his chair.

'She'd stand by you, I'm sure of it,' Fox went on. 'If you told her, I mean. She wouldn't believe any of it.'

'I'll do it in my own time, if that's all right with you, Inspector.' Fox took the hint and held up his hands in surrender. Breck rubbed his own hands together.

'So,' he said, perching himself on the arm of the chair, 'what have we got exactly?'

'Your guess is as good as mine.' Fox paused. 'Have you contacted your credit card company about that debit?'

Breck stared at him. 'What makes you ask all of a sudden?'

'Just popped into my head.'

'I've been on to them. The payment to SEIL was an online transaction, so there's not much they can say.'

'Anyone with your card details could have done it?'

'As long as they knew the security number, plus maybe my address and postcode.'

'So we're not really any further forward?'

'I can't prove it wasn't me, if that's what you're suggesting.' Breck got to his feet again. 'Still got a nagging doubt, Malcolm?'

'No.'

'Try to sound a bit more convincing.'

Before he could answer, Fox's phone rang. It was Annie Inglis. 'Hey, Annie,' Fox said, 'what can I do for you?'

'Nothing really.'

Breck had gestured that he would leave the room. Without waiting, he was already on his way. Fox leaned back in his chair with the phone to his ear, then recoiled in pain. His back throbbed a fresh complaint.

'How are things at the Chop Shop?' he asked through gritted teeth. 'Have they given you a replacement for Gilchrist yet?'

'Still working solo.'

'That can't be good.'

'It's not.'

'How's Duncan?'

'He's fine. How about you, Malcolm?'

'I've got my feet up.'

'Really?'

'Well, sort of.' He listened to her laugh.

'How soon will you be back at work?'

'That's up to Grampian.'

'I've met DI Stoddart. She seems very ... efficient.'

'Was she asking you about me?'

'Just in passing.'

'I was supposed to come in today for another session on the rack.'

'So she said.'

'I told her I was ill.'

'But you're all right really?'

'Actually, I've got a few aches and pains.'

'This time of year, who hasn't?'

'A bit more sympathy wouldn't go amiss.'

She laughed again. 'Do you want me to drop by after work? Bring you some grapes and Lucozade?'

Fox was touching his fingers to his bruised and battered face. 'It's a tempting offer, but no thanks.'

'Don't say I didn't ask.'

'I'll be fine in a few days, Annie. Listen, there's something I wanted to ask you. A while back, you warned me that the Australian police were getting ready to pounce on Simeon Latham. When I talked to Gilchrist about it, he said much the same.'

'Yes?'

'Well, the cop you put me on to in Melbourne seems to have other ideas.'

'You know I can't talk about this, Malcolm.' Inglis's voice had hardened.

'I'm just wondering who it is that's lying to me, Annie.' Breck had stuck his head round the door and was indicating that he was about to leave. Fox shook his head and listened as a beep in his ear told him Inglis had hung up. He snapped shut the device and waved Breck back into the room.

'DI Stoddart,' he said, 'has been pumping Annie Inglis for information.'

'She's thorough, if nothing else,' Breck commented.

Fox was thoughtful as he let his fingers drift across his swollen cheek. 'You shouldn't be part of this, Jamie. What you should be doing is clearing your name.'

'And how do I do that without them realising *you* must have tipped me off?' Breck shook his head slowly. 'Got to clear your name before I can clear mine – so what's next on the day's agenda?'

Fox looked at the front of his phone – three o'clock had come and gone. 'Lunch?' he suggested.

'Another supermarket run?' Breck guessed. Fox nodded, reaching into his pocket for money.

'My shout,' he said. 'You paid for breakfast ...'

Breck took the ten-pound note but stood his ground. 'And after?'

'Dundee's an option – but again, it's something I can do for myself.'

Breck pointed at Fox's face. 'I've seen the results of your solo efforts. So you won't mind if I tag along?'

After Breck had gone, Fox rose to his feet and walked to the window. He stared out at the street, his mind dazed. Then he went to the kitchen and helped himself to more painkillers. Annabel's glass was waiting to be washed. There was a pale smear of pink lipstick on the rim. Was her boyfriend too good to be true? Then again, was *she*? Could she be feeding titbits back to the inquiry? Handing Malcolm Fox to Billy Giles on the understanding that Giles would then go easy on her lover? The list of people Fox felt he could trust was short, its margins filled with ifs and buts and question marks.

Back at the coffee table, he picked up a sheaf of photocopied sheets – the transcript of the cabbie's interview. It struck him that Vince might have had good reason for hesitating before leaving the taxi. He'd been agitated. He had a location in mind but showed some reluctance. At Marooned he'd tried picking a fight, then at the bus stop there had been a second confrontation. The doormen at the Oliver shouldn't have let him in, but did. Why was that? Jamie Breck had said that Joanna Broughton didn't want the place getting a reputation, yet Vince Faulkner was allowed to drink himself into a near-stupor. Two to three hours he'd been there ... When Vince's body had been found, he'd had only a few notes and coins in his pockets. Had he gone to the Cowgate to borrow money, or because he'd suddenly come into some?

Sifting through all the material, it struck Fox that here was another huge favour Annabel Cartwright had done him, without even really knowing him. She was helping because he was Jamie's friend ...

'I trust *you*, Annabel,' he said to himself. Then, after a moment: 'Okay, maybe eighty per cent.'

He was back in the kitchen, pouring more tap water into his glass, when he realised his old mobile was ringing and headed through to the living room to find it. But whoever was calling gave up before he got there. Fox checked the number – another mobile – and called back.

'I just missed you,' he said when the phone was picked up at the other end.

'It's Max Dearborn.'

'How are things with you, Max?'

'Nose to the grindstone.'

'Any sign of the errant developer?'

'No.'

'But that's what he's become, right? Errant rather than deceased?'

'It's one possibility among many.'

'I can only think of five, Max. He's dead and it was an accident; or he topped himself; or someone took care of him.'

'That's three ...'

'And if he's alive, he either faked his suicide or someone else did it for him, meaning he's been snatched.'

'Wouldn't the wife have had a ransom note by now?'

'Maybe she's just not telling you, Max. From what I know of Joanna Broughton, she'd want to deal with something like that in her own way.'

'That's a point,' Dearborn conceded. 'Speaking of which, her PR man's on the warpath again.'

'I've not been near her ...'

'It's a reporter he's got in his sights.' Dearborn sounded tired. Fox reckoned he knew why he'd called – no hidden agenda, but rather the need to talk, to blow off a little steam, to gossip with someone outside the circle of wagons. Fox imagined Dearborn in a half-empty CID office, everyone flagging after the first few days of toil. Waiting for a break in the case, and made lethargic by too many sandwiches and chocolate bars. Maybe Dearborn had his chair pushed back, necktie undone, feet up on the desk ...

'What's the reporter done?'

'Not much. She's got hold of a rumour that Brogan was tied up in something.'

'Yes?'

'Trying to bribe a councillor. It's something to do with all these flats Brogan's been putting up. Suddenly nobody's buying. He was hoping the council might.'

'What would the council want with them?'

'Social housing – city's short a few thousand homes, or hadn't you noticed?'

'Sounds as if Brogan might have had the solution.'

'If the price was right ...'

'And how was a solitary councillor going to sugar the deal?'

'Helps if the councillor sits on the Housing Board.'

'Ah,' Fox said. Then, after a pause: 'I still don't see much that's wrong with it.'

'To be frank, me neither.'

'So who told you all this? Not Gordon Lovatt?'

'The reporter.'

'And why are you telling me?'

'Because you've got form when it comes to getting up people's noses. Next time you see Joanna Broughton or Gordon Lovatt, you might drop it into the conversation.'

'In the hope that they'll do what, exactly?'

'Maybe nothing ... maybe something.'

'Seems to me you owe this reporter a favour, but can't stick your own head above the parapet. Mine, on the other hand ...'

'It was just a thought. The reporter's name is Linda Dearborn, by the way.'

'That's quite a coincidence, Max.'

'It would be, if she wasn't my baby sister. Let me give you her number ...' He did so, and Fox jotted it down. He could hear another phone ringing somewhere in Max Dearborn's vicinity. 'Got to go.'

'Any news about Brogan, you'll let me know?' Fox reminded him. But Dearborn had already ended the call. Fox scratched his head and tried to order his thoughts. There was something he should have asked, so he sent Dearborn a text.

Name of councillor?

It was five minutes before he received a reply:

Ernie Wishaw.

Fox was still staring at the name when Breck returned with the food. Breck didn't appear to have noticed any change in him. He unloaded packets of sandwiches and crisps on to the coffee table, along with a couple of bottles of lemonade. He was halfway through asking Fox if he preferred prawn salad or ham and mustard when he broke off.

'Did someone die?' he asked.

Fox shook his head slowly. 'Your councillor ...'

'Which one?'

'With the lorry business.'

'What about him?' Breck's face showed puzzlement.

'He might connect to Charlie Brogan.'

Breck thought for a moment. 'Because of the casino?'

'There's a journalist looking to prove that Brogan was giving a backhander to Ernie Wishaw.'

Breck slowly unwrapped his sandwich, sliding it on to the same plate that had earlier held his croissant.

'Brogan,' Fox continued to explain, 'wanted to offload some of his white elephants on to the council. Wishaw was going to make sure the council didn't get too much of a bargain.'

Breck shrugged. 'Sounds feasible. Who's the journalist?'

'Max Dearborn's sister.'

'And who's Max Dearborn?'

'A DS at Leith. He's on the team investigating Brogan's little disappearing act.'

Breck looked at Fox. 'Not suicide?'

Fox just shrugged. 'If the reporter's right, you could get your hands on Ernie Wishaw after all.' Fox paused. 'If you were Brogan and you wanted to twist his arm, maybe you'd show him a good time first.'

'At the wife's casino?'

'Give him a pile of chips to play with ...'

'I'm not sure Wishaw's that gullible.'

'Depends on the deal Brogan was offering.'

Breck was still looking at him. There was a sandwich in his hand, but he'd forgotten about it. Prawns were falling loose and landing back on the plate. 'This is a rumour, right? So far, that's all it is?'

Fox shrugged again. He'd peeled open the ham sandwich, staring at the filling, but his appetite was gone. He reached for the lemonade instead. When he unscrewed it, it fizzed out of the neck and made a puddle around itself on the table. He got up and fetched a cloth from the kitchen. Breck still had to make a start on his own sandwich.

'Can't be many prawns left in there,' Fox warned him. Breck noticed what had happened and started replacing the prawns between the two triangles of brown bread.

'Linda Dearborn,' he said at last. 'That's her name?'

'You know her?' Fox asked, busy wiping up the spillage.

'I remember her now. When Wishaw's drug-running driver was arrested, she came sniffing around. I think her general argument was, Wishaw had to have known.'

'I seem to recall that was *your* general argument, too.'

Breck smiled at this. 'I only spoke to her that one time ...' His voice drifted off.

'Seems she's kept the councillor on her radar.'

'It does, doesn't it? Reckon she's worth talking to?'

'If we can keep our names out of the story. Problem is, if she gets a quote from us, we'd be her "unnamed police sources".'

'What's wrong with that?'

'Her brother's part of the Brogan inquiry.'

Breck nodded his understanding. 'Everyone would assume it was him.'

'So I doubt she'd let us stay "unnamed".'

'Then why did Dearborn tell you in the first place?'

'I think he wants me to take it to Joanna Broughton.'

'Why?'

'In the hope that she blows a fuse and maybe lets something slip.'

'That won't happen.'

'What about Ernie Wishaw?'

'He's hardly going to incriminate himself, is he?'

'You watched him for a while … where's he most vulnerable?'

'I'd have to think about that.'

'In the meantime, how about this – we tell him we'll forget about the bung he sent to the driver's wife, so long as he fills us in on the deal Charlie Brogan was offering.'

'Are you serious? We don't even have warrant cards.'

'You're right.' Silence filled the room for a few moments, until Jamie Breck broke it.

'You're going to do it anyway,' he stated.

'Probably,' Fox conceded.

'Why?'

'Because Brogan's the key to everything.'

'Are you sure of that?'

Fox thought for a second. 'No,' he decided. 'I'm not really sure of that at all.'

That evening, Fox found himself back at the Cowgate. He stayed in his car, watching passers-by, on the lookout for faces he knew. There were just the two: Annabel Cartwright and Billy Giles. Fox slid far down into his seat, even though it sent spasms of pain down his spine. Cartwright was first – talking to another member of the inquiry team. The man seemed to be following her orders. He had a fresh bunch of flyers with him. They moved along the street and he lost sight of them. Then, ten minutes later, it was the turn of Billy Giles, sauntering along as if he owned the place. He was chewing on a stubby cigar and had his hands stuffed deep into his pockets. The night was overcast and mild, with hardly any breeze. When Giles headed off in the same direction as Cartwright and her colleague, Fox pushed himself back up out of his hiding place. Three quarters of an hour later, a car drove past – the driver had picked up all three detectives. Giles was talking animatedly, gesturing with his arms, the others listening tiredly. Fox waited a further thirty minutes, then got out of his own car and locked it. Pete Scott was not on duty outside Rondo. There were two doormen tonight, one black and one white. They paid Fox not the slightest attention. One of them was showing the other something amusing on the screen of his phone.

'That's terrible!' Fox heard one of them say, but in a tone that suggested the opposite. He kept walking. It wasn't even ten o'clock, and he didn't know why he was bothering. If he'd wanted to do this right – a re-enactment scenario – he would have come here after midnight. The lane was deserted. The neon sign still said SAUNA. Fox studied the territory around him and decided he was safe from attack. Nevertheless, he kept his head half turned as he walked down the alley, stopping at the door. He pressed the buzzer and stared into the camera lens. When nothing happened, he pressed again. He couldn't hear anything from inside. There was no glass; nothing but the glinting eye of the camera. He waved his fingers in front of it, leaned down close to it, even gave it an exploratory tap. Then he tried the door handle, but it wouldn't budge. He bunched up a fist and rapped three times, then three more. Still nothing.

Eventually he turned to go, pausing next to where he'd lain unconscious not twenty-four hours before. He crouched down and lifted a circular object from the ground. It was the missing button from his trouser waistband. He pocketed it, got back to his feet and headed for home.

There was a detour to take first, however, and it was a long one. In daylight, the A198 out of the city was a meandering coastal road with eye-catching views. Fox remembered that it had been a weekend favourite with his ex-wife. They would stop at Aberlady for lunch, or Gullane for a stroll along the edges of the golf course. There were car parks leading to the seashore, and for the adventurous there was the mass of Berwick Law to climb. Tantallon Castle, just the other side of North Berwick, was as far as they ever got before heading across country. There might be a bacon roll at the Museum of Flight or fish and chips in Haddington. But

North Berwick was Elaine's favourite. She would peer through one of the Sea Life Centre's telescopes or wander along the beach, coaxing him to catch up with her (he was always the ambler, she the strider). North Berwick was Fox's destination tonight. He knew the route, but took it slowly: the road was twisty and unpredictable. Cars sped past him, their modified exhausts roaring, the drivers overtaking on blind bends and flashing their lights. These drivers were young, the other seats crammed with whooping friends. Maybe they were from the city, but Fox thought them more likely to be locals. This time of night, what else was there to do in East Lothian?

When he reached North Berwick, he headed for a particular narrow street not far from the shore. There was a house there he'd parked outside before, though never in his own car. The house was single-storey, but had been extended into the roof space, a balcony allowing views towards several islands and outcrops – Fidra, Craigleith, Bass Rock – not that any were visible tonight. The wind had risen, but the temperature remained a few degrees the right side of zero. Elaine had always wanted to live on the coast. Fox's objection had been purely selfish: he hadn't fancied the commute. But that same commute did not seem to worry Glen Heaton. Heaton had lived in this town for eight years. The Complaints had looked into his purchase of the house. These days it was probably worth half a million plus. No way should he have been able to afford it, a point put to him more than once during their several interviews. Heaton had told them to look at the paperwork.

'Nothing dodgy,' he'd stated.

And: 'You lot are just jealous.'

And: 'It eats you up that someone's done better than you.'

This was the house where Fox parked now, turning off his engine in the realisation that an idling motor might cause curtains to twitch. The next house along was a bed and breakfast, its front garden converted into a driveway where three cars sat. This time of year, Fox doubted any of them belonged to tourists. Heaton's own car – an Alfa – would be stowed in its garage to the rear of the property. The car was two years old and had cost its owner just under twenty grand. Heaton had spent almost the same amount on holidays in the twelve months leading up to the conclusion of the inquiry – jaunts to Barbados, Miami and the Seychelles. One of those trips, he and his wife had opted for business class, while the others had been economy plus. Four- and five-star resort hotels waiting for them. Sadly, the Complaints' budget had not stretched to surveillance of these breaks. On the drive here tonight, Fox had caught some news headlines on his radio. Questions were being asked about MPs' allowances. It wasn't that anyone was being corrupt, apparently, but they were playing the system for all it was worth. Fox reckoned this tied in to the furore about bankers' bonuses and pensions. People wanted to scream that it was unfair, but, there being little they could do about it, attention had turned to politicians with their snouts in the trough instead.

Just jealous ...

Heaton's accusation had rankled because it was accurate. Tony Kaye in particular had seethed and spat as he listed the outgoings and purchases.

'How's he doing it on his salary?' he kept asking anyone who would listen. The answer was: he wasn't. Many of the transactions were paid in cash, and Heaton couldn't explain why. Fox stared at the house and imagined Glen Heaton in bed with his wife. Then he considered the son she didn't yet know about – not unless Heaton had confessed. The son was eighteen and lived in Glasgow with his mother. Added to which there was Sonya Michie, again kept secret from the wife. But then in Fox's experience, often the wives didn't want to know. They suspected ... they sort of knew anyway ... but they were happy to feign ignorance and get on with their lives.

'What are you doing here, Malcolm?' Fox muttered to himself. He was half hoping Heaton might appear on the doorstep in his dressing gown. He would walk to the car and get in. Then they could talk. Fox had told Breck that Charlie Brogan was at the centre of everything, but something had been niggling him even as he'd said it. Glen Heaton was more than unfinished business. There was a poison in the man that to Fox's mind had infected more carriers than had come to light as yet. They were still walking around, some of them only dimly aware of the contagion. Sonya Michie was one of them, for sure. But now Fox was wondering about Jack Broughton and Bull Wauchope, too. He had wound his window down. He could smell and hear the sea. There wasn't another soul about. He wondered: did it bother him that the world wasn't entirely fair? That justice was seldom sufficient? There would always be people ready to pocket a wad of banknotes in exchange for a favour. There would always be people who played the system and wrung out every penny. Some people – lots of people – would keep getting away with it.

'But you're not one of them,' he told himself.

And then he saw something – movement at the door of Heaton's bungalow. The door itself was opening, a man standing silhouetted against the lit hallway. He was wearing pyjamas and – yes – tying the belt of his white towelling robe. Glen Heaton was peering into the darkness, his focus directed at Fox's Volvo. Fox cursed beneath his breath and turned the ignition. The parking space wasn't huge and it took a bit of manoeuvring not to hit the vehicles in front and behind as he eased his own car out. Not that it mattered – Heaton seemed content to stand there, hands in pockets. Fox stared straight ahead as he drove off, headlights on full beam in an attempt to dazzle the man in the robe. Right, then right again, and he was on his way back towards Edinburgh, the image staying with him throughout.

Glen Heaton standing there, as if delivered to him.

And he, Malcolm Fox, had bottled it.

Thursday 19 February 2009

22

Thursday morning, Fox woke up to a text from Caroline Stoddart.

Feeling better?

As a matter of fact, he was. The swelling was starting to go down, and his palms only stung a little when he rubbed them together. His chin was okay, so long as he didn't touch it. He reckoned he might postpone shaving that particular spot for another day or two. As for his back, it hurt when he twisted or leaned too far in one direction, but it was manageable, so he texted her back:

Yes.

Her next and final text told him to be at Fettes at ten. Fox sent a message of his own to Jamie Breck, letting him know he'd be tied up until lunchtime. Breck called back immediately.

'Is it Stoddart?'

'The one and only.'

'Do you know what you're going to say?'

'I'm going to reiterate that I had nothing to do with Vince's death and that none of this is your fault.'

'It's a plan, I suppose. What about afterwards?'

'Thought I might go speak to Ernie Wishaw.'

'Why?'

'He's a councillor, isn't he? Maybe I've got a problem I want him to help me with.' Fox paused. 'No point you being there, Jamie.'

Breck gave a snort. 'Try and stop me.'

'Haven't you got a game of Quidnunc to be playing?'

'I'm the one who *knows* about Wishaw – or had you forgotten?'

'But you've never met him?'

'No.'

'It's risky, Jamie – if word gets back to Stoddart or Giles …'

'If you're going, I'm going,' Breck stated. 'End of story.'

But first there was the little matter of Fettes and the Grampian Complaints. The three officers – Stoddart, Wilson and Mason – assumed positions as before. When Stoddart saw the state of Fox's face, she stopped what she was doing.

'What happened to you?'

'I fell down the stairs.'

Her eyes narrowed. 'Isn't that usually your sister's excuse?'

'At least it means I wasn't shitting you yesterday.' Fox accepted the clip-on microphone from Mason and fixed it to his shirt before sitting down.

'I suppose not,' Stoddart was saying in reply to Fox's remark. 'But I was just about to congratulate you ...'

'On what?'

'Not getting into any more trouble in the interim.' She paused. 'Now I'm not so sure.'

Fox leaned forward a little in his chair, though the effort cost him a twang of pain. 'You calling me a liar, Inspector Stoddart?' he asked accusingly.

'No,' she answered, sifting through her paperwork. Fox ran his fingers down the laminated visitor's pass that hung around his neck.

'Any news from the Faulkner inquiry?' he asked innocently.

'I wouldn't know.' She glanced up from her work. 'Why *did* you attack DS Dickson?'

'I was emotionally fragile.'

'Would you mind repeating that?'

'My sister had just lost her partner,' he was happy to explain. 'That had an effect on me, which I hadn't reckoned with. It was only afterwards that I realised the force had made a mistake.'

'The force?'

'In not cancelling my duties and making me take a few days' compassionate leave.'

Stoddart sat back in her chair. 'You're shifting the blame?'

Fox shrugged. 'I'm just saying. But how come you were watching me, Inspector? Who was it ordered the surveillance, and what story did they use?'

Stoddart gave a cold smile. 'That's confidential information.'

'I'm glad to hear it – too many leaks around here for my liking ...' He sat back, mimicking her posture.

'Shall we get started?' she asked.

'Ready when you are,' Fox told her.

An hour and a half later, he was handing his pass back to Frank on the front desk, grateful not to have bumped into anyone he knew – it would only have meant lying about his bumps and bruises. On the other hand, Tony Kaye, Annie Inglis and the others would probably find out anyway. Fettes was like that. On his way to his car, Fox took a call on his old mobile. It was Jude, just wanting a chat.

'How you doing, sis?' he asked her.

'I'm okay.'

'Are your pals still rallying round?'

'Everybody's been great.'

'That's good to hear.'

'How about Dad – have you seen him?'

'I'm probably in *his* bad books as well …'

'I didn't say you were in my bad books,' she chided him.

'I'll try to visit at the weekend. Maybe we could take Dad out somewhere.' Fox was behind the steering wheel by now. 'Any news of them releasing the body?'

'Nobody's told me anything – could you maybe put in a word?'

'I don't see why not – everybody on the team loves me to bits.'

'Are you being sarcastic, Malcolm?'

'Maybe just a little.' He started the ignition. 'You sure you're okay?'

'I think I sound better than you do, actually.'

'You're probably right. I'll ring you tomorrow if I can.'

He ended the call and put the car into first. He was just easing his foot off the clutch when his new phone rang. He exhaled loudly and answered.

'Where are you?' The voice sounded breathless.

'Tony, is that you?'

'Where the hell are you?' Tony Kaye growled.

'I'm on Lothian Road.' The car was exiting its parking bay.

'You're rubbish at this game, Foxy. I've been lying to my wife since the morning after the honeymoon …'

'I'm not sure what you're getting at.' Fox almost dropped the phone when a body flung itself against the front of the Volvo. He slammed on the brakes. 'Stupid bastard!'

Tony Kaye had righted himself and stood with his hands cupped to his chest, trying to get his breathing back under control. His mobile was clutched in his right hand, his tongue lolling from his mouth. Fox left the car running and got out.

'Can't remember when I last ran that far,' his friend was

spluttering. 'Egg-and-spoon race probably ... last year of primary school.' Kaye tried to spit, but the long thread of saliva just hung there until he wiped it away with a handkerchief. He took a few more gulps of air. 'I cheated, mind – used chewing gum to fix the egg to the spoon ...'

'You couldn't have heard already,' Fox was saying.

'Wildfire,' Kaye was able to gasp. 'So who did it and why didn't you tell me?'

'First explain to me how you know.'

'Bumped into Stoddart's boys in the toilet.' Kaye paused, and Fox knew what he wanted.

'I was jumped,' Fox duly obliged.

'When was this?'

'Night before last.'

'Thanks for the heads-up.' Kaye sounded genuinely slighted. 'Where did all this happen?'

'Outside a sauna on the Cowgate. The inquiry got word that a cab dropped Vince Faulkner nearby. I was retracing his steps.'

Kaye was studying Fox's injuries. 'Whoever it was let you off lightly.'

Fox gave a twitch of the head in acknowledgement. 'Anyway ... I'm touched by your show of concern.'

'I was hoping for something a bit more gruesome.' Kaye tried to sound peeved. 'You know ... something I could post on YouTube...'

'You're all heart, Sergeant Kaye. Anything happening I should know about?'

Kaye gave a shrug. 'McEwan seemed to think there might be a job for us in the north-east ...'

'He mentioned it to me a couple of weeks back. It's been given to Strathclyde, right?'

Kaye stared at him. 'How do you know that?'

'McEwan told me. Shame, too – I'd have liked some ammo to tease Stoddart and her boys with ...' Fox broke off. Kaye could see he was thinking of something.

'What?' he asked.

'Nothing,' Fox assured him.

'Don't give me that ...'

'Why are you miffed about Strathclyde getting it?'

'Because they're rubbish, Foxy! Everybody knows that. Last time I looked, our success rate was twice what theirs is.'

Fox nodded slowly. 'That's true,' he said.

The two men stood in silence for a moment. Kaye leaned his backside against the front wheel arch of the Volvo. 'Was it just a coincidence?' he asked.

'The attack?' Fox watched as Kaye nodded his head. 'It wasn't a mugging; nothing got taken.'

'Someone could have interrupted ...'

Fox gnawed at his bottom lip. He was remembering Jack Broughton. Broughton hadn't said much of anything at all about what he'd seen or not seen. 'These things happen,' he eventually offered.

'Remember that night we were in a bar and some arsehole went for us with pepper spray?' Kaye chuckled quietly.

'Did you ever track him down?'

Kaye's face tightened a little. 'You don't want to know.'

'Is that what you'd have done to Vince Faulkner – kicked the crap out of him?'

'Would the world have lost anything in the process?'

Fox knew how he wanted to reply – he wanted to say 'yes'. But then Kaye would have asked 'What exactly?' and Fox didn't have an answer for that ...

'I've got to get going,' he said instead.

'Anything else I should know about?'

Fox shook his head, but then thought of a question. 'You said you lied to your wife the morning after the honeymoon?'

'Yes.'

'What was the lie?'

'I told her she was really something in the sack ...'

The Gyle hadn't really existed when Malcolm Fox had been growing up in the city. The land must have been there, of course, but with nothing on it and no roads leading to it. He remembered walking to the airport one day with friends, so they could go plane-spotting. And he would take his bike along the canal, reaching Wester Hailes and beyond. Maybe the Gyle had been fields or wasteland, meriting no place in his memory. These days, it was more a city within a city, with its own railway station and vast corporate buildings and a shopping complex. Ernie Wishaw's haulage business had its HQ in an industrial estate, next door to a parcel delivery company. Lorry cabs sat in a row on the pale concrete apron. Empty trailers had been unhitched and lined up in similar fashion. There were also stacked pallets and a couple of fuel pumps, and bundles of rubbish awaiting collection. The perimeter fencing, unlike neighbouring properties, lacked any windblown shreds of plastic and polythene. There was a well-equipped garage where a couple of mechanics wrestled with what sounded to Fox like an air-brake problem. They had a radio playing and one of them was singing along.

Jamie Breck had arrived first, content to wait in his car outside the compound until Fox trundled up. They entered the open gates as a convoy of two, and parked in front of the garage. There was a door to the right with a sign on it saying OFFICE. The two men greeted one another with a nod.

'How do you want to run this?' Breck asked, stretching his neck muscles.

'How about I play the bad cop,' Fox suggested. 'And you play the bad cop too.' Then he offered a smile and a wink. 'Let's just see what he has to say.' He pushed open the door, expecting the room beyond to be cramped, but it was long and light and airy. There were four women and two men working telephones and computers from their individual desks. A photocopier was humming, a laser printer printing, and a fax machine halfway through sending a document. There were two smaller offices off to one side. One of these was empty; in the other sat a woman who removed her glasses as Fox and Breck walked in, the better to scrutinise these new arrivals. She rose to her feet, smoothing her skirt before leaving the office to greet them.

'I'm Inspector Fox,' Fox said, handing over one of his business cards. 'Is there any chance of a word with Mr Wishaw?'

The woman's glasses hung around her neck on a cord. She slipped them back on so she could study the writing on the card.

'What seems to be the problem?' she asked.

'Just something we need to talk to Mr Wishaw about.'

'I'm *Mrs* Wishaw. Whatever it is, I'm sure I can help.'

'You really can't,' Fox informed her, looking around the room. 'My colleague called not fifteen minutes ago and was told Mr Wishaw was here.'

The woman turned her attention to Breck.

'Isn't that his Maserati outside?' Breck decided to ask.

Mrs Wishaw looked from one detective to the other. 'He's very busy,' she countered. 'You probably know that he's a councillor as well as running a successful business.'

'We only need five minutes,' Fox said, holding up his right hand, fingers splayed.

Mrs Wishaw had noticed that the desks were quiet. The staff were holding their phones to their faces, but they were no longer talking. Fingers had ceased clattering against keyboards.

'He's next door.'

'You mean the garage?'

Mrs Wishaw nodded: she meant the garage.

As they left the office, Breck added some information for Fox's benefit. 'She's his second wife, used to be one of the desk-jockeys …'

'Right,' Fox said.

The two mechanics were finishing off the job. One was tall and brawny and young. He was gathering together all the tools they'd used. The other was much older, with wavy silver hair receding at the temples. He was below five and a half feet and the waistband of his blue overalls was bulging. He was concentrating on wiping his oily hands on an even oilier rag.

'Mr Wishaw,' Breck said, having recognised him at last.

'You two look like cops,' Wishaw stated.

'That's because we are,' Fox told him.

Wishaw glowered at him from under a set of dark, bushy eyebrows, then turned towards the mechanic.

'Aly, off you go and get a coffee or something.'

The three men waited until Aly had done as he'd been told. Wishaw stuffed the rag into the pocket of his overalls and wandered over towards a workbench. There was a concertina-style toolbox there and he hauled it open.

'Notice anything?' he asked.

'Everything's in the right place,' Fox stated after a few seconds.

'That's right. Know why that is?'

'Because you're anal?' Breck offered. Wishaw tried him with the glower, but he had decided that Fox was the man worth talking to.

'Business is all about confidence – reason the banks have started teetering is because people are losing confidence. Someone wants to work with me, maybe offer me a contract, I always bring them here. They see two things – a boss who's not afraid of hard work, and a boss who makes sure everything runs like clockwork.'

'That's why all the lorries are lined up outside?'

'And why they've been given a good wash, too. Same goes for my drivers …'

'Do you hand them the soap personally?' Breck couldn't help asking. Wishaw ignored him.

'If they're going to be late on a pick-up or delivery, they call ahead and explain why. And the explanation better be twenty-two carat, because *I'm* the very next person they call. Know what I do then?'

'You phone the customer and apologise?' Fox guessed. Wishaw gave a brusque nod.

'It's the way things get done.'

'It tends not to be how councils work,' Fox argued.

Wishaw threw his head back and hooted. 'I know *that*. Amount of red tape I've tried getting rid of ... Nights I've sat in that chamber and argued till I'm blue in the face.'

'You sit on the housing committee,' Fox said. 'Is that right?'

Wishaw was quiet for a moment. 'What is it you want?' he asked.

'We want to ask you about a man called Charles Brogan.'

'Charlie.' Wishaw bowed his head and shook it slowly. 'Hell of a thing.'

'How well did you know him?'

'I met him a number of times – council business and suchlike. We got invites to the same sorts of parties and functions.'

'You knew him pretty well then?'

'I knew him to talk to.'

'When was the last time you spoke to him?'

Wishaw's eyes met Fox's. 'You've probably been through his phone records – you tell me.'

Fox swallowed and tried to sound nonchalant. 'I'd rather you did the talking, sir.'

Wishaw considered this. 'Couple of days before he died,' he finally admitted. 'Only for five minutes or so.'

'I meant to ask ... Did your firm ever do any work for CBBJ?' Fox watched Wishaw shake his head. 'So you weren't owed money?'

'Thankfully.' Wishaw had taken the rag from his pocket and was wiping his fingers more thoroughly, making little or no difference.

'But the call was business?' Fox persisted calmly.

'I suppose so.'

'Was he offering you another bung?' Breck interrupted. 'Probably *begging* you by then ...'

'*What* did you say?' The rush of blood to Wishaw's face was impressive in its immediacy. 'Would you be happy to repeat that in front of a lawyer?'

'All my colleague meant was ...' Fox had his hands held up in supplication.

'I know damned well what he meant!' The man's face was the colour of cooked beetroot; flecks of white were appearing at the corners of his mouth.

'Come clean on Brogan,' Breck was saying, 'and we might forget all about the bung *you* handed to your driver's family. Remember him? With the dope stashed in the fuel tank?'

Fox turned away from the spluttering Wishaw and propelled Jamie Breck backwards towards the garage opening. When they were out of earshot, Breck gave Fox the most fleeting of winks.

'That felt good,' he whispered.

'Slight change of plan,' Fox whispered back. 'You stay here; I'm going to be good cop ...' He removed his hand from Breck's chest and turned back towards Wishaw, reaching him in a few short strides.

'Sorry about that,' he apologised. 'Younger officers don't always have the ...' He sought the right word. 'Decorum,' he decided. Wishaw was rubbing hard at his palms with the rag.

'Outrageous,' he said. 'Such an accusation ... totally unfounded ...'

'Ah, but it's not, is it?' Fox said gently. 'You *did* give the man's family a sum of money – what it comes down to after that is interpretation. That's the mistake my colleague made, isn't it?'

Wishaw's silence seemed to concede as much. 'Outrageous,' he echoed, but with only half as much force as before.

'It's Charles Brogan we were talking about,' Fox reminded him. Wishaw gave a sigh.

'Thing about men like Charlie ... His whole generation ...' But he broke off, and Fox knew a bit more effort was required. He pretended to be studying the garage.

'You're a lucky man, Mr Wishaw. Except we both know luck has little or nothing to do with it – that fleet of lorries, the Maserati ... they're the result of hard work rather than luck. You've as good as said so yourself.'

'Yes,' Wishaw agreed. This was a subject he could talk about. 'Sheer bloody hard work – I would say "graft" but you'd probably take it the wrong way.'

Fox decided this was worth a full-throated chuckle.

'That's what so many people don't realise,' Wishaw went on, buoyed by the effect of his words on the detective. 'I've worked my arse off, and I do the same thing in the council chamber – to try to make a *difference*. But these days, people just want to sit back and let the money and all that goes with it find *them*. That's not the way it works! There are businessmen out there ...' Wishaw made a stabbing motion with one finger, 'who think money should come easy.'

'Money from nothing?' Fox guessed.

'As good as,' Wishaw agreed. 'Buy a parcel of land, sit on it for a year and then sell at a profit. Or a house or a bunch of flats or whatever it might be. If you've got cash in a bank, you want a double-digit rate of interest – doesn't matter to you how the bank finances it. Money from thin air, that's what it seems like. And nobody asks any questions because that might break the spell.'

'Your own company's surviving, though?'

'It's hard going, I won't deny it.'

'But you'll work your way through it?'

Wishaw nodded vigorously. 'Which is why I resent it when ... when ...' He was wagging a finger towards Jamie Breck.

'He didn't mean anything, sir. We're just trying to build up a picture of why Charles Brogan did what he did.'

'Charlie ...' Wishaw calmed again, his eyes losing focus as he remembered the man he'd known. 'Charlie was incredibly likeable – genial company, all of that. But he was a product of his time. In a nutshell, he got greedy. That's what it boils down to. He thought that money should come *easy*, and for the first few years it really did. But that can make you soft and complacent and gullible ...' Wishaw paused. 'And stupid. Above all, it can make you incredibly stupid ... yet for a while you're *still* making money.' He raised a hand. 'I'm not saying Charlie was the worst, not even in the bottom fifty or hundred! At least he created things – he caused buildings to rise.'

Fox seemed to recall that Brogan had said much the same thing in one of his newspaper interviews. 'But that becomes a problem when nobody wants those buildings,' he suggested.

Wishaw's mouth twitched. 'It's when your investors want to be paid back. Empty buildings might be an investment if you wait long enough – same goes for land. What's worthless one year can turn to gold the next. But none of that's relevant if you've promised a quick return to your investors.'

Fox was giving Wishaw his full attention. 'Who *were* Mr Brogan's investors?'

It took Wishaw fully fifteen seconds to answer that he didn't know. 'I'm just thankful I'm not one of the ones waiting for Salamander Point to turn a profit.' He was trying for levity, and that told Malcolm Fox something.

Told him he'd just been lied to.

'That last time you spoke with him – did he call you or did you call him?'

Wishaw blinked a couple of times and fixed the detective with a look. 'You must know that from the logs.'

'I just want confirmation.'

But there was a change taking place behind Wishaw's eyes. 'Should my lawyer be here?' he asked.

'I don't think that's necessary.'

'I'm beginning to wonder. The man had money troubles and he took his own life – end of story.'

'Not for the police, Mr Wishaw. As far as we're concerned, when someone disappears or dies ... that's the story just beginning.'

'I suppose that's true,' Wishaw offered. 'But I've told you all I can.'

'Except for the details of that final phone call.'

Wishaw considered his response for a further ten or fifteen seconds. 'It was nothing,' he decided. 'Nothing at all ...' He looked down at his overalls. 'I need to get changed. There's council business this afternoon – another dispute with the tram contractor.' He offered a curt nod and made to move past Fox.

'You're sure you never had any business dealings with Mr Brogan?' Fox asked. 'Not even a tender for some work?'

'No.'

'And he wasn't trying to persuade you to help him lay some of his tower blocks off on the council?' Wishaw just glared, bringing a smile to Fox's lips. 'You know a man called Paul Meldrum, Mr Wishaw?'

The change of tack took Wishaw by surprise. 'Yes,' he admitted.

'He works for a firm called Lovatt, Meikle, Meldrum,' Fox went on. 'They're in PR, but Meldrum's area of expertise is lobbying.'

'I'm not entirely sure where this is going ...'

'I was just wondering if it was maybe Charles Brogan who put you on to the firm in the first place.'

'Might have been,' Wishaw conceded. 'Is it important?'

'Not really, sir. Thanks again for your time.' Fox paused for a few beats, then leaned in towards Wishaw. 'And maybe next time we'll have that lawyer present,' he added in an undertone.

'Libel comes with a hefty price tag ...' Wishaw was about to add Fox's name, but realised he didn't know it. 'I'm sorry,' he said, 'I don't think you introduced yourself ...'

'I gave my card to your daughter,' Fox answered.

'My …?' Realisation dawned on Wishaw. 'That was my wife.'

'Then you should be ashamed,' Fox said, deciding this was as good a parting shot as any.

23

'Something I should maybe have told you,' Jamie Breck said. They had dropped Fox's car back at the house and were now heading north out of the city. Fox was a nervous passenger at the best of times, and he wasn't liking the RX8. He felt too low to the ground and the sports seat restricted his movement. Breck – a vital couple of inches shorter and probably half the girth – fitted in well, but not Fox. Cars like this were not built for people his size, and certainly not ones with injured backs.

'What?' Fox asked. Another thing: sometimes it felt as if the Mazda was about to mount the kerb; other times as if it were straying out into the opposite lane. Breck always seemed to wait until the final moment before making the correction.

'It's about Ernie Wishaw – I didn't let his case drop exactly.'

Fox was in two minds about whether to let the conversation continue or suggest that Breck should shut up and concentrate on driving. Curiosity got the better of him.

'How do you mean?'

'I mean I've been doing some digging – strictly in my own time. I'm one hundred per cent sure he was taking a cut from the trafficking. His lorries head over to Europe on a weekly basis. Always tempting to jack up the profit by bringing back some contraband.'

'That usually means booze and cigarettes.'

Breck nodded. There was a sudden vibration in the car as the driver's-side tyres once more connected with the cat's eyes down the middle of the carriageway. Breck made the adjustment and started talking. 'Booze and cigarettes for sure, plus porn and anything else that might turn a profit. Once you know you're not getting caught, you might decide to up the stakes a little.' He paused.

'Or it could be that someone just comes along and makes you the right offer.'

Fox considered this. 'Bruce Wauchope's in jail for drug-dealing.'

'Indeed he is.'

'You think his son's ...?'

'I can't prove anything as yet.'

'But if he was, he might turn to Ernie Wishaw for advice?'

'Wishaw's had the equivalent of a near-death experience – one of his guys is doing time, and he was the thickness of a Rizla paper away from joining him.'

'So Wishaw wouldn't smuggle dope on Bull Wauchope's behalf?'

'Actually I think he would,' Breck said quietly. 'All it needs is for someone to scare him enough.'

Fox thought about it. Yes – the threat of violence against his precious wife or his even more precious fleet of lorries ... 'Think we might find an answer in Dundee?'

'Isn't it lucky we're already headed there?'

And so they were – they'd already passed through Barnton and were sweeping out into the countryside, the road broadening into a proper dual carriageway, passing Dalmeny and South Queensferry on their right. In a moment, the Forth Bridges would be visible.

'Why are you just telling me this now?' Fox asked.

'Maybe I have a problem with trust, Malcolm. Have you forgotten how long it took *you* to tell me I was a suspected paedophile?'

'That's different – you were under investigation.'

'And *you*, my friend, were a suspect in the killing of Vince Faulkner. Didn't take me long to see that Billy Giles was wrong in his assumption ...'

Fox took a moment to digest this. 'So how did you go about your own little inquiry into Ernie Wishaw?'

'I spoke to the driver's wife and her brother. I did some digging to see if there was any sudden cash swilling around – new TV or car, that sort of thing.'

'And?'

Breck just shrugged. 'I even went to Saughton as a visitor.'

'You spoke with the lorry-driver?'

'He wasn't giving anything away.'

'But he knew who you were?' Fox watched Breck nod. 'So it could have got back to Wishaw – or anyone else for that matter.'

'I suppose.'

Fox was thoughtful. 'Could Wishaw's driver have been working for Bull Wauchope? Wauchope Senior's doing time for bringing dope in by sea. Maybe intercontinental lorries started to look a better bet to his son.'

'Maybe,' Breck conceded. 'You'll have heard the stories as often as me – port officials sometimes "oiling the wheels".'

'They take a bung and don't check the cargo too thoroughly?'

Breck was nodding. Fox reached into his pocket for his phone and a slip of paper – the one with the number of Max Dearborn's sister.

'Who are you calling?' Breck asked.

'A friend, maybe.' He had the ringing tone, and a moment later the call was answered by a female voice.

'Is that Linda Dearborn?' Fox asked.

'Speaking.'

'My name's Malcolm Fox. I'm a colleague of Max's.'

'Yes, he's mentioned you. Word is, you're on suspension.'

'Funny, I've not read about it in the paper ...'

'Plenty time yet, Malcolm.' Her voice had a teasing quality to it. This was probably her method, Fox reasoned: be chatty, gossipy, maybe your new best friend ... and then repeat any confidences for the paying public.

'Max tells me you're looking into Charles Brogan's disappearance.'

'Not exactly,' she corrected him. 'It's Brogan's method of doing business I'm interested in.'

'In particular, whether he was trying to bribe a city councillor?'

'Yes.'

'And as a result, Joanna Broughton's set Gordon Lovatt on you.'

'Mmm. They're an intriguing couple, Brogan and Broughton.'

'Joanna, you mean?'

There was a momentary silence on the line. 'You're right to add Father Jack to the mix,' she eventually said.

'You reckon Brogan has done a Reggie Perrin on us?'

'Or he's crossed the pa-in-law in some way.'

'And what way would that be?'

'Malcolm ...' She almost sang his name. '*You're* the detective, not me. My job's to vacuum up the crumbs. Think of me as a housemaid ...'

'That won't be easy when I know your true identity, Linda.'

'And what's that?'

'A hard-nosed investigative reporter – which is what I need you to be for me right now.'

'You've got me intrigued, big boy.'

'It would be useful to know how Brogan's company is organised

– maybe it's a case of companies plural ... we don't know the extent of his empire. He'll have shareholders, people he owed money to. Who exactly are they?'

'Companies House is the place to start ... I've already got quite a lot of info, including the details of his accountants. I suppose I could talk to them, but I'm not sure how helpful they'd be ... to a journalist, I mean. On the other hand, they'd *have* to talk to the police.'

'Sadly, as you've already noted, I'm suspended from duty.'

'Which begs the question – what's all this in aid of?'

'It's in aid of whatever the opposite of suspension is,' Fox told her. They were just arriving at the road bridge. It was, as ever, magnificent. To the right sat the complex, intertwined geometry of the Forth Rail Bridge. There was talk of a new bridge being built to relieve the strain on the present road bridge. Some of the cables were showing their age. But where was the money to come from? Linda Dearborn was saying that she'd see what she could do.

'One other thing that might be fun for both of us ...' Fox added.

'Do tell.'

'You could look up Lovatt's firm at the same time, get an idea of just how far their tentacles stretch.' Fox ended the call and Breck turned the radio back up a little.

'Think we can trust her?' he asked.

'I'm not that stupid, Jamie.'

'Glad to hear it.'

Forty minutes later they were on the outskirts of Dundee. The trip had been Breck's idea. He hadn't been to the city on business before, but a cop he'd gone through training with had ended up in Tayside CID. One phone call later, the friend had agreed to meet with them 'on the quiet'.

'How many roundabouts can one city have?' Breck complained as he followed the signs towards the waterfront. He'd been told to park next to the train station and cross the road to where the *Discovery* was docked. Fox asked why the boat was moored there.

'I think it was built in Dundee.'

Fox nodded. 'Shackleton took it to the Arctic, right?'

'Arctic ... Antarctic ... who knows?'

Whoever had the answer, it wasn't Mark Kelly. He was a DS, same rank as Breck, and he was waiting for them by the metal fence in front of the ship. Fox pretended an interest in the mast and rigging while the two friends shared a brief hug and exchanged comments about hair loss and body mass. When Breck asked about the boat, Kelly said he'd no idea.

'We going on board or what?' Breck asked.

'It's just a landmark, Jamie – I seem to remember navigation's not your strong point and Dundee's a tough gig for the first-timer. Come on ...' He led them back across the road and past another roundabout. Their destination was a café, whose clientele seemed to be biding their time until they could be elsewhere. Once seated with their coffees, the real conversation began.

'I took a look at Bull's file,' Kelly said, keeping his voice low.

'The file didn't come with you,' Breck commented.

'Couldn't do it, Jamie. Alarm bells would have sounded.'

'Then let's hope your memory's better than it used to be.'

Kelly accepted this with a smile. 'Bull keeps being lucky – bullets bounce off him ... metaphorically speaking.'

'Has anyone tried the other kind?' Fox interrupted.

'There are stories ... But it seems Bull's been taking a few tips from his old man. He used to be quite a physical sort, if you get my meaning.'

'And now?'

'Now he's building bridges rather than knocking them down.'

'This all sounds like code to me,' Jamie Breck complained. 'Can we go somewhere a bit more private so you can just spit it out?'

Kelly leaned across the table towards him. 'Bull's been driving up and down Scotland with his trusted lieutenant, meeting some of the other players – the ones that count. Aberdeen one day, Lanarkshire the next.'

'Has this been going on a while?' Fox asked.

'A few months ... maybe a bit longer. It took time for us to notice what was happening.'

'You thought maybe he was writing a guidebook?' Breck asked.

Kelly just glowered at him. 'We've no idea *what* he was doing.'

'But you can hazard a guess,' Fox said.

Kelly took a deep breath. 'Maybe he's playing peacemaker on his dad's behalf. Or could be he's scared that with the old man inside, a competitor will try muscling in.'

'Then he could be trying to extend his own reach,' Fox added. 'Tentacles again ...'

Kelly nodded at this. 'On the surface, of course, he's a legitimate businessman.'

'Of course.'

'But not too many of those need muscle like Terry Vass.'

'His lieutenant?' Fox guessed.

'With a criminal record the approximate length of *War and Peace*.'

'I'm assuming drugs play a part in all of this,' Breck interrupted.

'I'm sure they do,' Kelly snorted.

'But you've got no proof?'

Kelly shrugged. 'Any help you can give ...' He looked from one man to the other. 'Actually, you were pretty vague on the phone, Jamie. Maybe I should be asking what this is all about.'

'It's complicated,' Breck replied.

'But it might,' Fox interrupted, 'have to do with a murder and a missing person.'

'The missing person being Charlie Brogan,' Breck added.

'Never heard of him,' Kelly said, stirring his spoon in his cup.

'He's a developer in Edinburgh ... don't you watch the news, Mark?'

Kelly gave another shrug. 'Bad time to be a developer ... we had one top himself a couple of months back.' He paused. 'Hang on ... is this the guy with the boat?'

'What did you just say?' Fox asked.

'I asked if it was the guy who went missing from his boat.'

Fox was shaking his head. 'Before that – you've got your own dead developer?'

Kelly nodded again. He was still stirring his coffee and it was driving Fox demented. Another minute or two and he'd be snatching the spoon and tossing it the length of the café.

'Don't recall the name,' Kelly was saying. 'There's a bunch of high-rises they're demolishing. He jumped from one of the upper floors.' Kelly noticed that Fox and Breck were staring fixedly at one another. 'You don't think there's a connection ...?'

Now the two men were staring at him.

Jamie Breck's study.

Darkness had fallen. Food had been fetched from a Chinese takeaway, but half of it sat congealing on the worktop in the kitchen. Breck had opened a bottle of lager for himself, while the takeaway had sold Fox a couple of cans of Irn-Bru. Breck had shifted over a little to make room for Fox's chair in front of the computer screen.

'And there we were accusing Dundee of being parochial,' Fox said as Breck found the news item. There was a photograph of the 'tragic suicide'. He was smiling at somebody's wedding. There was a big, bold carnation pinned to his jacket lapel. The story put his age at sixty, but the photo showed a man of thirty-five or forty.

His name was Philip Norquay and he'd lived in the city all his life – local high school, local university, local businessman. He'd come to property developing 'almost by accident' – his parents had owned a shop, making their home in the flat above. On their death, there had been lots of interest in the property, leading the son to do some detective work. Turned out there were plans for a new housing estate nearby. Norquay hung on to his parents' place until he could contact a supermarket group, who were glad of the chance to knock it down and rebuild, paying over the odds for the privilege.

That had given Norquay a taste, and by the time he was forty he'd built up a fair-sized portfolio of rental premises, moving on to full-scale development opportunities when his chance came. He'd made a name for himself by spearheading an attempt to buy the stadiums belonging to both the city's football clubs. A new joint-share stadium would be built outside Dundee as part of the deal, but negotiations collapsed.

'Charlie Brogan wanted to buy into Celtic at one time,' Fox told Breck.

'He had plans to pave Paradise?'

Still, Norquay was vocal in his support for the regeneration of the city, pitching in when the council put forward a proposal to regenerate the waterfront.

'Just like Brogan,' Breck commented.

'They were going to get rid of that roundabout we walked past.' Fox was tapping his finger against the computer screen.

'And reroute the roadway – makes sense,' Breck agreed. 'Read further down, though.'

The next few paragraphs explained Norquay's fall from grace. He had overstretched himself financially, buying up one of the ugliest pieces of real estate around, a hotchpotch of 1960s high-rise blocks on the city's periphery. His plan was to knock the whole thing down and start again, but difficulties had presented themselves almost immediately. The buildings were stuffed with asbestos, which made them expensive to demolish. Then old mine-workings were discovered, meaning half the land was unsuitable for construction without spending a fortune on underpinning. In his enthusiasm for the project, Norquay had paid over the odds as it was. When the market tumbled south, so did confidence. Still, his suicide had come as a shock to all who knew him. He had been at a formal dinner that evening, and had seemed relaxed and jovial. His wife had sensed no change in him that might indicate growing despair. 'Philip was a fighter,' she had told one reporter.

‘Remind you of anyone?’ Fox asked Breck.

‘Maybe,’ Breck conceded. ‘But Norquay’s dead for certain, not just AWOL.’

‘He didn’t leave a note … didn’t visit his lawyer to make sure his will was up to date …’

Breck scrolled a little further down the page, then clicked on a link to an associated story. It didn’t add anything to their knowledge. According to the search engine, there were more than 13,000 matches still to go, but Fox had risen to his feet. There wasn’t much to see from the window, but he looked anyway.

‘Reckon they’re watching us?’ Breck asked him.

‘No … not really.’ Fox sipped from his can. There was a slight tremor running through him, and he didn’t know whether to blame the sugar, the caffeine, or Breck’s driving on the trip back from Dundee.

‘You don’t think he killed himself?’ Breck asked.

‘Do you?’

Breck considered for a moment. ‘Guy was haemorrhaging money … probably about to lose everything … and here was this white elephant just sitting there mocking him. He climbs to the top and decides to end it.’

‘Except everyone says he wasn’t the type.’

‘Maybe they just didn’t know him.’ Breck leaned back with his hands behind his head. ‘Okay, then – what’s the alternative?’

‘He could have been pushed.’ Fox gnawed at his bottom lip. ‘He was at a dinner … told everyone he was headed straight home … instead, he jumps into his BMW and makes for the asbestos jungle he’s just bought. I can think of better ways to die, Jamie.’

‘Me too.’ Breck paused. ‘Could he have been meeting someone?’

‘Either that or they followed him – can you get your pal on the phone?’

‘Mark?’ Breck picked up his rented mobile. ‘What am I asking him?’

‘Mind if I do the talking?’

‘No.’ Breck punched in the number and handed over the phone. Fox pressed it to his ear.

‘That you, Jamie?’ Mark Kelly answered.

‘Mark, it’s Malcolm Fox. Jamie’s here next to me.’

‘What’s got you so excited, Malcolm?’

‘We were just looking at some of the stuff on the internet about Philip Norquay.’

‘I hope you’re on overtime.’

'We do this as a hobby, Mark. Listen, one thing you could help us with …'

'Fire away.'

'Did anyone think to check Norquay's phone records?'

Kelly considered for a moment. 'I don't suppose it ever came up. The guy killed himself; there wasn't anything you'd describe as an "investigation". What's your thinking, Malcolm?'

'Just wondering what took him to the block of flats … the straw that broke the camel's back …'

'I suppose I could ask the widow.'

'Or give us her details and we'll do it,' Fox suggested. There was silence on the line. 'Mark? You there?'

'You don't think he jumped,' Kelly stated.

'Chances are, that's exactly what he did, but with this thing in Edinburgh …'

'How are the two connected?'

'Again, I'm not sure they are …'

'But they might be.' It was statement rather than question. Kelly exhaled noisily, causing static on the line. 'You think we might have missed something?'

'I'm not trying to score points here …'

'Okay, look – if I get the info to you, and you *do* find anything …'

'We come to you first. That's not a problem, Mark. How long till you get back to us?'

'Depends how merry the widow is. Talk to you soon.'

The phone went dead and Fox handed it back to Breck. 'He thinks we'll try to throw some custard in Tayside's face.'

'It might come to that,' Breck said.

Fox nodded. 'But if so, he wants to be the one to break the news.'

'Wouldn't do his career any harm. Did he say how long we'd have to wait?'

Fox shook his head.

'So what do we do now?'

'I think I'm going to go home.'

'I can run you.'

Fox shook his head again. 'The walk will do me good. I'm sure you'll want an hour or two on your game.' He wafted his hand over the top of the computer.

'Funny thing is,' Breck told him, 'it's lost some of its appeal, now the real world's turned more interesting …'

Friday 20 February 2009

24

Next morning at eleven a.m., Fox had a meeting with Linda Dearborn. There was no resemblance to her brother – she was petite and fizzing with energy, and her outfit would have had church ministers walking into lamp posts. The miniskirt was pleated, the bare, tanned legs reaching all the way down to pale-brown cowboy boots. Beneath her suede jacket she wore a blouse with the first four buttons undone, showing ample bronzed cleavage. Just a hint of make-up, and straw-blonde shoulder-length hair.

She had picked the rendezvous – a café called Tea-Tree Tea on Bread Street. There was a bearded guy behind the counter and he tutted audibly when Fox ordered coffee. Fox had arrived twenty minutes early, giving him time to scan the newspaper. He'd added a cheese scone to his order, and settled himself at a table by the window. The sun outside had some warmth to it, hinting that spring was maybe finally on its way. Linda Dearborn arrived for the meeting ten minutes early. She smiled as if in recognition.

'Linda?' he asked anyway.

'I hate to say it,' she laughed, 'but you *do* look like a cop. I think it's the posture, or the way your eyes flit around all the time – Max is just the same.' She had placed her heavy-looking satchel on the chair next to Fox.

'Well, I'm not sure *you* look like a news-hound,' Fox responded.

'It's my day off.'

'You've chosen a brave get-up.' She didn't seem to understand. 'Bare legs in winter.'

She looked down at them. 'With what this tan cost, I can't afford to hide them. Some of us suffer for our art, and my legs *are* a work of art, don't you think?'

'What can I get you?'

But she was already bounding towards the counter. The proprietor had perked up, and knew her order before she got the chance to tell him. Lapsang souchong with a slice of lemon. Fox pretended to read his paper while the two of them chatted. Dearborn stood on tiptoes with her elbows on the counter. She twirled a hank of hair while she talked. Fox tried not to think how attractive she was. She was Max Dearborn's sister. She was a journalist.

The proprietor insisted on carrying the tea to the table for her. She thanked him with a crinkling of her nose, then sat down next to Fox rather than across the table from him, having removed her satchel from the chair. She crossed one leg over the other while he assumed an interest in the art on the walls around them.

'Nice place,' he said.

'It's handy – my flat's on Gardner's Crescent.'

Fox nodded and turned his attention to the window. There were two shops across the street. One was a hairdresser's, the other a vet's. Linda Dearborn had leaned down to find something in her bag. When she placed the laptop on the table, she peered down the front of her own blouse.

'Almost a wardrobe malfunction there,' she pretended to apologise.

'Does the act always work?' Fox asked, fixing his eyes on hers.

'Mostly,' she eventually conceded.

'Well, it's not that I don't appreciate the effort, but maybe we could ...' He tapped the laptop. Dearborn gave a little pout but lifted the screen anyway and switched the machine on. Fox looked away as she typed in her password. Twenty seconds and a couple of clicks later and she was angling the screen towards him.

'Companies House is all well and good,' she began. 'But it helps that my newspaper hasn't yet scaled down its business desk. The accountants aren't even halfway through dealing with everything Mr Brogan left behind, but what seems clear is that CBBJ was buoyed in the early days by large injections of cash. As far as anyone can tell, these weren't always accompanied by effective paperwork.'

'Meaning?'

'We don't know where the money came from. But there are plenty of other actual shareholders.'

'Would one of them happen to be called Wauchope Leisure?'

Dearborn ran one long-nailed finger down the mouse pad, the names and numbers on the screen scrolling with her.

'Not quite,' she said, placing the cursor over a name and highlighting it – ScotFuture (Wauchope).

'Would that company be Dundee-based, by any chance?' Fox asked.

Dearborn just nodded. 'Remember you asked me to look at Lovatt, Meikle, Meldrum's client base? They just happen to represent a company called Wauchope Leisure. As far as I can ascertain, LMM's job was to disguise the sleaze factor in a series of adverts for lap-dancing clubs up and down the country. Meantime, Wauchope's managing director has been put in jail ...'

'Fancy that,' Fox mused. When the journalist saw she wasn't going to get anything more out of him, she turned her attention back to the screen.

'There are a lot of small companies listed here – private companies, meaning they don't have to file much in the way of information about themselves. The lads on the business desk were intrigued. Charles Brogan seems to have had friends all over the country – Inverness, Aberdeen, Glasgow, Kilmarnock, Motherwell, Paisley ... and further afield, too – Newcastle, Liverpool, Dublin ...'

'I don't suppose these friendships survived the financial meltdown,' Fox mused.

'No, I don't suppose they did. Anyone who bought into Salamander Point, for example ... well, nobody seems to think they'll get back more than five pence in the pound.'

'Ouch.'

'And our benighted banks take yet another hit – Brogan had loans totalling just over eighteen million, and he was behind on his payments.'

'Could they go after his widow?'

'Unlikely – that's the beauty of a limited company.'

'Is Joanna Broughton's name on none of the paperwork? She wasn't company secretary or anything?'

Dearborn was shaking her head. 'She didn't hold a single share.'

'Yet her initials are right there in the company's name.'

'That's why I dug back a little further. She *was* a partner at one time, but her husband bought her out, around the same time she started her casino.'

'Does CBBJ happen to own a slice of the Oliver?'

'I don't think so.' She cupped her chin in her hand. 'And neither does Wauchope Leisure. So where's this all leading, Malcolm?'

'You tell me.'

'You think some of the money in CBBJ was dirty?'

'Is that just an inspired guess?'

She smiled. 'It's what my business editor thinks. Problem is, the paper trail is almost impossible to follow.'

'Maybe if you gave it a bit longer …'

She stared at him. Her eyes were almost violet. He wondered if they were tinted lenses. 'Maybe,' she said. Then: 'By the way, how's suspension treating you?'

'Can't complain.'

'That's funny … sort of.'

'Because I'm in the Complaints, you mean?' He watched her nod.

'Story is, you were trampling all over your brother-in-law's murder.'

'He wasn't my brother-in-law.' Fox paused. 'And it's *not* a story.'

'Oh, but it might be, if you let it.' The tip of her tongue protruded from between her lips.

'Grieving Cop Errs on the Side of Zeal – that's about as much as you could do with it.'

'But now all that zeal seems aimed at Charles Brogan …'

'Do you reckon your own zeal will get you anywhere?'

'My editor describes me as "tenacious".'

'But so far you can't prove a link between Brogan and Ernie Wishaw?'

'I know they met several times.'

'But nobody saw any money change hands?' Fox guessed. Dearborn angled her head to one side.

'Strange, isn't it?' she asked. 'The way he went missing just after your friend Vince died? Took me about fifteen minutes to make the connection – Vince worked at Salamander Point.' She looked like a schoolgirl with a gold star on her latest essay. 'I'm right, aren't I?' And, when he didn't say anything: 'See, Malcolm? I'm not just a pretty face.'

'I never thought you were.'

'Hot water?' a voice from behind them called. It was the proprietor, standing with a fresh pot in his hand.

Fox had parked his car on a yellow line outside. A warden was hovering as he emerged from the café. The man was wondering whether to honour the POLICE sign Fox had left on the inside of the windscreen. When Fox scowled at him, the warden decided there might be easier pickings elsewhere. Fox had offered Linda Dearborn a lift, but she'd said she was happy walking. Her destination was George Street, 'for a little window shopping'. Fox could bet that she liked walking, knowing male heads were turning as she passed them; knowing eyes were fixed on her from cars and vans and office windows. He was turning the key in the ignition when his phone – his new phone – sounded. The number belonged to Jamie Breck.

'Morning,' Fox said, answering.

'I've just had a call from Mark Kelly.'

'What's he got for us?'

'He visited Norquay's widow. She didn't seem fazed by his request.'

'She showed him hubby's phone bills?'

'Mark says the whole house is a shrine. She's bought a job lot of photo frames. There are hundreds of family pics strewn across the living-room floor as she sorts them all out. She took him into her husband's den – the paperwork was immaculate. She's got it all boxed in chronological order – bank statements, bills and receipts, credit card stuff ...'

'And phone bills?' Fox prompted.

'Right.' Fox listened as Breck picked up a sheet of paper. 'Luckily he opted to have everything itemised – calls in as well as calls out. Towards the end of that dinner he was at, he got a call from a local number. It's a payphone in a bar called Lowther's. Mark tells me it's pretty grim, but slap-bang in the centre of town.'

'Okay.'

'Call lasted two minutes and forty seconds.'

'And do we know his state of mind immediately afterwards?'

'Mark hadn't thought to go that particular extra mile ...'

'But you've asked him now?'

'He's going to talk to the friends who were with Norquay at the dinner.'

'I don't suppose it'll get us much further.'

'No ...' Breck drew the word out, and Fox knew there was something else.

'In your own time, Jamie,' he prompted.

'Well, Mark knows Lowther's by repute – there's often a bit of trouble there on a Saturday night, except actually the trouble always seems to happen a hundred yards or so from the pub itself.'

'Out on the street, you mean?'

'If an argument starts, it's always taken outside.'

'And why would that be?' Fox asked, already with an inkling of the answer.

'Nobody wants to get on the wrong side of the owners.'

'Wauchope Leisure Holdings?'

'Who else?' Jamie Breck said.

'In a way, that's a bit of a shame – means none of the punters are going to tell us who made the call.'

'Probably not,' Breck agreed. 'But it's certainly got Mark interested.'

'He needs to ca' canny.'

'Don't worry about him. How did your meeting with Linda Dearborn go? Was she asking after me?'

'Your name didn't quite come up.'

'She's a little stunner, isn't she?'

'She's also pretty good at her job. There's a link between Wauchope and Brogan's company. Do you think we could tie Wauchope to Norquay's outfit too?'

'We can try ... or rather, Mark can – it's a Tayside shout.'

'Wauchope's company also employs a PR firm ...'

'Let me guess – LMM?'

'They ran an advertising campaign for lap-bars.'

'On the sides of buses – I remember that. Do we need to talk to them about it? Their HQ's slap-bang next to the Parliament ...'

'Maybe for later,' Fox advised. 'Get back on the phone to your friend in Tayside and see if he can find anything else to tie Wauchope to our Dundee developer.'

'Will do. What's next on your own list, Malcolm?'

'Family,' Fox said, signalling out into traffic.

Jude opened the door. When she saw it was him, she turned and headed back to the living room, knowing he would follow. Her hair and clothes looked like they could do with a wash, and she was sunken-cheeked. There was a cigarette waiting for her in the ashtray on the arm of her chair.

'I thought you weren't coming round till the weekend,' she said. 'This isn't a good day for me to go see Dad.'

Fox noted the two empty wine bottles on the breakfast bar and the remains of the bottle of cheap vodka on the coffee table. Jude was seated and pretending an interest in the television, but her eyes were heavy-lidded.

'You okay, sis?' he asked.

'Why shouldn't I be?' She looked up at him and her eyes widened. 'What happened to you?'

Fox rubbed his face with his fingers. 'I fell down some stairs.'

Her look hardened, but then she turned away, lifting the cigarette and sucking on it. Fox wandered into the kitchen and filled the kettle. He couldn't see any tea or coffee, and there was no milk in the fridge. Plenty of food, though – it didn't look as though she'd eaten anything since her shopping trip.

'Has your pal Sandra not been in?' Fox called to his sister.

'Not for a few days. She's phoned me a couple of times, just to check.'

'How about Mrs Pettifer next door?'

'Visiting her brother in Hull. He's had a stroke or something.'

'So you're having to manage on your own?'

'I'm not an invalid.'

'You're not exactly taking care of yourself either.'

'Fuck off, Malcolm.' She slung her legs over the arm of the chair, almost knocking the ashtray to the floor.

Fox allowed her a few moments to calm down. 'When I was round here the other day, you seemed to be coping ...' Opening cupboards, he found a fresh jar of instant coffee. He rinsed two mugs, and decided to add two spoonfuls to Jude's.

'You okay with black?' he asked. She didn't answer. 'What are you doing for money?'

'There's some in the account.'

'But probably not much ...'

'When I'm reduced to begging on the street, I'll let you know.'

He picked up some of the mail from the breakfast bar. There was a letter explaining that the mortgage repayments were being reduced in line with the recent cut in interest rates. 'Did Vince have life insurance?' he asked.

'Yes.'

'Have you done anything about it?'

'Sandra did ... phoned them and then got me to sign a letter.'

'Well, that's something.' Fox was sifting through the rest of the mail, some of which had yet to be opened. There was an O2 bill addressed to Mr V. Faulkner. Fox peeled it open, eyes on his sister's back. He gave a little twitch of the mouth when he saw that it wasn't itemised. A hundred and twelve pounds was owing. The kettle came to the boil and Fox took Jude's mug through to her.

'You could do with some milk,' he said, handing it over. She stubbed out her cigarette and took the drink from him. 'And maybe not so much wine and spirits.'

'You're not my dad.'

'I'm the next best thing.' He reached into his jacket pocket for his wallet. When she saw what he was doing, she flew from her chair and headed into the kitchen, pulling open one of the drawers and coming back into the living room brandishing a wad of banknotes, which she flung up into the air in front of him.

'See?' she said. 'I don't need any of your bloody charity!'

Fox stared down at the notes strewn across the carpet. Jude was back in her chair, staring at the TV, knowing he was awaiting an explanation.

'I found it,' she obliged. 'About two grand in total.'

'Found it where?'

'Hidden in Vince's room upstairs. Lucky I got to it before your lot turned the place over – they might've pocketed it.'

'Where did it come from?'

Jude managed a shrug. 'Winnings from the casino?' she guessed. 'Maybe that's where he was on all those nights he didn't bother coming home.'

'He was there on the Saturday,' Fox said quietly, crouching down and beginning to gather up the cash. 'When he left, he took a taxi to the Cowgate ...'

She wasn't really listening to him. 'The sod kept it from me, Malcolm. Hid it away in that bloody room of his with his porn mags and DVDs. I didn't want anyone to know he was like that ... that's why I didn't say anything.' She looked at him again. 'What happened to your face?'

'I got into a fight.' He placed the money on the coffee table.

'Did you win?'

'Not yet.' This produced a thin but palpable smile. She picked up her drink and blew across its surface. 'Shouldn't be too hot,' he told her. 'I added some cold from the tap.' She took a slurp and squirmed. 'A bit strong?' he guessed.

She nodded, but took another mouthful.

'There's tinned soup in the cupboard ...'

'I'm fine with this,' she told him, but he went into the kitchen anyway and got out a pot. The hob was spotless, evidence that nothing had been cooked for a few days. No dishes in the sink, just mugs and glasses. Fox emptied the soup into the pot. It was cream of chicken – the same stuff their mum used to give them when they were sick.

'Jude,' he called, 'the police gave you back Vince's personal items, right?'

'Yes,' she said.

'Could I take a look at them?'

'Envelope in the drawer.' She pointed towards a unit in the living room. It had shelves above, drawers and cupboards below. He found the large padded envelope in the first drawer. Below it were several folded sheets of unused Christmas paper. Fox reached into the envelope, interested in only one thing – Faulkner's mobile phone. It had been dusted for prints, and was also edged with dirt. At some point, it had been lying on the ground. When Fox tried switching it on, nothing happened.

'Got the charger?' he asked his sister.

'Upstairs landing.'

He gave the soup a stir, then headed for the stairs and brought the charger down, plugging it into the spare socket next to the kettle. When he attached it to the phone, a tiny pulsing green light came on. Fox left it while he poured the soup into a bowl and found a clean spoon. There was bread in a bag, but it had begun to go mouldy. He cut away the green bits and laid what was left on the edge of the bowl.

'You'll have to sit at the table for this,' he said, sliding the coffee table closer to Jude's chair. She swung her legs on to the floor and put her mug on the table.

'I'm not really hungry,' she warned him.

'But you're going to eat anyway.'

'Or what?'

'Or I'm grounding you, young lady.' It was a passable imitation of their father, and Jude smiled again before picking up her spoon.

'What's so important about Vince's phone?'

'Just wondering if there's anyone we've not talked to yet.'

'The other ones ... Giles and his lot ... they went through all that.'

'Maybe I just don't think they're as good as I am.'

She took her first mouthful of soup, savouring its aftertaste. 'Know what this reminds me of?' she said.

He nodded. 'I was just thinking the same thing myself.' He went back to the kitchen and switched on the phone.

'His pass number's four zeros,' Jude called to him.

Figured: Vince was too lazy to change the default setting. On the other hand, maybe it also proved that he had little – if anything – to hide from Jude. Fox punched in the numbers. Vince's screen-saver was a photograph from 1966. It showed Bobby Moore hoisting the World Cup. It took Fox a few moments to figure out how to navigate the phone, but eventually he got the call log. There were almost two hundred entries. He reckoned that Giles's team would have been interested only in the most recent additions, but Fox went back further. He got a notepad from his pocket and started jotting down the numbers that recurred, adding date, time and duration. Some were listed by name – Jude, Ronnie, garage, Marooned, Oliver – but many weren't.

'How's the soup?' he asked Jude.

'I ate it all up like a good girl.' She had risen from her chair, bringing the empty bowl into the kitchen and depositing it in the sink. Then she leaned across and pecked him on the cheek.

'What's that for?'

'I just felt like it.' She studied the numbers on his pad.

'Any of them look familiar?' he asked.

'Not really. You think maybe the person who ...?' She broke off, unable to finish the sentence. She cleared her throat and found a different form of words. 'You think it was someone he knew?'

Fox shrugged. Some of the numbers appeared only once. He decided to try one at random and took out his own phone. The call was answered by a woman.

'Wedgwood,' she said in a sing-song voice.

'Sorry?'

'Wedgwood Restaurant.'

Fox ended the call and turned to Jude. 'Wedgwood?' he prompted.

She nodded. 'We had dinner there in December.' She smiled at the memory.

'Just the two of you, or were the Hendrys in tow?'

'Just the two of us – we *did* manage a social life without Sandra and Ronnie.'

Fox acknowledged this with a grunt. There was one number that appeared eleven times between October and January. He asked Jude again if she recognised it and she shook her head, so he made the call.

'Hello?' The voice was quiet, hesitant. It was a woman again, but not a stranger.

'Ms Broughton?' Fox asked. There was no answer. 'This is Inspector Fox. I gave you a lift from Leith Police Station ...' It was a few more moments before she spoke.

'Gordon Lovatt wasn't very happy about that, Inspector. Did Charlie's diary reach its destination?'

'Yes.'

'And did you take a peek?'

Fox took a deep breath. 'Ms Broughton, I'm calling you from Vince Faulkner's phone.'

'Yes?'

'You remember the name?'

'You mentioned him. Then you went to my casino to watch the CCTV footage.'

'From the Saturday night, yes. But what I'm wondering now is, why does he have your number, and why did the two of you speak on eleven separate occasions between October and January?' The silence at the other end stretched past twenty seconds. Fox gave Jude a look to gauge her reaction. She placed her hand on his arm, as if to reassure him.

'Ms Broughton?' Fox prompted.

'It's not my phone,' he heard her state. 'It's Charlie's. The two of them must have been discussing work.'

Fox stared at his sister again. 'Mr Faulkner was pretty low down the food chain.'

'It's the only explanation,' Broughton said. Fox thought for a moment.

'You're keeping your husband's phone switched on . . .' There was another lengthy pause on the line.

'In case people call. He had very many business contacts, Inspector. There's a chance some of them don't know what's happened.'

'That makes sense, I suppose.'

'You *suppose*?'

'But there's one thing that doesn't,' Fox went on. The silence stretched again.

'And what's that?' Broughton eventually asked.

'Why wasn't the phone on the boat?'

'It *was* on the boat,' she growled. 'It was returned to me afterwards. You understand that I'll be telling Gordon Lovatt about this conversation? He's bound to interpret it as further harassment.'

'Tell him he can interpret it any way he likes. And thanks for speaking to me, Ms Broughton.' Fox ended the call and placed the phone on the worktop.

'So that's what you're like when you're working,' Jude commented. Fox gave a shrug. 'Broughton as in Joanna Broughton?' she went on. 'The one who owns the Oliver?'

'That's her. Vince seems to have known her husband pretty well.'

'He sent over champagne one night ...'

'Yes, he did. Did you ever see him talk to Vince?'

Jude nodded. 'They spoke that night. And I think there was another time we bumped into him there ...' She looked at her brother. 'Where do *you* think that money came from, Malcolm? Was Vince mixed up in something?'

Fox gave Jude's good arm a squeeze, offering a smile but no words. She lingered a moment, then headed back to the living room and the television. Fox was thinking of his meeting with Joanna Broughton ... the penthouse and its bare white walls ... meeting Jack Broughton and Gordon Lovatt at the lift ... sitting in the car with Charlie Brogan's diary ...

And did you take a peek?

Maybe not thoroughly enough. Pretty much all that he remembered were the TV shows Brogan kept tabs on. Jude was watching something on the television involving houses and warmer climes. Television ... TV for short ...

TV.

'Oh, Christ,' Fox said suddenly. Jude turned towards him.

'Are you all right?'

He'd placed a hand to his head and his knees were just about holding. His other hand was grasping the edge of the worktop.

'Bloody idiot,' he muttered.

'Malcolm?'

'I'm an idiot, Jude – that's all there is to it.'

'Not better than Giles and his team?'

Fox shook his head, then wished he hadn't. The room swam and he had to steady himself.

'You look terrible,' Jude was saying. 'Can I do anything? When was the last time you ate?'

But Fox was making for the living-room door. 'I'll call you,' he said. 'But I've got to go now.'

'Is it about Vince? Tell me, Malcolm – is it?'

'Maybe,' was as much as Fox could manage to say.

25

'Slow down,' Jamie Breck said. He was dressed as if for jogging and his hair was wet from the shower. 'You look like you've just bitten through a mains cable.'

They had reached Breck's living room. There was ambient music on the hi-fi. Breck sat down and used a remote control to lessen the volume. Malcolm Fox was pacing up and down.

'How can you be so laid-back?' Fox asked, accusingly.

'What else am I supposed to do?'

'Someone's tried setting you up as a paedophile.'

'True – and if I start complaining, everyone knows *you* told me.'

'You should do it anyway.'

But Breck was shaking his head. 'We find out *why* it happened – after that, everything falls into place.'

Fox paused in his walking. 'You think you know?'

Breck folded his arms. 'It's both of us. They brought us together knowing we'd get along ... start to trust one another. You'd see it was a set-up and maybe tell me. Meantime, I'd be letting you walk all over the Faulkner case. Once that was established, we could both be kicked into touch.'

'It's other cops, then? Has to be.' Fox had started pacing again.

'What's on your mind, Malcolm?'

'Vince and Brogan kept phoning one another; means they weren't just boss and employee. The day I took Joanna Broughton home, she gave me Brogan's diary to hand in at Leith. There were a lot of mentions of programmes he wanted to watch. TV – 7.45 ... TV – 10.00 ... that sort of thing.' Fox stopped pacing again and stared at Breck. 'Remember what Mark Kelly said? Bull Wauchope's side-kick?'

'Terry Vass,' Breck said quietly, nodding to himself. 'Same initials.'

'They weren't TV shows, Jamie. Brogan must have been meeting Vass. Now why would that be? Why would Wauchope keep sending his enforcer down to Edinburgh?'

'Brogan owed him money.'

'Brogan owed him money,' Fox echoed. 'And here's another thing – Joanna Broughton keeps her hubby's phone next to her, even now. I called and it took her about five seconds to answer.'

'So?'

'She says it's because people might call who don't know what's happened.'

'Seems plausible,' Breck said with a shrug. Fox gnawed at his bottom lip, then got out his phone and called Max Dearborn.

'Max, it's Malcolm Fox.'

'Linda says you talked to her.'

'This morning. I'm going to help her if I can, but listen ... I've got a quick question – was Charlie Brogan's phone on the boat?'

'We had it checked, then gave it back to the wife.'

Fox's shoulders slumped. He placed his palm over the mouthpiece. 'It was on the boat,' he told Breck.

'Why do you want to know?' Dearborn was asking.

'It's probably nothing, Max. In fact, it *is* nothing.' But Breck was clicking his fingers, trying to get Fox's attention. 'Hang on a sec,' Fox said, placing his hand over the mouthpiece again.

'Wouldn't someone like Brogan have more than one phone?' Breck asked, voice just above a whisper. Fox took a moment to digest this, then spoke to Dearborn again.

'Max ... do you happen to know the number of the phone?'

'It'll take me a minute.' Dearborn was obviously in the inquiry room. There was a rustling sound as he cupped the phone between shoulder and chin, then a clacking sound as he worked at a keyboard.

'How are things anyway?' Fox decided to ask.

'Still no trace of the sod, one way or the other.'

'You keeping a watch on the widow?'

'We're thinking about it.'

'She'd know it was happening.'

'Maybe ... Okay, here's the number.' Dearborn reeled it off.

'Thanks, Max,' Fox said, ending the call and looking at Breck. 'Good tip,' he said with a nod.

'The numbers don't match?' Breck guessed.

'No.'

'So the phone she's keeping beside her isn't the one that was left on the boat?'

'No.'

'Yet she told you it was?'

'She did.'

'Might be the sort of thing better discussed in person?'

'If we can get to her,' Fox mused. Breck suddenly sat bolt upright.

'Time is it?' he asked.

'Just gone one.'

Breck cursed under his breath. 'I'm due at Fettes at half past.'

'That might be a bit tight – unless you don't bother changing.'

Breck had risen to his feet. He studied himself. 'That's an idea,' he said.

'Here's another one – I'm coming with you.'

Breck stared at him. 'Why?'

'Because we have no idea who we can trust on our own patch.'

Breck's eyes narrowed. 'Stoddart?'

Malcolm Fox slipped his hands into his pockets and offered a shrug.

'She's the Complaints,' Breck protested.

'So am I, remember. Let's fight about it on the way. If you're not convinced, I won't get out of the car ...'

Fox didn't get out of the car. It was his car and he sat in the driver's seat with the radio playing, watching as Breck marched into Police HQ. He drummed his fingers on the steering wheel, staring ahead of him, but with his eyes focused on nothing. After five minutes, he heard a noise and turned his head. Breck was coming back, and he was not alone. Inspector Caroline Stoddart looked less than enthusiastic. Her two colleagues, Wilson and Mason, watched from the doorway. Fox got out of the car, not knowing quite what to say. Breck skipped forward and opened the passenger-side door for Stoddart. She glared at Fox.

'You two were told to cease communication.'

'We're bad boys,' Breck seemed to concur. Stoddart stood her ground for a moment, then ducked her head and got into the car. Breck offered Fox a wink before climbing into the back. Fox stood for a further moment, staring at Wilson and Mason. They turned and headed back indoors.

'Let's get this little pantomime over with,' Stoddart was saying. Fox sat back down and closed his door. 'All right,' she went on, 'you've got five minutes.'

'Might take a bit longer,' Breck warned her. Then, to Fox: 'We'd be better doing this elsewhere – if walls have ears, then windows definitely have eyes.'

Fox looked at the building, realised Breck had a point, and switched the engine on.

'Am I being abducted?' Stoddart complained.

'You can leave any time you like,' Breck assured her. 'But what we're about to tell you ... trust me, this isn't exactly the best place.'

'Do I just drive around?' Fox asked, eyes on the rearview mirror. He was aware of Stoddart next to him, tugging at the hem of her skirt.

'As long as you can drive and talk at the same time,' Breck responded.

So Malcolm Fox drove.

Their route took them around the periphery of the Botanic Gardens and uphill towards the city centre. Traffic became sluggish, and Fox said less, concentrating his attention on the road. Breck filled in, and soon they were crossing the top of Leith Walk. Royal Terrace, then Abbeyhill, and down past the Parliament building and the Palace of Holyrood, before entering Holyrood Park itself. Past St Margaret's Loch and entering the one-way section that snaked around the immensity of Arthur's Seat. It felt like the middle of nowhere. There were stretches where no signs of habitation could be glimpsed; just heath and hill. The drive had lasted almost thirty minutes, and Stoddart was asking Fox to pull over.

'A bad place to leave us,' Breck warned her. 'Taxis don't come by here.'

She looked around her. 'Where *is* here?'

Fox had brought the car to a stop next to Dunsapie Loch. A couple of joggers trotted past. A young mother had paused with her baby buggy. There was a nest in the middle of the loch. In a few weeks, a pair of swans would be setting up home.

'Another side of Edinburgh,' Breck was explaining to Stoddart. 'I'd be happy to act the tour guide some time ...'

She said nothing to this, just opened her door and tried to get out. She flinched, perhaps thinking they were holding her down, but it was only her seat belt. She unlocked it and stepped from the car, slamming the door behind her.

'What now?' Breck muttered. Fox met his eyes in the rearview. Breck had been sounding enthusiastic and confident, but it had been a front. Inwardly, he was all nerves.

'Give her a minute,' Fox said. Stoddart was standing with arms folded, legs slightly apart, her eyes on the loch and the view beyond.

'But say she walks ... say she goes straight to your boss or mine?'

'Then that's what she does.'

Breck stared out at her. 'She thinks we're spinning her a line.'

'Maybe.'

'Conniving together ever since we were put on suspension ... and this is all we could come up with! That's what she's thinking.'

'Jamie, you don't know what she's thinking,' Fox muttered, hands wringing the life out of the steering wheel.

'She's *corporate*, Malcolm – same as you used to be. She's not about to break ranks.'

'She just did.' Fox paused until he had Breck's full attention. 'She got into the car, didn't she? Left her cronies back at the homestead. That's not exactly company policy.'

'Good point,' Breck agreed. Then: 'Where's she going?'

The answer was: she was heading towards an incline away from the road. She had to clamber up it, slipping a couple of times in her sensible shoes. Fox didn't think there was anything on the other side until you reached Duddingston. She paused at the top of the outcrop, then turned her head towards the car.

'Let's go see the lady,' Fox said, drawing the key from the ignition.

She had found a dry, moss-fringed rock to sit on. She was huddled over, arms on her knees, wind whipping at her hair. The pose made her look younger. She could have been a teenager, mulling over some perceived injustice.

'You asked a good question,' she told Fox. He had crouched down next to her, Breck standing off to one side with his hands stuffed into the front of his fleece. 'It's the timing – that's the one thing that niggles in all this.'

'Just the one?' Breck gave a hoot of disbelief.

'Nothing else you've told me has any proof attached, but Inspector Fox appeared on our radar several days before Vince Faulkner's murder. I've wondered at that myself.'

'Good for you,' Breck said, while Fox's eyes warned him to shut up.

'Someone must have given you a reason,' Fox stated quietly.

Stoddart shook her head. 'It doesn't always work like that.' Then, after a pause: 'You should know ...'

Yes, he knew. Someone higher up the command chain just had to give you the nod. They were the ones taking care of the paperwork. They were the ones who would take responsibility. All you had to do was watch and record what you saw. There had been a case a few years back – a force down in England. A Chief Constable who suspected a junior officer of an affair with his wife had put a 24/7 surveillance on the man. As far as the team was concerned, the paperwork was in order and the Boss could do as he pleased.

'Who did you get the order from?' Fox asked quietly.

'My boss,' she eventually answered. 'But *he* got it from the DCC.' Meaning the Deputy Chief Constable, Grampian Police.

'So someone must have gone to the DCC,' Breck was saying. Roles had been reversed: Breck had started pacing now, while Fox felt an almost unnatural calm.

'There's something else ...' Stoddart broke off and raised her eyes to the heavens. 'I could get in so much trouble for this.'

'Meaning you believe us?' Fox asked her.

'Maybe,' she replied. 'See, there's this ...' She sought the right words. 'There's been a rumour that something went badly wrong on a murder case a few months back. The victim was a kid, and CID went after his family – turned out the killer had form and was living only a couple of streets away. There was cover-up after cover-up, trying to paper over the cracks.'

'You think that's what the Complaints in Edinburgh were going to be looking into?' Fox asked. Stoddart shrugged.

'It's become Strathclyde's case instead,' she said.

'But everyone knows Strathclyde are second-raters.'

'Yes, they are,' Stoddart agreed.

Fox was thoughtful. 'Does that sound like a trade-off to you? The bosses in Edinburgh saying that if Aberdeen puts one of our men under surveillance, we'll find an excuse not to come chasing you?'

'Maybe,' she said again. She had clasped her hands between her knees, and one of her feet was pumping up and down.

'Are you cold? Do you want to go back to the car?'

'What do I tell Wilson and Mason?'

'Depends how much you trust them,' Breck said. He was taking swipes with his trainers at the tufts of grass. 'Reason we came to you in the first place is, *we* don't know who we can trust.'

'I can see that ...' She looked from Fox to Breck and back again. 'So what are you going to do?'

'We might try talking to Terry Vass,' Fox said.

'So if we're found floating face-down in the Tay,' Breck went on, 'at least *you'll* know where to start.'

Stoddart managed the beginnings of a smile. 'It *is* a bit chilly up here,' she said, getting to her feet.

'Colder than Aberdeen?' Fox teased. But she took the question seriously.

'In a funny way, yes.' The three of them started back towards the car. 'I know I've not been here long, but there's something about this city ... something lacking.'

'Blame the trams,' Breck joked. 'It's what everybody else does.'

But Fox stayed silent. He thought he knew what she meant. People in Edinburgh might be quick to take offence, but they were slow to do anything about it other than seethe. And meantime, on the outside, they seemed reticent and unemotional. It was as if there were some vast game of poker being played, and no one wanted to give anything away. He caught Stoddart's eye and nodded slowly, but she was retreating back into her own shell and didn't respond. What would she say at Fettes? How would she frame her report? Might she begin to resent them for dragging her into their story, a story she wanted no part of? As they reached the car, she stopped with her hand on the door handle.

'Maybe I'll walk,' she said.

'You sure?' Breck asked. But Fox knew she'd made up her mind.

'It's downhill from here,' he explained, pointing. 'You'll come to Holyrood Park Road and that leads out on to Dalkeith Road. Should be taxis there ...'

'I'll be fine.' She slid her hands into her pockets. 'You've given me a lot to think about.' Then she paused and fixed Breck with a look. 'But I'll still need you to come in for interview, DS Breck. Say tomorrow at nine?'

Breck scowled. 'Tomorrow's Saturday.'

'We don't take weekends off, DS Breck, not on the taxpayer's tab.' She waved and headed down the footpath. Breck got into the passenger seat and shut the door. 'What's the point of pulling me in for another Q and A? We've just filled her in on every sodding thing.'

'It's for her colleagues' benefit. So they don't get more suspicious than they probably already are.' Fox started the car and released the handbrake. Ten seconds later, they were passing her. She kept her eyes to the ground, as if the car and its occupants were strangers to her.

'Have we just made a huge fucking mistake?' Breck asked.

'If so,' Fox reassured him, 'we can always blame the trams.'

26

That evening, Breck was going for a meal with Annabel Cartwright. Fox had asked which restaurant.

'Tom Kitchin's place – booked it before all this blew up.' Breck had paused. 'I'm sure we could squeeze in an extra chair ...' But Fox had shaken his head.

'Brogan used to take Joanna there,' he commented.

'How do you know?'

'It was in his diary.'

Afterwards, thinking back on this exchange, he'd felt gratified that Breck had asked him to come to the meal. It was the act of a friend, or at the very least the act of a man with little to hide. Fox had asked Breck if he was any nearer to telling Annabel about the website.

'Later,' was all Breck had said.

Fox had gone out to his car and driven to Minter's, texting Tony Kaye to let him know he was on his way. When he was five minutes from his destination, a reply had arrived from Kaye: Cant make it sorry TK. Another minute later, there was a PS: Joe n gilchrist might be there.

Fox wasn't sure that he wanted to see Joe Naysmith and his new best friend. On the other hand, he couldn't be bothered turning back, and the deal was sealed when a car drew out of a parking bay just as Fox was arriving. He backed the Volvo in and checked that he didn't need to pay for a ticket at this hour. Turned out he'd beaten the system by a good five minutes. He locked the car and crossed the road to Minter's. There wasn't anyone standing at the bar, and no quiz show on the TV. The barmaid was young, with tattooed arms and pink streaks in her hair. Fox looked around. The woman Kaye knew was chatting with a friend at a corner table. Recognising Fox, she gave him a wave. Fox dredged up her name: Margaret Sime. The drink in front of her looked like a brandy and soda. Her cigarettes and lighter sat at the ready. Fox nodded back a greeting and ordered a tomato juice.

'Do you want it spicy?' the barmaid asked. Her accent was Eastern European.

'Thanks,' Fox said. 'And a round of drinks for the table over there.' Then, as she went about her business: 'Are you Polish?'

'Latvian,' she corrected him.

'Sorry.'

She shrugged. 'I get that a lot. You Scots are used to the Poles invading your country.'

'I hear a lot of them are heading home.'

She nodded at this. 'The pound is not so strong, and people are getting angry.'

'About the exchange rate?'

She shook the bottle of tomato juice before opening it. 'What I mean is, jobs are becoming difficult to find. You don't mind immigrants when they're not stealing work from you.'

'Is that what you're doing?'

She was adding Tabasco to the drink. 'Nobody's complained as yet – not to my face.'

'What would you do if they did?'

She made a claw of her free hand. The nails were long and looked sharp. 'I bite, too,' she added. Then she rang up the drinks. Fox was trying to decide where to sit when the door opened and Naysmith came in, followed by Gilchrist. Fox noticed that Joe's whole demeanour had changed. He rolled his shoulders when he walked, as if filled with new confidence. His smile to Fox was that of an equal rather than an understudy. A couple of paces behind him, Gilchrist had his hands in his pockets, seemingly pleased with the transformation and ready to take credit for it.

'Hiya, Foxy,' Naysmith said, voice louder than usual.

'Joe,' Fox said. 'What are you having?'

'Pint of lager, thanks.'

Gilchrist added that he'd take a half of cider. The barmaid had just returned from delivering the drinks to Mrs Sime and her friend. She started pouring as Fox dug into his pocket for more cash.

'How's it going?' Naysmith was asking. He went so far as to place a hand on Fox's shoulder, as if to console him. Fox glared at the hand until it was removed. Gilchrist pursed his lips, trying to suppress a grin.

'Still suspended,' Fox answered Naysmith. 'What's keeping Kaye from his usual skinful?'

'Crisis at home,' Naysmith explained. 'Mrs Kaye says if he doesn't start spending some time there, she's going to walk.'

'So now we know who wears the trousers,' Gilchrist added from over Naysmith's shoulder. Naysmith laughed and nodded.

Fox didn't know whether to be impressed or outraged. It had taken the interloper only a few days to turn Joe Naysmith around. The notion of Joe making jokes about Tony Kaye ... laughing at domestic troubles ... gossiping within hearing distance of a barmaid ... With Fox out of the picture, Kaye was team leader, and now his authority was being eroded from within. Malcolm Fox didn't like it. He didn't like the way Joe had changed, or had let himself be remoulded.

'What happened to your face?' Gilchrist was asking.

'None of your business,' Fox answered.

'Let's grab a seat,' Naysmith was saying, oblivious to Fox's scowl of disapproval. Gilchrist had seen it, though, and understood perfectly. The smile he gave was lopsided and humourless. Divide and conquer – Fox had seen it before in his career. A team was seldom a *team*. There would always be the naysayer, the dissenting voice, the stirrer. You either gelded them or you moved them elsewhere. One cop he'd known had been offered a promotion to pastures new but had asked for it to be offered to a rival. Why? To move the bastard on and leave the rest of the crew intact. Fox wasn't sure he'd have done the same. Maybe now he would, but not until recently. Until recently, he'd have taken the promotion and moved on, leaving his old team to its troubles.

'Bloody quiet in the office,' Naysmith was saying. 'Bob's talking about us taking on some of the meat-and-potatoes stuff.'

'I'm not missed, then?' Fox asked.

'Of course you are.'

'But if I was still there, you wouldn't be.' Fox gestured towards Gilchrist.

'It's not as cloak-and-dagger as I was expecting,' Gilchrist complained. 'Joe's told me about some of your previous work. I wouldn't have minded a piece of that.'

'Don't go getting too comfy,' Fox warned him. 'I could be back at my desk any day.'

'It'll happen, Malcolm,' Naysmith assured him. But Fox was

staring at Gilchrist, and Gilchrist didn't seem so sure. Fox got to his feet, the legs of his chair scraping against the floor. 'Joe,' he said, 'I need a word with your compadre.' Then, this time to Gilchrist: 'Outside.'

It sounded like an order because that was what it was. Gilchrist, however, was in no rush. He took another sip of cider and slowly placed the glass on its beer mat. 'That okay with you?' he asked Naysmith. Joe Naysmith nodded uncertainly. Fox had waited as long as he could and was now striding towards the door.

'See you later,' the barmaid called to him.

'For definite,' he answered her.

Outside, he took several deep breaths. His heart was pumping and there was a hissing in his ears. Gilchrist didn't just annoy him – it went well beyond that. The door behind him swung open. Fox grabbed Gilchrist by his lapels and drew him forwards, then slammed him back against the stone wall. Gilchrist was staring at Fox's bunched fists. He could boast almost half his opponent's body weight and none of his indignation. There wasn't going to be a fight.

'Do what you've got to do,' was all he said, turning his head so Fox couldn't make eye contact.

'You're a turd,' Fox said, his voice rasping. 'What's worse, you're the turd who got me into this. So I'm going to ask you again – who was it brought Jamie Breck to you?'

'Why does it matter?'

'It just does.'

'You going to slap me about a bit? We could compare bruises after.'

Fox pulled Gilchrist forward, then hurled him into the wall again.

'McEwan's going to love this when I ...'

'Tell him whatever you like,' Fox said. 'All I want to know is – whose idea was it?'

'You already know.'

'I don't.'

'I think you do ... you just don't want to believe it. She wanted me gone, Fox. Never, ever liked me. Sure, I was keen on a move, but I didn't have anything to negotiate with. *She* did.'

Fox had loosened his grip. 'You mean Annie Inglis?'

Now Gilchrist turned his eyes towards him. 'Who else?'

'You're lying.'

'Fine ... doesn't matter. You asked me the question and I've given you the only answer I've got. Inglis was the one who said we were going to ask the Complaints for help – and it was *your* name she had.'

'Was it Inglis who called you that night to cancel the surveillance?'

Gilchrist hesitated, and Fox knew that whatever came out of his mouth, it wouldn't be the truth.

'You're still a turd,' Fox stated, breaking the silence. 'I want you to lay off Joe.'

'Lay off him? I can't get *away* from him! You and Kaye must have treated him like shit.'

Fox released his grip completely, his hands falling to his sides. 'I'm coming back,' he said quietly.

'And that's when they move me elsewhere – anywhere Annie Inglis isn't.' Gilchrist was straightening his jacket. 'Are we finished here?'

Fox shook his head. 'Whether it was Annie Inglis or you, the order had to come from somebody upstairs.'

'So go ask Inglis.'

'I'll definitely do that.' Fox paused, remembering something. 'Do you recall me asking what was happening about Simeon Latham? You told me the Aussies were readying to go to trial. But when I spoke to someone on the inquiry, they contradicted that.'

'So?'

'So you lied.'

Gilchrist shook his head. 'It's what I was told. How often do you want me to say it – go ask your girlfriend.' He looked Fox up and down. 'Except she's not, is she? Not now she's got what she needed from you.' Gilchrist gave a smirk. 'There was that look of desperation about you, first time you walked into the office, wearing your braces and your red tie, hoping they'd get you noticed. Annie Inglis is good at her job, Fox. She's good at pretending to be what she's not – she does it each and every day online …'

The door was opening. Fox expected to see Naysmith, but it was Margaret Sime, cigarette at the ready. She assessed the scene in an instant.

'No nonsense, lads,' she warned them.

'We done?' Gilchrist asked Fox.

Fox just nodded, and Gilchrist headed back inside.

'Since I first set eyes on that young man,' Margaret Sime commented as she lit her cigarette, 'I've had just the one thought.'

'What's that?' Fox felt compelled to ask.

'He's got a face deserving of a good hard skelp.'

'Sorry I let you down, Mrs Sime,' Fox apologised.

He spent an hour on the sofa, with the TV playing, sound turned down. He was wondering what sort of conversation he could have with Detective Sergeant Annie Inglis. She had invited him into her home ... made up with him after their falling-out. Was he really now going to accuse her of setting him up in the first place? Was he going to accept Gilchrist at face value? If so, then Inglis had set Jamie Breck up, too ...

Fox thought about Deputy Chief Constable Adam Traynor, confronting him with Bad Billy Giles in the interview room at Torphichen. Then he spooled further back, to the Complaints office, McEwan teasing him: *Chief thinks there's the whiff of something septic up in Aberdeen* ... After the chat with Stoddart, Fox's thinking was that a deal had been done. But if all of this had been the Chief Constable's idea, why would he have hinted to McEwan that the team might have to investigate Grampian Police? No, it had to be Traynor, didn't it? And that was when Fox knew he had his question. He swung his legs off the sofa and reached over to the coffee table for his phone, punching in Annie Inglis's number. When she answered, he hesitated.

'Hello?' she said, her voice taking on an edge. 'Hello?'

'It's me,' Fox eventually admitted. He was gouging his thumb into the space between his eyebrows, just above the bridge of his nose, eyes screwed shut.

'Malcolm? What's the matter? You sound—'

'Just a yes or no answer, Annie. That's all I need, and I won't bother you again.'

There was silence on the line. When she spoke, it was with a tone of concern. 'Malcolm, what's happened? Do you want me to come over?'

'One question, Annie,' he persisted.

'I'm not sure I want to hear it. You're in a bit of a state, Malcolm. Maybe wait till tomorrow ...'

'Annie ...' He swallowed hard. 'What did Traynor promise you?' He listened to the silence. 'If you brought me in on Jamie Breck, he'd move Gilchrist out – was that the deal? Was that all it took?'

'Malcolm ...'

'Just answer!'

'I'm putting the phone down.'

'I deserve to be told, Annie! This whole thing's a stitch-up and it wouldn't have worked without you!'

But he was talking to the dial tone. She'd hung up on him. Fox cursed and considered calling her again, but he doubted she would answer. He could drive to her flat, keep his finger pressed to her buzzer, but she wouldn't let him in. She was too wise.

Too wise and too calculating.

Good at pretending to be what she's not ...

Fox paced the room. He had half a mind to call Jamie, but Jamie was wining and dining Annabel. And how come he was doing that? Why wasn't he pacing his own living room, snarling at the unfairness of it all? Fox grabbed his phone again and made the call.

'Hang on a sec,' Breck said upon answering. 'I'm taking this outside.' Then, to Annabel: 'It's Malcolm, sweetheart.'

'Tell her I'm sorry for butting in,' Fox said.

'I will, when I get back to the table.'

'Nice dinner?'

'What is it that can't wait till morning, Malcolm?' Fox listened to the sound of a door opening and closing. The atmosphere changed – Breck had stepped out of the restaurant. Fox thought he could hear distant traffic, the sounds of the city at night.

'If it wasn't urgent, Jamie ...'

'But obviously it is, so let's hear it.'

Fox began to walk a diagonal of the room, and explained as best he could. Breck didn't interrupt once, except to posit the theory that Gilchrist, being so keen to take a beating, might well be a masochist. When Fox finished, there was silence for a good fifteen seconds.

'Yes,' Breck eventually said. 'Well ...'

'You mean you'd already figured this out?' Fox blurted out, sinking down on to the sofa.

'I'm a gamer, Malcolm. *Role-playing* games – and that's just what this has been. There are roles someone knew we'd end up playing – I'd get to like you; you'd come to trust me ... and we'd end up with our careers blown to smithereens because of it. It's down to our *natures*, Malcolm.' Breck paused. 'We've been played.'

'By one of our own? Our Deputy Chief Constable?'

'I'm not sure that really matters. What's more important is the *why*.'

'And have you come to any other conclusions? Ones you've seen fit to keep from me?'

'We're back in the game, Malcolm. We got blown up once, but

they misjudged us – we've got a second life, and that's down to our natures, too.'

'I'm not sure I follow …'

'You don't need to. All this work we've been doing …' Breck paused to correct himself. 'Work *you've* been doing … it's leading to one thing and one thing only.'

'And what's that?'

'Endgame.' Breck paused once more. 'They're going to have to destroy us again, and that's when we'll know the who and the why.'

'How can you sound so bloody calm?'

'Because that's how I feel.' Breck gave a laugh – a tired laugh, but a laugh all the same. 'Remember when we talked in the car on the way back from the casino?'

'I remember.'

'You're not a spectator any more.'

'Is that necessarily a good thing?'

'I don't know – what do you think?'

'I just want this done and dusted, one way or the other.'

'That doesn't sound like the old, cautious Malcolm Fox.'

'Sorry I interrupted your dinner, Jamie.'

'I'm sure we'll talk tomorrow, Malcolm. Maybe I'll call after my meeting with Stoddart. Meantime, I've got razorfish and carpaccio of scallop waiting for me …'

'Rather you than me.' Fox ended the call and went into the kitchen. Appletiser … various fruit teas … Rooiboos … decaf coffee … none of it appealed. He wanted something altogether edgier and more life-affirming. He thought back to the spiced tomato juice in Minter's and imagined it with the added injection of a thirty-five-centilitre shot of Smirnoff.

'In your dreams, Foxy,' he told himself. But he could taste it all the same, smooth at the back of his throat, and then the burn as it trickled its way downwards into his belly. Vodka had been his childhood drink, swigs stolen from the cupboard where the bottles were kept. Through his teenage years he'd shifted to rum, Southern Comfort, Glayva and whisky, coming back to vodka again for a short second honeymoon before a dangerous liaison with gin. Then whisky again – the good stuff this time round. And always with beer and wine, wine and beer. Lunches and dinners and in-betweeners. Kidding himself that a champagne breakfast with Elaine didn't count …

Kahlua – he'd never drunk Kahlua. Nor had he got far with the huge variety of alcopops. If he wanted lemonade in his vodka, he would add it himself – along with a few splashes of Angostura. As a five-year-old, for an experiment, he'd mixed a couple of spoonfuls of Creamola Foam into a glass of vodka. His father had torn a strip off him for that, and had moved the alcohol to a higher shelf in the pantry. Not high enough, though ...

Fox went back through to the living room and decided to close the curtains. There was a car parked across the street. Its lights were off but its engine was still running. There was a figure in the driver's seat. Fox finished the job at hand, then headed upstairs in darkness. In the main bedroom, he stuck close to the walls as he approached the window. The car was a dark-coloured, sleek-looking saloon. The angle didn't allow him any view of the number plate. Fox thought he could hear music. Yes – coming from the car. Nothing he recognised, but growing in volume. A neighbour across the street opened their own curtains to peer out, but then closed them again and didn't come to the door. A black cab stopped to let a couple out. They'd obviously been to the late-night shopping in town. The wife was toting a couple of expensive-looking carrier bags. The husband's name was Joe Sillars – Fox had met him a few times to talk to. They'd only been in the street a couple of months. Husband and wife stared at the loudly parked car as their cab rumbled away. They had a quick word with one another and decided not to get involved. The driver acknowledged this by sliding his front windows down. And now Fox recognised the song. It was called 'The Saints Are Coming'. It was by an old punk outfit called The Skids. Fox had heard it at many a party in his youth. But he'd listened to it more recently, too ...

After Glen Heaton had mentioned it at one of their interviews.

Bloody fantastic song ... a real rallying call ...

Fox had asked him if he thought of himself as one of the saints, but Heaton had just punched the air, belting out the first couple of lines.

The music outside had stopped, but then started again. The bloody thing was on repeat. A fist was emerging into the night from the driver's-side window.

Glen Heaton was singing his heart out.

Fox walked downstairs on unsteady legs. He stopped in the doorway outside the living room. There were things he could do, calls he could make. He could hear bass and drums join the guitar as Heaton cranked the volume up another notch. Fox grabbed his jacket and headed outside, pausing for a moment on the doorstep ...

Then down the garden path, breathing the night air …

Opening the gate …

Crossing the road …

Heaton watching him all the time, fist no longer visible but still singing along. When Fox was a couple of feet away, the music died. The silence was punctuated only by the Alfa's engine ticking over.

'Knew you'd twig eventually,' Heaton said.

'What are you doing here?'

'You're not the only one who can sit around outside people's houses.'

'Is that what this is?'

'Did you think I hadn't clocked you? Skulking in the dark, scuttling away as soon as you saw me coming … But I'm bigger than you, Fox. I saw *you* coming and I'm still here.'

'What do you want, Heaton?'

'It'll never come to trial – you know that, right?'

'You'll be tried fairly in a court of law and then you'll go to jail.'

Heaton puffed out his cheeks and exhaled. 'There's no telling some people.'

'Did your pal Giles give you my address? Maybe you just wanted to check the bruises.'

'Now that you mention it …' Heaton angled his head. 'Not that you were much of a looker to start with. Still, I must stand whoever did it a couple of drinks.'

'You're saying it wasn't you?'

Heaton gave a smirk. 'Trust me, I wouldn't be slow to take the credit.'

'So you weren't visiting your girlfriend's sauna on Tuesday night?' Fox's spirits lifted when he saw the effect his words had. 'Sonya Michie, Heaton – we know all about her, even if your wife doesn't. Then there's your son …'

The driver's-side door flew open. Fox stood back, putting some distance between himself and Heaton. It struck him that they were the same height and probably much the same weight. There was more muscle on Heaton – the Complaints had followed him to his gym a few times – and almost certainly more aggression in him. But they weren't so dissimilar. Heaton seemed to think better about making a move. Instead, he started to light a cigarette, flicking the spent match on to the roadway so it fell just short of Fox's shoes.

'What sort of cop,' he drawled, 'gets his kicks playing Peeping

Tom? Raking through rubbish bins … sneaking around behind people's backs.'

Fox thought about folding his arms, but didn't – he needed to be ready in case Heaton tried something. 'How is it,' he asked back, 'we never connected you to Jack Broughton?'

Heaton glared at him. 'Maybe because there *is* no connection.'

'Sonya Michie's a connection.' Fox watched Heaton's face muscles stiffen.

'Careful what you say,' Heaton cautioned. 'Besides, she's ancient history.'

'Not so ancient. A few months back you were still seeing her. You stopped to have a chat with her outside the Cowgate sauna.'

Heaton took a couple of seconds to work it out. 'Breck told you,' he said with a sneer.

'Jack Broughton's a sleeping partner in the sauna,' Fox went on. 'Bit more meat to add to your file. Something you might end up being asked about at the trial.'

Slowly, Heaton folded his arms, meaning he wasn't about to attack. Fox allowed his shoulders to unknot a little. 'I've already told you – it won't come to that.'

'You ever been inside that sauna, Heaton? Is that where you met her? Maybe you bumped into Jack Broughton there. Or it could have been the lap-dancing bar on Lothian Road, the one owned by Bull Wauchope …'

'Never been near the place.' The cigarette stayed in the corner of Heaton's mouth as he spoke.

'You've been to the Oliver, though?'

'The casino?' Heaton's eyes narrowed; it could just have been the smoke, but Fox didn't think so. 'Yeah, I've lost the odd quid there.'

'So you'll know Broughton's daughter – she runs the show.'

'She's wearing well,' Heaton acknowledged with a nod of the head.

'Did she ever introduce you to her husband?'

'Charlie Brogan? Never had the pleasure.'

'What about Bull Wauchope?'

Heaton shook his head. 'And the company that owns the sauna belongs to Bull's old man rather than Bull himself.'

'But Bull's in charge for the foreseeable,' Fox argued.

'Might be a short tenure. I hear Bruce Senior's spending a small fortune on lawyers. They're picking the original case apart, looking for anything that screams mistrial.'

'So Bull's not got long to make his mark ...' Fox was thoughtful.

'What's any of this got to do with you, Fox?'

'That's my business.'

'Well, let's see if I can guess.' Heaton unfolded his arms and removed the cigarette from his mouth, flicking ash on to the ground. 'Your sister's man gets himself killed. He worked on a building project. That project was about to doom Charlie Brogan to bankruptcy.' Heaton paused. 'And you're trying to connect Brogan to Bull Wauchope?'

'The connection's already there,' Fox stated.

'Bull's not a stupid man ... some people think he is, and that suits him – means they underestimate him, right up to the moment when he pulverises them.'

'Did Charlie Brogan underestimate him?'

Heaton smiled to himself. 'Why should I tell you anything?'

'They say confession's good for the soul.' Fox paused. 'And maybe I could see to it that the stuff in your file about Sonya Michie gets lost in the system.'

'You think it bothers me that much?' Heaton watched as Fox shrugged. 'You'd have crossed a line, Fox – hard to go back to the Complaints after that.'

'I doubt I'm going back anyway.'

Heaton stared at him for a full quarter-minute. 'When it comes time for the Fiscal to talk to you ...'

'I could say mistakes were made. I could suddenly remember that some procedure or other wasn't followed ...'

'Then they'd have to chuck the case out,' Heaton said quietly. 'Ten minutes ago, you said it was going to trial.'

Fox nodded slowly.

'What's changed?'

'Me,' Fox stated. 'I've changed. See, I've decided right of this minute that *you're* not important. You'll fuck up in future and someone will nab you then. For now, you're a low priority. I want answers to other questions.'

Heaton managed a wry smile. 'How do I know you'll do it?'

'You don't.'

'Case like this, Fiscal might take months or years getting it ready for trial. And all that time, I'm at home with my feet up and the salary going into my bank account.'

'But that's not you, Glen. It's not what you were made for. You'd go stir-crazy.'

Heaton was thoughtful. 'So the state of play is: I've no guarantees

I can trust you, there's stuff you want from me, and we still hate one another's guts?'

'In a nutshell,' Fox agreed.

'Do I get to come inside?' Heaton nodded towards Fox's house.

'No.'

'In that case, get in the car – I'm freezing my balls off out here.' Heaton didn't wait for Fox to agree. He got back in behind the steering wheel, closed the door and slid the window shut. Fox stood his ground for a few seconds more, watching Heaton avoid eye contact. Then he walked around to the car's passenger side and got in. The interior of the Alfa smelt new: leather and polish and carpets.

'You don't smoke in the car,' he commented. 'Is that because your wife doesn't like it?'

Heaton gave a snort.

'So say your piece,' Fox prompted.

'You're right about Bull not having long to make his mark. His plan was to act as a broker for all the other bosses. He told them he could launder their dirty money by putting it into property and property development.'

'Did Jack Broughton tell you this?' Fox asked. Heaton turned his head towards him.

'Charlie Brogan told me.'

'You said you'd never met him.'

'I lied. But here's the thing … now you know this, there's every chance you'll end up the same way as him.'

'There was a developer in Dundee …' Fox was thinking aloud. 'When he lost Wauchope some money, he turned up dead. Did Terry Vass kill him?'

Heaton's eyebrows lifted a millimetre. 'You seem to know a hell of a lot.'

'I'm getting there. So Brogan and the Dundee developer suddenly had a bunch of negative equity, and Wauchope wanted his money out – because it wasn't actually his. What's Vince Faulkner got to do with any of this?'

'You ever see Charlie Brogan? He never had much *heft*.'

'Vince was like his … bodyguard?'

'That's maybe too strong. But when you go to a meeting, you want someone at your back.'

Fox took a moment to mull this over. 'Remember a few months back? One of Ernie Wishaw's drivers was caught with a consignment of dope …'

'I remember.'

'Rumour is, you were feeding information back to Wishaw.'

'Breck again,' Glen Heaton spat.

'You're a regular gun for hire, aren't you? And that means you know a lot ... Is that why they need to protect you?'

'What do you mean?'

'Ever since I handed your case over to the Fiscal's office, there've been people following me, trying to set me up and scare me off.'

'I don't know anything about that.'

'Your good friend Billy Giles hasn't dropped any hints?'

'I'm finished talking, Fox. Just remember what I said – way things are going, you might not be around to see me stand trial.'

'Not that that's going to happen.'

'Exactly.' Heaton paused. 'Now get out of my fucking car.'

Fox stayed put. 'When people speak up for you, they say you always got results. You'd do a favour for one villain, and that villain would repay the debt with a titbit about a competitor. Is that what's happening here, Heaton? Someone's told you to give me Wauchope?'

Heaton stared at him. 'Get out of the car,' he repeated.

Fox got out. The music blared back into life as Heaton revved the engine hard before setting off. A neighbour peered from behind the curtains of her living-room window. Fox didn't bother trying to apologise. What was the point? He stuffed his hands into his pockets and headed back indoors.

Saturday 21 February 2009

27

'What makes you think you can trust him?' Jamie Breck asked.

'You reckon he was lying?'

Fox and Breck were discussing Glen Heaton. They were seated in Fox's Volvo. It was eight o'clock in the morning. Daylight was definitely coming earlier as spring stopped cowering. Breck didn't respond to Fox's question; probably because he didn't have the answer. He held a cardboard beaker of coffee in both hands. It was from a baker's and was now lukewarm as well as weak. Fox had already emptied his out of the driver's-side window. They were parked by a set of wrought-iron gates, waiting for those gates to open.

'Twenty minutes,' Breck muttered, checking his watch.

'Kids don't wear watches any more, have you noticed that?'

'What?' Breck turned his head towards him.

'They use their phones – that's how they tell the time.'

'What are you talking about?'

'Just making conversation. How was the carpaccio last night?'

'Fine – Tom's a great chef.'

'Did you apologise to Annabel for my phone call?'

'She forgives you, and I still don't think you can trust Glen Heaton.'

'Who said I was going to trust him? Someone's using him to send us a message. What we do with it is up to us.'

'You've thought it through?' Breck stared at Fox, but then something caught his attention. 'Hang on … what's that noise?'

It was the low humming of a motor, accompanied by the rattle of a metal grille as it slowly opened. Fox turned the key in the ignition and waited. SeeBee House boasted an underground car park, and one of the residents was about to head out. From his vantage point, Fox could only see the top few inches of the grille that protected the slope down into the car park, but it was sliding upwards all right. And now he could make out the purring of a car engine.

'Porsche,' Breck drawled. 'Bet you any money you like.'

Yes, a silver Porsche, driven by a man who didn't really need the sunglasses he was wearing. It was light out, but there was no sun as yet. The gates seemed to shiver, then opened inwards slowly. The Porsche had to bide its time, though it sounded impatient. As soon as the gap allowed, it sped out of the compound and past Fox's car. Fox drove inside and parked at the front door, just as on his previous visit. He was out of the car before the gates had started to close again.

'Did you recognise him?' Breck asked.

'You mean the driver?' Fox nodded. 'Gordon Lovatt.'

'Bit early for a PR meeting, isn't it?'

Fox agreed that it was. He was standing by the intercom, his finger pressed to the bell for the penthouse. There was a little camera watching him, and he stared into its lens.

'What do you want?' a voice asked from the speaker.

'Just a quick word, Ms Broughton.'

'What about?'

'Mr Brogan. There's some news.'

'I'm not dressed yet.'

'I thought you were used to hosting meetings in your nightie.'

'What do you mean?'

'I could have sworn I just saw Gordon Lovatt's Porsche ...'

As the silence stretched, Fox locked eyes with Jamie Breck. Breck was whistling, but without making any noise.

'It really can't wait?' Joanna Broughton's voice crackled from the metal speaker.

'It really can't,' Fox confirmed.

The door buzzed as if in irritation. Fox pushed at it and it opened.

The foyer was deserted. Fox led the way to the triplex's private lift and pushed the button. It arrived and they got in. Fox pressed the button and the P sign lit up, the doors beginning to close. He recalled meeting Jack Broughton and Gordon Lovatt on his previous visit. They had gained access to the compound without needing anyone to open the gates for them. At the time, Fox had reckoned Jack Broughton must own one of the little remote-opening boxes

– gifted to him by Daddy's little girl – but now he was beginning to wonder.

When they reached Joanna Broughton's floor, the door to her apartment was standing open in readiness. Joanna Broughton was fully dressed, her hair and make-up immaculate.

'Fast work,' Fox commented.

'What is it you want to tell me?' she asked. She sounded in a hurry, but that wasn't Fox's problem.

'You know DS Breck?' he asked by way of introduction, as Breck busied himself closing the door. Breck waved a hand in greeting, without making eye contact. He was too busy examining the view.

'Nice,' he said. 'Very nice.'

'Yours for three million,' she snapped, folding her arms and placing one foot in front of the other, ready for combat.

'I imagine Mr Brogan *would* sell, too,' Fox said, sliding his hands into his pockets. 'But the market's against him, and it would still be a drop in the ocean.' He paused, locking his eyes on Broughton's. 'How much is he into them for, Joanna?'

'I don't know what you mean.'

'Bull Wauchope and his syndicate,' Fox informed her. 'We've been trying to work it out, DS Breck and me. Could be anywhere from ten to a hundred million. CBBJ owns a lot more real estate than either of us realised. A journalist's been doing some research. Hunting lodges in the Highlands with thousands of acres attached ... a couple of islands ... land in Dubai ... a few dozen flats on spec sites in London and Bristol and Cardiff ... All of it bought at the height of the boom, a boom nobody thought was about to be punctured. He was in the middle of setting up a company in Bermuda, wasn't he? That's something else the journalist learned. Soon it would all have been offshore and a damned sight more secret. But then everybody got twitchy and wanted their money back. Wanted it in the same cold, hard cash they'd given him to launder in the first place.'

During this speech, Joanna Broughton's face had shown no emotion. She hadn't so much as blinked. But when Fox paused, she turned away and headed for one of the cream leather sofas, settling herself there and making sure her knee-length skirt didn't reveal anything she didn't want it to.

'You said you had news,' she said coolly. 'I'm not hearing any.'

'What was Gordon Lovatt doing here?'

She glared at him. 'The police force is leaking like a sieve – mostly to that reporter you mentioned. Gordon is preparing a response.'

She paused. 'I dare say *you've* been speaking to her, too ... dripping poison into her ear ...'

'That's from *Hamlet*, isn't it?' Breck said, hands behind his back, pretending still to be interested in the panorama.

'That time I dropped you home,' Fox started to ask, regaining her attention, 'when I mentioned Vince Faulkner's name it didn't seem to mean anything to you.'

'Why should it?'

'Your husband used him on occasions – specifically, occasions when he feared he might be in for a thumping.'

'I don't know what you're talking about.'

'How about the name Terry Vass?'

She was shaking her head, refusing to meet his eyes.

'I'm guessing it was pretty late in the day before Mr Brogan told you what was going on. I'm also betting you're furious with him about it. Wouldn't do for your father to find out what sort of numpty you've gone and got hitched to.' Fox's voice softened a little. 'But Charlie needed your help, Joanna, and you've been giving it, furious or not. That phone you keep beside you, the one you said came from the boat ... you lied to us about that. Your story's holed at the waterline and I think the pair of you are sinking ...'

Her eyes were growing glassy with tears, but she angled her head skywards so as to trap them there.

'We need to speak to him,' Fox went on, measuring out his words. 'He hasn't fooled the investigators and I very much doubt he's had more luck with Bull Wauchope. Criminals the length and breadth of the country will be on the lookout for him. There's a good chance they'll get to him before we do – and I think you know what that means. I don't suppose he had much time for planning. He saw what happened to Vince Faulkner and knew he had to do something quick.' Fox gestured towards the empty walls. 'On the other hand, he flogged off the family jewels. I'm guessing some of the money was an attempt to stave off Wauchope. The rest'll be paying his way right now and for the foreseeable.' He paused again, but there was no reaction from the figure on the sofa. Her whole body seemed frozen and she could have been posing for a portrait in oils.

'Is he even in the country?' Fox asked her. 'I'm guessing he is – hard not to leave a trail otherwise. He could even be in one of the flats on the floors below ... sneaking up here at night ... living like a hermit in the daytime ...'

'I want you to leave.'

'If you care about him, you'll talk to him about this. We're not his friends, Joanna, but we're far and away his best bet. What did you tell your father? Did you even think of asking him for help?' Her eyes burned into his. 'Probably not,' he went on. 'Because you can look after yourself, and Jack's never had much faith in your husband anyway ... that's how it is with fathers and daughters.' Fox offered a shrug.

'Get out,' she repeated, with fresh venom.

Fox was holding a business card by the tips of his thumb and forefinger. 'My new number's on the back,' he explained, setting it on the arm of the sofa. 'We figured it out,' he reminded her. 'Wauchope will figure it out – and he *will* come asking, Joanna.'

'My dad would have something to say about that. He'll have something to say about *you*, too!'

Fox shook his head slowly. 'Jack's tired – you can see it in his eyes, the way he walks. I know you still respect him, but that's because you remember him the way he was. Maybe you were even more than a little scared of him. But that's all changed. Think about it – if Charlie had been scared of him, he'd never have got involved with Wauchope and the others. He'd have run a mile, for fear of offending the infamous Jack Broughton.' Fox bent at the knees a little, the better to sustain eye contact. 'Some of the stuff Wauchope owns in Edinburgh ... I'm guessing it used to be part of your father's empire. He's been letting Wauchope buy into it because he knows the future when he sees it. These days, Jack's not much more than a minority shareholder. And Wauchope knows weakness when he sees it. Bull wants your husband, Joanna, and I'm not sure you can stop that happening on your own.'

This time, Joanna Broughton was unable to stop the tears. She wiped them away with the arm of her blouse, smearing mascara across both cheeks.

'Go,' she said, her voice barely above a whisper.

'You'll talk to Charlie?'

'Just go, will you?' She pushed her shoulders back and filled her lungs with oxygen. '*Get out!*' she screamed. '*I want you out of here!*'

'My card's there when you need it,' Fox reminded her.

'Out.'

'We're going.'

In the lift on the way down, Breck nodded in appreciation of his partner's performance.

'Couldn't really fault it,' he commented. Fox shrugged away the compliment.

'Let's see if it gets us anywhere,' he cautioned.

Outside, a large black BMW with tinted windows was being parked next to the Volvo. When the driver emerged, Fox recognised him.

'It's Mr Broughton, isn't it?' he asked.

Jack Broughton stared at the proffered hand but decided against shaking it.

'You probably don't recognise me,' Fox went on. 'I was in a bit of a state last time we met.'

'You're that cop ... you were here once before.'

Fox nodded. 'But I was also attacked one night in the Cowgate ...'

Broughton's eyes narrowed as he studied Fox afresh. 'I hope you've not been upsetting Joanna?'

'Perish the thought. That sauna on the Cowgate ... you used to own it, didn't you?'

'I owned the building – whatever happens inside is nobody's business, so long as it's legal.'

'With the Wauchopes in charge, there's not much hope of that.'

It took Jack Broughton a few moments to decide not to respond. 'I'm taking my daughter out for breakfast,' he said, making to move past Fox. When the two men were side by side, he paused. 'I'll let you in on a secret, though ... I *did* see something that night. There were two of them. I only saw them from behind, but ... well, you get a feeling for these things after a while.'

'What sort of feeling?'

'They were cops – and bloody good luck to them.'

He used his own key to enter the building. Fox stared at the door. *Two of them* ... Yes, one to kneel on his back, while one swung a foot at his jaw. Two cops.

'He's just trying to rattle you,' Jamie Breck commented. Fox turned towards him.

'You reckon?' Fox wasn't so sure. Breck was checking his watch.

'I need to be at Fettes for my session with Stoddart ...'

'I'll take you.' Fox unlocked the Volvo and started to get in, fastening his seat belt but then just sitting there, hands on the steering wheel.

'In your own time,' Breck prompted him.

'Sure.' Fox started the engine and angled the car towards the gate, which had already started opening inwards.

'You're not taking the old bastard seriously?' Breck asked.

'Of course not, but do me a favour, will you?'

'What?'

'Call Annabel and ask her a question.'

Breck dug into his pocket for his phone. 'What is it you want to know?'

'The team handing out the Vince Faulkner flyers on Tuesday night …'

'You *are* taking him seriously.'

'Two cops, Jamie … one of them dying for payback …'

Breck eventually got it. 'Dickson and Hall,' he stated.

'Dickson and Hall,' Malcolm Fox concurred.

It was afternoon when the text arrived on Fox's mobile. Breck had gone to meet Annabel for a coffee. There was some apologising to be done. They'd been planning to spend Saturday night in Amsterdam, flying back Sunday evening, and now Breck was cancelling. Fox had told him not to, but Breck had been adamant.

'I need to be around for this,' he'd explained.

'What if there *is* no "this"?' Fox had retorted.

But now here was a text – Waverley 7 p.m. buy ticket Dundee n wait WH Smith. There was no name, and when Fox called the number there was no reply. But he knew all the same. He paced his living room for a few minutes, then called Jamie Breck.

'You still with Annabel?' he asked.

'She's gone to the loo. I think she's starting to hate me, Malcolm.'

'You can make it up to her later. How did it go with Stoddart?'

'As you suspected, I think it was for the benefit of her colleagues more than anything else.'

'Did either of them think to ask you about the little jaunt we took with their boss?'

'She didn't give them the chance – escorted me on to and off the premises; never left the room for a minute.'

'That's good …'

Breck could tell from his tone that something had happened. 'Tell me,' he prompted.

'We've got a meet. Seven tonight at Waverley station. He wants us to buy tickets to Dundee.'

'Dundee? Am I missing something or is that the last place he'd hide?'

'Plenty of stops between here and there.' Fox took Breck's silence for agreement. 'Once we've got the tickets, he wants us to wait by the newsagent's.'

'Why?'

'I don't know.'

'You didn't ask him?'

'It was a text message.'

'Did you try calling back?'

'No one's answering.'

'We should give the number to someone ... get them to put a trace on it ... Can we even be sure it's from him? Did he give his name?'

'No.'

'So it might not be?'

'I don't know.'

'Annabel's coming back,' Breck said.

'You should take her out tonight ...'

'You don't get rid of me that easily. I'll see you there at seven.'

The phone went dead. Fox slipped it back into his pocket and rubbed at his temples. He lifted a book from one of the piles and placed it on the half-filled shelf.

'It's a start,' he told himself.

He took a taxi to the station. The driver's conversation revolved around tram works and traffic diversions. 'See the council,' he would say at one moment and 'See the government' the next. 'And don't get me started about the banks ...'

Fox had no intention of getting him started; the real problem was getting him to stop. Fox was trying to imagine himself into a role. He was a commuter on his way home from a tiring day. Maybe he worked Saturdays; maybe he'd been shopping. He would step from his taxi, head into the booking office, and pay for a ticket. The driver had even asked him – 'This you on your way home?' – without seeming interested in any answer.

'Wouldn't blame you for emigrating, pal ... whole country's a bloody shambles ...'

The cab bumped its way down the slope into the station proper and pulled into a waiting bay. Fox paid the driver, adding a tip. The man was wishing him well for the rest of the weekend as Fox closed the door. It was six forty by the station clock. Plenty of time. The post-shopping rush had died back a bit, though the concourse was still busy. A train had obviously arrived from London. There was a lengthy queue at the taxi rank. He pitied whichever tourist or traveller ended up with the driver he'd just waved off. The booking office had another queue, but there were self-serve machines. Fox used his bank card and bought two off-peak returns.

You're leaving a trail, he warned himself. But if things turned sour, that might be a plus – it would give the cops who came looking for him something to work with. He wandered past the coffee stall and the bar and the Burger King, then headed towards the platforms. There were people resting their backs against the window of the WH Smith. The place was doing a good trade, and Fox wasted a couple of minutes looking at the range of books and magazines. Even so, it was still seven minutes shy of the hour.

'Hello, copper,' a voice barked from behind. Fox swirled towards it. Jamie Breck was grinning.

'Need to sharpen those spider senses, Malcolm,' he said. 'I've been here a while.' Breck held up a ticket. 'Got you this.'

In reply, Fox held up his own. 'Snap,' he said. Then: 'How long since you arrived?'

'Half an hour – decided to scope the place out, and saw you doing the same.'

'I'm wondering if maybe he wants to meet us here.'

'It's a bit public,' Breck replied, his voice full of doubt. 'Just that wee bit *exposed*.' He seemed to remember something. 'You know what you were saying? About him maybe living downstairs from the penthouse ...?'

Fox shook his head. 'It would put Joanna in the firing line.'

'Isn't she there already? When he scarpered, why did *she* stick around?'

'She's got a casino to run, Jamie. Besides, if they'd both done a midnight flit, Wauchope would have been on to them all the quicker.'

Breck nodded his agreement. 'How come I'm the one being fast-tracked when you're the better cop?'

Fox shrugged. 'Maybe you bribed someone ...?'

Breck gave a snort and checked his watch against the large digital clock above the departure and arrival boards. 'There's a train to Dundee, leaves on the dot of seven. If we miss that, next one's half past. What do you think?'

'Maybe we get on the train we're told to catch and he jumps on at a station down the line.'

Breck nodded slowly. 'Or?'

'Or he meets us here. But you said it yourself – it's risky.'

'Or we're being led a dance,' Breck offered.

Fox gave a twitch of the mouth. 'Was Annabel okay in the end?'

'Dinner midweek at Prestonfield House, and Amsterdam the next window we get.'

'She's a tough negotiator.'

'I thought it best to cave in straight away. You were right, by the way ...'

'Dickson and Hall?'

Breck nodded again. 'Handing out flyers the night you got jumped. Any plans for a revenge attack?' Breck watched Fox shake his head, then checked the station clock again. 'Seven's been and gone.'

'Yes.'

'And here we are, standing outside WH Smith.'

'I can't disagree.'

'And nothing's happening.' Breck shuffled his feet. Fox was studying the passing parade of travellers. Some had obviously enjoyed a drink; maybe one or two of them had been to the football. They were voluble as they chatted with their friends. It was Saturday night and people from outside the city were arriving with only one aim in mind. Fox had even heard the Rondo mentioned as a probable destination for later.

Breck was studying his watch. 'Just relax,' Fox told him.

'Are you on medication?' Breck asked. 'Don't tell me you're not fretting.'

'My insides are dancing,' Fox admitted.

More people passed them, some at a gallop in a bid to make this or that seven o'clock departure – there were delays on a few of the trains. The announcer explained as much through the Tannoy. Fox could make out the gist of what she was saying.

'He's late,' he stated. Breck just nodded. The phone in Fox's hand started to ring. He peered at the screen: same number the text had come from, but this time it was an actual call. He pressed the phone to his ear and answered. 'Yes?' he said.

The voice was unnaturally deep. Had to be fake – someone putting it on. 'Leave by the back exit. Wait by the lights on Market Street.' The phone went dead.

'Message received and understood,' Fox muttered. Then, to Breck: 'Come on.'

'Where are we going?'

'He wants us on Market Street.' Fox crossed the concourse, heading for the stairs.

'Why?'

'Because he's watched too many *Bourne* films.'
'Did you recognise the voice?'
'I've never spoken to him.'
'So maybe it's *not* him.'
'If this was Quidnunc and not real life, how would you play it?'
'I'd forge alliances.'
Fox looked at him. 'Not much time for that.'
'Besides which, who'd want to side with us?' Breck added.
'Good question ...' When they reached the top of the footbridge, Fox had to pause to catch his breath. 'Imagine what I'd be like if I smoked,' he managed to say.
'Half a stone lighter?' Breck replied. Then: 'What are we supposed to do when we get there?'
'Await further instructions.'
Breck stared at him. 'Tell me he didn't use those words.'
Fox shook his head and started moving again. A further flight of steps and they emerged out on to the pavement. There were traffic lights to their right. Fox looked around, seeking their tormentor. The City Art Centre was in darkness. People scurried past, heads down. North Bridge was overhead to their left, buses nose to tail as they waited for the lights to change at Princes Street.
Breck was staring at the train tickets. 'I hope he's going to refund us,' he said.
'I think we're at the very rear of that particular queue, Jamie.'
'You're probably right.'
Fox's phone rang again. He put it to his ear. The voice had changed, unable to sustain its previous tone.
'Cross the road and head for Jeffrey Street. Once you're past the bridge, look for a church.' The caller hung up. Fox turned to Breck.
'I think we're about to repent our sins,' he said, readying to cross at the lights. Fox wasn't really expecting any church to be open to visitors on a Saturday night, so when they arrived at the doors to Old St Paul's he stood there, looking to left and right. He checked that he was still getting a signal on his phone – Edinburgh was full of dead zones.
'What now?' Breck asked. 'More waiting?'
'More waiting,' Fox agreed.
'Whatever else happens, this guy's getting a slap from me.' Breck paused. 'Do you think he's watching us?'
'Maybe.'
Breck looked up and down the street. 'Not too many candidates,'

he concluded. It was quieter here than on Market Street. There was a single-decker bus parked outside the Jurys Inn, but no sign of its passengers. 'Could he be staying there?'

'Maybe.'

Breck swore beneath his breath while Fox studied the wall of the church. There was a couple of signs, one indicating that Old St Paul's belonged to the Scottish Episcopal Church, the other giving a taste of its history. The church had been founded in 1689, and was an eighteenth-century refuge for Jacobites. It proclaimed itself a place 'for all who seek faith'.

'Amen to that,' Fox was muttering under his breath as his phone sounded again. He put it to his ear and had already uttered a terse 'Yes?' when he realised it was an incoming text. There was just the one capitalised word:

INSIDE.

He showed Breck the screen, and Breck reached out to turn the door handle. With the slightest of pushes, the door opened inwards. There was a flight of stone steps. Fox used the handrail as he climbed. When he turned the corner at the top, he was in a church much larger than its exterior had suggested. There were modern-looking paintings at one end, a pulpit and altar at the other, with a chapel off. A young man was sweeping between the pews. He didn't pay them any attention, even though Breck was staring at him. But Fox's attention had shifted to the lit chapel. A huge painting covered most of one wall. Some folding chairs had been placed in front of it. He sat down on one and saw that the painting comprised four square canvases, placed together to make up a vast swirl of white material. Was it meant to be a cloak or a shroud? He couldn't tell, but he was mesmerised by it.

'Is that him?' Breck was whispering. He meant the floor-sweeper.

'Too young,' Fox stated.

'This is just stupid.' Breck ran his fingers through his hair.

'Sit down,' Fox suggested. 'Take the weight off.'

Breck didn't look convinced, but he sat down anyway.

'One of the paintings Brogan sold,' Fox said quietly, 'looked a bit like this, only smaller.' He was remembering the photo of the penthouse's interior, the one published in the newspaper.

'Is that why he's brought us here?'

Fox just shrugged and let his gaze move across the painting. Someone was coming up the stairs. Their footsteps sounded like busy sandpaper. Breck had turned to watch. The footsteps were quieter as they entered the chapel. Breck had risen to his feet, nudging Fox, but Fox was continuing to study the painting. The new arrival crossed in front of him and sat down on the next chair along.

'The artist's name is Alison Watt,' Charles Brogan said. 'I know a bit about art, Inspector.'

'Must've been a wrench to sell it all ...' Fox turned his head and found himself looking at the drowned man. Brogan had removed a lumberjack-style hat, revealing that his already thinning hair had been shaved off.

'Did the missus do that?' Fox asked.

Brogan ran a hand across his skull. He was wearing fingerless black woollen gloves. He looked to have lost some weight and his skin was sallow. He finished rubbing his head and dragged his fingers down around his jaw. He hadn't shaved in a while. The black workman's jacket could have been borrowed from one of his building sites. The denims had seen better days, as had the scuffed boots. As disguises went, it wasn't bad.

Then again, it wasn't great.

'You weren't followed,' Brogan said. 'And you didn't bring the cavalry with you.'

'How come we didn't spot you at Waverley?'

'I was on the overhead walkway. When I called on the phone and saw you answer, I knew you were my guys.'

'Except we're *not* your guys,' Breck corrected him.

Brogan just shrugged. Fox turned his head a little and fixed him with a stare. 'What happened to Vince Faulkner?' he asked.

Brogan was quiet for a moment. He turned his attention to the painting. 'I'm sorry that happened,' he said at last.

'You sent him to meet with Terry Vass, didn't you?'

Brogan nodded slowly.

'And Vass decided to send you a message,' Fox stated.

'If I'd gone to the sauna ...' Brogan's voice drifted off.

'That was the deal, was it? Vass was expecting to see you, but Vince turned up instead?' For the first time, Fox felt a pang of sorrow for Faulkner's fate. Brogan had found out about the man's history of violence, and had thought him a useful 'soldier'. Vince would have loved playing that role. Maybe he'd goaded Terry Vass, and maybe not. But he had died horribly.

'You knew from Vince's personnel file that he had previous,' Fox went on. 'You could have gone to Jack Broughton to borrow some muscle, but you had to be your own man, which is why you opted for Vince. He came to you on Saturday night. He'd just clobbered his girlfriend and was angry and ashamed, drinking away the memory of it. Barman at the casino says he should never have got past the door – makes me think you'd primed the bouncers for his arrival …' Fox paused, but Brogan wasn't taking his eyes off the painting. 'You needed him to go meet Vass, so he could take a beating on your behalf. Suited you just fine that he was too drunk to refuse.' There was a bitter taste at the back of Fox's throat. He tried swallowing it down.

'I was desperate,' Brogan muttered.

'The cabbie who dropped him near the sauna says he nearly changed his mind about going – he was sobering up fast and he was scared.'

'Then he shouldn't have played the tough guy.' Brogan managed a quick glance in his tormentor's direction.

Fox was thinking again of Vince Faulkner. With his hidden stash of money at home, payment for past services rendered …

'Was he killed at the sauna?' Breck interrupted. 'Maybe Forensics could take a look.'

But Brogan shook his head. 'They took him somewhere else … kept him there.'

'How do you know?' Fox was giving Brogan his full attention. He watched the man swallow before he answered.

'They phoned me. They put Vince on …' He squeezed shut his eyes, trying to block out the memory. 'I never want to hear anything like that again.'

'You might,' Fox said. 'When they come for Joanna.'

Brogan opened his eyes and glowered at Fox. 'I'd kill them,' he spat. 'They know that.'

'Maybe.'

'And if I didn't, Jack would.'

'Jack's what all this is about, isn't it?' Fox asked. 'You were doing something you thought might impress your father-in-law – playing money-man for the big boys. I'm not saying Jack Broughton knew, but you were thinking maybe it would get back to him some day and he'd start to respect you just a little bit more.'

Brogan's face tightened, and Fox knew he'd struck a nerve.

'But here's the thing, Charlie,' Fox went on. 'When they come for Joanna – and they *will* come for her – Jack's not going to go after them.' Fox paused. 'He's going to come gunning for *you*. You're the one he'll blame.'

Brogan seemed to consider this. 'I'm in hell,' he said weakly, eyes back on the painting.

'That's why you're here,' Fox said. 'You know we're your only chance.'

'What can you do?' Brogan was bowing his head as if in prayer.

'I don't know.'

With head still bowed, Brogan turned his neck so he could watch Fox's face.

'I really don't,' Fox stated with a shrug of the shoulders. Then, to Breck: 'Have you got any ideas?'

'One or two,' Breck replied after a moment's consideration.

'That's all right, then,' Fox said. 'But Charlie … you're going to have to tell us everything. And it's got to be done properly.'

Brogan considered this. 'I really thought it would work,' he muttered to himself at last.

Fox gave a snort. 'Vince's body was found Tuesday afternoon; a few hours later you're suddenly checking your will at your solicitor's office, and by Thursday you're supposed to be dead?' He shook his head slowly. 'No, Charlie, it was never going to work.'

'The deck shoes were a nice touch, though,' Breck conceded. 'Left bobbing about on the water like that …'

'They were Joanna's idea.'

'And she helped you come ashore, too?' Fox guessed. 'Dinghy, was it?'

'I swam.' Brogan puffed out his chest a little. 'Time was, I could have swum the whole estuary …'

'Good for you,' Breck said.

Fox had thought of something else. 'The money from the paintings … it was to tide you over, right? Did Wauchope find out you were holding on to it? Is that what finally blew his fuse?'

'Men like Bull Wauchope, their fuses are long blown.'

'You know Glen Heaton, don't you? When I started sticking my oar in, did you have Joanna go see him? Did she tell him to fill me in on Bull Wauchope?'

Brogan gave a resigned smile. 'You said it yourself, Inspector – you're the one card left in this lousy hand I've been dealt …'

There was the sound of someone clearing their throat nearby. All three turned, expecting trouble, but it was only the cleaner.

'Sorry,' the man said, 'but I've got to lock up now. Don't blame you for loitering, though.' He nodded in the direction of the painting. 'It's a great thing, isn't it? So true to life …'

'True to life,' Fox agreed. But it was a shroud, and it reminded him of Vince Faulkner's ice-cold corpse, lying in the darkness of a mortuary drawer. All because of the shaven-headed fat man who was staring at the painting one final time.

All because Charlie Brogan had something to prove to the world.

It was Annabel Cartwright who met them at Torphichen. She'd already checked that Billy Giles and his team had left for the night. There was a desk sergeant on duty, but he was on the telephone when they arrived. Cartwright ushered them through the door and along the corridor to the interview room. She'd brought a videotape for the camera and audiotape for the recorder. Once everything was set up, Fox mentioned that it would be best for all concerned if she left them to it. She gave the curtest of nods and left the room. She hadn't so much as acknowledged Jamie Breck's existence.

'The debts are piling up,' Breck commented to Fox.

'Let's get on with this,' Fox replied.

An hour later, they had as much as they needed. Fox pocketed both sets of tapes and they left the station without seeing anyone. There was a locked patrol car outside. Fox looked to left and right, thinking back to the day he'd taken that first walk with Jamie Breck.

'What now?' Brogan asked, fixing his hat to his head.

'Is it safe, wherever you're staying?' Fox asked him.

'Yes.'

'Does Joanna know the address?'

Brogan gave him a look, and Fox rolled his eyes. 'If she knows, then it's not safe.'

'She'd never tell.'

'Maybe so ...' Fox didn't bother with the rest of the sentence. 'We keep in touch by phone, right?' He waited until Brogan had nodded his agreement. 'Okay then. Keep your head down for another day or two while I discuss options with DS Breck.'

Brogan nodded again. A taxi had swept around the corner, its 'hire' light illuminated. Brogan stuck out a hand and the driver signalled to stop. Brogan got in and closed the door after him. Whatever destination he gave the driver, neither Fox nor Breck heard it. They watched the cab as it headed for the Morrison Street junction.

'What now?' Breck asked.

'I thought you were the one with the ideas.'

'You might not like them.'

'If they're better than nothing, they're worth hearing.' They started walking uphill towards the traffic lights. There was a pub just across the road.

'What did you think of Brogan?' Breck asked.

'I wanted to punch him in the face.'

'That would have looked good on the video,' Breck said with the hint of a smile.

'Wouldn't it, though,' Fox agreed. 'I should have done it when we were in that chapel.'

'In the sight of God?' Breck's voice feigned outrage at the notion. Fox reached out and touched his shoulder.

'These ideas of yours, Jamie ...'

'To be honest, there's only the one.' Breck paused. 'And you're really not going to like it.'

'Because it's risky?' Fox guessed.

'Because it's stupid,' Breck corrected him.

Sunday 22 February 2009

28

Dundee the following night, and people were out to have one last good time before the working week began again.

Fox and Breck sat in Fox's car. Back in Edinburgh, Breck had suggested taking his Mazda, 'for a change', but Fox had declined, explaining that he just couldn't get comfortable.

'I'm not built for a sports car, Jamie.'

So they had travelled to Dundee in the Volvo and were parked on the street outside Lowther's bar. Breck had interrupted Mark Kelly's weekend that afternoon with a request for recent photos of Bull Wauchope and Terry Vass. The resulting printouts from Dundee CID were in the glove compartment, having been committed to memory. So far, no one entering or leaving Lowther's had offered a precise match – though some came close.

'Not exactly a cocktail clientele, is it?' Breck commented, as they studied three men who had come outside to smoke cigarettes, check texts on their phones and hawk gobbets of phlegm on to the pavement. One man kept rearranging his crotch; another offered gravel-toned enticements to any young women who dared to pass within his orbit. All three men wore T-shirts stretched over distended stomachs. All three sported tattooed forearms and gold chains around their necks and wrists. What hair they had was gelled and spiky, faces shiny and fat and pockmarked. One was missing most of his front teeth.

'So do we just walk in there or what?' Breck was asking.

'It's your plan, Jamie – you tell me.'

'We could sit here all night otherwise.'

They had already been to the address they had for Wauchope Leisure Holdings. It was one of a row of shops on an estate to the north of the city centre. The door had looked solid, and the blinds in the unwashed window had been shut tight. No answer to their knock. Lowther's was all they had left – it was the pub owned by Wauchope, the pub with the payphone. Someone in there had lured one property developer to his death and harried another into faking his own suicide.

Lowther's was all they had ...

Breck seemed to realise as much and pushed open the passenger-side door. Fox pulled the key from the ignition and followed suit. The three men still hadn't noticed them. They were laughing about something, a message or a photo on one of their phones. Breck found himself standing just behind them.

'Can anyone join in?' he asked.

The men turned as one. Fox had caught up with his partner by now, but didn't fancy their chances. The good humour had disappeared from all three faces.

'That's some smell of bacon coming off you two,' one of the men stated, while another spat on the pavement, just missing Breck's shoes.

'Need a word with Bull,' Breck went on, folding his arms. 'Inside, is he?'

'Why would he want to waste his breath on a twat like you?' the first man went on. 'Away you go and take Gene fucking Hunt with you.' He nodded towards Fox while his two friends grinned.

'We're not looking for trouble,' Breck continued. 'But we're always happy to provide it when necessary. Three of you in the same holding cell – gets a bit crowded on a weekend.'

'I'm shaking in my fucking boots.'

'Is he inside or not? That's all we're asking.'

Fox had risen up on to his toes so he could peer in through the pub window. The bottom half was frosted glass, the top half clear. A couple of drinkers glared back at him, but he'd already seen enough.

'He's inside,' he stated, answering Breck's question. He made to move past the men, but they stood shoulder to shoulder, blocking the door. 'Bull won't thank you for this,' he explained to the leader. 'Think about it for a second – right now it's just the two of us he's dealing with. But if we have to round up a posse, we'll be sure to bring him out with his hands cuffed behind his back. It'll be into the van and down to headquarters for the night. If you think that's what he'd want, fair play to you. But I'm guessing you're wrong, and he'll know who's to blame when the blues and twos come screeching to a halt …' Fox took a step back, raising his hands in a show of surrender. 'Just think it over, that's all I'm saying. Maybe go talk to him, see what he says.' He pointed across the road. 'We'll wait by the car.' Then he started walking, Breck following him.

'Nicely played,' Breck commented in an undertone.

'That remains to be seen.' But by the time they reached the Volvo, the ringleader had disappeared inside, the door swinging behind him. Fox and Breck bided their time. A face neither of them knew appeared at the window of the pub.

'You saw him?' Breck asked.

'Holding court at the bar,' Fox confirmed. 'Amount of jewellery he's toting, I'm surprised he can lift a glass.'

It was another couple of minutes before the door opened. No one emerged, but something was either said or signalled. The two smokers flicked away their cigarettes and headed inside.

'Now what?' Breck asked. It was a fair question. 'Do we just stand here while they have a good laugh at us?' A few more faces had appeared at the window. One man flicked the V sign. 'Maybe that posse of yours isn't such a bad idea.'

'It's a terrible idea,' Fox corrected him.

'Don't tell me you want us to walk in there without back-up?'

'Is that what you'd do in Quidnunc, Jamie – wait for reinforcements before you make a move?'

'By this stage of the game, I'd be mob-handed, same as the person I'm fighting.'

'Then we'll just have to be a mob of two.' Fox paused. 'But meantime, we'd be warmer in the car.'

'We make a better impression standing our ground.'

'Is that from Quidnunc again? Place probably won't close for another three or four hours.'

'It won't take that long.'

Sure enough, after only a few minutes, they started to hear the sound of an engine. It was whining as it approached at speed, and when it turned the nearest corner its tyres squealed. There was no attempt to pull in kerbside. The driver just slammed the brakes on with the car still in the middle of the road. It was a Ford Sierra, but with a modified engine and an oversized exhaust pipe. The driver let it growl one last time before allowing it to idle. The tyres had left marks on the road and there was a smell of burning rubber.

'*Top Gear*'s got a lot to answer for,' Fox commented.

The man who eventually emerged from the back seat was big and scowling. He'd worn the same face in the photo on the printout. The

Sierra rose the best part of an inch on its shocks once relieved of its passenger. He rolled from the waist as he walked. He was wearing a short-sleeved shirt the size of a two-man tent, baggy jeans and white trainers. His hair was black, slicked back from the forehead and over the ears, falling to just past his neck. He sported a gold tooth at the front of his mouth but no baubles or obvious body-art. His eyes seemed tiny, but piercing at the same time.

'What do you want?' he asked. 'Second thoughts – don't answer that. Just get in the car and vamoose.'

'We can't do that, Terry,' Fox said, managing to sound apologetic. 'We need to speak to Bull first.'

'I don't want to hear another word from you,' Terry Vass said, jabbing a finger in Fox's direction. 'Just you and your bum-chum hit the fucking road.'

There was silence for a moment before Jamie Breck uttered a single word. The word was 'Interesting.' This caught Vass's attention.

'What's that?'

Breck offered a shrug. 'It's just that when people use homophobic insults, it's often a sign.'

Vass's face darkened further. 'What sort of sign?'

Breck shrugged again and seemed to be searching for the right phrase. 'Subconscious ... leanings,' he offered.

Vass lunged at him, but Breck was nimble. He ducked beneath the huge man's outstretched arm and stepped past him. He bounced on his toes, ready for the next move.

'Terry,' Fox said, his voice a little louder than before, demanding to be heard. 'We don't need any of this. Bull's got you here so you can find out what we want. It was meant to be for his ears only, but here's the gist – we've got Charlie Brogan.'

Vass had been glowering at Breck, readying for another assault, but Fox's words hit home. His breathing steadied and his shoulders relaxed a fraction.

'I don't mean he's in custody,' Fox went on. 'I mean *we've* got him. And we want a trade.'

Vass turned towards Fox. 'A what?'

'A trade,' Fox repeated. 'Go tell your boss that. We'll be waiting in the car.' He was already opening the driver's-side door. Vass watched as he got in and closed it after him. Then he turned his attention back to Breck, who was still up on his toes, halfway between the Volvo and the Sierra. From the car interior, Fox had only a partial view. He was hoping Breck wouldn't rile the giant any further. But Vass seemed to dismiss his tormentor with a wave of the hand, and trundled towards the door of Lowther's. Breck waited a few seconds, then returned to the Volvo and got in.

'Scary bloke,' he commented.

'Didn't stop you poking him with a stick.'

'Happens in online games all the time.' Breck paused. 'Besides, I've always had fast reflexes – nice to test them now and then.'

'Want some gum?'

Breck nodded and reached out towards the packet Fox was holding. The hand hardly trembled at all. They sat in silence, chewing and watching the world pass by. Some women were on a hen night. They wore identical pink T-shirts emblazoned with the words 'We Are The Four And Twenty Virgins'. A group of local men were tagging along behind, trying out their various chat-up lines. Half a dozen teenagers slouched past, dressed in black hooded tops and baseball caps. The Sierra got a few stares. It hadn't moved, and traffic was having to negotiate it. One or two cars sounded their horns. The driver kept his hands glued to the steering wheel and the engine ticking over.

'Reckon that's a full-time job?' Breck asked. Fox went on chewing and watching. When the pub door next swung open, it was only a couple of smokers. They seemed interested in Fox and Breck, but stuck to their own side of the road. The door opened again, and this time it was one of the three men from earlier. He almost jogged towards the Volvo, leaning down at the driver's-side window. Fox ignored him, so the man tapped on the glass. Fox gave it a few more seconds, then lowered the window.

'Bull says to come in,' the man said.

'Tell him he can go fuck himself.' Fox slid the window back up. The man stared through the glass as though he couldn't believe what he'd just heard. He tapped again, but Fox just shook his head. The messenger stood up and slunk back the way he'd come.

'Reckon he'll find another way of phrasing it?' Breck asked.

'Probably.'

'You didn't fancy going in, then?'

'I like it better here.'

'Me too.' Breck leaned back a little in his seat. More minutes passed, and then Vass appeared, holding the door open for Bull Wauchope. He was everything Fox had expected. There was a feral look to him. He was never going to be half the man his father was, and he knew it. He carried weight, but very little of it was muscle. His arms were flabby, and the belt around his jeans was straining at its last notch. The short hair was greasy, as was the complexion. Acne around the throat, almost certainly exacerbated by the cheap-looking gold chains. The ink tattoos on the backs of both hands looked self-inflicted, probably dating to adolescence. Rings on most of his fingers – dart-player chic. The young man looked brash and smug, the result of having grown up untouchable, thanks to a father feared by all. Vass was a couple of steps behind his boss. Fox slid his window down again.

'You,' he said to Wauchope, 'can get in the back, but I don't want your gorilla stinking up my car.' Wauchope didn't pause for a second.

'Stay here,' he ordered Vass. Then he hauled open the door and got in, slamming it shut after him.

'Everyone seems to think you're cops,' he said. 'And if you're not, I'll eat Terry's cock.'

'That makes it very tempting to lie,' Fox said.

'Got the car wired for sound?'

'No.'

'Am I supposed to believe that?'

'Here's what I want you to know,' Fox began. 'We've got Charlie Brogan's location. You'll have worked out by now that his little disappearing act was just that – an act. The cops are thinking the same way, and that means they'll have him in a day or two.' He paused. 'Which doesn't give you much time, Bull.'

'I'm listening.'

'That's good, because what I'm doing right now is incriminating myself – that's why I can guarantee you we're not taping this.'

'Keep talking.'

'We know where he is and we know you want him. We're willing to trade.'

'You want money?'

Fox shook his head. 'It's not Glen Heaton you're dealing with here.' He paused. 'We want our lives back.' He stared at Wauchope in the rearview mirror. 'Don't you know who we are?'

'Not a clue.'

'My name's Malcolm Fox. This is Jamie Breck.' Fox watched Wauchope's reaction. The man was looking at Breck. 'We've been set up and we think you're at the root of it. Tell us we're wrong.'

Wauchope turned his attention back to the mirror. 'I'm still listening,' he told Fox's reflection.

'We want everything cleared up, clean slate, that sort of thing. But we also want Glen Heaton. No way he gets to walk.'

'You seem to credit me with a lot of clout.'

'The clout might not be yours – might belong to your dad. But I get the feeling it's there.'

'Your pal doesn't say much.'

'Only when there's something to add,' Breck stated, breaking his silence.

'This must be the most half-arsed entrapment any of you spunk-bags has ever tried to pull.'

'You decide the time and place,' Fox went on, 'and we'll be there. But we'll have questions for you, and you don't get to see Brogan until we're happy.'

'What sort of questions?'

'The sort we need answers to.' Fox reached a hand over the back of his seat. It was holding a scrap of paper with his mobile number on it. 'Remember, you've got maybe one or two days at most. When they arrest Brogan, they'll offer him a deal. It'll be you they really want. And with him still alive, what are you going to offer your investors?' Fox paused, allowing this to sink in. Wauchope had taken the slip of paper from him, their fingers grazing momentarily.

'Are we done?' the man asked.

'One last thing …' Fox watched Wauchope pause with his hand on the door handle. 'You've got to give us Vass, too.'

'Why?' Wauchope sounded genuinely curious.

'He killed Vince Faulkner. Vince was my sister's bloke.'

Fox kept watching Wauchope in the mirror as comprehension started to set in: this was family. That explained a lot. Where family was involved, the normal rules did not apply. The man didn't say anything – he still didn't trust the car not to be wired – but he locked eyes with Fox and nodded slowly. Then he started clambering out, before pausing to stick his head back inside. 'You I've never heard of,' he announced to Fox. He closed the door and headed back to Lowther's. Vass walked alongside him, and Wauchope draped an arm over his shoulder.

'You any good at reading signs?' Fox asked Jamie Breck.

'He's telling us Vass might just be expendable,' Breck answered quietly. Fox turned towards him.

'Do I get another "well played"?'

'What did he mean at the end?'

Fox had been wondering that too. 'I suppose he meant what he said – he's never heard of me.' He shifted in his seat.

'Why the slip of paper rather than a business card?'

'Less info he has on me, the better.' Fox paused. *You I've never heard of* ... He spat his gum out of the window. 'All of a sudden, I'm starving. How about you?'

'I could go an Indian.' Breck looked around. 'I'm just not sure we'd be safe in Dundee.'

'You're right – when Wauchope calls, we want to be as far from here as possible.'

'So we've got time to set everything up?' Breck nodded his agreement. 'You warned everybody to be ready?'

'I warned them.'

'How's my crazy plan shaping up so far?'

'We're still breathing,' Fox answered, starting the engine. 'That's saying something, I suppose.' He peered in his rearview mirror as he drove off. The Sierra was still parked in the middle of the road, as if it owned the place.

Which in a funny way, Malcolm Fox reasoned, it did.

Monday 23 February 2009

29

Monday afternoon, Breck and Fox were playing cards at Breck's house when the call came. They'd been drinking tea and coffee all day. Three newspapers had been read from cover to cover. TV news had been watched, music listened to, and there'd been phone calls to Annabel and Jude. Lunch had comprised supermarket sandwiches and chocolate eclairs. The sun had been shining earlier, bringing a little warmth with it, but now the sky was a sheet of unbroken cloud the colour of old dishwater.

'It's him,' Fox said, glancing at the phone's tiny screen.

'How do you know?'

'I don't recognise the number.' Fox waggled the phone at Breck but didn't answer it.

'Don't tease the man,' Breck chided him. He was attempting levity, but Fox could see he was anxious. Fox pressed the answer button and placed the phone to his ear.

'Malcolm Fox speaking.' He realised his own voice sounded higher than usual – Breck wasn't the only one suffering nerves.

'It's me.' Bull Wauchope's voice. He probably thought he was being clever, not identifying himself by name. As if the latest technology couldn't match a voice to its owner as surely as fingerprints.

'Yes?'

'I'm still not sure I get it.'

'There's nothing to get – we meet, we ask you a few questions. If we're happy with what we hear, you get your little reward.'

'Just like that?'

'Just like that.'

'So why don't we do it over the phone?'

'Because a phone could be bugged, couldn't it? Same as my car yesterday. I'm just trying to put your mind at rest ...'

'I choose where we meet?'

'Somewhere you know you'll be safe.'

'I like Lowther's.'

'Fine, but I don't want too many people around – could it be after closing time?' Fox was looking at Breck and Breck winked back – he had bet twenty quid Wauchope would choose the pub.

'I'll make sure everybody's gone by eleven.'

'Then we'll be there at quarter past.'

'But not with Brogan?'

'Not till we've had our little chat.'

'I'll need proof you know where he is.'

'Not a problem.'

'And I swear to God, if you try anything I'll have you nailed to the wall before your buddies can kick the door down.'

'Understood. But I want us to be clear on something – Heaton and Vass are not negotiable.'

'Give me Brogan and they're yours.' The line went dead. Fox held the phone in his hands for a moment.

'Well?' Breck asked.

'We've got more calls to make.' Fox held the phone in front of him and found the number he was looking for.

'Five hours till we have to leave,' Breck calculated. 'Is that enough time?'

'It better be,' Malcolm Fox said as the first of his calls was answered.

They parked the car outside Lowther's at precisely one minute to eleven. People were leaving, not all of them happy at having their evening curtailed. But the grumbling was muted, and even then it only started once they were safely on the street. At five past, Terry Vass emerged. He recognised the Volvo but ignored it. His job seemed to be reconnaissance. He walked up and down the street, looking for signs that Fox and Breck had brought company. Seemingly satisfied, he headed inside again. At ten past, Fox asked Breck if he was ready.

'Few more minutes,' Breck replied with a glance at his watch. They sat in silence, and saw the bar staff making to leave, shrugging themselves into their jackets, lighting cigarettes as they headed home. Vass came out of the pub again, this time signalling for them that it was time. Fox looked at Breck and nodded. Breck fetched the laptop from the back seat and they crossed the road. There hadn't been time for anyone to do more than the most cursory amount of tidying up. A few chairs had been placed upside down on tables, and the top of the bar was lined with dirty glasses. The fruit machine's lights were flashing, tempting players who no longer existed.

At a corner table sat Bull Wauchope. His arms were draped along the edge of the bench behind him.

'Search them,' he ordered.

Vass stood in front of the two detectives. 'Take off your jackets and undo your shirts.'

'As long as you're not after *The Full Monty*,' Breck said, placing the laptop on the nearest table. They slid their jackets off and unbuttoned their shirts, untucking them so Vass could check for wires. He patted down each jacket, squeezing the pockets and reaching in to check they only had wallets and phones.

'Trousers, Terry,' Wauchope barked, so Vass ran his hands down their legs, too, checking their ankles and socks.

'Nothing,' he said, struggling to get back to his feet.

'Take their phones off them – don't want anyone eavesdropping, do we?'

Vass ended up with three phones. 'This one's got two,' he told his boss, nodding towards Fox.

Wauchope stared at Fox and Breck, then pointed to the chairs on the other side of the table. Breck placed the laptop between them. 'Okay if I plug this in?' he asked, looking down at the floor for the nearest socket.

'What's it for?' Wauchope demanded.

'Proof,' Fox told him. 'And since I don't have a phone, I'll need to borrow yours.' He had his hand held out.

'Give him his phone back,' Wauchope ordered Terry Vass. Then: 'But I'm warning you …'

'Crucifixion's not high on my wish list,' Fox assured him.

Breck had found a socket on the skirting board below the bench. Fox punched buttons on his phone and held it to his ear. Wauchope's eyes had narrowed. They were flitting between the two men.

'We're ready, Tony,' Fox said when the call was answered. Then he snapped the phone shut and tossed it towards Vass. Breck had powered up the laptop and turned it so it was facing Wauchope.

'Give it a minute,' he said, leaning over so he could make a few adjustments.

'Mind if I ...?' Fox nodded towards the bench. Wauchope's head twitched, which Fox took for agreement. He sat down next to the man so he too could view the screen. Wauchope's body odour was almost overpowering.

'What we've got,' Fox explained, trying to keep his breathing shallow, 'is a webcam.' On the screen, a three-inch-square box had opened. There was a face there, Charles Brogan's face.

'Who's Tony?' Wauchope asked.

'Just someone doing me a favour.'

'He's operating the camera?'

'Didn't think Brogan could be trusted to do it for himself.'

Wauchope leaned forward. Brogan's head was moving from side to side as he stretched the muscles in his neck. There was no sound. 'Why's the picture so small?'

'Blame the laptop,' Fox explained. 'Wages Breck's on, he can't always afford quality.'

'I could magnify it,' Breck added, 'but you'd lose definition.'

Wauchope just grunted. Then, a few seconds later: 'You're telling me this is live?' Instead of answering, Fox gestured for the phone again.

'One way to prove it,' he offered.

Vass looked to his boss for permission, then handed the phone over. Fox waited until he was connected.

'Tony,' he said, 'tell him we need a wave.'

The face on the computer turned to one side, as if listening to an instruction. Then Charlie Brogan gave a half-hearted wave of one hand. Fox snapped shut the phone again, holding on to it this time. Wauchope kept staring at the screen.

'So now you know we've got him,' Fox said.

'I know he's in police custody,' Wauchope corrected him, but Fox shook his head.

'You've got friends in Lothian and Borders, Bull – you *know* he's not handed himself in.'

Wauchope turned to look at him. 'What is it you want?'

'I want to know why my colleague here was targeted.'

Wauchope considered for a second, then turned his attention back to the screen. 'He can't hear me?' he asked.

'No,' Fox confirmed.

Wauchope leaned his face right in against the screen. 'Going to get you, you fucker!' he yelled. Flecks of saliva spattered Brogan's head and shoulders.

'Will that be enough to appease the gangs in Lanarkshire and

Aberdeen?' Fox asked. Wauchope turned to him again.

'It's a start,' he confirmed. 'I told them he'd die.'

'When he disappeared from the boat ... you could've tried taking the credit.' Fox saw Wauchope's face change. 'You did, didn't you? You told them you'd had him executed? That's why he can't turn up alive and kicking ...'

Wauchope was staring at him again. Breck cleared his throat.

'Malcolm ... maybe we're cheating ourselves here.'

'How do you mean?' Fox asked.

'We're trading him for a few scraps of information. Seems to me he's worth a whole lot more now.'

'Don't go getting greedy,' Wauchope snarled.

'Then start talking,' Fox said. He had risen and shifted to the seat next to Breck. Wauchope's eyes were on the screen again. There was a sheen of sweat on his forehead. He had an inch of lager left in his glass, and he drained it, wiping his mouth with the back of his hand. He made a smacking sound with his lips, then stared across the table.

'I don't trust you,' he said.

'The feeling's mutual,' Fox answered. 'If it comes to it, it's us two against you and your gorilla – I'm not entirely sure I fancy those odds.'

Wauchope almost smiled, but didn't. He glanced in Vass's direction. The man-mountain was resting his weight against the top of the bar, arms folded, breathing noisily through his mouth. Fox knew what Wauchope was thinking: if he stuck to the deal, he really was going to lose his lieutenant. When Wauchope turned his attention back to Fox, Fox knew the decision had been made.

Terry Vass could be replaced.

But there was something else: Vass couldn't be handed over to the police; he might start talking. Fox gave the briefest of nods, letting Wauchope know this was the gangster's problem and no one else's.

'Where is he?' Wauchope asked, jabbing a fat finger at the screen.

'We need to hear the story first.'

'What's to tell?' Wauchope said with a shrug. 'You already know the way it happened. Your pal here was sniffing around a councillor called Wishaw, but Brogan needed Wishaw.'

'Why?'

'He was the last lifebelt on the *Titanic*. Brogan's plan was to get the council to buy his unfinished flats and all that spare land he had on his books. They'd then have a place to put all the dregs on their waiting lists. Wishaw was supposed to be made head of housing, but it never happened. Still, he sat on the committee – there was a chance he could swing it. But then he got panicky, said the police were hassling him about some drug thing from way back.' Wauchope was looking at Breck. 'So it's all your fault, really.'

'I had to be discredited?' Breck asked. Wauchope nodded and leaned back against the bench. It creaked under the strain.

'You already knew Ernie Wishaw, didn't you?' Fox asked Wauchope. 'Glen Heaton had done you a favour, made sure Wishaw didn't get dragged into the case against his driver. That meant Wishaw owed *you*, but at the same time *you* owed Heaton, and Heaton wanted a favour – if he went to trial, stuff would start spilling out. That couldn't happen. Your job was to set me up for Vince Faulkner's murder.'

'I really don't know what you're talking about.' Wauchope gave a slow shake of the head. 'Like I said before, I only know about *him*.' He stabbed a finger in Jamie Breck's direction, and it was Breck who responded.

'You had to have someone inside the force. Someone who knew what was happening in Australia. Someone with access to my credit card …'

'Think I'm going to tell you?'

'If you want Brogan, you're going to have to,' Fox interrupted. 'Only problem is, it's not going to go down well with your dad, is it?'

Wauchope glared at him. 'You already know,' he said.

'I'm the Complaints, Bull. Other cops are an open book to me. I just had to go back through the files far enough.' Fox paused. 'Long before he became Deputy Chief Constable, Adam Traynor worked right here on Tayside. He had a couple of run-ins with your dad, but nothing ever came to trial. Funny that … the way those cases kept falling apart … Did you ask your dad to put you in touch?'

Wauchope kept glaring. The silence lengthened. When he eventually moved his head, the signal was ambiguous.

'Is that a yes?' Fox asked.

'It's a yes,' the gangster said.

'Traynor arranged all the details?'

'Yes.'

'For old times' sake?'

'He owed Dad a few favours – plenty of cops owe my dad favours, Fox.'

'Probably explains why it took Tayside so long to lock him up.' Fox watched the scowl spread across the son's face. 'So Brogan needs DS Breck kicked into touch and you arrange the details. But then what happens? He sets Vince Faulkner on you?'

'Faulkner was amateur hour. Terry saw him as a living, breathing insult.'

'You didn't give an order?'

Wauchope shook his head. 'First I knew of it was when Terry phoned me.'

Fox turned in his chair so he was half facing the man at the bar. 'The argument got out of hand? You whacked him a bit too hard? See, Brogan has a different take – he says Faulkner was tortured and his screams fed down the phone to send him a message.' When Vass said nothing, Fox turned back to Wauchope. 'Did Brogan lie to me?'

'What do you say, Terry?' the gangster called to his lieutenant. Then, to Fox: 'Like I said, Terry felt insulted. Maybe the phone call was to let Brogan know.' Wauchope gazed at the screen again. 'He's still sitting there. Can you get your pal to punch him or something?'

'Where was Vince Faulkner killed? That sauna of yours in the Cowgate?'

Wauchope turned his attention back to Vass. 'Terry?'

'Back of the van,' Vass muttered.

'I didn't catch that,' Fox complained.

'Terry took one of the vans down to Edinburgh,' Wauchope explained. 'You didn't really mean for him to die, did you, Terry? You just thought you were putting him in hospital.'

Fox didn't bother checking Vass's reaction. 'Where do I come in?' he asked instead.

'You don't,' Wauchope said with a shrug. 'Not as far as I'm concerned.'

'I was under surveillance ... then I got put on to DS Breck's case. No coincidence.'

'Nothing to do with me.'

'I need more than that,' Fox said.

'There *isn't* any more than that!' Wauchope slapped his palm against the surface of the table.

'Then you need to ask another favour from Traynor – because if you really don't know, maybe he does.'

Wauchope wagged a finger. 'No more favours till I've got my hands on Charlie Brogan.'

The two men stared at one another.

'I hand him over,' Fox guessed, 'and you rip him to pieces in front of an invited audience?'

'That's the deal we had.'

Fox turned towards Breck. 'You were right,' he said. 'We folded when we should have raised.'

'We can still raise,' Breck commented.

'Not if you want to leave here without the help of paramedics,' Wauchope growled. 'Fun's over – all I want from you now is the address.'

Fox drew a beer mat towards himself and took out a pen. 'It's quarter to twelve now,' he said. 'It's going to take you an hour and a bit to get to Edinburgh. At half past one, my pal walks out of the house. Once he's gone, you can go in whenever you like.' He had written down an address. He pushed the mat in Wauchope's direction.

'And if this is all a ruse?' the gangster asked.

'Come and get us,' Fox answered with a shrug. Wauchope slid a fingernail under the mat and lifted it to peer at the address.

'Is this a joke?' he asked.

'No joke,' Fox assured him, tucking the pen back into his pocket. 'There are dozens of finished properties still on the books at Salamander Point. Some of them are even furnished – an enticement to buy, I suppose.'

Wauchope was staring past Fox towards Terry Vass. 'First place we should have looked,' he rasped.

'You're cleverer than Breck and me, then,' Fox stated. 'It was number three or four on our list.' He paused. 'Are we done here?'

Wauchope fixed him with another long, cold stare. Breck was unplugging the laptop and shutting it down.

'We're done,' the gangster eventually said. And then: 'Terry, go fetch the van …'

30

Fox and Breck drove back to Edinburgh at speed and with Breck on his phone for most of the way. Their destination was Police HQ at Fettes. Tony Kaye's Nissan was parked outside the main entrance. Fox pulled up next to him and got out, Breck following suit. Kaye came to meet them, while Charles Brogan stayed in the Nissan's passenger seat.

'He all right?' Fox asked.

'Scared shitless,' Kaye answered with a smile.

'He heard the whole thing?'

'Clear as a bell.'

'So he's convinced it's us or nothing?'

'He's convinced. Doesn't mean he's happy about it.'

'He did well, though,' Jamie Breck said. 'If Wauchope had screamed at me like that, I'd have started running for the hills.'

'I kept the volume low,' Kaye explained. 'And there was a bit of prep beforehand ...'

Breck had bent a little at the knees so he could give Brogan a thumbs-up sign, while Brogan resolutely ignored him.

'Have you tried playing it back?' Fox was asking Kaye.

'It's fine – sound and vision, and copied on to an external hard drive, date- and time-stamped.'

'What would we have done if he'd spotted the camera?' Breck asked Fox.

'Told him the truth,' Fox replied. 'It's built into the laptop, meaning there's nothing to be done about it.'

'He'd have wanted it covered up.'

'We'd still have the audio.' Fox looked to Kaye for confirmation. Kaye nodded back at him and Fox patted his friend's arm. Truth to tell, he'd harboured doubts about Tony Kaye, had even wondered for a time if Kaye might have been got at. He felt a little bad about that ... but not *too* bad.

Fox's phone rang and he answered it. It was Bob McEwan, letting them know the squad was in position at Salamander Point.

'The van's got to go to Forensics,' Fox reminded him. 'Could well be the same one they used with Vince Faulkner.'

'Relax, Malcolm,' McEwan said, ending the call.

'He says we should relax,' Fox informed Breck and Kaye.

'Want to go watch the fun?' Breck asked. Fox checked his watch.

'If they catch so much as a glimpse of us,' he warned, 'they'll know something's up.'

'What about our resident scaredy-cat?' Kaye gestured towards Brogan.

'We keep him at HQ for the interview – I'd hate for him to have an "accident".'

'You're saying Leith's not safe?'

'Is anywhere?' Fox asked, sounding deadly serious.

It was another five minutes before the surveillance vehicle arrived, driven by Joe Naysmith and with Gilchrist as his passenger. Fox hauled open the driver's-side door.

'Well?' he asked.

Naysmith jumped down from the van and Breck tossed him the three-pin adaptor. This, rather than the laptop's mains cable, was what he'd plugged into the wall socket at the pub. The device only looked like an adaptor, but was actually a bug with its own transmitter and a range of seventy-five metres. Terry Vass had looked up and down the street, but the van had been parked around the corner.

'Picked up every word,' Naysmith said, beaming a smile.

'And duly recorded.' Gilchrist was holding a freshly burned CD in his hand.

Breck started counting off on his fingers. 'Brogan's evidence ... plus the laptop ... plus the surveillance ...'

'Any evidence Forensics can lift from the van,' Fox added. 'And the fact they're about to be caught red-handed ...'

'Just about wraps it up,' Breck concluded. 'Doesn't it?'

'Just about,' Fox seemed to agree. The two men stared at one another.

'All right then,' Fox relented. 'Let's go.'

*

It took them only a few minutes to reach Salamander Point, helped by the fact that the roads were deserted. They had borrowed Kaye's car to make them less recognisable to Wauchope and Vass. Fox was in the driving seat, slowing only marginally for red lights and then going through them if there was no other traffic.

'We're not going to get much of a view if we stay in the car,' Breck complained. 'There's nowhere nearby to park.' So they left the Nissan on a side street and walked around the perimeter of the site. The temporary fencing had been removed from that part of Salamander Point boasting finished abodes. Grass had been laid, and a few trees and shrubs planted. The address handed to Wauchope belonged to one of the few actual houses. It was semi-detached and stood in a row of six. There was light coming from its upstairs window. Fox had plumped for it because there was less chance of neighbours getting in the way. Many of the flats were occupied, but four of the six houses stood empty. Fox and Breck kept their distance, peering from behind a brick wall that sheltered the neighbours' dustbins from general view. There was no sign of life from any of the properties.

'We can't have missed them,' Breck whispered. 'Maybe the van wouldn't start, or they got cold feet ...'

'Ssh,' Fox advised. 'Listen.'

The low rumble of an engine. A scruffy white van slowly turning the corner into the cul-de-sac. Each homeowner had a parking bay, but these were grouped together at the rear of the row of houses. The roadway was to be kept clear at all times, and boasted an unbroken run of double yellow lines. Not that this bothered the van. Its headlights had been turned off, and it pulled to a stop in the middle of the tarmac. When the engine died, Fox realised he was holding his breath. The burning bulb in the upstairs bedroom had been Tony Kaye's idea. A good one, too. The van doors creaked open and two men got out. Fox recognised both of them. They padded over to the front door of the house, Wauchope's face illuminated by the screen of his phone. Fox realised he was checking the time. When he nodded, Vass tried the door handle. Having opened it a fraction, proof that it hadn't been locked, they pulled it closed again and went to check through the downstairs window. Then Bull Wauchope took a couple of steps back and angled his head towards the lit window upstairs. He seemed to whisper something to Vass, who nodded his agreement. Vass retreated to the van, looking to left and right, and returned carrying a length of clothes line and a roll of tape.

It was Wauchope who pushed the door open, but he let Vass lead the way. When both men were inside, Fox nodded towards Breck. They left their hiding place and started crossing the road. They were halfway to the door when they heard the shouts. Suddenly the doors of the houses on either side flew open, officers pouring out and following Wauchope and Vass inside. There were figures in the upstairs window – more officers. They were dressed in black and protected by visors and stab vests. They carried pepper spray and truncheons. There were yelled commands and the sounds of a struggle. Fox and Breck had no means of identifying themselves to their colleagues, so stayed outside on the path, moving aside when the team started pouring back out again. Wauchope and Vass had been handcuffed and were led downstairs, an officer behind them toting an evidence bag containing the clothes line and tape. Breck stayed to watch, but Fox had walked over to the van. He used the sleeve of his jacket when he turned the handle, opening its back doors and staring at the shadowy interior. Neighbours were finally coming out, alerted to the commotion. Officers were reassuring them that there was nothing to be worried about. Fox kept staring. He could make out Terry Vass's voice, cursing the arresting officers. Police cars were arriving on the scene, lights flashing, bringing out more spectators. Fox flipped his mobile phone open, using the light from its screen as a torch. A sheet of plywood separated the rear compartment from the front seats. Wedged in against the furthest corner was a big, ugly-looking steel hammer. It looked stained, matted with something very like human hair. The phone's screen went dark again, but Fox only turned his head away from the scene when he felt Jamie Breck's hand land lightly on his shoulder.

'You okay, Malcolm?' Breck was asking.

'I'm not sure,' Fox admitted. He saw that Bob McEwan was standing in the doorway of the house, hands in pockets. McEwan spotted Fox and Breck, but made no gesture of recognition. Instead, he turned and wandered back indoors.

Tuesday 24 February 2009

31

Four in the morning and Fox was back home.

Wauchope and Vass would spend the night in separate cells, though Wauchope's lawyer – the one working hard to spring Bruce Senior from jail – was already on his way from Dundee. Charlie Brogan would be interviewed again in the morning. At some point, Fox knew he had to explain it all to Jude. But that could wait. He also needed to call Linda Dearborn – she was owed an exclusive, and Fox knew he could offer her a choice of several. He had assumed he'd be feeling lighter, but there was still the sense of a weight pressing down on him. He placed a couple more books on one of the shelves, then sat back down with a mug of tea. When he heard a car come to a stop outside, he turned his head towards the window. The living-room lights were off, the curtains still open. The car idled, then its headlights were switched off, followed by its engine. A door opened and closed. Fox held the mug in both hands, his elbows resting on his knees. The caller didn't use the bell; they knocked instead, knowing he'd be waiting.

It was another few seconds before he rose to his feet, leaving the mug on the coffee table. When he opened the door, Bob McEwan was standing there.

'Everything all right?' McEwan asked.

Fox nodded slowly and ushered his boss inside. He'd spent a good part of Sunday convincing McEwan to go along with Jamie Breck's plan. Back in the living room, Fox switched on the ceiling light.

'Tony Kaye tells me you managed to record the whole lot.'

'The whole lot,' Fox echoed. Then, after a pause: 'Well … not quite. Do you want a drink?'

'A whisky, maybe.'

'No alcohol in the house.'

'Not even for special occasions, Malcolm?'

Fox shook his head. McEwan had spotted the mug. 'Tea, then,' he decided.

The two men went through to the kitchen. Fox filled the kettle and switched it on.

'Did they give you any trouble?' he asked.

McEwan put his hands in his trouser pockets. 'Vass took a couple of swings, but you'd warned the lads he would.' He pulled a handkerchief from his pocket and blew his nose. 'This cold of mine's getting worse ...'

Fox just nodded and reached into the cupboard for a mug. It had a drawing of Edinburgh Castle on the side. He hesitated, then placed the mug on the worktop.

'I can't do this,' he muttered, pushing past McEwan.

'Do what?' McEwan asked.

Fox was standing by the window when McEwan arrived in the living room a few moments later.

'What's wrong?' McEwan asked.

Fox kept his back to McEwan and started to speak. 'Remember what you said to me, Bob? All those years back when I joined the Complaints? You said "No favours." What you meant was, we had to treat everyone the same – friend or stranger, if they were bent, we took them down.'

'I remember,' McEwan said quietly. Fox heard him take a seat.

'Adam Traynor wanted a favour from you – he wanted a cop put under surveillance. You said it would be best if the Chop Shop did the asking – that was the proper channel, after all.'

'Is that right, Malcolm?'

'I can't see any other way it could have happened.' Fox took a deep breath. 'This would have been the Thursday or Friday. I was busy dotting the i's and crossing the t's on Glen Heaton ... handing the whole thing over to the Procurator Fiscal. But there was something you told me that Friday – you said there might be a case for us in Aberdeen.' Finally Fox turned towards McEwan. 'And that gave you an idea. Maybe you already knew a bit about Jamie Breck ... what kind of officer he was. You reckoned me and him would get on. I'd be intrigued by him, begin to see in him lots of things I'm not ... You did a deal with Grampian – they'd start tailing *me* and you'd do what you could to make sure the inquiry into them was as soft as it could be.'

Fox walked towards his chair and sat down opposite McEwan.

McEwan was staring at the piles of books on the floor next to him. He would even pick one up from time to time and pretend to study it before putting it back.

'You had that whole weekend to think it over,' Fox went on, 'to make sure it felt right. I'd be set the task of watching Jamie Breck. The more I found out about him, the more I'd start to trust *him* rather than the evidence. And from what you'd come to know about me, you were sure I'd put my foot in it somehow. That was all you needed … for me to make a mistake. Same sort of fall Breck himself was being set up for, and for exactly the same reasons.' Fox paused. 'Which, if true, puts you in the selfsame class as Bull Wauchope and Charlie Brogan …' He let the accusation linger, while McEwan riffled the pages of another book.

'If true,' McEwan eventually echoed.

'The only real coincidence was, Breck ended up on the Faulkner inquiry – gold dust, as far as you were concerned. It gave me a whole new set of ways of falling flat on my face …'

Fox paused again, giving McEwan another opportunity to speak, an opportunity McEwan found it easy to refuse.

'When I was going through Traynor's file, I took a look at yours too, Bob. It reminded me of something you'd said right back at the start of the Heaton inquiry – that you had to take a back seat. And you were quite right – you'd worked in the same office as him, after all. Only for a short time, but these things can come back to haunt us once defence teams get hold of them. But your file told a different story. Glen Heaton was your partner way back in the day – he was just starting out and you were the one teaching him the ropes. You wanted my reputation tarnished so his lawyer could use it against us in court. You wanted the Complaints to *fail*. Your own team, Bob …'

McEwan looked up for the first time. 'And to your way of thinking, this is the only way it plays out?' he asked.

'Remember when you told me Breck and Heaton weren't the best of friends? You said you'd spoken to someone at Torphichen … but it was your old pal Heaton you actually spoke to, wasn't it? We don't *get* to help our old pals,' Fox continued, leaning forward with the top half of his body. 'We're the Complaints.'

McEwan cleared his throat. 'Glen Heaton gets the job done, Malcolm.'

'So I keep hearing, but that's the excuse we're always given!' Fox waited for McEwan to say something more, but he just tossed the book he was holding on to the coffee table and leaned back a little on the sofa.

'I thought it was Wauchope helping Heaton,' Fox admitted with a rueful smile.

'Bull Wauchope and Terry Vass are bad men, Malcolm.'

'Meaning you're not?' Fox stared at his boss. After a few moments of silence, he gave a sigh. 'In the morning,' he said, 'you're going to take everything on Wauchope and Brogan and Vince Faulkner to the Chief ...'

'Everything?' McEwan echoed.

'You're going to have to tell him about Traynor and you're going to make sure Jamie Breck gets reinstated without the hint of a slur or a stain on his character.

McEwan nodded slowly. 'And what about us?'

'Last thing you do before leaving the Chief's office is hand him your resignation – that gives you a few hours to come up with any excuse you like. I want DI Stoddart put back in her box and I want to be told I'm returned to duty. But not with you running the show.'

'And if I refuse?'

'Then it's *my* turn to talk to the Chief.'

'It'd be my word against yours.'

'You really want to take that chance? Be my guest ...' Fox got to his feet. 'I suppose I'll find out in a few hours' time.'

McEwan stared at him and started reaching into his pocket, pulling out a phone. 'I'm thrilled at your high regard for me,' he said quietly, pushing buttons. When his call was answered, he spoke only four words.

'You better come in.'

Fox heard another car door open and close. McEwan had exited the living room long enough to let in the new arrival. There was a quick, muttered conversation in the hall. Fox had risen to his feet. Surely McEwan hadn't brought Glen Heaton with him ... But if he had, Fox was ready. The door opened, and McEwan led a distinguished-looking man into the room.

'Malcolm,' he said by way of introduction, 'you've maybe not met the Chief Constable ...'

The Chief's name was Jim Byars and he held out a hand for Fox to shake. He was in his late fifties, with thick silver hair combed straight back from the forehead.

'Sir,' Fox said by way of greeting.

'Bob here tells me you've grabbed the wrong end of the stick,'

Byars said. His eyes were deep-set but probing. 'Maybe we should all sit down, eh?'

The Chief Constable waited until they were settled, then turned towards Fox. 'You looked at Adam Traynor's file, didn't you?'

'Yes, sir.'

'Notice anything?'

Fox nodded slowly. 'Some of your own comments were in there … Reading between the lines, it looked to me as if you never really rated Traynor as a possible successor.'

Byars turned his attention to McEwan. 'He's a sharp one, Bob.'

'Yes, sir,' McEwan agreed. 'On occasion.'

Byars was facing Fox again. 'As it happens, you're quite right – there had always been whispers about Adam Traynor.'

'Dating back to his days in Dundee?' Fox guessed.

'Suspicions that he'd kept the wrong company in the past. Bruce Wauchope for one …'

'It was probably Wauchope who introduced Traynor to Glen Heaton,' Bob McEwan interrupted, fixing Fox with a look. 'You're right to say that me and Heaton go back a long way … but I'd never sell out one of my men, Malcolm.'

Fox swallowed. Blood had begun to colour his cheeks.

'Bob here,' the Chief Constable went on, 'knew something was up – no way Traynor should have sanctioned a surveillance operation on you without Bob being kept in the loop. Bob already knew I had some concerns about my deputy, concerns *he* was now sharing. DI Stoddart has had a word with *her* DCC up in Grampian, and he's admitted it was Traynor who ordered your surveillance.'

'He's admitted it? Just like that?'

The Chief Constable offered a shrug. 'On the understanding that we keep a few details to ourselves.'

'In other words, we don't go shouting from the rooftops that Traynor offered him a deal – if Grampian kept tabs on me, the Complaints in Edinburgh wouldn't take on the Aberdeen inquiry?'

'Something along those lines … Look, I can appreciate you're upset …'

'Not half as upset as me,' McEwan interrupted, eyes on Fox. 'You really thought I was behind all this?'

'You're not the one who was left out there as cannon-fodder,' Fox muttered. He slumped back in his chair and ran a hand through his hair. He was remembering something his father had said to him – *You've got to be careful … Machinery … it's not to be trusted* … Maybe the old boy hadn't been so confused after all. The police force consisted of a series of connected mechanisms, any one of which could be tampered with, or become misaligned, or need patching up …

'Why did Traynor pull the Breck surveillance?' he eventually asked. It was McEwan who answered.

'Best guess is, he already had enough on both of you to kick you out of the park. The longer the Breck thing went on, the more suspicions it was bound to raise.'

'Breck's credit card payment to SEIL went back five weeks,' Fox commented.

McEwan nodded. 'This whole thing had been a while in the planning. Probably they were waiting to see if he'd notice it and query it.'

'Or it could be that all they needed,' Fox added, 'was for Wishaw to know Jamie Breck *would* be kicked out of the park at some time, and so wouldn't keep on nipping at his heels …' He thought for a moment. 'Breck's credit card details …'

'He worked alongside Glen Heaton,' McEwan reminded him. 'Heaton likes to know everything there is to know – no telling when it'll come in handy.'

'He copied out the details?'

McEwan offered a shrug. 'Best guess,' he offered. The Chief Constable looked from one man to the other, then pressed his hands to his knees, readying to rise to his feet.

'It was Traynor?' Fox asked. McEwan nodded.

'Traynor,' he agreed. 'Heaton asked a favour, and Traynor saw a way to kill two birds.'

'But when I accused you just now … before you hauled the Chief in … why didn't you say something?'

'Can't a man have a bit of fun?' Bob McEwan said. But then his face darkened. 'Although you and me *will* be having words about those conclusions you jumped to.'

'Yes, sir,' Fox managed to reply, watching the Chief Constable head towards the door. 'One thing, sir,' he called out to him. 'I think I'm owed …'

Jim Byars paused. *'Owed?'*

'Owed,' Fox repeated. 'I want Dickson and Hall taken down a peg.'

Byars looked to McEwan for an explanation. 'They're Billy Giles's men,' McEwan obliged.

'They gave me a doing,' Fox added, indicating what remained of the damage to his face.

'I see,' the Chief Constable said. Then, after a moment's thought: 'There *are* channels, you know?'

Fox made no answer, and it was left to McEwan to step in.

'I think Malcolm knows that, sir,' he told Byars. 'He is the Complaints, after all . . .'

32

Fox stopped for a double espresso at a Starbucks near Annie Inglis's street. He hadn't had any sleep at all. The café seemed to comprise students with essay deadlines and mothers who'd just dropped their children at day-care. The background music was 1980s electro-pop. Fox took a stool next to the door and watched cars queuing at the Holy Corner junction. The caffeine didn't seem to be having any immediate effect, but he decided against a refill. Besides, it was time.

He drove his car the hundred yards to Inglis's tenement and sat there, waiting. As before, Duncan was the first to leave. Fox watched him trudge sleepily schoolwards, then got out of the Volvo and made for the tenement's main door. He was about to press the buzzer marked Inglis when he heard footsteps descending the stone stairwell. He bided his time, and when the door was opened from within, Annie Inglis herself was standing there. Her eyebrows shot up when she saw him.

'Malcolm!' she gasped. 'What in hell's name ...?'

'Have you heard?' he asked.

'Heard what?' She looked him up and down. 'Have you started sleeping rough?'

He ignored this, keeping his eyes fixed on hers. 'Traynor's career's on its way to the knacker's yard,' he stated. 'You need to be careful he doesn't take you with him.'

She stared at him, saying nothing.

'When Gilchrist got that call,' Fox went on, repeating words he'd rehearsed time and again in his head, 'the call telling him to pull the Breck surveillance ... it was you on the other end, wasn't it?'

'Malcolm ...'

'You owe me this, Annie.' He'd taken a step towards her so that their faces were only inches apart. She played with her bag's shoulder strap. 'You really do,' he nudged her.

'I didn't know it was a set-up, Malcolm – you've got to believe that. Would I have given you that contact in the Melbourne police if I hadn't trusted you?'

'You were just following orders, is that it? But you were getting something in return, Annie – Gilchrist was going to be removed from the picture. That's not the way it usually goes with orders.' Fox was shaking his head. 'If you didn't know, you at least suspected ... and yet you still went along with it. That day I told Stoddart I was ill, I'm betting you volunteered to call me and check I wasn't just pulling a fast one. That's why you offered to come to the house – just to make doubly sure.' It was Fox's turn to look her up and down. 'You're some piece of work.'

'I did as I was told.' Her face showed that even to her own ears, this sounded weak.

'Traynor specified that you should get the Complaints to help you nail Jamie Breck. He gave you my name ...' He paused. 'Traynor, rather than Bob McEwan?'

'Chief Inspector McEwan?' Inglis's eyebrows lifted a little. 'He had nothing to do with it.'

Fox nodded slowly, then angled his head towards the sky. 'You helped set two innocent men up for a fall,' he told her. He lowered his head to stare at her again.

'I really didn't know...'

'Inviting me to your flat – wasn't that a bit of a risk? Did you just want to string me along, keep me sweet?'

'Couldn't it be that I just liked you – maybe wanted to warn you?'

'But you didn't.'

'When I realised you'd looked in my file ...'

'Yes?'

'How could I know Adam hadn't pencilled something there – or wouldn't in future?'

'Adam?' Fox's eyes narrowed. 'You mean Traynor?'

'There's a bit of history there.' She closed her eyes for a second. The silence stretched.

'History?' he eventually echoed, but she just shook her head. 'And you did all of this without questioning, without Traynor needing to explain any of it?'

'There was the evidence against Breck ...'

'I'm talking about *me*, Annie. Traynor insisted it had to be *me* – and when I told you there might be a conflict, he got you to reel me back in again.' His eyes narrowed. 'You never thought to ask him? My career starts hurtling down the hillside, and you do absolutely nothing?'

'He told me you were a liability – that your friends in the Complaints were covering up for you ...'

'Did you ever bother asking for proof? He watched her shake her head again. 'Something to bear in mind for next time, then,' he went on as he turned away from her. 'A little bit of proof never hurts ...'

Unless it's on the side of a bottle.

He returned home and managed a couple of hours on the sofa with his eyes closed. He'd bought a roll of bin bags and was going to fill them with the various piles of books. The whole lot could go to a charity shop. After a shower and change of clothes, he felt at least half awake, though still numb. Jamie Breck had left messages on his mobile, but he didn't feel like responding. Instead, he drove to Saughtonhall and picked up Jude.

'Notice anything?' she asked as she got into the car.

'New jeans?' he guessed.

'They've taken the cast off,' she corrected him, waving her arm in his face. 'Should never have been on in the first place, according to the doctor who removed it.' She looked at him. 'Some detective you are.'

'If only you knew, sis ...'

On the way to Lauder Lodge, he told her some of the story. She listened intently, tears leaking from her eyes. When he apologised for upsetting her, she told him it was all right. She needed to hear it.

'All of it.'

He sat in reception while she visited the bathroom, splashing cold water on her face. The staff were going about their business – just like any other day.

Mitch Fox was waiting for them in Mrs Sanderson's room, the two of them seated opposite one another as if they'd been friends all their lives. Jude kissed her father on his forehead.

'Got rid of that cast,' he commented approvingly.

'You're quicker than your son.'

Fox squeezed his father's shoulder by way of greeting and pecked Audrey Sanderson on her powdered cheek.

'Your cold's cleared up,' she told him.

'Yours too.' He turned towards his father. 'I've been meaning to ask – have you still got money in the Dunfermline Building Society? Looks a bit ropy, from what I hear.'

'The lad worries too much,' Mrs Sanderson said with a chuckle.

'You told me three fifteen,' Mitch chided him, tapping his wrist, even though there was no watch there.

'Traffic,' Fox explained. 'They need to get those roadworks at Portobello roundabout finished. And someone's taken it into their head that this would be a good time to start replacing gas mains, as if the trams weren't causing enough chaos. There's a zebra crossing in the Grassmarket, seems to be taking them months to install it. Tourists will be in town soon, and God knows what they'll make of it all. Bits of roof keep falling off buildings, according to the *Evening News*. City's a deathtrap, the whole of Scotland's in meltdown, and for all I know the rest of the world's about to follow ...' He broke off when he realised the other three people in the small room were looking at him.

'Stop complaining,' Fox's father said into the silence, speaking for all of them.